A Counterfeit Princess

# A Counterfeit Princess

Doug Bedwell

Space Bear Press
Cloverdale, Indiana

This book is a work of fiction.  The characters, incidents, and dialogue are drawn from the author's imagination.  No direct reference to any specific events, organizations, dragons, or persons is intended.



And *please*, no spoilers!

For information, please contact:
  Space Bear Press
  P.O. Box 182
  Cloverdale, IN    46120

  On the web at:  SpaceBearPress.com
  On Facebook at:  Facebook.com/spacebearpress

Bedwell, Doug
        [Fantasy; Adventure]
        A Counterfeit Princess
        First Print Edition: August 1, 2018
        ISBN-13: 978-1-943219-07-0

Original Cover Artwork © Amy Nagi – www.amynagi.com
Cover and Interior Layout and Design by Doug Bedwell
Photo of the Author by Doug Bedwell
Map Artwork by Mark Hansen – theherostale.blogspot.com
Map Design, Layout, and Editing by Doug Bedwell

"Nothing was changed, everything was changed,
by my having seen the dragon."

                                     – John Gardner, *Grendel*

# The Great Island

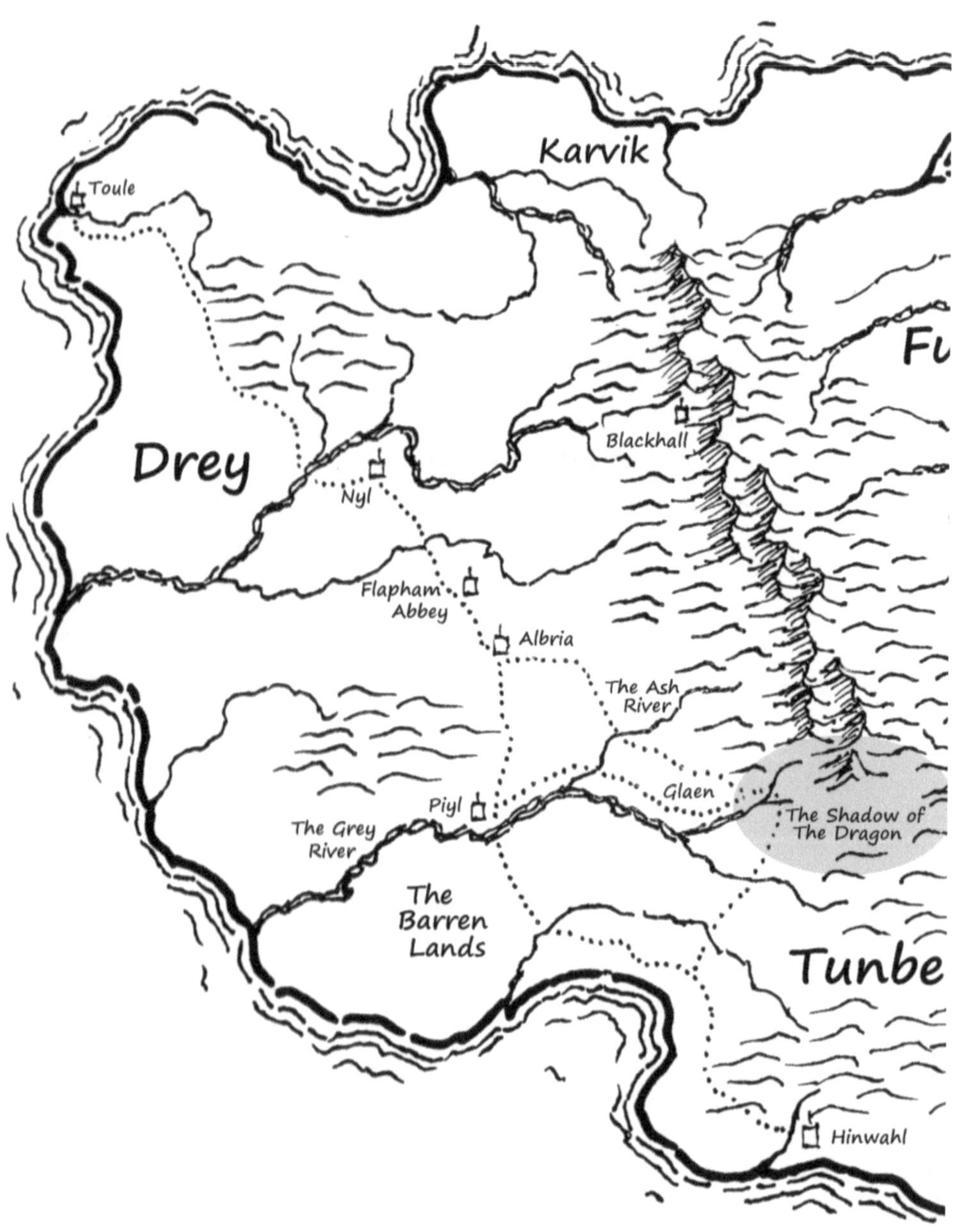

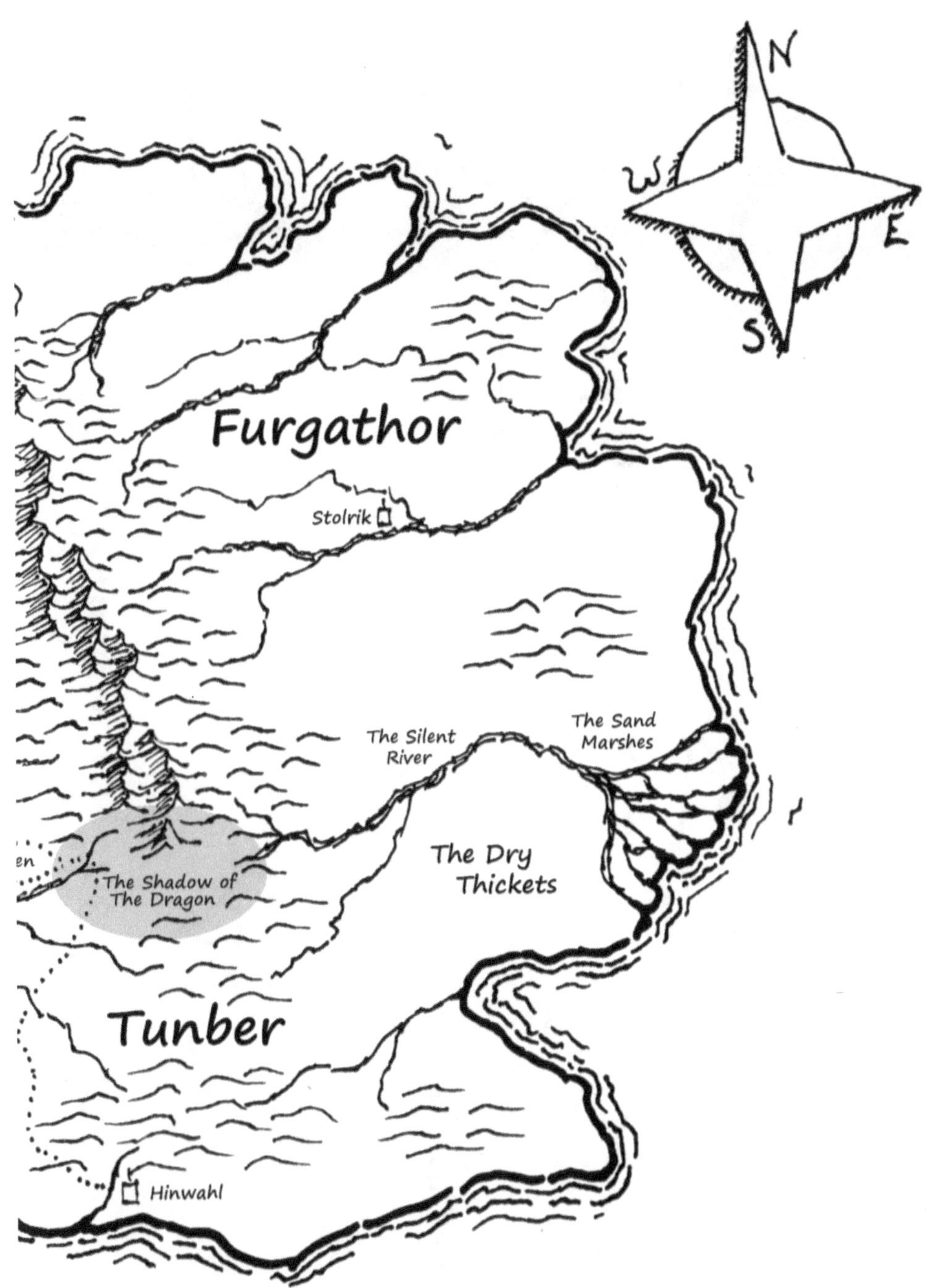
N
W
E
S
Furgathor
Stolrik
The Silent
River
The Sand
Marshes
The Dry
Thickets
en
The Shadow of
The Dragon
Tunber
Hinwahl

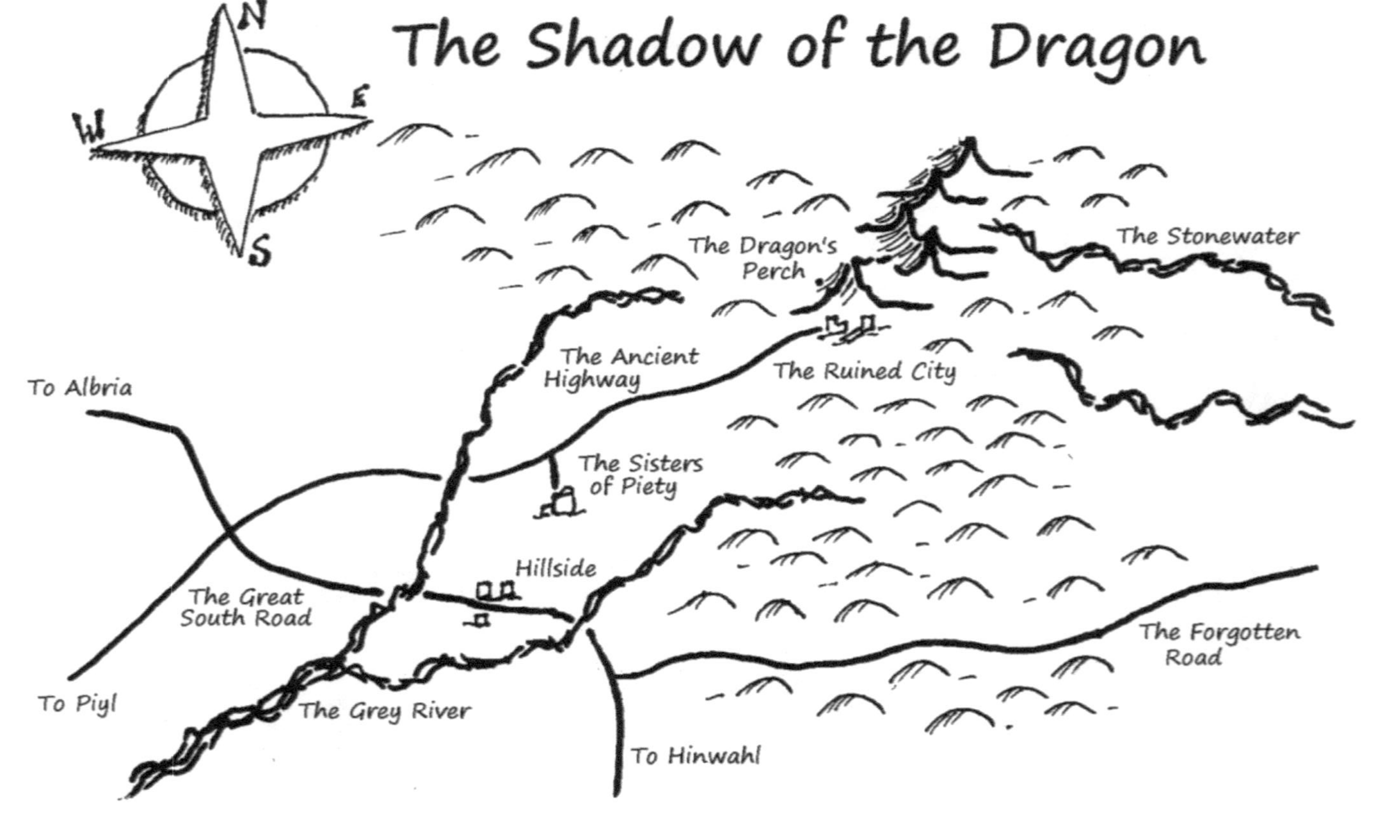
The Shadow of the Dragon
N
S
E
W
The Dragon's Perch
The Stonewater
To Albria
The Ancient Highway
The Ruined City
The Sisters of Piety
Hillside
The Great South Road
The Forgotten Road
To Piyl
The Grey River
To Hinwahl

# Contents


Prologue:
The Old Dragon                    page viii

Book One:
A Counterfeit Princess            page 1

Book Two:
The Dragon's Thief                page 95

Book Three:
Prophecy and War                  page 175

Book Four:
The Dragon's Treasure             page 263

--------------------

Acknowledgements                  page 325

About the Author                  page 327

# Prologue:
## The Old Dragon

Near the summit of the Last Mountain, at the southern end of the long chain of low peaks known as the Boundary Range, lived a dragon. He had been there longer than anyone could remember. He had been there since the fall of the old kingdom, which was a time so far in the distant past that it was almost forgotten. Only a handful of myths and legends of the old kingdom remained, and even its proper name was lost.

In its day, the old kingdom had conquered every corner of the great island. From the eastern shores to the mountains, from the mountains to the Great Western Sea. Every hill and valley, every river and stream, every forest and prairie and brushland and bog was within its vast dominion. Great cities rose, and kings ruled, and peasants toiled, and laws were written, and the lawbreakers were put to death.

Nothing remained of that kingdom now but ruins, scattered here and there across the land. The dragon had made those ruins; they were his creation. He had crafted them with great labor, and diligent artistry. Where before there had been only cities and towns, he had shaped great fields of magnificent rubble. Where once there had stood nothing but castles and towers, he had sculpted a landscape of shattered walls and scattered moss-covered stone. These things were his handiwork, formed from a raw wilderness of man. Using only his native cunning and strength and fire, he alone had brought the world into a new age.

But, as it has often been said, though men may die and civilizations rise and fall, mankind lingers on. The old kingdom vanished, but a few fields and farms remained, and those spread and grew until there were once again villages and towns.

The dragon waited, and he watched.

And where there are towns, there are tradesmen, and men who gather wealth. And when there is wealth, there must be scholars to count it, thieves to steal it, soldiers to guard it, and priests to justify it all and bury the dead. And some men gather enough wealth to become lords and lawgivers; and eventually a handful of those men become kings.

And so it was on the dragon's great island.  Dozens of kings rose to power and made war, and some kingdoms fell while others grew, until only three kingdoms remained, and all the lands were divided between them.  And the dragon's great island became known as *The Land of the Three Realms.*

East of the mountains was Furgathor, a kingdom which stretched from the stony ravines of Karvik in the far north, to the banks of the Silent River in the south; from the eastern slopes of the Boundary Range to the sandy shores of the Great Eastern Sea.

To the south was the realm called Tunber, where people lived mostly in the fertile region of hills between the scrublands and the Southern Sea.  In the west, its northern border was the Grey River, which cut through the great open prairies.  In the east, the Silent River divided Tunber from Furgathor, flowing down from the Last Mountain in a slow and lazy course until it spread itself over the broad expanse of freshwater bogs known as the Sand Marshes.

The third kingdom was Drey, largest of the three, and the strongest in terms of its manpower and resources, if not the wealthiest in terms of gold.  It was a sprawling and varied realm, encompassing all the lands between the Boundary Range and the Western Sea.

These three kingdoms were now at peace with each other, and so it had remained for many years.  But mankind is a restless creature, and soon the kings of the three realms looked across their own lands toward their neighbors.  And they looked back to the time of the old kingdom, and ahead to an imagined time when the old kingdom might be restored.

From his perch near the top of the Last Mountain, still the dragon watched.  He was old now, and tired.  Ancient philosopher, guardian of time; a living furnace of memory, and power, and understanding.  Long ago, he had set a new age in motion, and soon that age would be ending.  His work, and his time, were nearly complete.

He sat, and he watched, and he waited.

# Book One:

# A Counterfeit Princess

## (Spring)

# Chapter 1:
## The Abbey at Flapham

It was mid-morning, and Notwot the prophet was badly hung over. This was by no means unusual, and on any ordinary morning, the boy would have wisely left him to sleep it off, a process that often lasted well into the afternoon.

But it was now clear that on this day standard protocols of prophet management would not suffice, and the boy was already scrambling up the broad stone steps of the little tower, hurrying to the prophet's bedchamber with two full buckets of cold water.

The abbey at Flapham was devoted to the worship of Mosig, a minor god of farmers. Mosig's chief interests were the growing of grain and the brewing of beer, and for many generations the abbey had served as both chapel and brewhouse for the impoverished denizens of the surrounding farmland.

The abbey compound was laid out something like a small city, with a central temple and about a dozen other buildings, all surrounded by a six-foot stone wall. The wall was not a fortification of war, but a simple deterrent to wild beasts from the nearby forest, or to any country rogues who might be inclined to snoop around in search of valuables.

In fact, there were quite a number of valuable things kept in the abbey – religious artifacts, ceremonial chalices, some nice tapestries, and a not insubstantial pile of coins. The coins were mostly hidden in a small oaken chest in a secret room underneath the kitchens. The rest were securely stored in the personal cash reserves of the abbot and the prophet, the whereabouts of which they kept entirely to themselves.

Historically, the abbey had been nearly as poor as the farmers who worshipped there. However that was not the case any longer. In fact, even in the current era of general deprivation, the abbey was thriving.

There were two primary reasons for this remarkable turn of fortune. The first was the prophet Notwot. Ever since he began to experience sacred visions some twelve years before, persons great and small had travelled from many miles around to seek his advice and hear him speak of the future. These pilgrims not only made more and larger offerings to Mosig than they had before the advent of the prophet, they also purchased more of the abbey's beer. Profits soared.

The second reason for Flapham Abbey's wealth was the leadership of the abbot Risby, who was a prudent business manager and an effective promoter of the abbey's primary revenue stream. Under Risby's careful management, the abbey ran like clockwork. The guards rotated duties in regular shifts, the livestock were well-tended, the beverage inventory was carefully charted, the gardens were neatly weeded, and so on.

But not so this morning. The usual routines had given way, and the boy with the buckets was not alone in his haste. Throughout the abbey grounds, everyone seemed to be in motion. The gardeners were chasing chickens back into their coops, the off-duty guards were being roused and rushed to their posts, the cooks were stoking the ovens, and the cleaning girls were scrambling about, gathering up their mops and brooms before disappearing into their little wooden hut to wait for the all clear.

In his personal chamber, even the abbot Risby was halfway to panic, and hurriedly changing into his most impressive vestments. He'd been worried that something like this might happen. Try as he might to keep his most notorious employee sober, old Notwot was three days into one of his characteristic week-long benders, and was definitely in no condition to meet with customers.

This was not an ideal time for a royal delegation to come riding up to the front gates of Flapham Abbey.

----------------------------------------------------

At one time, Flapham Abbey's central temple had been quite small – barely larger than an average farmer's hut. But with the abbey's improved fortunes of late, that original stone building had been strategically expanded. It was now over sixty feet in length from front to back, though for most of that length it was not much wider or taller than before. If seen from above, it was in the shape of a great hammer, with a long slender handle and a wider, rectangular head.

In the handle, there were no windows.  The air was heavy, and the only light came from candle sconces along the walls.  Benches were set to either side, with a narrow aisle between them.  To reach the altar – which stood at the far end in the center of the hammer's head – visitors had to traverse that darkly claustrophobic corridor, listening to the echoes of their own footsteps on the bare stone floor.  The effect was similar to walking through a narrow underground passage, to reach a larger cavern.

In contrast, the altar chamber was spacious, and well-lit from high open windows.  Even for returning visitors already accustomed to the place, the transition from the constricting gloom of the handle to the bright and well-ventilated head of the hammer made for an effective bit of architectural theatricality.

The prophet was perched unsteadily on a wide stone bench, directly in front of the main altar.  He was looking down, and ever so slowly tilting his head from side to side, as if he were intently studying his own feet.  He was dressed in a simple robe which seemed to be made from some sort of rough, coarse cloth like burlap.  Aside from some decorative green stitching, the robe was entirely a deep amber brown: Mosig's favorite color.

The boy and the priests had worked a remarkable transformation on the old prophet.  Not twenty minutes before, he had looked in every way like a man at the end of a three-day drunk.  Now, he looked like a man who had only been drunk for a day and a half, tops.

"So far, so good," thought Risby, as he led Lord Fodge forward down the narrow corridor.  Fodge was the king's minister of finance.  He had made the journey from the palace alone, with only a small escort of soldiers.  This was a considerable relief to the abbot.  When his sentries had first reported the royal banner approaching over the horizon, he'd immediately feared the worst.  Had the king come himself, the visit might have lasted for days, and feeding the royal retinue would have been very taxing for the abbey's larder.  As it was, there was some hope that total expenses for the visit could be kept low, and with any luck, the abbey might turn a handsome profit on the deal.

The abbot walked slowly, to maximize the effect of the temple's design.  Old Notwot lacked polish even on his best days, and in his current condition was likely to dispense with decorum altogether. Risby knew full well that if he wanted there to be any sense of gravitas to this encounter, he would have to create it himself.

About ten feet from the prophet, just past the point where the corridor of the handle opened into the larger chamber of the head, the abbot stopped and knelt, signaling to Lord Fodge that he should do the same. He raised his arms to either side and silently counted to ten, letting the sense of anticipation build before taking the plunge.

"Oh Notwot, wisest of the wise," he intoned solemnly, "we have a visitor... from the king."

The old prophet leaned forward, and squinted blearily in the general direction of Risby and the stranger. He closed his eyes tight again, scrunched his face into a grimace, and thrust out his open hand toward the boy, who was standing to one side.

The boy rushed forward with a large flagon, which he placed in the prophet's outstretched hand. The prophet held it there while the boy filled it to the brim with a dark foamy liquid, which he poured from a stoppered wooden cask.

"Sacred potion," the abbot whispered to Fodge.

The prophet opened one eye and gave Risby a long, baleful stare. He took a stout pull at the flagon, then extended it back toward the boy, who quickly topped it off again.

"Hair of the werewolf," the prophet corrected, before belching resonantly. Risby felt a little piece of himself painfully dying inside. He did not interrupt again.

The old prophet turned an appraising bloodshot eye toward Fodge, and the two men looked at each other like a pair of old card players, each trying to guess at the other's bluff. After a few moments, the prophet grunted sagely, and spoke.

"Hrmp... You have a question."

Fodge nodded slightly in affirmation. He'd had the entire journey to contemplate the ideal phrasing, and he took great care to speak it clearly and precisely, word for word.

"The *king*..." he said with due emphasis, "wishes to know how the *dragon*... might be slain."

Fodge closed his eyes briefly, and gave another courteous nod, to make it entirely clear that he was finished.

"Rrrmphff..." said the prophet, with a scowl. He peered at Fodge for several seconds, even more intently than before, then lowered his gaze to that dark and frothy liquid, held in the flagon which he was now clutching tightly with both hands.

# Chapter 2:
## The Mind of the Prophet

Old Notwot stared silently into his beer for a long time, as if the answers to all of life's mysteries might be found there, etched in foam. He sat, and he stared, and he thought.

*Prat that Risby... My aching skull... A curse on all mornings... Oh the gods, what did I drink last night?... Mulch and gardens... What was it they wanted?... From the king, eh? Well, that's a ripe chicken, isn't it?... Prims and prattle... Somebody's head will be off about this... By Mosig's brown balls, I'd part with mine... Where is that boy with my beer?... It's in your hand you old sot; you're looking at it... Ah, yes, so I am... He's a good lad... Kings and courtiers... Damn the lot of them... What was I thinking?... Nothing and everything... How did that song go, the one about the prince and the serving girl?... Doesn't matter...*

*The Dragon, ey?... what harm's the old worm done to any of them, I'd like to know... Keeps to himself; guilty of history... dull echoes... water and beer... But they forget. Aye, they forget... morning isn't always this bright, is it?... Ruins of the old kingdom... Then Abzag, bless the old girl... Is any of it true?... Old life makes way for the new... What was I thinking again?... Can't solve the whole world in a morning... bits and pieces, bits and pieces... First the question in hand, then back to bed.*

*How does a dragon die?... all things rise and fall... barley in the fields... barley to beer and back again... how did that song go?... "A lady, a knight, a lord, a law. A curse on the world, and feed the oxen straw."... yes, that was the tune... can't remember any more of it... Doesn't matter...*

*Armies and war... it always comes to that, I suppose... Dark days... Then a new age, perhaps? Perhaps... But that wasn't the question, was it. Never the right question; the whole world, forever only looking to the next stair... Easier going up than coming down... Yes, yes... Was morning always this bright?... the dawn and the dusk of a darkening day, dreams of dragons with little to say... Ha!... I quite like that... I'll never remember it.... Bits and pieces, bits and pieces... Can't solve the whole world in a morning... First the question in hand, then back to bed... Doesn't matter... Yes... Yes, I suppose that will do.*

He looked up from his beer again, and spoke aloud.

# Chapter 3:
## Prophecy

"Feed him a princess," the old man mumbled with enthusiastic certainty. Then he paused, and took a long pull at his flagon. He'd meant to leave it at that, but couldn't help himself. "If that doesn't choke the old worm, nothing will," he added.

The prophet laughed at his own joke, miserably, and wrapped his arms around his aching skull. He lost his balance and rolled off the bench, into a heap on the floor. The boy rushed forward just in time to catch the flagon before it spilled, carefully handing it back to the old man as he helped him into his seat again.

"Yes, yes..." the prophet continued, once he had gathered himself. "First the princess, then the... the... oh, the stabby things... the..."

"Swords?" suggested the boy, quietly.

"Swords!" shouted the prophet, grimacing at the sound of his own booming voice. He paused for several seconds, muttering incomprehensible sounds, trying to recalibrate his vocal apparatus to a more moderate volume. "Yes," he eventually added, nodding clumsily. "Then comes the sword, the axe, whatever else. Blades and handles, tools of war, bloodshed and death will surely follow; all that sort of nonsense. Echoes of time, everywhere. Everywhere."

He emptied the last drops from the flagon, handed it carelessly to the boy, and lolled his head back, staring up at the ceiling. Fodge and Risby knelt there in silence, waiting for his next words. Only when he began to snore did they realize that he was fast asleep.

------------------------------------------------------

Once the abbot and the stranger had exited the temple, the boy gently roused his sleeping master, and helped him stumble out the back way and across the abbey grounds toward his little tower. The prophet kept his hood over his face, not to conceal it from prying eyes, but to shield it from the mid-day sunshine, which seemed impossibly bright. The abbey grounds were empty, as the guards and the other priests were still attending to the visitor and his escort, by the entrance at the far end of the compound.  All the abbey's laborers and most of the servants had been sent to their own quarters an hour before, to hide there until the royal guest departed.

Climbing the staircase to the prophet's chamber was something of a challenge, but it was easier going up than it had been coming down. The old man kept muttering quietly to himself the entire time.  Most of what he said was little more than random grunts and incoherent mumbles as he climbed the stairs, but when they reached the top he paused for a moment, leaning against the wooden door, and looked the boy very deliberately in the eye.

"Never the right question," he said, slowly shaking his head.  "Had you noticed that?"

The boy was puzzled; he'd heard the words very clearly, but he didn't understand what the old man had meant by them.  He waited for an explanation, some sort of clarifying remark, but Notwot just looked at him with a keenly whimsical stare.

"No sir?..."  the boy replied cautiously, when he could stand the silence no longer.

"The treasure isn't what they think," the old man said, with a grin, "no, not at all.  But precious... oh, yes!  More precious by far."

With that, the old man turned back to the closed door and released the iron catch.  He gently pushed the heavy door open and stumbled unsteadily inside.  The boy helped his master out of his ceremonial garb and back into bed, covering him with a light blanket.  Notwot rolled himself onto his side and pulled the blanket up.

"Thank you, lad, thank you."  said the old man.  "You're a great help, and the best of the lot.  Now off with you.  You can find better things to do than hover about me, surely.  And fetch that cleaning girl up here.  You know the one I like."

The boy silently nodded that he did, and gave a quick bow of reverence before scuttling himself out the door and down the tower stairs.

-----------------------------------------------------

Risby took the offered coinpurse with a courteous nod, neither opening it nor inquiring as to its contents. He considered it unwise to haggle over price when dealing with the king.

"He doesn't seem well," said Fodge. He'd never been face-to-face with the prophet before, and hadn't been at all sure what to expect from the encounter.

"Yes, it's a difficult business," said the abbot, soberly. "A great burden, you know, wisdom and visions and all that. Very draining. It wears on a man." He unconsciously jingled the little bag of coins, trying to guess at its value.

"Yes, of course," replied Fodge, who was feeling increasingly skeptical about the whole business. "An unfortunate prophecy, wouldn't you say?"

Alarm bells began to ring inside Risby's skull. Any dealings with the king were perilous, but with the payment already in hand, he'd begun to think that they'd all survived the encounter nicely. Now he was worried. The last thing he needed was an unhappy royal customer. Why couldn't the old drunk have come up with something more vague, less fraught with potential negative repercussions? Anyone with a scrap of business sense should have known better. Risby craned his neck ever so slightly, and turned his full attention to damage control.

"Unfortunate?" the abbot asked innocently. "In what way?"

"Are you mad?!?" said Fodge, incredulously. "The king only has the one daughter, you know that as well as I do. We can't rightly go feeding Her Royal Princess – the sole heir to the throne – to some scaly monstrosity in the hills!"

"Oh, I don't think that's necessary..." replied Risby, trying his best to sound genuinely unconcerned. "Dress up some peasant girl or other. Surely a dragon won't know the difference."

The financial minister was aghast, and made no effort to hide it. "I beg your pardon... Are you suggesting some sort of... counterfeit?"

Now Risby's heart was racing. He had been hoping the abbey might receive some small cut of the profits, if the dragon was really slain. In fact, he'd already been fantasizing about what he might do with the loot. But now he could almost hear the prospect of that royal reward slipping away, like the hoofbeats of a lone horse disappearing into the night. His head began to swim. He lost his composure, and blurted out the first thing that popped into his mind.

"Oh, but of course!" Risby heard himself saying. "Yes, yes, a fake princess, obviously. Just as good. Not a thing to worry about. We do it all the time."

The abbot's last few words, *We do it all the time*, hung gently in the air like a freshly dead pickpocket swinging from the gallows. Had he been given a week to plan, it is unlikely that Risby could have come up with a more obvious lie, and he winced so hard at saying it that he had to look down for a moment to gather himself. He'd blown it. He'd overplayed his hand, and instantly wished that he hadn't said anything at all. But he had, and there was nothing to be done now except to try and make the best of it. He looked up at Fodge again, forcing a smile onto his face that absolutely screamed *I just lied to you. Let us both pretend that I didn't.*

# Chapter 4:
## Lord Fodge

At a patient, methodical pace, it was a three-day ride on horseback from Flapham Abbey back to the Royal Palace at Nyl. This was just as well because Lord Fodge had quite a lot of thinking to do, and was very glad to have a few quiet days in which to do it. He was not inclined to hurry home.

He found himself in the unfortunate circumstance of serving a king whose ambition exceeded his resources. For nearly seven years Fodge had successfully managed the rebuilding and expansion of King Othelwaite's royal palace, despite cost over-runs and shortages of manpower. But that work was now complete, and the king was turning his mind toward dreams of conquest.

After centuries of war, the Land of the Three Realms had been at peace (or nearly so) for over thirty years now: ever since Othelwaite's grandfather, Arvallin the Great, had conquered the last few independent provinces west of the mountains and north of the Grey River. Before Arvallin's time, the kingdom of Drey had not existed, and now it was arguably the most powerful realm of the three.

But Othelwaite wanted more. According to legend, the heirs of Arvallin would one day conquer every part of the great island. Such stories likely began as standard tropes of regal propaganda conceived in his grandfather's time, but to Othelwaite that made little difference. In his mind, the myths he'd been taught in his childhood foretold his own personal destiny; and so he dreamed of restoring the glory of the old kingdom, with himself as master of it all. To that end, he had built the most magnificent palace, an unshakable fortress from which he could rule unchallenged. It was a grand monument in stone, designed to strike awe into the hearts of his allies, terrify his foes, and guard his treasure.

But that, in part, was the problem: Othelwaite had very little treasure left to guard. Construction of his great palace had so badly depleted the royal treasury that funds to pay his army were running low. Worse still, he was not only running out of money, but also food.

So many of Drey's young men had been conscripted into service – either to build the king's fortress, or to join his army, or to man the great mines at Blackhall – that too few had been left to plow and plant the fields.  It was now only mid-spring, but Lord Fodge already knew that come fall, the harvest would be poor.  By winter, at the latest, the king would be unable either to pay his overgrown army or to feed it.  Already, Othelwaite's soldiers were "foraging" here and there in an effort to extend supplies, but that would only delay the inevitable, and it was causing great hardship throughout the realm.  There was not only the usual grumbling from the peasants, but also anger from the tradesmen and merchants, and now even hints of rebellion among the clergy as well.

Othelwaite had painted himself into a corner.  Fodge guessed that the realm could be sustained through the summer, and then the fall harvest might offer a respite while it lasted.  But the king needed a war soon, or his great house of cards would come crashing down around him.  It might be delayed for a few seasons, but if things remained as they were the end result was now unavoidable.

But war presented a problem of geography.  Tunber could not be invaded without crossing the great Grey River, and then marching an army south through many miles of barren lands.  An attack on Furgathor would require an army marching north, around the mountains and across the harsh and broken terrain of Karvik.  And any campaign, either against Furgathor to the north or Tunber to the south, would leave Drey's borders exposed to a sudden attack from the other kingdom.

The only alternate route for invasion was through the foothills below the Last Mountain, under the shadow of the dragon.  From there, an army would be well-positioned both to attack and defend against either neighbor.  But it was impossible.  No armies could pass that way as long as the dragon lived.

And so, in the hopeful death of the dragon, Othelwaite saw a solution to all his problems.  A route for invasion would open, and the untold wealth hidden in the dragon's hoard would provide the funds to pay his armies.  Food could then be purchased abroad, or taken through conquest.  If only the dragon could be slain, every obstacle to the king's ambition would be removed.

But now it appeared — assuming that the prophecy was to be believed — that slaying the dragon would require the expenditure of a princess, and that was no small matter.  Princesses are valuable commodities, and even under the best of circumstances are generally in short supply.  Fodge wondered briefly if some friendly kingdom might have a princess or two to spare, but he didn't pursue that line of thought with much optimism.  Recent diplomatic relations with Tunber had been cordial enough, but their king, Mulrin the Second, had only two sons and no daughters.  He wasn't sure if there were any available princesses in Furgathor, though King Edral was far less friendly toward Drey, and unlikely to willingly offer his assistance.  There was even less hope in obtaining a princess from the kings of the Western Corsairs, across the sea.  They were far away, and were unsteady trading partners at best: not to be trusted.

And anyway, the entire line of reasoning was absurd.  What king would willingly surrender a daughter, just so Othelwaite could slay the dragon and conquer the world?  The only monarch Fodge knew of that might be willing to part with a daughter just for a chance at the dragon's gold was his own boss.  But that was entirely out of the question.  Othelwaite only had the one child, and even were he willing to feed her to the dragon (a very real possibility), the princess herself would never go for it.  Self-sacrifice was not a characteristic royal trait.

Fodge wasn't at all sure who would prevail if it came to an outright power struggle between father and daughter.  Princess Dophne was every bit as ambitious and ruthless as her father, and Fodge suspected she had been quietly forging alliances of her own for some time.  There were more than a few provincial lords who had no love for Othelwaite, and who might look favorably on the prospect of replacing him with a clever young queen.

But to Lord Fodge, at least in practical terms, those details made little difference.  No matter how such a scenario might play out, he was quite certain that he would not be around to see the final outcome.  Either the princess or the king, and possibly both, would almost certainly order his execution, probably sooner rather than later.  By the time the dust settled on their royal conflict, Lord Fodge, the former financial minister, would be long dead and gone.

The more Fodge thought about it, the more convinced he was that he was facing a no-win situation.  If the prophecy was true – and Fodge was not convinced it was – then that meant the dragon couldn't be killed without the expenditure of a princess.  But no princess was readily expendable, and so the mere mention of that proposition to – well, to pretty much *anyone* – would likely cost Fodge his head.  But by the same token, if Fodge returned to the king without a suitable plan for obtaining the dragon's gold, that also would likely result in work for the royal headsman.  For Fodge, all paths seemed to lead inexorably toward the same unpalatable conclusion.

But no matter how Fodge put the pieces together, his thoughts always returned to the abbot's absurd suggestion of a counterfeit princess.  It wouldn't work... prophecies could not be cheated.  But then again, what did it matter?  Perhaps the prophet was a fraud, and all that was really needed to slay the dragon was a few knights of sufficient valor, willing to make the attempt.  As far as he knew, no one had even *tried* to kill the dragon for a great many years, possibly not since the fall of the old kingdom.

And if an attack on the dragon failed, what of it?  By not offering up a real princess, the stakes in such an attempt could be kept quite low.  And Fodge was certain that the king wouldn't blink an eye at risking a small handful of knights and soldiers either way; he had plenty to spare.  In such circumstances, it was likely that a failure could be plausibly blamed on almost anything, and Fodge might manage to escape with his neck intact after all.  At the very least, even if the attempt ended in a catastrophic failure, it would still buy him a little more time, which in Lord Fodge's case was the most precious commodity of all.

By the second day of the return journey, Fodge had fully convinced himself that this was the most workable plan, and his thinking had shifted from considering *what to do*, to instead contemplating *how best to do it*.

# Chapter 5:
## A Quiet Proclamation

And so it was decided that a tournament would be held in the capital city of Nyl, beginning on the first day following the new moon. Three champions would be chosen to undertake a bold and dangerous quest, for the greater glory of King Othelwaite and the entire kingdom of Drey. Upon completion of this quest – the nature of which was not clearly indicated – one of those knights would win the hand of the Princess Dophne in marriage.

Riders had been sent to discretely carry the news to every province in the realm. These messengers were under strict orders to speak only with the lord of each province, and not to breathe a word about the tournament to another solitary soul. Othelwaite hoped to lure in the best knights of the kingdom, but he didn't want the city to turn into a carnival. This entire scheme to slay the dragon was – at its heart – a business venture, and something of a gamble to boot. The less fanfare that surrounded it, the better.

It was nearly a week later – just as the first knights began to arrive in Nyl – that Princess Dophne first got wind of what was about to go down. She was not pleased.

-------------------------------------------------

It was a lovely late spring morning when the doors to the king's breakfast chamber burst open and Her Royal Princess Dophne stalked across the floor toward her father's noshing table. The king, who had been carefully plotting a strategic assault on a large silver serving tray laden with savory bacon cutlets, looked up with alarm, and took a deep breath to brace himself. He'd been expecting this, and was surprised it had taken her this long to call him out. He only wished she'd waited until after breakfast. It was trouble enough arguing with her on the best of days, and having to do so on an empty stomach only made things worse.

"You're holding a tournament," she stated abruptly. "Why wasn't I told?"

"Oh dear," said the king, in mock disappointment, "and I so wanted it to be a surprise."

"Is it true then, what I'm hearing?  Have you really promised my hand in marriage to the winner?"

"We are holding a tournament," the king explained patiently, "to choose the bravest knights in all the land to go and slay the dragon. It's a sacred quest.  We had to offer them *something*.  You can't have a tournament without a prize."

"I will not marry some ridiculous knight," Princess Dophne declared firmly.  "I'm not throwing away my inheritance just to fill your treasury."

"Precious Darling," King Othelwaite replied, "my treasury *is* your inheritance."

"It is not.  *Drey* is my inheritance, the whole realm.  All of it.  It is mine, and I intend to have it."

"And you will, Raindrop, you will.  All in due time, of course."  The king delighted in calling his daughter by pet names.  He knew it irritated her.

"Not if I'm married," she responded angrily.  "It'll belong to my husband – Sir Bentspear, or Sir Rustbucket, or whoever it turns out to be.  I'll choose my own husband, thank you, and not until *after* I'm queen."

"But I'll be dead and gone by then," the king replied, "and I'd so hate to miss your wedding."

"Just as I would hate to miss your funeral," his daughter answered, without amusement.

"I'll be sure to reserve the best seat for you," said the king.  "But I'm only teasing.  You won't really have to marry the knight who slays the dragon, whoever that turns out to be.  That's just the sort of lie daddies have to tell sometimes, to get what they want."

"Don't patronize me, Your Majesty," she replied icily.

"You should be grateful, really," said the king, shifting suddenly to a far more serious tone.  "By all rights, I could be sending *you*, you know."

"Sending me?... Where?"

Othelwaite looked his daughter squarely in the eye.

"According to the prophecy," the king said, pausing a moment for emphasis, "the dragon can't be slain until he devours a princess. A *princess*, mind you. It's fortunate for you that Lord Fodge has arranged for a substitute. But I must warn you not to test my fatherly affection too far."

His point made, the king turned his attention once again to his breakfast, as if the princess were no longer there. It was his way of making it clear that their nice little father-daughter chat was over. Dophne stood there for some time, silently smoldering. Then she smiled politely, curtsied, and casually walked away.

Once she had finally gone, King Othelwaite slumped into his chair, closed his eyes, and rubbed his forehead. Why did he have to have such a difficult daughter? Why couldn't she have been one of those shallow, simpering types, like so many of her mother's handmaidens had been? Then he could have happily married her off to some distant prince ages ago and been done with her. As it was, she was a constant thorn in his side, and – he was well aware – the chief danger to his rule. She was sharp and cunning and resourceful, and was admired by far too many of his lords and soldiers for comfort. And no one could deny that she was beautiful, or at least that she was rich enough to seem so.

Ever since he'd first seen her – more than nineteen years ago, as a squawling newborn in the queen's bassinet – he'd always felt that there was far too much of himself in her, and not nearly enough of her mother. Or perhaps there was too little of either of them. It made his head hurt just thinking about it.

It occurred to him that he might have erred in telling her the details of the prophecy, but it hardly mattered. He trusted Fodge's discretion, but eventually others would have to know, and Othelwaite was wise enough to understand that, as with the tournament, such things could not be kept secret for long. Prophecies, dragons, quests, and affairs of state always seemed to emerge into the light, often at the most inappropriate times.

# Chapter 6:
## Aglor of Glaen

The king's messengers travelled swiftly, but it was many miles from Nyl to the furthest reaches of Drey. And so, even as the first eager knights from the nearby provinces were beginning to arrive at the capital, some of the more distant lords had still not yet even received their invitations.

One of the last to hear of the tournament was Vildar, Lord of Glaen, whose lands lay at the southeastern corner of the kingdom, along the banks of the Grey River. Glaen was a rich and fertile region. Wheat and other grains were grown there in great open fields, and the rolling hills at the eastern end of the province were filled with herds of livestock, particularly horses. The finest, most handsome mounts in all of Drey were bred and raised in Glaen, and were often sold at equally handsome prices to lords and wealthy merchants throughout the realm. "As good as from Glaen" was a common exaggeration used by stablemasters of other provinces when they wanted to brag on the quality of their own foals.

Lord Vildar was much too old to take part in the tournament himself. But his two sons, Aglor and Valand, were not only the right age for such an undertaking, but were also conveniently unmarried. Of the two, there was no question that Aglor was the better candidate. He was not only older than Valand, but also a more prudent and skillful soldier.

For his part, Valand was quick to admit that his elder brother was the better knight in almost every way; he did not begrudge Aglor his opportunity. In fact, Valand was eager to help him prepare for the long journey to Nyl, and to counsel him with a few sage words of his youthful wisdom.

"It's an awfully long ride to Nyl," Valand pointed out. "I would think you could get your head beaten in right here in Glaen, and save yourself the trip."

Aglor smiled. "Ah, yes," he said, "but you've neglected to consider that there are no princesses here, and that is an important factor in the equation."

"Why would you want to marry the princess anyway, I have to wonder."

"Well..." replied Aglor, "there *is* the chance to become king – which some might regard as a desirable perk – but aside from that, the princess is young, and rich, and is said to be very beautiful."

"She can't be as beautiful as the barmaid at the Speckled Crow," said Valand, with a wry smirk. He crossed his arms as if he had just won the argument.

Aglor shook his head with amusement. "Peasant girls will be the death of you, brother."

"I can think of worse ways to die. Fighting in a royal tournament, for one, or going on some ridiculous quest is another."

"There are things one has to do to move forward in life."

"That's why it's so lovely being second-born," said Valand, cheerfully. "As far as I can see, this all works out purely to my advantage. If you somehow win, I'll be brother to the king. And if you manage instead to get your head chopped off, I'll suddenly find myself first in line to become the next Lord of Glaen."

"All in due time, of course," said Aglor.

"Oh, of course. Don't mistake me; I'm in no hurry, one way or the other. But in either case, I would seem to hold a winning hand."

"Cards will be the death of you, brother."

"Come now... which will it be, cards or peasant girls? I can't die from both."

"I wouldn't be so sure," said Aglor. I think you're clever enough that you could find a way."

"It is safer, I think, to gamble at cards and peasant girls than to toy with fate. The pleasures of winning are real enough, and the penalties for losing are far less dire. I am perfectly happy to let you take on the real risks in life, if you're crazy enough to do it. And after all is said and done, I'll gladly pick up whatever loose coins fall from your pockets."

Aglor smiled. "You are an endless fountain of encouragement."

"I do what I can for you, but you are already so far gone. And here," Valand said, retrieving his brother's sword from its hanging-place on the wall, "you might find a use for this. Don't say I never helped you."

"I would not have forgotten it," Aglor replied. He took the sword and gave his brother a sincere and affectionate hug. "Look after our father and try to stay out of trouble, at least for as long as I am gone. I hope that's not too much to ask?"

Valand smiled and shook his head. "You know I will," he said. "Oh, and Aglor, in all sincerity, do try *not* to get your head chopped off. I've really no desire at all to be the next Lord of Glaen, but I might not mind being brother to the king."

# Chapter 7:
## The Choosing of Champions

Despite the limited publicity and the severe lack of advance notice, nearly a hundred knights arrived at Nyl for the royal tournament. Gallant young hopefuls from across the realm – mostly the sons and grandsons of provincial lords – dropped whatever other plans they might have made like pennies into a well. A chance to marry into the royal line – and perhaps one day become king – was worth any personal risk, or any scheduling inconvenience. It was rumored that two of the young men had even postponed previously planned nuptials with lesser brides, all for the slender chance of securing a far more profitable match. There was also the lure of Princess Dophne's (almost) legendary beauty, but for most of the hopefuls that was at best a secondary incentive.

Interestingly, no one seemed to be concerned about what sort of quest the three winners would eventually be sent on. The young hopefuls didn't waste their attention on such matters. They were focused on the immediate task at hand, and couldn't be bothered worrying about anything beyond their next step up the political staircase.

The tournament stretched over four days, and true to the nature of such events, it was exceedingly violent. The contestants were put through a wide range of challenges, encompassing everything from horsemanship to archery to group battle tactics. But of course, the chief attraction for spectators was the individual dueling.

Duels were fought only using blunted weapons, and many precautions were taken to minimize the chance of serious injuries among the contestants. No one, fortunately enough, was killed. But bones were broken, blood was spilled, scars were given, and serious contusions were too commonplace to even draw notice. Given the extraordinary opportunity at stake for the winners, the combatants were not inclined to be merciful with each other. Sportsmanship be damned, this was war; or at least it was as close to war as most of the entrants had ever personally experienced.

At the end of the second day, the group of contestants was cut in half, and at the end of the third, only fifteen knights were allowed to continue.  At the end of the fourth day, the three victors were finally named.

The first chosen was a tall young knight named Rudrik.  He was the eldest son of Lord Hargrave, who was master of the province of Toule and the great port city of the same name.  Toule lay along Drey's northwestern coast, and was a large and relatively wealthy region.  Much of that area was heavily forested, and farms were scarce.  But while it lacked in farming, the province thrived on its fisheries and shipyards.  The tall ships of Toule had a high reputation, and Lord Hargrave was a respected and influential man, particularly among the noble families of Drey's more northern provinces.

In the tournament, Rudrik had fared brilliantly in the tests of arms, particularly in archery and open dueling on foot.  In hand-to-hand combat, his weapon of choice was a long-bladed spear.  This was not a javelin designed to be thrown, but a stout pole with a heavy blade – a weapon to be held in both hands, either slicing or stabbing with reach and power.  It had served him well in the forests around Toule, hunting bears and wild boar, and presented a formidable challenge for the opponents he had faced in each of his individual duels.

Rudrik had fared less well in some of the other tests, such as horsemanship and battle tactics.  He preferred to fight on foot, and had little interest in strategy.  He consistently chose the simplest and most direct approach to every situation, confident that skill and courage alone could overcome any obstacle.  All notions of subtlety or nuance were lost on him.

The second knight chosen was Beldrin, the eldest son of Lord Torinal, master of the province of Blackhall.  The region took its name from a steep-sided canyon, carved deep into the mountains by the Mortise River.  Blackhall Canyon was so sheer and so deep that darkness reigned there for much of the day.  Only in the morning and evening, when the sun was aligned with the river, did direct light reach the bottom.  This was where Drey's richest mines could be found, and great quantities of coal and iron and other metals were extracted from the cloven mountain.  Labor there was always in short supply, and every year poor young men would be brought in from other provinces, to toil and eventually die in the mines.

Beldrin was the shortest of the three knights chosen, but also the strongest.  Broad in the shoulders and powerfully built from head to toe, he dominated in the tests of strength, and simply overpowered most of his dueling opponents.  His preferred weapon was a great two-handed axe, and he fought with very little armor and no shield.  This allowed him great mobility.  None of his opponents had been able to effectively land their first blow against him, and none of them had gotten the chance for a second.  All the duels he fought were like reflections of himself: they were brutal and short.

Though no one questioned his courage or prowess, Beldrin was not popular among the other knights at the tournament.  He lacked the noble graces that most of the other contestants valued.  He laughed easily – often at inappropriate times – and was quick to mock those he defeated, and even his own attendants.  This was in keeping with his upbringing – a reflection of his father's management of the great mines at Blackhall, where most of the workers were little more than slave labor.

The final champion chosen was Aglor, the son of Lord Vildar, who had distinguished himself in the contests of horsemanship, as well as in the tests of group battle tactics.  Having been born and raised in Glaen, Aglor had spent his life among horses, and had a natural understanding of them; consequently, he was an expert rider.  Of the three knights chosen, he was the only one who preferred to fight from horseback.

And unlike Beldrin, Aglor was quite popular among the other competitors.  He was handsome and courteous, smiled politely even at servants, and considered his words carefully when he spoke.  He was cautious without cowardice, noble without arrogance, and wise beyond his years.  Not a few of the other knights at the tournament cheered when he was announced as the third champion.

Officially, the champions had been chosen by a secret panel of judges, but in truth, Lord Fodge had made the final selections himself, and his choices were based as much on politics as on merit.  It was not lost on him that the prophet had never clearly specified exactly how the dragon would be killed, and had made no mention at all of what sort of man would do the killing. If the prophecy proved true (which he still doubted) then any man of sufficient luck or courage might equally serve the task. Fodge certainly knew that prophecies rarely turned out quite as expected.

And then there was the matter of the princess Dophne. If the man who killed the dragon was to have her hand in marriage, Fodge felt it would be prudent to choose knights who might make a plausible match for her. By picking the eldest sons of wealthy and prominent lords – and selecting them from three very different parts of the realm – he hoped to minimize the likelihood that the princess's betrothal would somehow incite a general rebellion or civil war. Wars of succession were a harsh fact of history, which he did not want to see revisited.

Of course, King Othelwaite had already told his daughter that she wouldn't really have to marry the man who slew the dragon, but that little detail had not been passed along to Lord Fodge. Regardless however, it is unlikely that Fodge would have done anything differently, even had he known. It was impossible for him to guard against every contingency. He could only make the choices that seemed to him least likely to lead toward certain disaster.

In the afternoon of the day following the tournament, a grand banquet was held to honor the three young champions. They were suitably wined and dined, and everyone in attendance spoke glowingly of their skill and their prowess and their virtue. Some of what was said was true.

Interestingly, despite his prominent role in arranging the tournament and choosing the champions, Lord Fodge did not attend the feast. Even as it was going on, he still had one more essential piece of unfinished business to attend to.

# Chapter 8:
## The Turnip Thief

Sergeant Gask of the Royal Guards stood patiently just inside the rear entrance to Lord Fodge's private chambers.  Behind him, two of his men were holding what looked at a glance to be a pile of dirty rags.  Only on closer inspection did it become obvious that it was actually a bedraggled young girl, down on her knees.

Lord Fodge looked the girl over appraisingly.

"She seems to be about the right size... is she in good health?"

"I suppose so," the sergeant answered.  "Half-starved maybe, but she's stronger than she looks.  Her teeth are good, I can tell you that much."

"Oh?" asked Fodge, curiously.

"She bit one of the men, when we caught her."  The sergeant laughed. "Best keep your hands in your pockets."

"How old is she?"

"No idea; thirteen, fourteen maybe.  I can never tell."

"How old are you?"  Fodge asked the girl.  She said nothing, but looked up at him and scowled.

"You won't get any answers from her," said the sergeant.  "Doesn't talk much, this one."

"Where did you find her?"

"In the markets.  Robbing one of the merchants; stealing beets or something like that."

"A turnip," the girl said suddenly.  "I took one turnip, and he owed it to me."

"Did he now?" asked Fodge suspiciously.  "And why is that?"

The girl gave no reply.  She stared angrily at the floor.

"Where do you come from?" Fodge asked.  "Who are your parents?"

"I don't remember."

The sergeant laughed again. "Like I said, you'll get no answers from her! She's an orphan, I'd wager. Lots of the little beggars wandering the streets. Or parents couldn't feed her, turned her out. Once they're old enough, they cut them loose. Peasants, bah, they don't care one way or the other. I'll tell you, the things I see on watch sometimes would keep you awake at night..."

Fodge raised a hand to interrupt. "Yes, yes. Thank you, Sergeant," he said firmly. "I am well aware that poverty exists."

"Sorry, Lordship."

Fodge drummed his fingers, thoughtfully. The girl would do. She was a little darker than he would have liked, and her hair was too short, but those were minor quibbles. She seemed healthy, and was small and slender enough to fit the dress they'd chosen. Those were the most important things.

"Well done, Sergeant," he said with a decisive nod. "Keep her tonight, and Captain Harbek will collect her in the morning."

"Very good, Lordship," the sergeant replied. "That's bad luck for you, girl."

"What?" said the girl, suddenly horrified. "You're going to hang me for stealing a turnip?!"

Now it was Lord Fodge's turn to laugh. Not a deep belly-laugh; just a fleeting moment of sardonic delight. He looked down at the girl and shook his head slowly.

"Hanged?" he said, still smiling in spite of himself. "Hanged, did you say? No, no, no... not at all; something far worse than that. We're going to make a princess out of you."

# Chapter 9:
## The Caravan Departs

The next morning, in the dark hours before dawn, a small caravan assembled in a courtyard near the city gates of Nyl.  A troop of twelve soldiers, led by Captain Harbek of the Royal Guards, would escort the three young knights on their journey south.  The early hour had been chosen to ensure that the caravan departed with as little fanfare as possible.  The quest to slay the dragon was, officially at least, still to be kept a secret.

Travelling with the knights would be a cook, a scholar, and two drivers leading horse-drawn wagons.  The first wagon carried the food and the tents and the other gear.  The second carried a locked cedar chest, which contained a marvellous dress that the princess Dophne had long ago outgrown.  That wagon also carried the large iron cage which held the ragged peasant girl.

Lord Fodge was there to see them off.

"Brave knights," he began, "you have won the king's tournament, and shown great skill and courage.  You have done honor to yourselves and your family names.  By virtue of your virtue, you have been chosen.  Now, the time has come to reveal the task that lies before you.  Your quest, if you agree to the challenge, is to ride forth, and slay the dragon."

The knights stirred in their saddles, but Fodge did not pause to allow a response, either yes or no.

"You may die," he continued, without apparent concern, "but it has been *foretold* that the bravest and most true of heart among you will prevail, and the dragon will be slain."

This was not precisely what the prophet Notwot had actually said. Lord Fodge had chosen to take some liberties with the original prophecy, in order to make it sound a little more noble – and a little more straightforward – for those who would have to do the hard part. He figured that what the knights didn't know wouldn't hurt them, or if it did end up hurting them, they wouldn't be in any position to complain.

"It's a worthy challenge, Your Grace," Aglor said. "But one thing puzzles me still. The girl, in the prison cage, is she a part of our quest? And if so, why?"

"You surprise me, Aglor," said Lord Fodge, who was not, in fact, surprised. "Consider your strategy. The girl is merely a wastrel, a vagabond, condemned for an act of thievery. But now she is to become a princess, or so she will seem to the dragon, once she is properly attired. By setting her in a place of your own choosing, you can lure the dragon into ambush. The beast is not to be taken lightly, and it would not be wise to face him in his lair, where he would have every advantage."

If the knights found any flaw with this plan, they did not say so. The king's command was the king's command, after all, even if the king wasn't actually there to say it. And it was not their place to question a divine prophecy. Now that the true nature of their quest had finally been revealed to them, they were eager to begin. It would not do to dwell needlessly on a minor point of tactics.

Ironically enough, almost everyone there had already known what the quest would be, even before Fodge made his little speech. The three knights were, in fact, the last to find out. Captain Harbek had been told several days before, when the king first selected him to lead the caravan, and he had revealed it to his men. Even the girl in the cage had learned of her fate beforehand. She'd been told during her encounter with Lord Fodge the night before.

Each of the knights swore that he would slay the dragon or die in the attempt. Fodge wished them success and good fortune, and he watched as the caravan quietly slipped out of the city gates and disappeared into the morning fog. Once they were gone, the financial minister bundled himself in his cloak to ward off the dew, and returned to his private chambers. This would be a good time, he reasoned, to return to his home province, and perhaps to make arrangements for a longer journey, in case that became suddenly necessary.

-------------------------------------------------

By the time the sun had risen, the caravan was far from the city walls. They passed through long stretches of forest, occasionally broken by clusters of farms, small villages, or open fields. Often they would encounter other travellers. Many of the folk upon the road were beggars – vagabonds and refugees of one sort or another – fleeing in all directions (or so it seemed) either from poverty or from brigands or famine or some other natural or manmade disaster. There were more prosperous sorts of folk on the road as well: farmers with heavy carts, pilgrims headed to various shrines, and even merchants laden with wares, all coming and going from the capital city. All of those they passed marvelled at the three knights, and many were curious about the girl in the cage, but the soldiers glowered fiercely at anyone who got too close, and discouraged the asking of questions.

For much of that day, however, they found themselves alone upon the road, and it was fine weather for travel. The sun was bright, but the air was cool, and a light breeze was in their faces. The scents of the forest and the fields were rich and heartening, and all the men were flush with enthusiasm and pride as they set out on this bold adventure.

The three knights rode at the back of the caravan, and turned out to be excellent travelling companions. Rudrik and Beldrin knew dozens of old tales of heroism and valor, and they told them well. Many of their stories began with a familiar cast of characters – a young knight, a monster, and a beautiful damsel in distress – and the plots would typically progress along similar lines: The knight would do battle with the monster, against all odds he would prevail, and in the end he would marry the fair maiden, retiring to a happy old age fully financed by the monster's treasure.

Interestingly, the heroes in these tales were almost always *rescuing* the damsels. None of the stories mentioned anything about feeding the fair maiden to the monster, but no one seemed bothered by that particular incongruity.

For his part, Aglor preferred to sing. Some of the songs he knew were comical, and others were terribly sad. He sang a long and tragic ballad of a beautiful girl who fell in love with a common soldier. But her father – a powerful lord – did not approve, and sent her far away to live in a monastery. She remained there for many years. But when word came to her that the soldier had died in battle, she fell deeply into grief; and after a time, she took her own life.

Aglor had a good voice, and sang with such passion and sorrow that some of the soldiers openly wept. Then he made them laugh again, with a comic song about a thief and an innkeeper's daughter. And so they passed the first part of their journey, in daydreams of heroism and valor and romance.

The one man who had little interest in the knights' storytelling was Captain Harbek. He rode alone at the front of the caravan, and if he was moved by their tales, either to merriment or sorrow, it did not show. Many years before, as a young soldier still in his teens, he had fought under the command of Arvallin the Great in the final battle that had unified Drey. He was the only man present who had actually seen war, and he had little use for young men's tales of heroism.

He was grim as a rule, and pragmatic in his approach to all things. But those under his command adored him. To a man, they believed that he had been marked by the goddess Abzag for some great destiny, and that they themselves were made only to trail in his wake. They would follow him to the dragon – or wherever else he chose to lead – and gladly die there, if that was their lot.

The caravan made good progress on their first day's ride and did not stop until it was nearly dark. The knights were eager, and wanted to press on through the night, but Captain Harbek refused. He reminded them that the dragon had been there for centuries, and would still be there in another week or a month or a year. No one was going to get there ahead of them. There was no need to hurry.

They made camp in an open field, near a patch of woods where a stream crossed the main road, and settled in for the night.

# Chapter 10:
## The Girl in the Cage

It was nearly midnight. The caravan was encamped, and the soldiers were gambling. The scholar, fascinated but unwelcome to the game, lingered at the edge of the firelight and tried not to draw their attention. He was hoping that a fight would break out; watching men brawl with each other was one of his favorite pastimes. But it didn't seem that tonight's game would head in that direction.

"They aren't drunk enough," he thought to himself. Disappointed, he walked away back toward his own little tent.

The scholar considered himself fortunate to have been sent along on this great quest to slay the dragon. He'd been chosen by Lord Fodge, partly to make a written record of the journey for posterity's sake, but more importantly to tally up the loot after the dragon was slain. His chief responsibility was to make very certain that none of the dragon's hoard was "misplaced" through shoddy book-keeping.

The scholar's proper name was Orbert, but no one called him that; he was addressed as "Scholar" by almost everyone. And, by the same token, he called no one else by their proper name either. Everyone he met was either too important for him to speak to on such familiar terms, or too unimportant (in his eyes) to be bothered with. This unfortunate calculus of his unique social standing was one of the many reasons that he had no friends.

As he made his way back to his tent, the scholar stopped for a moment at the quiet sound of a female voice. He pursed his lips in annoyance. Ever since the caravan had set out from Nyl, the girl in the cage had been nothing but trouble. She'd shouted and argued a great deal at first, but since then she'd spoken only intermittently. Why she wouldn't just keep silent entirely was an utter mystery to him. He couldn't imagine her having anything worthwhile to say.

The scholar wanted nothing to do with the girl, but he wondered if – perhaps with a good talking to – she would see reason and leave everyone else in peace. He decided to try comforting her with a few helpful words of advice.

"Can't you be silent, you wretched child?" he suggested, kindly.

The girl looked up and snarled at him. "Go away, prat." she said.

"There, you see?" said the scholar, as if he'd just scored a winning point of rhetoric. "Insults. You're burden enough as it is, girl. You could at least show some gratitude."

"Gratitude...?"

"You don't seem to realize what an opportunity this is. Yesterday you were only a nameless street urchin, but today you're part of a great quest. And yet all you can do is complain. *I'm hungry... I'm thirsty... I'm cold... I don't want to be eaten by a dragon...* On and on and on. It's tiresome."

"Stand in the fire and roast yourself," the girl replied.

"You've no sense of what's important, that's your problem," the scholar continued, helpfully. "All these great and noble men around you, and then the dragon's treasure of course. You're just a cog in the wheels... you could be replaced, you know."

"Then replace me," she snapped back. "I'm no good for anything, you said it yourself. So turn me loose and replace me with someone better."

"Nonsense. You're the ideal nobody. All you need is a more objective appreciation of how unimportant you really are. Someone should have taught you that long ago."

"I could tell you what *you* are," said the girl. "I could tell you that you're an abject cretin; that you're the slime that grows on dead things at the bottom of a dried cesspool. I could tell you all of that, but I won't, because I'm above that sort of honesty."

The scholar snorted with offense, turned on his heel and disappeared into the shadows. There was clearly no point; she'd never learn manners by the time they reached the dragon. He found himself wondering just how convincing of a fake princess she would be. He didn't think she was pretty enough, not like a real princess at all. But perhaps the dragon couldn't tell.

"May the old worm choke on her," he thought, "let *him* teach her a lesson."

Once he had gone, the girl curled up in her cage and tried to sleep. Despite the scholar's assessment, she had never been just a nameless street urchin.  She had indeed been poor and hungry for a long time, but she had a name, and that name was Trea.

She detested the scholar, but got little satisfaction out of arguing with him.  She certainly had no fear of him, or even the soldiers for that matter.  They were under orders to make certain that she reached the dragon unharmed, or harmed as little as possible.  Then there were the knights; they wouldn't lower themselves even to bother with her.  In their eyes, she was a problem for lesser men.  The only person in the entire caravan she really feared was Harbek.  He was the one who set the boundaries on her punishments, and kept the others in line.  Even the knights – who at least in terms of social status were well above him – did not question his decisions.  He generally let them do as they wished, but if push ever came to shove, there was no question that Captain Harbek of the Royal Guards was the real leader of this expedition, and Trea, for her part, was simply the human cargo.

# Chapter 11:
## The Caravan at Flapham

It was fast approaching the sunset of their second day since leaving Nyl when the caravan arrived at Flapham Abbey. The abbey guards opened the gates, and greeted the travellers cheerfully.

This time, Risby was well prepared for guests. After Lord Fodge's visit, he had sent one of his younger priests to Nyl to keep an open ear for any news that might relate to Notwot's prophecy, and so he had heard all about the royal tournament. Knowing that the victors' caravan would almost certainly travel past Flapham Abbey – as it lay along the most efficient route from Nyl to the dragon – Risby had made careful plans to ensure that the abbey provided these anticipated guests with a more polished experience than the king's financial minister had received.

Risby even knew the names of the three young knights chosen as champions. And, as each could be identified by the distinctive colors of his livery, the abbot was able to greet them by turns as they rode through the gate.

"Hail, Rudrik of Toule! All praise your skill and virtue! Hail Beldrin of Blackhall! Mighty warrior, as strong as the mountains! Hail Aglor of Glaen! Master horseman, proud son of a noble line. Never has our humble abbey hosted such honored guests as these young champions."

If Captain Harbek felt slighted at not being included in this roll call of honor, he did not show it. But he was the one who rode forward and answered Risby's well-rehearsed greeting.

"I am Captain Harbek of the Royal Guard," he said, "and these are the king's champions, as you seem to know. We will stay here tonight, and tomorrow morning we will depart again."

"Greetings, Captain," said Risby. He'd expected the three knights to be the ones in charge of things, and for a fleeting moment he was thrown off his script. But he recovered quickly, and did his best to amend the oversight. "Your coming was foretold, and we have been expecting you. Everything is made ready for your comfort."

Harbek frowned and nodded thoughtfully. "Where will I find the prophet?" he asked. "I wish to speak with him as soon as may be."

Risby had been expecting this as well. "I am sorry to say that the prophet is indisposed. He is most unwell, and is unable to greet visitors at this time. However, we are delighted to welcome such esteemed guests as yourselves. We are, of course, but poor humble servants of Mosig. Nevertheless, we will do what we can to make your visit a comfortable one. I would be remiss if I did not also mention that there is beer available for purchase, if any of your men might find that to be of interest."

---

In fact, the prophet was not simply unwell or indisposed, he was dying, and would be gone from the world before the caravan ever reached the dragon. His words to Lord Fodge would be his final prophecy, and he had hardly left his room in the tower since the financial minister's visit.

The boy had doted on his master the entire time. He loved the old man, as did all the abbey's servants and laborers. Notwot was a kindly soul, in spite of his unpolished exterior. Now, everyone who lived at the abbey was left wondering what would become of them when he was gone.

Risby wondered too. Without the prestige of the prophet, Flapham Abbey might well be expected to once again dwindle into obscurity. His one hope was the dragon. If the monster were slain, the abbey's share of the fame and the treasure would almost certainly put Mosig's little sanctuary securely on easy street, at least for the rest of Risby's life, which was all Risby really cared about. And if by some chance the dragon were not slain, well, for Risby that was unthinkable, so he tried not to think about that possibility at all.

---

It was well past midnight and the half-moon had already set, when Trea was awakened by a quiet knocking sound. She opened her eyes to see a strange young man, who could not have been much older than she was. He was gently tapping on the side of her cage with a wooden cup.

"Would you like some water?" he asked in a whisper.

Trea instantly sat up, fully awake. She looked around in the darkness and realized she was still in the cage in the wagon, and still inside the abbey wall. She could see two soldiers, sitting on the ground nearby. She guessed they'd been ordered to guard her, but they seemed to be asleep.

She'd had little to eat or drink for days, and was desperately thirsty. "Please," she said in a whisper, as the boy reached the wooden cup through the riveted iron bands of the cage and handed it to her. The water was clear and cool as she drank. He refilled the cup, and she drank again.

"Mosig teaches us to show kindness to the poor," the boy said. "I'm sorry for your suffering. I can't imagine what terrible crimes you might have committed, or why you've been brought here under so much guard. But that doesn't really matter."

Trea coughed. She'd tried to drink too fast, and some of the water had gone the wrong way. The boy jumped at the sound, but the sleeping soldiers did not stir.

"I've done nothing!" she whispered urgently. "Can you let me out?"

"No," said the boy. "It's forbidden, and I wouldn't even know how. Forgive me, I can only do so much."

"But they are taking me to the dragon!"

The boy pulled back suddenly, and put his hand over his mouth.

"You are not a princess," he said, in astonishment.

"They mean to dress me as one!" she pleaded. "Can you let me out? If you do not help me to escape, I will die."

"But you're not a princess," he said, his eyes wide with alarm. "This wasn't the prophecy."

"What do you mean?"

"This wasn't the prophecy," said the boy again. "I heard my master speak it in the temple. I was there. This is all wrong."

"Let me out!" she shouted, desperately. That was enough to rouse the guards, who stumbled hastily to their feet.

"You boy!" one of them growled, "away from there. She's no business of yours."

"I'm sorry," the boy said. Whether he was apologizing to the girl or the guards, even he did not know.

"Off with you, then," said the other guard. "And you'll get worse than a beating if we catch you around that cage again."

The boy backed away for several steps, and then hurried off into the night.

# Chapter 12:
## The Journey South

After the caravan departed Flapham Abbey, Trea did not try to talk to anyone any longer, not even the driver of the wagon that carried her. He was an old peasant, half-deaf and tired of the world. He had no interest in the caged girl behind him, or indeed in anything beyond his next meal and the chance to sleep each night.

Trea stared at the back of his head, and watched his gnarled hands mechanically guiding the horses slowly down the stony road. Deep in her heart, she wished that she too could simply stop thinking. But she could not. For mile after mile, she could only look at the passing landscape, and listen to the steady creaking of the wagon and the slow clop of the horses. It is terrible to be an unwilling passenger in life, with little to do, no say in where you are going, and no desire to ever get there.

For the rest of the caravan, however, the visit to Flapham Abbey had left them in high spirits. The soldiers all agreed that the abbey's reputation for excellent beer was well-earned, and the three knights spent much of the next day in a good-natured argument over which of their provinces could claim to have the finest brew.

"They make a stout and proper beer at Flapham Abbey," said Rudrik. "It doesn't compare to the dark served in the Swordfish Inn at Toule, mind you, but it almost reminded me of home."

"The best grain makes the best beer," said Aglor, proudly. "And there is no finer grain in the world than what's grown in the rolling fields of Glaen. There isn't a bad beer to be found in the whole province, and that's the truth of it. Not that Flapham Abbey doesn't make a fine brew."

"Beer may be good enough for fishermen or farmers... but after a long day in the mines, a man needs something stronger," said Beldrin, who had never worked a day in the mines in his life. "Cider from the orchards to the west of Blackhall, along the banks of the Mortise River... that's a drink that will curl a man's beard."

The scholar Orbert, riding in front of the wagons, ignored the knights' ongoing debate. He had little interest in beer, and preferred to pass his time focused on more practical concerns, such as contemplating how he might estimate the value of the dragon's priceless treasures, and fretting over whether the scales he had brought would be large enough to accurately weigh the largest pieces in the monster's hoard.

Near the end of that day, they reached a large walled city called Albria. There, the main north-south road was crossed by another that ran east and west. Aglor spoke highly of an inn called *The Fox & Owl* which sat near the center of the town, but they did not stop to test his recommendation.

"Towns are trouble," said Captain Harbek, as he turned the caravan onto the road going east. The captain had travelled with soldiers often enough to know that the best way to avoid delays was to camp in the field, far from any unwanted distractions. He'd even been reluctant to visit Flapham Abbey, but agreed that it had probably been a worthwhile stop, despite the fact that they were not able to speak with the prophet.

As with so many of the smaller villages they had passed, the townsfolk of Albria swarmed around the caravan to beg for food and coins, to marvel at the handsome knights, and to gawk at the prisoner in the wagon. With such impressive guardians, they expected the cage to hold some fearsome brigand or horrible, screaming half-man. They were both disappointed and confused to discover that it only held an ordinary peasant girl, who sat miserably on the floor and said nothing. A few of the children tried throwing rocks and sticks at the cage, as they were accustomed to do, but the soldiers chased them off. Eventually, most of the townsfolk decided that it was poor sport anyway, and none of them followed the wagon beyond the eastern gate of the city wall.

"That main road we just left winds south for many more miles," Aglor explained to his companions, once they were beyond the crowds of onlookers, "until it strikes the Grey River and the ferry at Piyl. Most of the traffic that passes between Drey and Tunber comes that way. Perhaps a day's ride from here, or thereabouts, the road we're on now will turn south again.  A day or two after that we will cross the Ash River, which flows down cold from the mountains.  Beyond the river, this road runs almost due east toward the Last Mountain, and the shadow of the dragon."

Trea had never followed this road to the mountains, but she knew the main road well.  Years before, her grandfather had brought her that way, crossing the great river at the ferry, and then walking north toward the capital.  She remembered every little town they had passed through, though now it seemed like it had all happened a lifetime ago, and in a different world.

------------------------------------------------------

On the morning of their fourth day after leaving Flapham Abbey, the sun rose slowly above a silver mist, and a heavy dew covered the world.  The Ash River was behind them now, and they were entering the foothills that surrounded the south end of the Boundary Range mountains.  The three knights, as they usually did, rode at the rear of the column, where they could chat easily among themselves.

"Am I right in my reckoning?"  Rudrik asked.  "This is unfamiliar country to me, but unless I am much mistaken, we must be less than a day's ride from the dragon."

"I have been this way many times," said Aglor.  "This road marks the northern edge of my home province of Glaen, and all the lands you see to our right side are under the wise rule of my father.  We are approaching a crossroad, where the highway we are on meets the Great South Road that runs west toward Piyl and east into the hills along the Grey River.  But we will not take that road; our way follows a more northerly track toward the Last Mountain.  The further east we go, the more the farms and villages will dwindle until there are none at all."

"At least the highway is solid enough," Beldrin remarked, "I'd half expected we'd be riding along a cow path to get where we're going.  You've plenty of herdsmen in Glaen, but not your share of stonemasons, or so I'm told."

Over the course of their journey together, Aglor had grown accustomed to this sort of rudeness from Beldrin, and he let the remark pass.  "For now," he replied patiently, "the road we are on is still in good repair, and we'll have a clear path for a while yet. But by late this afternoon it will become much more difficult. Beyond the crossroads, we'll be following an ancient highway of the old kingdom. Few travellers go that way, and none go where we are headed."

"And we'll go slowly enough with these wagons as we climb through the hills, no doubt," Beldrin grumbled, "but perhaps we can still be there by nightfall."

Captain Harbek had ridden in silence, listening to the knights chatter, but now he spoke for the first time in many miles.

"We are not riding on to the dragon today," he said. "First, we must pay our respects to the Sisters of Piety."

Beldrin was instantly alarmed. "The Sisters of Piety?" he asked. "Are you mad? We'll never reach the dragon at all!"

Aglor nodded unhappily. "I feared that might be your design," he said. "I can't say that I like the idea."

"What use is there in toying with fate?" continued Beldrin, angrily. "As if the dragon were not enough!"

Harbek turned his palfrey across the path of the three knights and reined to a stop, blocking their way. He rose tall in his saddle.

"Who will put the girl into that royal dress?" he asked, as if he were scolding troublesome children. "Had you not thought of that? She must be cleaned; her hair must be combed and braided. Will you do it? Would you even know how? There are men in this camp I would not have brushing my horse; would you trust them to bathe her, without doing her injury or some greater harm? Who will dress her in royal finery and arrange her hair? I will not, for these are skills I do not have. We go to the Sisters; they will prepare the girl for the dragon."

The three knights stared at him in amazement, but did not argue further, nor indeed offer any reply at all. Satisfied that his point had been made, Harbek rode forward to the front of the caravan, leaving the three young knights far behind him, at the rear of the line.

Rudrik was the first to speak.

"Who are The Sisters of Piety?" he asked.

"Do they teach you nothing in Toule?" spat Beldrin, mockingly. He was furious at having been dressed down by Harbek, and was glad to seize upon Rudrik as a safer target to vent his frustration. "You've heard of Abzag, at least, I hope."

"They are the cloistered acolytes of Abzag," Aglor explained. "They live deep in the Shadow of the Dragon. There are no other dwellings so near to him."

"Every man who lives knows of Abzag the Destroyer," said Rudrik, "but I did not know that anyone worshipped her."

"They do not so much worship her," said Aglor, "as they admire and honor her, and follow her example to the world."

"Then they are very evil?"

"Yes and no. They are like the goddess herself – both evil and good, and neither. They live at peace, but honor war. They are healers of the sick and skilled in poisons. They can be both kind and terrible. They are strange women, and not to be trifled with."

"They are also supposed to be astonishing in bed," Beldrin added, with a raised eyebrow. "It is said that to be taken as a lover by a Sister of Piety is a good way to die."

"Ah," said Rudrik with a wry grin, "so I take it that is forbidden."

"Forbidden?" said Aglor. "No, certainly not. But it's perilous, for it calls the eye of Abzag to a man, and then for the rest of his life she watches him. If you dream of peace in your old age, you should look, but not touch."

"You seem to know a great deal about them," Beldrin said. "One might wonder how you became so expert in such things, but I suppose they *are* nearer to your lands than to Blackhall."

"I have been to their compound more than once," said Aglor, patiently ignoring Beldrin's efforts to goad him. "My father sends them gifts of sheep and goats, from time to time. He feels it is wise to be good neighbors, and I agree with him; I would not want these women for enemies. I have spoken with their Matron of the Order several times, and she has always been courteous to me. But I would not want to see her angry; she is a shrewd and formidable woman."

The knights rode in silence for a while, each occupied with his own thoughts.  At length, Aglor spoke again.

"There is one more thing you both should know.  The Sisters revere the dragon.  I do not claim to fully understand it.  But they see him often, either flying or perched on the mountain, and they have lived in his shadow for many years without harm.  In Glaen, it is even said that the matron speaks with the dragon at times.  How or why that might be, I do not know, and it is hard to believe, but I do not doubt it.  So be warned: the Sisters profess to be neutral in all conflicts, but I cannot think that news of our quest will please them.  When we arrive, I would advise you to be on your best behavior, and to speak as little as possible."

# Chapter 13:
## The Sisters of Piety

Though their compound was technically inside the borders of Drey, the Sisters of Piety did not consider themselves subjects of any of the three realms. They lived nestled among the foothills at the southern end of the Boundary Range, in the region informally known as *The Shadow of the Dragon*, a sort of no-man's-land below the Last Mountain. There, the official territories of the three kingdoms met, but in practice it was a place outside of their power or influence.

The Sisters revered Abzag the Destroyer, one of the major gods. According to legend, Abzag carried a pouch of seeds – the seeds of pestilence, disease, famine, and death, which she would scatter across the world. She was a deity of special concern to soldiers, as their lives often revolved around destruction, or being themselves destroyed. One did not pray to Abzag, nor worship her directly. She did not take, nor fulfill, nor even hear, requests. She was complete to herself, and answered to no will but her own.

Following that example, The Sisters were themselves self-sufficient, or nearly so. They traded little with the outside world, and valued learning and skill and craftsmanship among their acolytes. They grew most of their own food, raised their own animals, and made their own tools, clothing and furniture. They performed all their own physical labor, including masonry and the slaughter of livestock. They could kill either beasts or men without remorse, if they found the need. But they were monastics, not warriors.

They perceived the world as a constant circle, with creation, healing, destruction, and renewal, each as an essential aspect of the divine. They usually dressed in white, partly because it was the color of death, and partly because stains – such as blood and dirt – showed on it clearly. They took pride in their labors.

The Sisters' sanctuary could not be seen from the main road, but it was not hidden, for the path toward it was well-paved and clear. Beyond that side path, the ancient roadway wound along up into the mountains, toward a broad expanse of ancient ruins dating back to the old kingdom.  That road was long unused by anyone, except perhaps the Sisters themselves, and was now mostly overgrown with trees and brush.  No travellers ever followed that forbidding trail through the shadow of the dragon.

Their temple and most of their other buildings were set atop a low hill surrounded by a formidable wall.  A neatly paved lane ran from the main road to the gate, crossing a stone bridge that was built over the mountain stream that ran swiftly along the hill's foot.  Surrounding the outer wall were many wooden fences, marking well-tended fields and gardens, and several lightly forested pastures where livestock were grazed.

As the wagons turned off the main highway, Trea looked out from her cage at the surrounding hills.  She saw small flocks of sheep and goats, and here and there she could see women in white, shepherding them.  She had heard some of what Aglor had said about the Sisters, and wondered what was going to happen to her in this strange and mystical place.

Mostly, she wondered about food.  She'd had little to eat the entire journey, and had been given nothing at all since the night before.  She wondered if the soldiers planned to starve her to death before sending her to the dragon, or if they simply didn't feel it was worth the trouble feeding her any longer.

The knights and soldiers were strangely quiet as the caravan crossed the little bridge and approached the gate, and they all drew nearer to the wagons, as if they feared an attack.  Harbek rode at the front of the column, and showed no sign of concern.  Of the three knights, Beldrin seemed the most troubled, and his eyes shifted constantly left and right.  As for the scholar Orbert, he was huddled against one of the wagons, doing his best to look very small and inconsequential.  It was a skill that came quite easily to him.

As they approached the gate, the wagons rolled to a slow stop.  One of the great doors swung outward, only far enough for a single woman to step through.  She was stockily-built, neither slender nor fat, and her hair was black, with wisps of grey.

"The Sisters of Piety greet you," she said politely, with a bow of her head.  "You are welcome here, but you must remain outside the wall.

One of you may enter, if you wish, to speak with the matron. Which of you shall it be?"

-----------------------------------------------------

Everything within the matron's conference chamber was neatly arranged and well-made, but without ornament. There was no gold or silver to be seen; no painted decor; no elaborate carving. A heavy stone table was set with simple crockery, and surrounded by a few sturdy wooden chairs.

Captain Harbek stood with his helmet clasped politely in his hands, and waited. The matron walked to an open window, and looked out.

"It is a long journey from Nyl to our little sanctuary," she began probingly. "I have to wonder what would bring you all this way. Dare I guess that a certain someone sends his love?"

"It wasn't mentioned," said the Captain.

"No, I would have been surprised. Then, this is not a personal visit?"

"Strictly business," said Harbek.

"I see," said the matron. "And what business are we to discuss?"

"The king would be grateful..." Harbek began, formally. Then he hesitated. "I would be grateful," he corrected himself, "if the Sisters of Piety would offer their assistance in preparing a sacrifice."

"A sacrifice?" asked the matron, turning back to face him. "To Abzag?"

Harbek shook his head.

"Then what are we to sacrifice? And to whom?"

"The girl in the cage," said Harbek. "We would be grateful, if you would prepare her for the dragon."

"For the dragon?" said the matron, with surprise. "You would have us prepare her? In what way? How does one prepare a girl for the dragon?"

"Clean her up," said Harbek with a shrug. "Put her in a dress. We've brought a dress for her to wear. It's very nice."

"And why would you have us do this thing?" she asked, skeptically.

"Well, I can't rightly expect my men to do it, can I?"

The matron was not amused. "Why..." she repeated, locking the captain's eyes with hers, "do you plan to give this... child... to the dragon?" She spoke quietly, but her voice was stern and powerful, and filled with such menace that the captain felt a chill run through him. But he did not blink or falter.

"We have come to slay the dragon," he said, firmly. "In fulfillment of prophecy, this girl must die."

# Chapter 14:
## The Temple of Abzag

Trea woke to find herself lying alone on an old wooden cot at the center of the cold stone floor of the temple. She was cold and stiff and hungry, and bound up in a strange blue dress. The dress was also cold and stiff, but it was lovely. It was long and elegant, and studded with pearls that shimmered in the darkness. It had once belonged to the princess Dophne, but she had outgrown it some years before. Now it was a garnish for dragon food.

The room was very dark, with only a little moonlight trickling in from above. Trea wondered how long she had been asleep. Her legs were tied at the ankles with rope, and her wrists were locked in iron manacles, but she was at least able to sit up on the edge of the cot, take stock of herself, and peer around at the darkness of the room.

The Sisters of Piety had cleaned her up and tended to her cuts and bruises. They had also combed and braided her short brown hair, and dressed her in the princess's discarded gown. They'd been none too gentle about any of it. Trea had struggled with them at first – even bloodying one of their noses – but the Sisters were not easily daunted, and she was too tired and hungry for a long fight. She didn't have the strength, and eventually had to give it up.

The Temple of Abzag was unlike any building Trea had ever seen. On the outside, it was beautiful, with elaborate carvings of flowers and animals, and long friezes depicting hunts and storms and warfare. But the interior was very different. Inside, it was stark and empty, and aside from her little cot, there seemed to be no furniture at all. On the outside, the walls were flat and sharply squared, but the inside walls were rounded, unpainted, and entirely smooth. The floor was some sort of bare polished stone; not flat, but gently rolling like an uneven sea. In the darkness, with no obvious lines or corners, the space felt shapeless and eternal; an imitation of infinite nothingness.

Even the little door to the outside could not be seen, hidden cleverly by an overlapping fold of stone. The only light came from high windows, not in the walls, but in the ceiling. Trea couldn't help but wonder what happened to the water that got inside when it rained.

"Is anyone there?" she said, more to reassure herself than anything. But her voice was surprisingly quiet, as if the room were consuming the words even as she spoke them. Voices did not echo in that place, but dissolved swiftly into silence.

Then Trea heard, or thought she heard, the creak of a door. But the sound was faint, as if at a great distance. She turned to look, and saw a flicker of candlelight, curving along one of the stone walls. Then the flame of the candle appeared, and then one of the Sisters entered, carrying a basket in one hand and the candle in the other.

"You're awake," the woman with the candle said. "I didn't want to disturb you while you slept. Are you hungry? I've brought food."

Trea scowled and gave no answer. It had been more than a full day since she'd last eaten, and she was ravenously hungry, but she wasn't going to give this Sister of Piety the satisfaction of hearing her admit it.

"You're still angry," the woman with the candle said, as she drew closer. Her voice was serene and quiet, and Trea found it soothing somehow. "They told me you broke Sister Mildren's nose. I wish I had seen it."

The woman knelt beside the little cot, and Trea was finally able to see her clearly. All the other Sisters of Piety that Trea had encountered were well into their thirties, if not older. But to her surprise, this was a young girl close to her own age, hardly a woman at all. Her hair was light and long and her face seemed delicate and beautiful in the dim light. She was dressed in the same sort of simple gown that most of the Sisters wore, and on this cool clear night she had a white blanket wrapped about her shoulders for warmth.

Even in her weakened condition, Trea guessed that she could best this girl in a fight. If she could, it might be her only chance of escape. But in the end she might have to kill the girl, and was she willing to do that, even for a chance at her own freedom? For a moment, she was torn between desperation and her own better nature. Then the girl smiled at her, and spoke as if she had read Trea's thoughts.

"I do not have the keys to free you, and there are soldiers standing guard outside the temple door. I was only allowed to come here because someone had to bring you food, and so the matron chose me.

She's hoping you'll strangle me with your manacles, I expect.  You can if you like.  I am only a dream of Abzag, and this is a good enough place to die."

---------------------------------------------------

The young Sister of Piety had brought a waterskin, and Trea drank from it greedily.  There was a surprising amount of food in the basket as well.  It held a large loaf of bread, two wedges of cheese, a few cold strips of roasted mutton, and even a little bowl of strawberries.  To Trea, it was a feast.  The bread was soft and fresh, and the rest of the food was every bit as good.  The strawberries were so sweet and delicious that she almost wept, tasting them.  She had not had so full a meal for as long as she could remember.

The young Sister of Piety ate nothing, but sat patiently, helping Trea serve herself whenever the need arose.  Trea had some use of her hands, but the manacles made it clumsy for her to do even simple things, such as tearing the bread or breaking off pieces of cheese.  She had not, of course, been allowed a knife or fork.

When she had finished, the girl set what little was left neatly back into the basket.  It suddenly occurred to Trea that she had quite probably just eaten her final meal.  She wondered if this girl knew that, or would care if she did.

"You know what they're going to do to me tomorrow?"  It was a question, and yet not a question at all.

"Oh yes," the girl said.  "It's all anyone has talked about since you arrived.  I envy you a little.  Are you frightened?"

Trea didn't answer her for a long time.

"No, I don't think I am," she said.  "I'm angry, if anything.  It isn't fair, but nothing ever is.  That never changes, I suppose."

"How were you chosen?"

"I was caught stealing food... not stealing... It doesn't matter.  I don't think they even cared what I did.  I was nobody."

"Were the soldiers cruel to you?"  the girl asked, quietly.

Trea paused.  She had not expected any sort of sympathy.  She'd been treated so poorly for so long that she'd forgotten what it was like.

"Yes," she said.  "No worse than the other times, but I don't think they wanted the bruises to show.  The worst was the one who kicked me."

"He kicked you?"

"Yes, after I bit his hand."

"Oh, you bit him!?!  That must have been wonderful," said the girl, her eyes sparkling with delight.  "How did he taste?"

Trea was so startled by the girl's question that she couldn't even answer.  She just stared at her, both puzzled and alarmed.

"I am told that men taste like chicken," the girl explained, "though I do not presume to know.  One of the older Sisters told me.  It may have been a jest.  But I'm also told that jokes are funniest when they are true.  I'm afraid I don't really understand it all.  I am not good with jokes.  Perhaps that's why I'm so disliked."

"The others don't like you?"

"No.  The matron told me once that I was... this is how she put it... *a little too close to the goddess*... But I don't know if that is really why.  For the others, it may simply be because I am too young, or because I do not understand their jokes.  I don't mind.  And I like to think that Abzag would approve, if she cared about such things."

The girl had a disturbingly offhand way of making the strangest remarks.  As Trea looked at her in the candlelight, she hardly seemed real, as if she were made of mists and moonlight.  Trea found herself asking a question she'd not intended to ask.

"What is your name?"

"I am called Malessa.  I am a Novice of Abzag the Destroyer.  She is my life and my doom.  Do you have a name?"

"I'm called Trea."

"I must leave you now, Trea.  You will need your sleep, and I have already stayed longer than I should.  But it is my great delight to have met you.  I feel that we will be friends."

"I die tomorrow."

The girl smiled at this, and shook her head.  "You are a person of importance," she said, "and we will see each other again."

Trea shook her head sadly, but said nothing.  The girl was sweet, and kind, and deeply insane.  There was no point in arguing.

"You can have my blanket, if you like," said the Novice of Abzag.  "The night is cold, and I am far too comfortable.  It will do me good to catch a chill, or pneumonia, if the goddess allows.  And you will have a long day tomorrow."

# Chapter 15:
## The Ancient Road

In the morning, Trea was returned to her cage in the wagon. The shackles were removed from her wrists, and her legs were untied. Then the guards slowly rolled the wagon down the neatly paved pathway toward the main gate, where the rest of the soldiers were waiting.

All the Sisters of Piety had turned out to watch the wagon go, and there were perhaps a hundred or more of them lining the path; some young, some old, all dressed in white. For them the dragon was a living expression of the goddess, and this was a sacred moment.

Trea scanned the line of women, looking for the girl who had visited her the night before, but she could not find her. The matron stood in front, tall and proud, and with a powerful air of authority. Trea also saw Sister Mildren, somewhere near the back, with a bandage across her nose. It was not until the wagon drew near the gate that she finally spotted Malessa, standing just apart from a group of novices clustered to one side.

The other young girls were whispering together, and some of them were giggling, but Malessa was only watching, silently, with her hands clasped before her. In the daylight, she looked almost ordinary – more tangible, more real than she had seemed in the shadows of the temple – and at first, Trea wasn't even certain she was the same girl. But then their eyes met, and she smiled, and Trea knew that it was her. Malessa raised her left hand and drew a circle in the air, before wiping it away again. It was the sacred sign of Abzag the Destroyer, and Trea wondered what she had meant by it, but she had no chance to ask. The wagon rolled on through the gate, and the great wooden doors swung shut behind her.

After the gate was closed and the caravan was gone, the matron stood for a long time, lost in thought. She remembered a young girl, many years before, who had loved a soldier. Her countenance softened, and for a moment she seemed an old woman, sad and tired, nothing more nor less.

One of the Sisters beside her spoke, and the moment passed.

"Is it true, Matron?"

"Some of it is true," the matron replied.

--------------------------------------------------

The rest of that morning, the little caravan trudged slowly up the mountain.  At a glance, the road they were following would have seemed to be merely an old cart-path or animal trail.  But though now badly overgrown, it had once been a broad and heavily-travelled highway, the main road into a great city of the old kingdom.  It was well-made, and even though many of the paving-stones were covered by soil or bracken or leaves, the roadbed itself was still firm, allowing the wagons to make a slow, steady ascent.

Some of the soldiers were set to walk in front, clearing any brush or logs or fallen stones from the path with swords and axes, and raw muscle when nothing else would do.  The rest of the soldiers took it in turns to lead the riderless horses at a slow walk.  Captain Harbek rode between the soldiers and the wagons and said little, unless it was to give direction to the men clearing the way.

The scholar Orbert rode beside the captain, his mind torn between excitement and terror.  To him, this had all seemed like a grand adventure when they first set out from Nyl, but now he was not so certain.  It is one thing to dream of dragons and battle and treasure, but quite another to realize that such things may be near at hand.

Trea sat on the floor of her cage, wearing the uncomfortable pearl-studded dress, and wrapped in the blanket that the young Sister of Piety had given her.  Captain Harbek, perhaps surprisingly, had allowed her to keep it.  He was not in the least concerned about her warmth or comfort, although the mountain air was crisp and cold.  His chief concern was the dress.  With all the rust and dirt that clung to the iron strapping of the cage, he reasoned that if she stayed wrapped in the blanket, it would help to keep the elegant dress clean.

The knights, as always, rode behind the wagons, talking quietly amongst themselves.  No songs were sung, nor stories told, and they rarely laughed as they had so often done earlier in the trip.  Though no one spoke of it, there was a sense among them that in daring to venture beyond the dwelling place of the Sisters of Piety, they had crossed a sort of threshold. What to that point had seemed little more than a pleasant holiday or hunting trip, was now a grim journey into earnest peril.

It was past noon, and the sun was still high above them when they reached the outskirts of the ruined city. Many broad terraces had been carved, centuries ago, into the side of the mountain. Those terraces had once been lined with neatly paved streets, and filled with buildings of every description, made of wood and brick and stone. Not a single building remained, at least not in its entirety. Mounds of rubble showed where the largest must once have stood, and of others there was little left but broken walls, or the crumbling remnants of their foundations. All the wood and thatching had long ago rotted or been burned away. Everywhere could be seen stones that were black and charred, a testament to the might of the dragon.

Within the ruined city, the overgrowth was lighter than it had been along the roadway. Most of the trees that grew there were stunted and bent, their twisted roots struggling to find a foothold between the paving stones, or in the shallow rocky ground. It was clear to see that here the bedrock of the mountain was never far below the surface, and in some places sharp outcroppings of natural stone showed through, where the ancient builders had left the sloping terrain unworked. What few large trees there were seemed almost as ancient as the ruins themselves, short and spreading, with massive trunks, and many dead or broken branches.

The caravan halted just inside the perimeter of the city proper, in what must have once been a narrow courtyard near the main gates. There, enough of the old walls remained to offer some concealment, in case the dragon happened to be out and about. They unloaded their tents and stores of food and other gear, and set up a makeshift base of operations. Harbek set most of his men to work clearing the area and tending to the horses, but four of them he sent out individually on foot to scout the ruins.

# Chapter 16:
## The Dead City

The four scouts had dispersed into the dead city, and there was little for the rest of the caravan to do but rest and wait. No fires were lit, and voices were kept low. They had not yet seen the dragon, nor any clear sign of him aside from the ancient ruins themselves. But it was certain that they were deep inside his domain, and he was far too close for comfort or carelessness.

His lair was thought to be somewhere above the city, close to the mountain's peak, though no one knew exactly where. But for the moment, that exact location hardly mattered. The plan was not to seek the dragon in his lair, but to set an ambush somewhere inside the ruins of the city, with the girl as bait. The scouts had been sent out in the hope that they could find a suitable spot.

The scholar Orbert nestled himself into a corner with paper and quill, and set to writing. He had been taking notes throughout the journey, whenever they stopped for any length of time, and now he was describing the slow ascent of the mountain. He wanted to keep everything in his records up to date, but mostly he wanted to distract himself from the terror he felt creeping through his bones, and the long wait for the scouts to return.

Others passed the time after their own fashion. Aglor tended to his horse, a magnificent dark grey stallion. Galfam was his name, and there was not a finer mount in all of Drey. He was tall at the shoulder, and powerfully built, but also nimble, and light of foot. Aglor believed that he was the only horse in the caravan, and perhaps in the world, bold enough to face the dragon without fear.

Rudrik sat on a block of stone, quietly sharpening his spear. He did it mostly from habit. The spear was already as sharp as it was ever going to get, but there was little else of use for him to do while they waited.

Beside him, Beldrin unsheathed the great axe that he always carried, and polished the blade lightly with a piece of fine cloth. He'd never had cause to draw the axe forth before, and none of the other travellers had seen it closely until that moment.  Now, every eye was upon it.

Much of the weapon looked rather ordinary.  The shaft was made of ash, or some other light-colored, strong-grained wood, and the grip was wrapped in black leather, with an ornate silver pommel below.  But the axe's head was truly astonishing to see.  It was made from some strange dark metal that seemed to shift in color when it moved from direct light to shadow.  A fine tracery of silver lines lay across its surface in an intricate and arcane design.  It was a beautiful, ominous weapon, and everything about it spoke of grace and power.

"I've heard that the weaponsmiths of Blackhall are masters of the craft," said Rudrik, "but I've never seen such an axe as that."

"Nor will you again," said Beldrin.  "There is none like it in all the world, and it was not made at Blackhall.  It's a treasure of my house, and a relic of the old kingdom.  It may even have been forged at this very spot, long ago, before this city was laid ruin.  Brogna is its name, and it has not drawn blood for nearly forty years.  My grandfather was the last to wield it in battle, and in all the years of his life and mine, it has never been sharpened, for there has never been the need.  There is some forgotten craft or sorcery of the old kingdom in it.  Its edges never dull, and it can slice through armor as easily as a knife cuts bread.  If any blade can cleave through the dragon's hide, it is this one.  This is why I will be the one to slay the dragon, and wed the princess."

"Not if I get to the beast first," said Rudrik, smiling.  "It's a marvellous weapon, but by the time you are close enough to use it, there may be little left for you to do."

"We shall see," said Beldrin.  He did not smile.

Aglor listened to their debate, but said nothing.  He thought it wiser to boast after the deed than before, or better yet, not to boast at all.  He saw no virtue in it.

------------------------------------------------------

By the time the last of the scouts had returned, the sun was low in the west and the shadows were long.  Each of the scouts gave a similar description of the ruined city, and all four of them had seen the dragon.

"He was sitting perched atop a tall shaft of rock," said the first scout, "further up the mountainside, and looking down upon the ruins. He sat there for a long time, motionless as if he were a part of the mountain. I was hidden behind a wall, but whenever I peered out, he was still there. I must have waited for more than an hour, but I couldn't move for fear of being seen. Then suddenly he was gone. Where he went, I do not know."

"That must have been the same perch where I saw him as well," said another. "I suspect he can see most of the city from there, and probably much of the road below. If he was perched there this morning, then I think it is likely that he has already seen us at some point."

The third scout nodded in agreement. "He is very dark in color; black, or nearly so. From a distance he could be mistaken for a shadow, or a ridge of granite, or a dark cleft in the mountainside. We might even have seen him as we approached the city, and not realized it. Unless he moved or took flight, he would be difficult to pick out from the landscape."

"I have better news," said the fourth scout. "I may have found our perfect spot. At the very heart of the city there is a great open plaza, surrounded by rubble and broken walls. It may have been a grand market, or some other sort of place where people would gather. It's level, and well-paved, without trees. At the center of the plaza, the girl could be easily seen from any direction, but men could lie well-hidden all around its perimeter."

Some of the other soldiers cheered (quietly) at hearing the fourth scout's report, and the knights all nodded their approval. Captain Harbek frowned, and scratched his ear.

"Can we get a wagon all the way there?" he asked. "I doubt that we could carry the cage that far, not with the girl still inside."

"Yes," the scout replied. "I scouted the route carefully. "We can get a wagon through, but it will take some time. Many of the roads are blocked with rubble. We'll have to steer a crooked path, but it can be done."

# Chapter 17:
## The Trap is Set

The caravan traced a circuitous route through the ruined city. Many of the streets were badly broken, or completely blocked by rubble. It took several hours, but the scouts had done their job well, and a clear route was eventually found. By the time they reached the stone plaza, the sun was down and the full moon was shining brightly.

The scholar, the cook, and the two drivers had remained behind at the base camp with the second wagon and most of the horses. They were not soldiers, and had no desire to see the battle with the dragon first-hand. Harbek was glad to be rid of them. This was a job for trained fighting men, and the last thing he wanted was to have some terrified amateurs fouling up the works.

Aside from the two that pulled the wagon, the only horse that came through the ruins was Galfam, whom Aglor led at a walk. It was almost certain that the dragon had already seen the caravan ascending the mountain, but there was still some hope that they could reach the plaza without being seen again, or more importantly, attacked. It was agreed by almost everyone that a troop of horses moving through the dead city would be more likely to draw the dragon's attention than a handful of men on foot slowly leading a single wagon.

Apparently, that part of the plan had succeeded. Though everyone kept a nervous watch on the sky – and on the mountainside whenever it came into view – they'd seen no further sign of the dragon. The knights and soldiers all hoped that he'd retired to his lair, or gone over to some other part of the mountain, and would not return until morning.

Trea, on the other hand, had given up on hoping. For her, whether the dragon attacked the caravan before they reached the plaza or after made little difference. Locked in the iron cage, she couldn't even hope for the chance to flee or hide. In the knights' stories, someone had always rescued the maiden in distress, but no one was going to rescue *her*. No one even wanted to. Dozens of possible scenarios played out in her head, but she could never come up with a version where she survived. She sat quietly in her cage and tried her best not to think about anything at all.

The plaza was exactly as the scout had described, and seemed like an ideal spot for an ambush. It was a broad, open circle, perhaps sixty yards across, and neatly paved with concentric rings of stone. There were no trees, not even the short spindly ones that they had seen elsewhere through the ruins. Here, the moss-covered stones were too closely set, and only a few feeble patches of grass could sprout unevenly in the cracks and fissures.

Several large roadways led in and out of the plaza, and all around it the crumbling remnants of broken walls and collapsed buildings provided ample cover where ambushers could lay hid. The three knights dispersed into the shadows around the perimeter, each choosing a hiding spot to his own liking. Harbek and the soldiers rolled the wagon to the exact center, and prepared to unload the cage with the girl.

The soldiers slipped heavy wooden poles through the cage's iron strapping. In this way, with four men to each side, the heavy cage could be lifted off the bed of the wagon, with the girl still inside. Then the horses would be led forward, pulling the wagon out from under the cage, which could then be lowered easily to the ground.

While the soldiers prepared to lift the cage, Harbek climbed up into the back of the wagon. He reached through the strapping and grabbed the blanket that Trea had been given.

"You won't be needing this any longer," he said, as he unwrapped the blanket, and pulled it out of her grasp, revealing the royal dress that had been hidden underneath.

Since it had been kept under lock and key for most of the journey – and after that it had been concealed by the blanket – most of the soldiers had not clearly seen the dress until that moment. It was magnificent. In the moonlight the pearls shimmered over many layers of rich, sapphire blue fabric of almost impossible beauty. The dress fit Trea perfectly, and clad in that remarkable gown the wretched, condemned urchin girl looked every inch a princess.

"It's a shame," said one of the soldiers, quietly. "It's an awfully nice dress." Some of the other soldiers nodded silently in agreement.

The wagon-horses screamed and reared up in panic. Trea suddenly felt the cage lift into the air and roll, nearly turning upside down. One of the top corners crashed onto the stone surface of the plaza, popping rivets and bending the rusted straps all along that side. Trea had no chance to brace herself, and landed hard on her shoulder. She was stunned, and it was several seconds before she could clear her head. What had happened? Had the horses panicked? Had the soldiers dropped the cage?

The upturned wagon was only a few feet away. It had flipped over completely, and Captain Harbek was underneath it, lying very still. Even in the moonlight Trea could see the blood pooling around his body. The tongue of the wagon had snapped, and the horses were fleeing into the ruined city, dragging the broken shards behind them. Men were running in every direction.

There was a shattering roar behind her, and Trea finally understood what had happened. The dragon, dark as the shadows and silent as moonlight, had swept down on them while the soldiers were distracted with the cage. He had been waiting with an ambush of his own.

# Chapter 18:
## The Knights and the Dragon

The plan had gone terribly wrong.  Captain Harbek lay dead beneath the toppled wagon, and his men were scattering in terror and confusion.  But not all was lost.  The dragon had come too soon, but the three knights were already in position at the perimeter of the great plaza.  Weapons in hand, they had been on their guard, and were ready for battle.

To the monster's right side was Aglor, astride the great horse Galfam, hidden behind a length of broken wall.  To the monster's rear was Beldrin, crouching low, wielding the great axe Brogna, dire relic of the old kingdom.

But neither of them had drawn the dragon's eye, for that was fixed upon Rudrik, proud and tall, fearless champion of the north.  He was the first to charge, and he did not strike from the side or the rear.  Rudrik of Toule had no use for subterfuge or cowardly cunning.  On his own two feet he stood, his courage as his only shield.  With his great spear clutched in both hands he charged from the front, headlong toward the dragon's snarling maw.

Not since the fall of the old kingdom had the monster faced such an assault from a warrior of such boldness, such fury and raw courage.  Rudrik sprinted across the open plaza, swiftly closing the gap between himself and the beast until he was near enough to strike.  the monster reared up, rolled his neck back like the curl of a whip, and a great stream of fire poured forth.  The grass and the mosses withered and died in an instant; the stones were charred black and the very air undulated with the searing heat of the dragonfire.

And so died Rudrik of Toule.

Beldrin however, had seized upon the dragon's distraction.  Even as the monster unleashed scorching destruction upon Rudrik, Beldrin charged him from behind.  Quick as a mongoose, he dove beneath a swipe of the beast's mighty tail, sprung nimbly to his feet again, and found himself close at the monster's side.

The moment was his. There, upon the open plaza of the ruined city, under the moonlight, Brogna glimmered with uncanny brightness, as if it were illumined from within. Beside the monster's exposed flank, the fierce young knight raised the dark axe high into the air, poised for a killing blow. His feet firmly set, Beldrin of Blackhall, strongest man in the entire kingdom of Drey, swung the great blade down with all the strength in his body, and Brogna – ancient relic of wars long forgotten, the black and silver blade that could not be dulled – flashed with the pale luminesence of doom.

The blow never fell. The dragon shifted his weight, and his lashing tail came sweeping from behind. That tail had broken towers, and shattered the walls of the mightiest fortresses of the old kingdom, and it had lost little of its power in the intervening years. The body of Beldrin was flung a hundred yards in the air, crashing against the remnants of a crumbling wall, where it burst like an overripe plum. The great axe Brogna, rent from his grasp, clattered harmlessly across the stones of the plaza.

And so died Beldrin of Blackhall.

But Aglor, master horseman of the open fields, had not been idle. Even as Beldrin ran toward the monster from the rear, Aglor had spurred Galfam forward. Powerful as a draft horse, nimble as a palfrey, the iron-grey horse reared and charged toward the dragon's side. Aglor had chosen the perfect moment, chosen the perfect spot from which to strike, and his cunning was rewarded. The distance between himself and the dragon was more than enough to allow Galfam to reach his full speed. The monster's head was still turned the opposite way, as the beast struck at Beldrin with his tail. The dragon did not see the gallant horseman coming, and had no time to turn or dodge or defend. With all his skill and strength, and with the full power of the charging stallion, Aglor aimed the knife-edged tip of his lance at the monster's breast, just above the forward arm, and just below his bat-like wing.

The lance struck home, and shattered into a hundred pieces against the dragon's scaly hide. No lance or spear or arrow could pierce that living armor, that battlement of chitin and bone. With the force of the impact, Aglor was thrown from his saddle, and Galfam ran off, riderless into the ruined city.

But Aglor was not yet beaten.  He was unhorsed, and badly shaken, but his shield was still on his arm.  He struggled to his feet, and drew his sword as the dragon turned to face the challenge of this third champion.

Once again, the dragon rolled his neck up and backward, and once again fire poured out of his gaping maw.  But Aglor was ready.  He had seen Rudrik die, and learned from it.  He had guessed what the dragon would do, and hid himself behind his shield.  Even that might not have saved him, but the dragon's fires were not limitless.  His furnace had not fully rekindled, and the flames that now licked at Aglor, dire and deadly as they were, did not have the full potency of those that had consumed Rudrik of Toule.  The paint on its surface bubbled and peeled, the wood smoldered and the iron that wrapped its edges glowed red, but the shield held, and Aglor of Glaen still lived.

The dragon was enraged.  His breath had vanquished armies, burned great cities to the ground.  Never before had any warrior so endured his all-consuming fire.  With a flap of his mighty wings, the beast reared up, towering over the brave young man with the sword and shield below him.

Aglor gasped for breath, and his body ached with pain, but hope stirred in his breast.  He suddenly knew what was about to happen.  The coming moment unveiled itself to his mind.  The monster was going to strike; its raised head would come crashing down, to crush and devour him in those fearsome jaws.  No blade could pierce the creature's hide, but the mouth, that was its weak spot!  There was no armor there, and with a bold thrust of his sword into that open maw, at just the right instant... that was how the dragon could be slain.

For the young knight and the dragon, time slowed to a crawl.  It was as if every instant were carved in stone, as if every movement took on a new meaning, all its own.  The head of the dragon plunged down, and the heroic young man thrust his steel blade upward in a desperate gamble.

It was a sucker's bet, and a wager that Aglor would lose.  His sword caught in the dragon's teeth, twisted, and snapped at the hilt.  Those monstrous jaws closed, the fangs sank deep, and Aglor, son of Vildar – the noblest and best of the king's chosen champions – was no more.

# Chapter 19:
## The Dragon and the Girl

Trea had a front-row seat for the battle between the knights and the dragon, but she wasn't sitting still and watching; she was trying to escape from the iron cage. Captain Harbek had the keys, but his body was out of reach, and the cage was much too heavy for her to move it any closer. Behind her, she heard the scorching roar of dragonfire, as Rudrik died.

It was then that she saw how badly the cage had been damaged. When it fell from the wagon the top had struck first, and it had then toppled onto its side. One of the corners was crushed, and many of the rivets that held the iron bands together had been sheared off or had popped loose. It was an old cage, badly rusted in many places; since it only had to hold a young girl, no one had been much concerned about its strength or its durability.

Trea scrambled to the damaged corner to see if she could squeeze through. There wasn't room, but with so many of the rivets gone – and some of the bands already bent – there was really only one strap that she would have to displace, and it was only held there by a single rivet. She spun around, rolled onto her back, and using her hands to hold herself in place, pushed against that strap with both feet.

It wouldn't budge. She kicked at it with her heels. Again. Again. Again. It seemed to be giving way. Again, again, and again she kicked, but it would not break free.

Then she heard a second roar of dragonfire. She turned to look, and saw Aglor, raising his sword as the dragon lunged at him. And then she saw him die.

Desperate now she kicked again and suddenly the rivet popped loose. She spun around, not even looking to see if the dragon was coming for her. With all the strength in her body, she pushed the bands apart, and they yielded ever so slightly.

She heard a scream, and realized that the dragon was stalking through the ruins now, hunting the soldiers. She raised her arms above her head, and tried to squeeze through the narrow opening she had made.

She got her arms and her head through, but the neck of the dress hooked on the twisted shard of a broken rivet. She was caught. Her shoulders were trapped. She could not bend her arms far enough to reach the snag, and could not twist herself free. She planted her feet against the ground and pushed as hard as she could. The fabric tore, pearls scattered across the stones, and her arms and shoulders were suddenly through the narrow opening.

She was bleeding. The gap she was trying to squeeze through was surrounded by jagged and broken pieces of metal, and she was cut and scratched in a dozen places. The dress was badly torn in twice that many spots, but she was nearly free. She pushed again and forced her torso through the opening, then her hips, and then her knees.

But that was as far as she could go. The broadly pleated hem of the long gown was hopelessly entangled in the jagged shards of metal. She could not draw her legs the rest of the way through, and didn't have the strength or leverage to free herself with her arms. She bent double at the waist, and tried to tear the fabric loose.

That was when the dragon returned. She had run out of time.

Trea did not hear the beast coming, but she felt a great rush of wind as he landed nearby. She stopped struggling with the dress, and with her feet still trapped inside the cage, pulled herself onto her hands and knees. She looked up.

The dragon was huge, though perhaps not as enormous as she'd once imagined him to be. His upper body and wings were a dark charcoal grey, nearly black, and the scales of his armored hide were as sleek as fine satin. Underneath, he was lighter grey, the color of rising clouds, not before a storm, but before a gentle summer rain. He towered over the girl, like the mountain itself. Trea closed her eyes.

Nothing happened.

She opened her eyes again and saw that the dragon had not moved. He was still standing there, looking down at her with a curious expression, like an old merchant appraising a stolen jewel. Then, with his eyes still fixed upon her, he eased himself gently down until his belly was nestled onto the surface of the plaza. Next he lowered his head, very slowly, like a single leaf drifting earthward on a windless day, until his chin was flat against the stones and his piercing blue eyes were level with hers.

She could smell the heat of his breath, like steam rising from smouldering ashes in a light rain. His teeth glistened like a hundred pearl daggers behind his scaly lips, slightly open. He was so close that she could have reached out a hand and touched him, had she dared. She did not try.

He lay that way for some time, silently considering the girl before him. She stared back at him, motionless, and waited for death.

It did not come. The dragon raised his head off the stones, and with a flap of his wings lifted into the air and was gone. Trea knew, without even thinking, that he was going to the base camp, where the scholar was hiding with the other horses. She understood somehow that the dragon would not rest until the caravan had been completely destroyed; not until every soldier, every single person was dead.

Everyone except her.

He had let her go.

She was stunned. She didn't know what to do. Ever since the caravan had departed from Nyl, she'd known exactly when and how her life was going to end. And then the moment came, and it didn't happen. She felt lost... confused... and as strange as it might have seemed, maybe even *disappointed*. It was, for her, that startling moment when some terrible fact that you've always known, always relied on, turns out to not be true.

She looked around at the wreckage and the bodies scattered about the plaza as if she were seeing them all for the first time. The overturned cart with the broken tongue. The dead captain underneath. The mortal remains of the young knights. Three of the soldiers who had never even made it into the ruins to hide. Then she looked at herself, and the dress that was still hopelessly entangled in the broken cage.

*She was more important than the dress.* It was so simple, and yet she had never thought of it in quite that way before. She reached up and grabbed the fabric at the neckline with both hands and pulled down.  The dress, already badly torn, ripped open.  She tore at the sleeves, and then the bodice.  She dragged herself out through the top, and within seconds she was free.

She looked around for something to cover herself with, and saw the blanket, still in the dead captain's hand.  "You won't be needing this," she said to him, as she took it and wrapped it around herself.

Amid the debris of the wagon was a short length of rope.  Trea guessed that it was the same one that had been used to bind her ankles in the temple of Abzag.  She took it, and tied it double around her waist.  It would serve well enough for a belt.

She paused, wondering what else she should take.  But there was nothing there that she wanted.  The blanket was hers, given to her by the young Sister of Piety.  Malessa was her name.  And the rope, by rights, was hers as well.  But the dead soldiers, she wanted nothing that had been theirs.  Their clothing, their weapons, their money if they had any... these things she would leave to the dragon.

# Chapter 20:
## The Aftermath

The Sisters of Piety had seen the flares of dragonfire in the night. With the first light of morning, the matron gathered all the novices – and the most able of the older Sisters – and set out, up the old road toward the ruins. If the dragon were slain, she felt that was something the young women should see. And if the dragon were not slain, well then, she thought that was something they should see as well.

More than forty of the Sisters made the slow ascent of the mountain. Most of them walked, but they also brought an ox-cart, which they took in turns to ride. Otherwise the cart was nearly empty, carrying only a few tools and a small supply of food and water. Not even the matron knew what, if anything, they would need when they arrived.

It was late morning when they reached the outskirts of the dead city. Even though they were on foot, and the ox-cart moved slowly, the Sisters reached the ruins in less time than it had taken the knights. Since the worst of the overgrowth had been cleared by the soldiers only the day before, the Sisters had an open trail.

They found the soldiers' base camp, but that seemed to raise more questions than it answered. It was clear at least that the dragon had been there. The Sisters found one of the soldiers' wagons broken into many pieces, and its former contents strewn about the area. There were no horses, nor any sign other than the wagon itself that any horses had been there. Nor did the Sisters find any of the men from the knights' caravan. What they did find was four sets of clothing – trousers, shirt, cloak, vest, hat and shoes – layed out in four different spots around the encampment. But the clothes were empty. There were bloodstains everywhere, and burn marks, and pieces of stone that seemed to be freshly broken.

"Gather the clothing, Niren," the matron said to one of the older Sisters, "and then lead the ox-cart to the great circle; I believe you know the way. Unless I am quite mistaken, we shall need it there. Malessa, you will come with me. The rest of you, I want you to search the ruins. If you find clothing, or anything else that belonged to the soldiers, bring it back here, and wait for the cart to return. If you find something you cannot carry, remember the spot, and fetch someone to help you with it."

"Matron?" one of the novices asked, "what are we to do if we find their bodies?"

"You will find no bodies," the matron replied.

-------------------------------------------------

Malessa wondered why she had been chosen to accompany the matron, instead of searching the ruins with the other novices. She suspected that the reason would eventually become clear, as reasons have a way of doing.

Malessa had never been inside the ruins before. In fact, since she had first become a novice of the order some years prior, she had rarely even been allowed outside the wall of the Sisters' compound. Now the matron was leading her northeast, toward what must once have been the center of the ruined city, and Malessa was almost breathless with excitement to be wandering in this desolate and sacred place. She found herself entranced by the splendor of such ancient and glorious destruction.

If the matron felt a similar sense of awe, she did not show it. She walked briskly through the maze of streets, occasionally climbing over a broken wall here or some small pile of rubble there, following a path she had travelled many times before. Malessa kept up with her easily enough, though she had to stay on her toes, and could not stop to bask in her surroundings in nearly the way that she would have liked.

But her diligence was rewarded when they reached the grand plaza, for this was where the real battle had been, and the impact of that event – so recent that the memory of it could be felt in the stones themselves – almost overwhelmed her. Tears streamed down her face. She wept not for sorrow, but in sheer religious ecstasy.

She wiped her eyes, and saw that the matron had walked away toward the center of the circle. The iron cage was there, partly crushed and lying on its side next to an overturned wagon. But Malessa felt herself drawn to a bright glimmer of reflected sunlight, far to one side of the plaza, at the base of a partial stone wall. She walked over, to see what it was.

It was an axe.  Its dark blade was ornately inlaid with fine tracings of silver that sparkled in the mid-day sun.  She reached down to pick it up, and discovered that it was surprisingly light in her hands.

"Matron," she said, walking back toward the center of the ring, "I have found something."

The matron was kneeling, not far from the iron cage, with her open hand pressed against a large bloodstain on the stones beside the upturned wagon.  There was clothing there as well, just as they had found at the men's base camp.  Malessa could see that these clothes had belonged to a soldier, possibly the Captain who'd led the caravan.  There was a chainmail shirt, and a helmet of leather and iron lying above it.

"Was that their captain?"  she asked.

The matron looked up suddenly, startled as if she had forgotten that Malessa was there.

"Yes, it was," she said.  "What have you found?"

"This," Malessa replied, holding up the axe.  "It's very light, and beautiful, but I don't understand why it is here.  There are clothes and armor all around the circle, but I see no other weapons."

The matron stared at the axe, wide-eyed for a moment, before she recovered herself.

"I will take that," she said.  "Where did you find it?"

"There, by that wall."  Malessa pointed with the axe, before handing it to the matron.  "There were no clothes anywhere near it.  I wonder how it came to be there."

The matron studied the axe carefully, turning it slowly to see how the sunlight reflected from it.  She traced the silver inlays on the blade with the fingers of her right hand.

"I think it is a relic of the old kingdom," Malessa said.

The matron turned and looked at the girl for a long time before she spoke.

"This is to be kept secret," she said.

------------------------------------------------------

By the time Sister Niren arrived with the ox-cart, Malessa and the matron had thoroughly searched the entire stone plaza. They'd found several more sets of the soldiers' clothing hidden among the surrounding ruins, but no other weapons, or any other signs of the men or their horses.

The matron had carefully wrapped the axe inside a heavy cloak, so that it could not be seen. She placed it near the front of the wagon – along with the captain's helmet and the shreds of the elegant blue dress – and gave explicit instructions that those three things were not to be touched.

Malessa had studied the cage and the dress for a long time, and found them nearly as puzzling as the axe had been. The hem of the dress was entangled in the broken cage, but it appeared that the girl had been torn out through the top of it. Or perhaps she'd torn herself out. There were spots of blood on the fabric, but far less than Malessa had seen on some of the other clothing.

It was even more curious to her that the pearls which had once decorated the gown were gone. When she'd seen the dress in the temple, there had been hundreds of them, all around the bodice and along the sleeves, but not a single one remained to be found, either on the dress, or on the paving stones nearby.

After they had loaded the clothing and what other debris they could find onto the ox-cart, they returned through the winding streets to the soldiers' base camp. The other Sisters had completed their search of the ruins, and were waiting for them. They'd recovered several more sets of clothing, but had seen no other token or news of the soldiers or the three knights. In all, they'd found twenty sets of men's clothing and the one shredded dress, which by the matron's arithmetic accounted for every member of the knights' caravan.

But Malessa thought that one member of the caravan might still *not* be accounted for. The blanket she'd given to the girl named Trea had apparently never been found. Nothing was said of it, and Malessa wondered if she was the only one among the Sisters who had even noticed its absence.

# Chapter 21:
## The Forest Stream

After her escape from the stone circle, Trea spent much of the night wandering blindly through the ruined city, looking for a way out. The streets were a tangled maze of shadows and rubble, and even in broad daylight, it would have been difficult to find a clear path. But for Trea, with the once-bright moon slowly vanishing behind a line of clouds, it was nearly impossible.

She tried to work her way eastward, and down, even though the ruins seemed forever to force her back up the mountain and to the west. She had no clear idea of where she was hoping to go, she only knew that she did not want to go back the same way that the caravan had come. If any of the soldiers had escaped from the dragon, they would almost certainly have fled down the ancient highway, back toward the Sisters of Piety. Trea had no desire to encounter anyone she might meet on that road.

After several hours, she was completely lost, and had begun to think that the ruined city was endless. She finally gave up, and crawled under an outcropping of stone that offered some semblance of shelter. Perhaps with the dawn, she told herself, she would be able to find a way out of the dead city.

When she woke again, it was daylight, but the ruins were cloaked in a thick morning fog. Trea still could not be certain of her direction, but at least she had some light to see. She was hungry, and very thirsty, but there was nothing she could do other than resume her search.

Fortunately, the hiding place she had chosen was not far from what had once been the city's outermost wall. She soon came to a broad line of broken stone that marked where the wall had stood, and beyond that there was only a sparse forest of pines. Once she was out of the ruined city's maze of streets, it was easy to follow the downward slope of the mountain.

Now her main concern was to find water. In time, all rivers flow to the sea, and Trea knew that if she could only find a stream, then eventually that would lead her to a town or a village. What would become of her then, she could not guess, but if she did not find food and water nothing else would matter. She would perish here on the mountainside.

Once the fog began to clear, she could see that she was indeed headed east, as she'd intended. But though she walked for hours, there was no stream to be found. She did find a dry creekbed, but it only ran a short way, till it vanished completely into fissures in the rock. Trea suspected that it slipped there into an underground cavern, but with no source of light and no weapon to defend herself, she knew better than to try looking for a cave. Wolves and bears and worse things by far made their lairs in those dark holes of stone.

The sun was past its peak, and was just beginning to descend when Trea finally heard the sound of running water. She stumbled toward it, and found a stream that was surprisingly broad and deep, flowing swiftly down a stairwell of cataracts into a wide pool, then flowing off to the southeast through the forest.

She drank deeply from the falls, and rested by the edge of the pool for a long while. Her head hurt, partly from hunger, but also because the braids the Sisters of Piety had put in her hair were much too tight. She untied the little strings of ribbon they had used to hold the braids in place, and bit by bit she set her hair free. When that was done, she drank some more water, then sat on the ground and leaned heavily against a large stone. In her exhaustion, she fell asleep again, though she had not meant to, and when she awoke the sun was sinking, and the shadows of the trees were growing longer.

She followed the little river downstream, walking along its western side. Though water and rest had revived her somewhat, she was still weak, and shaking from hunger. It had been nearly two days now since her last meal in the Temple of Abzag.

Just when she thought she could go no further, and was ready to lay herself down beside the river in the hope that she would never wake up again, she smelled a whiff of woodsmoke. Either the forest was burning, or someone had a campfire nearby. She continued down the stream, hoping against hope that some kindly hunter or fisherman might have set up his camp near the river.

Not ten minutes later, she found the source of the smoke, and to her great surprise it was not a hunter's camp, but a cottage. On the opposite side of the water, not far from the river's sandy edge, stood a little hut made of timbers and earth, with a tall stone chimney.

"Is there anyone there?" Trea called out, but she got no answer.

She would have to cross the river. The stream was not wide, maybe twenty feet across at its most narrow point, but she was sure it was too deep for her to simply wade. She would have to swim.

She took off the blanket, hoping to keep it dry. She folded it neatly, and tied it into a bundle with the rope she'd used as a belt. Then she flung it as hard as she could across the water. It landed on the sandy ground of the far bank with a thud, and did not tumble back down the gentle slope into the river, as she'd feared it might.

She waded in, and swam naked across the little river. The water was bitter cold, but the current was not too strong for her to manage. She was shivering when she reached the other side, and chilled to the bone. She shook off the water as best she could, and wrapped herself in the blanket again.

The cottage was small, but it looked warm and inviting. It had a thatched roof, and a wooden door with curtained windows to either side. Through the curtains she could see what looked like the glow of a fire.

She tapped on the door but again she got no answer; but if there was a fire, she reasoned, the hut's owner could not be far away. She looked through one of the windows, and saw what appeared to be a very old man, standing in front of a stone fireplace, with his back to the door.

"*A hermit, living alone in the forest*," she thought to herself. "*He must be. And more than a little deaf I expect.*"

She was far too cold and desperate to wait outside in the hope that he would notice her and invite her in. She pushed on the cottage door, and it creaked slowly open. She stepped inside.

# Chapter 22:
## The Hermit

"Ah," said the old man without looking up, "so you're finally here. I wondered. Yes, I wondered. The river is cold, but wooden huts are warm, when there's a fire at least."

Trea looked around the room in puzzlement. The hut seemed larger now than it had from the outside. There were three beds along the right side of the room, and two long wooden benches. Near the door there was a table with smaller benches set around it. To the left of the door there were several pegs, where clothing could be hung, and many empty shelves lined the left-hand wall. In the far left corner there was a cupboard, surrounded by what looked like several sacks of flour or other foodstuffs, and a number of large crockery jars. There was not a speck of dust to be seen anywhere. Late afternoon light filtered dimly into the room through three curtained windows.

The old man was easily the most curious thing in the room. He was grey and bent, and seemed blithely unconcerned by this strange girl's sudden arrival at his front door. In fact, he acted for all the world as if he had been expecting her. He was standing now in front of the fireplace, where a few small logs were slowly burning themselves down into a glowing bed of coals.

"Well, come in," the old hermit said, still without looking up. "Close the door; don't stand on ceremony."

He turned far enough to look at Trea over his shoulder for a moment, then bent back toward the fire, where he was stirring a smallish iron pot. A fine aroma of hot vegetable soup filled the room.

"You've been to a lot of trouble, haven't you?" the old man said, "Yes, yes. So I thought. Or else you wouldn't be here. But here you are! And seeing as much, I will offer you a choice. I can give you a bowl of soup or a bag of gold, which would you prefer?"

"The soup," said Trea, without hesitation. "Please."

"Ah-hah!" said the old hermit, as he turned to hand her a wooden bowl. "So you choose the soup? Interesting, interesting. Curious, isn't it? I wonder why, wonder why. Perhaps you don't believe I have a bag of gold to give you, but you can see that I have the soup. That's observation, calculation, a choice based on probability. There's intelligence in that, yes, yes, of a certain sort."

He ladled a generous portion of the hot stew into her bowl. She could see carrots and potatoes floating in the broth, along with a few herbs and beans. The smell of it was something wonderful.

"Gold is more precious than soup," the old man continued, "or so some might tell you. But why is that, I wonder? Here, you had the freedom to choose, and yet you took the soup. Interesting, interesting. Perhaps you didn't wish to be greedy, and so you took the less valuable choice. Possible, possible. That's virtue, or some might call it such, if that was the reason. Selflessness, not to seek more than you need. Hrmmm... There's a spoon for you on the table, and a napkin, if you like such things."

The old man dropped the ladle gently back into the stewpot and hobbled his way across the room toward one of the long wooden benches. Holding on to it for balance, he slowly turned himself around to face the girl again, and gingerly eased himself down until he was fully seated.

"Sit down," he said impatiently, "at the table, if you like, or there's a chair near the fire if you're cold. But don't mind me; I'm old and I've already eaten. Yes, more than enough. So you see? Have that, have some more. All that's in the pot, if you like. Don't stand on ceremony, and by the dragon sit yourself down already."

Trea decided to abandon her confusion, at least long enough to eat. "Thank you," she replied, as she sat on the little stool by the fireplace and set to work on her bowl of soup. The old hermit continued to ramble while she ate. Trea wasn't sure if he was talking to her, or to himself. She was too busy eating to follow what he was saying very closely.

"I could have offered you other choices, of course. I might have offered you a knife, or some other sort of weapon. Even two choices is a complicated matter, but then you bring weapons to the table. Yes, yes. You might have chosen the knife, then killed me with it, and eaten all the soup and searched the cottage to see if I really had the gold after all.  You might have claimed the lot!  Some would, you know.  Some might not have even waited for me to ask.  First notion of gold and they'd have gone for my gizzard.  Hah!  Yes, that's morality for you; or mortality.  Or perhaps it's just where those two lines of thought cross each other.  'X' marks the spot, doesn't it then?  Every time, every time.  Hrmm... "

His voice trailed off gradually, and eventually grew quiet.  Trea had emptied her bowl, and was about to ask if she could have some more.  But when she looked up, she saw that the old man's eyes were closed.  She wondered if he'd fallen asleep.

"May I have some more?"  she asked quietly.  She didn't want to wake him if he was sleeping, but she was still terribly hungry.

"EAT!!!!"  cried the old man, suddenly bursting with life.  "I told you as much before; didn't I say it more than once?  Eat, by the dragon.  I'm an old old man.  How would I drag your body to the river if you starved, I have to wonder?  One has to think of such things, you know, when one has the time.  But I'm not going to explain *time* to you.  No, no.  Time is a riddle you'll have to unwind after your own fashion.  Age helps with that, but it doesn't give you the answers.  Ah, but that's more than enough about time.  Now eat, child, eat.  Help yourself to the rest of the pot.  Just don't make me stand up again.  Not for a while yet.  Old bones.  Yes, dry old bones."

Trea refilled her bowl from the pot and returned to her seat by the fire.  The old man watched her in silence for a while, absently scratching his knees.

"But I'm speculating," he eventually said to her.  "Musing on the possibilities.  Putting words into your mouth perhaps, as well as soup.  And there's no need!  You could just tell me couldn't you?"

"Tell you what?"  Trea asked.  She was feeling better, now that she was on to her second bowl, and was finally able to divide her attention between the hermit and the soup.

"Tell me *why*, of course."  said the old man.  "Why the soup and not the gold?  You made the choice, not me."

"I was hungry."

"Ah, yes," he said, nodding. "You can't eat gold, can you? But you could have traded the gold for food, could you not?"

"Not here. I'd have to find a town."

"Ah-hah!" shouted the old man. "Excellent, excellent. Are you saying that value depends on context? That what is precious here and now might not be precious elsewhere... at a different place and time?"

"I suppose..." Trea said cautiously.

"Very good," he said, approvingly. "That's wisdom. I thought you had it in you; I was sure of it."

Trea wondered if this were some sort of trick – if the old man was playing a joke at her expense. Or perhaps he was just crazy. It flashed through her mind that everyone who had ever been kind to her was insane... this old man, the young Sister of Piety, even her grandfather. She couldn't help puzzling over why that was.

The old man hunched his head lower, and raised an eyebrow. When he spoke again, his voice was hushed, almost a whisper.

"The secret," he said, "is that gold, treasure and so on... it has no value. Not on its own merits. The stuff is useless, unless there's someone who craves it. Someone to sell it to. Someone who'll take it off your hands and give you something genuinely useful in return... Food, tools, land, servants, what-have-you... Whatever power gold might seem to have is pure illusion, entirely dependant on those who believe. On those who *worship*."

He said this last word sharply, abruptly, then turned his head to the side and spit, as if the very thought had left a bad taste in his mouth.

"Fools worship; the wise *consider*. Remember that," he said. "Gold doesn't create. It doesn't nourish. It doesn't even kill. Of itself, it is worthless. Meaningless. And thus, the dragon."

At the word *dragon*, Trea stopped eating. She felt a shiver in her bones. The old man noticed her reaction and smiled.

"Ah yes," he said, "but you already know a great deal about the dragon, don't you? Yes, yes. But you would like to know more, I think. Am I wrong?"

"You are not wrong," said Trea.  She tried to keep her voice from trembling at the merest thought of the beast.

"Gold," the hermit explained, "jewels, treasure, soldiers, heroes... and princesses, of course.  The dragon is a collector of beautiful and useless things."

"But he didn't collect me," Trea replied.  "He let me go."

"Ah-hah!" exclaimed the old man, his eyes sparking in the firelight. "Very true, very true.  And that was despite the fact that you were quite beautiful, weren't you?  With your hair neatly braided in that lovely blue dress.  How could that be?  Hrmm... One wonders.  One has to wonder.  Could it be that despite all of that, he somehow decided that you were not useless?"

The old man raised an eyebrow, and gazed levelly at her from across the room.

# Chapter 23:
## The Rope Circle

Trea woke up to find herself in one of the beds in the hermit's cottage. She looked around the room, but the old man was nowhere to be seen. Daylight was streaming in through the curtains, and the fire had long since burned itself out.

Trea didn't remember getting into the bed, or falling asleep. She did remember talking with the old man for a long, long time. He had done most of the talking, but at other times he had merely sat and listened.

He'd told her stories she had never heard before; stories quite unlike the heroic tales that the knights had told. He talked about the old kingdom, and how its people toiled, and its cities had grown, and spread across the great island. He spoke of how its kings became mighty, and powerful, and cruel, and how they craved greater glory, but there was nowhere left for them to conquer.

And he spoke of the coming of the dragon. How for a hundred years he burned the great cities and ravaged the land until every trace of the old kingdom was laid waste, and even its name was lost to time. And then began the *Years of Mist*, of which no record remained, when the dragon rested, the people of the land were scattered and few, and wilderness reclaimed the world.

They had talked of many other things after that – of history and the present day, and even the future – but she had somehow lost the thread that tied those thoughts together. Now they were like moths, fluttering aimlessly about a candle in her mind.

Somewhere during the course of the night, it seemed that she had slipped away from the waking world, where she was talking with the old man, and into a world of dreams, where she was talking with no one but herself. It was as if these separate versions of their conversation were somehow one and the same. Thinking back on it, the entire night seemed to her now more like a strange dream than something that really happened. And yet, here she was. The hut was real, the bed was real, the fire and the soup were real. She had been starving and lost in the woods, and now she was safe, and warm, and fed.

She pulled aside one of the curtains and looked out at the woods and the river.  The day was bright and clear, and the sun was already high.  Still she saw no sign of the hermit, but she hadn't really expected to.  He was a strange old man.  He had asked her questions that had no answers, and answered questions that she hadn't asked.  He'd known things that he could not possibly have known.  He had seen things that he could not possibly have seen.

She'd begun to think that even if the cottage and the river and the woods were real, the hermit himself was not.  Or rather, she suspected that he was something other than what he seemed to be, though what that other something might have been, she could not say.  Trea was certain that there was something else, something far deeper at work in all of this that she did not yet understand.  That frightened her, and yet, she felt strangely at ease in this equally real and otherworldly place.

But she knew that she could not stay.  She did not know where she might go, but she could not stay here for long.  If she had taken anything from the old man's philosophy, it was the understanding that she had some task to do, even if she didn't know what it was, and a debt to repay, even if she didn't know how.

She turned back to the room, and saw that there were changes from the night before.  Neither of the other beds had been slept in, but all the dinner things had been cleared away.  The cookpot was no longer in the fireplace; it was hanging from a hook along the ceiling.  She pulled it down for a moment to look at it, and found that it was empty and clean.  She saw that her bowl and napkin had been moved from the table to the cupboard, and had also been washed clean.  Whoever or whatever the old man was, he'd done the dishes before he left.

Her rope belt had been laid out on the table in a closed circle, nearly reaching to the table's edge.  Inside that circle were several things Trea had not seen before.  There was a small stack of neatly folded clothing, a burlap sack, and a long-bladed dagger with a black handle, encased in a dark leather sheath.

Trea puzzled at these things for several minutes without touching them.  The old man had apparently left them for her, and marked them out with her belt to make that clear, but she found the thought of them unsettling. The soup she had eaten the night before had been a gift, the old man had said as much. But these things, even if they had been left for her, she would have to take without his explicit permission.

She unfolded the clothing, and saw that it was not a dress or a gown, but garb for a boy or for a young man – trousers, a shirt and a vest – though they looked to be about her size. They were well-made, simple in design, and cut from ordinary cloth. The vest and trousers were black, or nearly so, and the shirt was a lighter grey. There were dark leather shoes, and a dark grey travelling cloak as well, with a hood.

She had to take the clothes. The white blanket had been better than nothing, but it wasn't a proper garment, even for the poorest peasant. She certainly couldn't go strolling into some town or village wearing that and nothing else. She'd surely be arrested or worse.

She pulled on the shirt and trousers, and was not surprised to find that they fit her reasonably well. They were loose around the waist and shoulders, and perhaps a bit too long at the hem, but those were problems easily managed. There was a belt, but it was attached to the scabbard of the dagger, and she was reluctant to touch that yet. She decided to tie the rope around her waist again, at least for the time being.

The shoes, she soon discovered, were sturdy, and fit her feet comfortably. She pulled on the vest and the cloak and walked outside to the river. Finding an eddy along the bank of the stream, where the water was reasonably still and clear, she knelt down close to it and took a long look at herself.

"You'd pass for a boy, at fifteen paces," she said aloud to her reflection. "Or a young man, I suppose... a short one, at least. But I can't imagine what the village girls might make of you."

Satisfied, she dusted herself off and walked back into the hut.

The burlap sack, she soon discovered, held about twenty dry biscuits. They would not make the most appetizing or satisfying of meals, but they would be a good deal better than starving in the wilderness. She picked up the sack and secured it to her rope belt.

Now, only the dagger remained.  She looked at it for a long time. Did she need it?  Did she even want it?

Everything else on the table – the clothing and the food – she had needed.  And yet, just by taking them she felt she had changed.  She knew somehow that taking the dagger would complete that transformation.  It would mark some sort of agreement, whether with the old man, or some hidden part of herself, she did not know.

Slowly, cautiously, she reached out her hand.  As she touched the strange black metal of the grip, a chill ran through her, as if she were being watched.  She pulled back her hand in alarm, looking all around the room, but no one was there.  She rushed to the door and opened it, but saw nothing aside from the river and the trees.

She closed the door again, and without thinking why, she bolted it. Compared to the broad daylight in the forest, the interior of the hut suddenly seemed very dark to her.  She turned and looked once more at the dagger.  She reached out, and wrapped her hand tightly around the handle.

For a moment she felt the chill again, but at the same time she felt a warmth flowing through her arm.  A few seconds later, the sensation had passed, and she felt entirely herself once more – neither warm nor cold – no different than she had ever been.

She drew the dagger out of its sheath, and was surprised to see that it did not seem to be made of iron, or indeed of any metal at all.  It was pure white, smooth and polished, and even in the dim light of the room it glimmered, faintly iridescent.  She was reminded at once of the pearls that had hung along the bodice of the elegant blue gown.  It was a terrifyingly marvellous thing.

She did not know what she might do with such a weapon, but she slipped it back into its sheath, and buckled the belt about her waist. The old hermit had meant for her to have it, and though she could not guess why, she understood that one day, perhaps very soon, she would need it.  It had to be taken, along with the rest.

--------------------------------------------------

Not long after Trea left the cottage, the trees along the banks of the little river had changed from firs and pines to maples, oaks, and other broadleafed hardwoods.  The slope of the ground became less steep and rocky, and began to look more like the familiar forests of the hills and valleys, instead of the richly-scented needle-carpeted mountainside. She continued to walk through those woods for most of the rest of that day.

The little river she was following was called the Stonewater, and it ran down swift and cold from the Last Mountain for many miles before it was finally swallowed up by the great Silent River, along its slow course to the sea.  Trea did not know the little river's name, but she knew that it was running eastward, away from the mountains, and away from the setting sun.

She came to a place where the river poured over a high stone bluff, plunging straight down in a splendid cascade for perhaps fifty feet, and into a deep pool that was hidden by the waterfall's churning spray of mist.  Looking out from that bluff, she saw low hills stretching away before her.  Far in the distance she could see a few scattered farms and towns, and beyond that nothing but the haze of twilight.

She was no longer in Drey.  She had passed through the shadow of the dragon, and was standing just inside the western boundary of Furgathor.

# Chapter 24:
## The Matron and the Novice

Malessa was standing just inside the closed doorway of the matron's chambers.

The matron was standing nearby, gazing out an open window. This room was at the top of her private tower, and from this high perch she could look out beyond the encircling wall of the compound, to the rolling pastures and the forest beyond. When skies were clear she could look far into the distance, high up the side of the mountain, toward the ruined city and the home of the dragon. But today, Githran had drawn a low veil of clouds across the morning sun. The matron could see the ancient road easily enough, but she could not see where it led.

Beside the window stood a heavy wooden table that the matron sometimes used as a writing desk. Lying on that table were two of the treasures they'd found in the ruined city: the shredded blue dress that had been tangled in the wreckage of the iron cage, and the ornate black and silver axe.

Malessa had never seen this room before, and did not know why the matron had summoned her now, though seeing the dress and the axe, she thought she could guess. She waited quietly. Several minutes passed before the matron finally turned to look at her.

"Tell me," the older woman began quietly, "do you know why I was chosen as Matron of the Order?"

This was not a question that Malessa had been expecting. She answered it as best she could.

"I have always understood that it was because you were close with the goddess."

"No," the matron replied firmly. "I have no special connection with the goddess. I was chosen for political reasons, not religious ones. My father was a person of some importance. He did not want me to... compete... with my younger brother for his inheritance. And so I was set aside. A sum of money was given to the Order, an agreement was reached by all parties concerned (myself excepted), and I was sent into a sort of sacramental exile. Here. To rule this little imitation of a kingdom."

The matron looked her in the eye, to gauge her response to this revelation, but Malessa had none. She nodded thoughtfully, but said nothing.

The matron picked up the axe, and turned it over in her hand.

"It was you who found this weapon in the dead city," she said. "And that troubles me."

*This* was a question that Malessa had been expecting.

"Am I to be punished?" she asked, eagerly. "Are you going to kill me with it?"

The matron's glance moved from the axe to the young novice, and hovered there in contemplation.

"You're a very peculiar girl," she said, eventually.

"So I am told by almost everyone."

"How is it...?" the matron began. But she hesitated, to phrase the question another way. "You said that you thought this axe was a relic of the old kingdom."

"Was I in error?"

"No," said the matron. "You were correct; it *is* a relic of the old kingdom. But I don't understand how you could have known such a thing."

"I'm very sorry, Matron," the girl replied, sincerely. "There are things that I don't know how I know them. How does one know which color is white and which is blue?"

The matron set the axe back on the table, and gingerly lifted the remains of the elegant dress.

"How indeed?" she said. "You spoke with the girl that last wore this dress. What can you tell me about her?"

"Her name was Trea, and she was very hungry," Malessa replied. "Many people had been cruel to her, and though she was slated to die, she was not afraid. She was angry – or so she said – I think at the injustice, more than anything else. She was a fascinating person."

"I see," said the matron. "Did you like her?"

"I did," admitted the girl. "Was that wrong of me?"

"Does it make you sad," the matron asked, "that she was devoured by the dragon?"

"No," Malessa replied. "Because she was not devoured. She escaped."

Now it was the matron's turn to be surprised.

"She escaped? You say that with great certainty, but no one can escape the dragon. We found her empty dress."

"I had given her a blanket," the young girl pointed out, "and it was not found in the ruins. Only she would have taken it. I think she still lives."

"Do you think that is why the prophecy failed?"

"I do not know. I don't know what the prophecy was."

The matron turned to the window, and stared out into the morning haze. It came to her that she did not know what the prophecy was either, not precisely. She only knew what Captain Harbek had told her, and even *that* might have been entirely wrong.

"If the dragon is slain," the older woman said, "then that will mark the end of an age. One circle will end, and another will begin."

"It's all the same circle, Matron."

The matron turned back to the room again, to contemplate the strange young girl who was still standing, innocently, in front of her closed door.

"I was right about you, child," she observed, "and wrong. You *are* nearer to the goddess than I am, but I was mistaken to see that as a fault. I now suspect that one day you will become Matron of the Order, perhaps even for the right reasons. But I cannot be certain of it. I am not gifted with foresight."

"I am."

"I know," the matron replied. "Go now; return to your duties. All that you and I have said here is to remain secret, is that understood? You are not to discuss it with the other members of the Order, though perhaps there will come a time to speak of it with your closest friends."

"I have no friends, Matron."

"You are mistaken," the matron replied. "You have at least one. Go now."

Malessa bowed her head, and slipped quietly out the door and down the tower stairs.

When she was gone, the matron walked to the large iron-bound chest which stood along the opposite wall. She unlocked it, and took two carefully wrapped bundles out of it. The first was the helm of Captain Harbek, retrieved from the ruined city. The second was an ancient sword. The sword had been forged from the same black metal as the axe that the girl had found, and it showed the same arcane tracings of silver along the blade. Its name was Vore, and it was also a relic of the old kingdom. It had once been – within living memory – the personal weapon of Arvallin the Great.

The matron had taken it, long ago. She had believed at the time that it was the only relic of the old kingdom that remained in the world, but she had been wrong. As she stood – staring at the sword and the axe, the dress and the helmet – she could see that she had been wrong about many things. She could not amend that now.

She carefully wrapped her four treasures, one by one, and returned them to the chest. First the sword, then the axe, then the shredded dress, and then the captain's helmet last of all. She closed the chest and locked it tight.

-- The End of Book One --

# Book Two:

# The Dragon's Thief


(Summer)

# Chapter 1:
## The Refugee

A month had passed since the knights' battle with the dragon, and the aftershocks of that event were beginning to be felt throughout the three realms. News of the failed attack travelled slowly. The Sisters of Piety, at least, had been in no hurry to inform the world of what had happened, and even they did not know the full story. No one did, not even the former urchin girl who was the caravan's sole human survivor.

Now, King Mulrin of Tunber sat on his throne and waited for one small piece of the greater mystery to unveil itself.

Kneeling on the floor in front of him was Princess Dophne of Drey. She looked lovely. She was dressed in a simple white gown studded with emeralds around the neckline and the sleeves; she wore no other jewelry, and her hair was unbraided, long and flowing about her shoulders. It was obvious to the king that these fashion choices were intended to convey not only the young woman's regal status, but also innocence, vulnerability, and desperation. Why she would choose to appear unannounced at his palace in such a guise as this was a puzzle to him, but he couldn't help admiring the skill with which she coordinated these not-so-subtle visual cues. It all seemed very genuine.

"Mighty King," the kneeling princess said quietly, "I have come to beg sanctuary."

Mulrin raised an eyebrow and peered a little more closely at the young woman before him. Her hands were clasped together, her head was bowed, and she seemed to be weeping. Her tears were plausible, given the circumstances, but they were merely window-dressing. Both the princess and the king understood that this meeting was a fulcrum point upon which the future course of all three realms now lay balanced. It called for sober judgment. All sentiment was purely for show.

"Why," the old man asked, cautiously, "would King Othelwaite's only daughter seek sanctuary in our little kingdom?"

Dophne did not immediately reply. First, she choked back a quiet sob and wiped a tear from her cheek. It was a nice touch, and Mulrin almost smiled, seeing how effectively she did it. He knew from long experience how difficult these things were to master.

After a carefully-timed pause, she finally answered him. "I am no longer safe in my father's realm," she said with a nicely understated tremor in her voice.

The old king adjusted himself on his throne, ever so slightly.

"Curious..." he replied. "Surely the heir of Drey is as precious to Othelwaite as my two sons, Halvik and Roal, are to me?..."

Mulrin gestured toward the young men who sat to his right. Halvik, the elder of the two, nodded once, politely acknowledging his father's remark. Roal pursed his lips and scratched at his thin beard, but made no other sign.

"If you are in some danger," the old man continued, "I would think your father could do more to protect you than I can."

"My father *is* the danger," Dophne replied. She raised her chin proudly now, and spoke with dignity and assurance. "He intends to offer me, as a sacrifice, to the dragon."

"The wily old bastard," muttered Roal, under his breath. His father heard him.

"Silence, Roal," the king said calmly, without looking away from the young woman before him. "We will not speak ill of our neighbor."

"I am sorry, Father," Roal replied.

"This is, to me, most curious," Mulrin said, lightly drumming his fingers on the armrest of his wooden throne. "Most curious indeed. There had been a rumor of sorts, that some of your father's soldiers were seen approaching the Last Mountain. I thought nothing of it at the time, but perhaps there was some truth in this matter after all?"

The old king knew far more than he was letting on. His spies in Drey had watched the royal tournament, and had marked the journey of the knights' caravan as far as the Sisters of Piety. It was only a few days ride from the foothills of the Last Mountain to the royal palace at Hinwahl, and though there might have been some confusion as to the finer details, Mulrin had, in fact, learned of the quest's failure even before Othelwaite had.

At first, his chief concern had been whether that incident would incite the dragon to a new campaign of destruction, but it seemed now that the dragon was content to remain a quiet enigma, as he had for so many years. What Mulrin had not anticipated was that Othelwaite's folly (as he regarded it) would turn to what now seemed a much more personal and self-inflicted injury.

"My father," said the young woman bitterly, "desperate to seize the dragon's gold, put his trust in a prophecy. It was a mad, foolish thing, doomed to failure from the start."

"I see," said the old king. "How unfortunate. Can you tell me what this prophecy was?"

"I know only that it called for the sacrifice of a princess. The attempt was made with a substitute... some peasant in one of my childhood dresses. That failed, as you seem to know. And so I fled, before my father could sacrifice *me*."

"Forgive me, child," said Mulrin, "But it seems unlikely that your father would sacrifice his sole heir, even for all the gold under the sky. Only a madman would bring an end to his own bloodline in such a way."

"My father has taken a new queen," the princess said, her voice dripping contempt. "The youngest daughter of Lord Hargrave of Toule, whom rumor for some time had made out to be one of his mistresses. But now it seems that the mighty king of Drey has set himself the task of fathering a new heir, or perhaps an entire pestilent swarm of them. I have heard it said that the blushing bride is already with child."

"I shall have to congratulate your father on his virility," said the old king, "when next I see him."

Halvik grinned, ever so slightly, at his father's remark. Roal coughed aloud, and put a fist to his lips, stifling a laugh. Mulrin pretended not to notice.

"In other circumstances," the king continued, "I would not hesitate to offer asylum to one so wronged as yourself. But this is a weighty matter. Our kingdoms have been at peace for many years. I seek no argument with Drey."

"I have allies of my own," the princess said proudly. "There are many lords in Drey who have no love for my father. Were the matter to come to war, his kingdom would be divided."

"Indeed?" the old king replied. "And yet, war is an uncertain business. The knights of Tunber are valiant, but they are few. The lords of your father's kingdom might be in disarray, but they are many. In the fog of battle, which would prevail? Some who might otherwise have lived would die, only *that* is certain. As for myself, I have lived a long life, of which I am justifiably proud. My father left me a kingdom in turmoil; yet through diplomacy I have unified it as he never could through war alone. I intend to pass that kingdom on to my sons, intact. And though conquest has its place, I prefer diplomacy rooted in strength. I will be judicious before I trifle with the prospect of war."

"I am not come here for trifles," said the young woman, firmly. "It is said that the heirs of Arvallin will unite the three realms and restore the old kingdom. Through me, you could bind your line to that great destiny."

Mulrin sat up a little straighter on his throne.

"You *are* forward," said the old man admiringly. "Are you proposing marriage to *me*, or to one of my sons?"

"As you will, My Lord."

Mulrin smiled. "An amusing thought," he said, "but I am much too old, and feel the weight of my years perhaps more fully than your vigorous father does. My eldest son is already betrothed to the Princess Nalya of Furgathor as you may or may not have known. That leaves only Roal, my youngest."

"I would have her," said Roal.

"Silence, Roal," said the king, warningly. He paused, locking his son with a stern glare. "There is much here to be considered."

At length, he turned his gaze once more to the young woman still kneeling before him.

"Repercussions aside," he said, "there is still the practical matter of simple propriety.  Lacking your father's consent, which it seems he certainly would not bestow, how could such a betrothal even be arranged?"

"I am a grown woman," Dophne replied indignantly, "and of royal blood.  Even were I still in my father's house, I would claim my own hand as mine alone to give."

The old king smiled again, but not so broadly as the first time.  "You are indeed an heir of Arvallin, for I have heard such words before.  But that is another story, and one that came to some grief, as I recall; not least of all my own, at the time.  Forever the circle spins, and such are the youthful memories of a sad old man.  Mists and vapor, all come to nothing.  Ancient history now, and perhaps of little matter to the world as we live it today.  Perhaps."

# Chapter 2:
## The Speckled Crow

Nestled in the foothills below the Last Mountain – only a few miles to the south of the Sisters of Piety, and still very much in the shadow of the dragon – stood a cluster of huts and small farmsteads known locally as "Hillside".  It was a town only in the most generous sense of the word.  There was no encircling wall, no open market, and no mayor or any other figure of civic authority.  As it lay just north of the Grey River, the place technically belonged to the province of Glaen, and was a part of Drey.  However, in practice it belonged to no one, not even those few impoverished souls who lived there.  It was above all else a waypoint, a temporary stop along the lightly travelled roads that ran west and south, to Drey and Tunber respectively.

Vagabonds and refugees would pass that way from time to time, as well as those who practiced other, less-savory professions.  Thieves and highwaymen made the inn there a regular port-of-call, as they fled trouble in one realm, only to seek it out again in another.  Spies from all three realms would ford the Grey River nearby, either on their way to new assignments, or returning home with whatever secrets they'd been able to gather.  Mulrin's men had passed that way, carrying news of the failed attack on the dragon.  Some weeks later the refugee princess Dophne had travelled through with two of her handmaidens, disguised as diplomatic envoys from the Sisters of Piety.

Soldiers from Glaen would come there now and again, either hunting for some fugitive or other, or half-heartedly patrolling that nearly-deserted corner of the realm.  But that was rare.  Most often, any soldiers that came to Hillside were off-duty, looking to briefly get themselves out from underneath their lord's authority, rather than enforce it.  It was a place where no real authority reigned, and yet – perhaps due to some invisible aura of civility that emanated from the Sisters of Piety, or simply because of the region's proximity to the dragon – an uneasy peace was kept, by a sort of mutual consent among all parties.  Though two men might be mortal enemies *beyond* the unmarked boundaries of Hillside, within the town itself they would most often leave each other alone.  There was ample time and space elsewhere for such conflicts to be resolved.

The chief attraction of the town was the Speckled Crow, a large, ramshackle inn.  And the chief attraction of the Speckled Crow was the innkeeper's eldest daughter, Mida.  Fair-haired and slender, she was as beautiful as a girl of eighteen years can be.  It was said that fully half the young men in Glaen were in love with her, and the other half hadn't seen her yet.  That was an exaggeration; some that had never seen her were in love with her as well.

The Speckled Crow was a quiet waystation between Drey and Tunber, particularly favored by those who hoped to avoid the tolls or the closer scrutiny that came with passage across the ferry at Piyl. Here at the foot of the mountains, the Grey River's many tributaries were yet to join its main flow, and even at its deepest points the water was little more than a gentle stream.  In the days of the old kingdom, there had been a broad and stately bridge across the Grey, less than a mile from where the inn now stood.  But only a few broken pillars of that bridge remained, as well as the many great blocks of stone that could still be seen lying on the riverbed in the dry fall, when the river was at its shallowest.

-----------------------------------------------------

It was a quiet night at the Crow, all things considered.  A handful of soldiers had come in, which sometimes led to trouble, but tonight they seemed to have little appetite for harassing the other guests.  They had made their way to the back room without incident, leaving the various rogues and travellers and local peasants in peace.

At a glance, the inn's great hall seemed nearly empty.  Tonight's guests had all avoided the room's well-lit center, choosing instead what privacy could be found at the benches and tables along the outer walls. No music was played.  No songs were sung.  There were no drunken jests, no revels, and no laughter.  The only sound was the low drone of half a dozen mumbled conversations taking place around the margins, and in the room's shadowy corners.

Saren, the innkeeper's younger daughter, wove her way through the wooden benches, talking in her hasty, animated way with the customers, and delivering ale and food as it was called for.  Her sister Mida had been sent to serve the soldiers in the back room.  Mida was the likely reason the soldiers had come to the inn at all, and letting her handle them was the safest way to ensure a peaceful night for all concerned. Most of the travellers passing through wouldn't know what they'd missed by not seeing her, and the rogues and regulars could always ogle her another time, after the soldiers were gone.

Seated near the open doorway to the kitchen, Gurin – the innkeeper and the two girls' father – was talking quietly with a strange old peasant; a refugee from somewhere up north.

"War is coming," the old peasant said, "mark my words. In this world, war is always coming. A man like Othelwaite bleeds the realm until there's nothing more he can steal from his own people. Next, his ambitions turn abroad. I've seen it before."

"You may be right in that," said Gurin, "but if there's war it won't come here. Armies can't march through Hillside, the dragon will see to that. Some might curse the old worm, but he's never done *me* harm. Let the wars happen elsewhere, so long as we're left alone here."

The old peasant nodded impatiently, waiting for the innkeeper to finish talking, but only half-listening to what he had to say. "People talk about Arvallin the Great," the old man continued, as soon as Gurin took a breath. "But I can remember his father, Marofyl. Marofyl the Cruel, he was called, and that was a name he well earned. That was my childhood, and those were dark times. We've had a few quiet years now, but the dark times are coming again to Drey, and elsewhere, I expect. And that means here as well, whatever you call this place. You shouldn't doubt me on that."

"I don't see how times could get much darker," said the innkeeper. "News from all three realms comes through here, and it's rarely good."

"Well, we're making for Tunber," said the old man, "if we can. Things are better there, or so I've heard. A man can raise a family, at least, and see his boys grow past childhood. There was a time I had three sons to call my own. No longer. Two of them I've lost to Othelwaite already: one to the mines at Blackhall, and the other to his damned fortress at Nyl. But he won't have this one."

He wrapped a bony arm around the small, dark-eyed boy sitting at his side. Across the table, his emaciated wife sat quietly, holding a young girl who could not have been older than five.

"At least neither was a soldier," the peasant continued. "I have that much to be glad of at least. They're both gone, to be sure, but they're not turned against me. Not turned against their mother or their own. It's a small blessing, as blessings go. But we've pitiful little else to be thankful for. We've done what we could, but this year, we decided would be our last. We gathered what we could carry of the early harvest and took to the forest. Soldiers walk the roads, but the forests are safe by comparison. What's a wild bear next to a troop of them, I ask you? A bear might eat *one* of you, and then only if he's hungry; but he'll most likely leave you alone. Soldiers, pah!" the old man spat on the floor, "they'll rob and beat you soon as look at you; murder you all if the mood takes them."

"We see a few soldiers come through Hillside," the innkeeper said. "Lord Vildar's men, mostly. There's some in the back room now. But they rarely give us trouble here."

"Aye, well you're a merchant, aren't you?" the old peasant said, pointing a crooked finger for emphasis. "That gives you standing a peasant doesn't have. And maybe your Lord Vildar is more a fair man than some. In the north there's no good fortune for the likes of us, and that's the truth of it."

"At least you've *had* sons," said Gurin, a bit defensively. "Me, with two daughters and no boys of my own at all. Now there's Mida, she's my oldest, and the pride of my heart. You've never seen a more beautiful girl than that. I'm waiting for the right match for her. Something to get me settled in my old age. She could have her pick of the lot, if I let her, but there's little enough to choose from comes through here. A son of a lord's been 'round here more than once though, and there's some hope in that, I'd like to think. For the wife and me, she's the only chance we've got at a better life in our old age."

"My youngest, though," continued the innkeeper, shaking his head with a frown, "that's her there with the red hair. She's like a lit match in a dark room. Where she came by that color, I'll never know. Her mother had a bit of ginger, years ago, but nothing like that, and it didn't come from me. There's something off with that girl since the day she was born, and I'm not afraid to tell you so. She's more than a handful and everyone around here knows it. I'd have married her off a year ago if I could find a taker. She's old enough... fifteen now, I think, or fourteen... I can never remember. She spends her days talking with the worst of the rabble that comes through. I don't know that I'll ever be rid of her. Not that she's not clever enough, mind you. A good bit too clever if you ask me. But at least she works hard, if you keep at her about it."

"Towns to the north are filled with unmarried girls," said the old peasant with a sympathetic nod. "Urchins running the streets. Families haven't enough to feed their own, much less take on another and raise some more. It's a bad situation from start to finish, and every day more boys lost to the mines and the builders and the soldiery. Me and mine, we're headed to Tunber, as I said, if our luck holds. It's carried us this far, but the coinpurse is light and the belly's empty every step of the way."

Gurin flinched ever so slightly. It had been a polite enough conversation while it lasted, but now that the talk had turned to money, he suspected the old peasant was after a bit of charity. Gurin, however, was a businessman, and not at all the charitable sort. He put on a professional smile and stood up, wiping his hands unconsciously on his apron.

"Well," he said, looking to end the conversation as quickly as possible, "we've a little shrine to Foll there by the fireplace. He's the guardian of inns and travellers, and I hope he'll keep watch on you. Good fortune with your journeys, then. Good fortune. Good night."

The innkeeper bustled hastily away, but the old peasant did not feel comforted.

---

In the wee hours of the morning, Gurin the innkeeper and his wife were fast asleep, but their two daughters were not. Saren and Mida shared the little room behind the kitchen, where they often talked late into the night.

"Were they bad tonight?" asked Saren. "Worse than usual, or the same?"

"I don't know," said Mida. "About the same, I guess. Always the same, really. Of course the same, just the same."

The two girls lay silent in the darkness for a while.

"I hate the soldiers," Mida said at length. "I hate smiling at them; I hate laughing at their jokes; I hate them drinking all night and pawing at me and fighting when they catch each other doing it."

"Someone will rescue you," Saren replied. "Someone always rescues the beautiful ones, isn't that how the stories go? That young merchant from Tunber, or Lord Vildar's son Valand, or even someone you've still not met..."

"I don't want to be rescued; no one's going to rescue me," Mida answered bitterly. "I want to *escape*, but I can't. I'm chained here. I belong to this miserable place, and were I anywhere else, the world would devour me, like a lump of sugar in a horse-stall."

Saren sighed, and stared up at the wooden ceiling. "At least you're wanted," she said. "I'm not wanted here or anywhere else, as far as I can see. You'll be made a far better match than I will, that much is certain."

"Sold to the highest bidder, you mean."

"Yes," the younger girl replied sadly, "Yes, that's what I mean. You'll have a future you don't want, and I'll have no future at all. We're in different traps but the same cage."

"Not both of us," Mida said. "I'm chained to this place, to our parents, but you're not. You're only chained to me. You could still escape."

Mida propped herself up on her elbow and gazed across the darkness at her younger sister.

"You can escape."

"I know," said Saren. "But I don't know how."

# Chapter 3:
## Fodge Returns

"What am I to do with you, Fodge?"  The king asked, tapping his hands together, his fingers fidgeting angrily in the air below his own chin.

"It is not clear to me," Lord Fodge replied diplomatically, "that you need do anything in particular with me at all."

The king was not satisfied with this answer, and Fodge knew it. The two men watched each other in silence for a few moments.

When news of the quest's failure had first reached King Othelwaite, he was furious, though perhaps not altogether surprised.  Heads would roll – he was certain of that much – though exactly *whose* heads remained to be determined.  The first and most obvious candidate, of course, was his errant minister of finance, the man standing before him now.

Fodge had been ordered to return to the castle immediately, or as immediately as could be arranged, and was provided with a generous security detail, to ensure that he did not lose his way.  As it happened, by the time the royal escort came to collect him, Lord Fodge was already awaiting their arrival.  On further reflection, he had decided not to flee the realm after all. Where could he go?  He had no reason to expect a warm welcome in either Furgathor or Tunber.  Given his reputation, and his status as a close confidant of King Othelwaite, he thought it more likely that he'd be put to the rack and tortured than given asylum.  And then there was the very real chance that he might simply get sent right back to Drey, either to be punished or executed, or perhaps even buried alive.  Quite possibly all three.

And so, after due consideration, Fodge reasoned that his best option was to hold his ground and talk his way out of it.  When in doubt, play to your strengths.  He took what little time he had to put his affairs in order, formally declared his eldest nephew as his heir (he had no children of his own) and prepared to return to Nyl as casually as could be managed under the circumstances.

"The royal treasury is still empty," Othelwaite fumed, "the dragon is still alive, and three of my finest knights – sons of three prominent lords – are dead!  Not to mention the loss of the captain of my royal guard.  Every element of your plan proved to be an utter catastrophe."

"I made no secret of the fact that our plan was a gamble," Fodge replied patiently.  "Some risk was necessary.  We could not be certain of success.  The goal, if you will remember, was to avoid needlessly endangering the life of the Princess Dophne."

"And there is another of the disasters you've brought me to. Princess Dophne is nowhere to be found!  Some of my spies believe that – fearing *she* might be sacrificed to the dragon next – she may even have fled the kingdom entirely!"

"May I remind Your Majesty," Fodge pointed out, "that it was *you*, not I, that revealed to the princess that one critical detail of the prophecy?  Had you not, she would have had little cause to flee."

"Reminding me of my errors, Fodge," the king growled pointedly, "is an excellent way to abbreviate your lifespan.  I am not in an agreeable humor."

"Yes, Majesty."

"This entire affair has been an ox-drawn funeral.  Someone must be punished, and if not *you*, whom?"

Fodge had been hoping for this question, and he had more than one answer ready.  "It seems to me," he said, "that it is not unlikely that the Sisters of Piety might have warned the dragon, or interfered perhaps in some other way.  It would be, of course, impossible to know that for certain."

"That is hardly a practical suggestion!"  the king barked angrily.  "I cannot safely take action against Ardelia or the Sisters of Piety while the dragon still lives, or I would have done so years ago.  You know that as well as I do."

"Then might I suggest exacting some punishment upon the Abbey at Flapham?"  Fodge ventured.  "As I understand it, Notwot himself – the abbey's somewhat dubious oracle – died shortly after making his unfortunate prophecy.  The shrine there is only dedicated to Mosig, a minor deity of minimal importance.  He is not, I think, the sort of figure that would likely be disposed to any sort of divine vengeance. The place itself has historically catered almost exclusively to the peasantry, and certainly has little real economic or spiritual value, especially now that the prophet is no longer in residence. And I might add that the idea of a substitute princess was in fact, the abbot's suggestion. I merely made the innocent error of taking him at his word."

That was it. Fodge had made his play. There was a long silence while he waited for Othelwaite's reply.

"You're a ruthless man, and a fairly good liar, Fodge," said the king, quietly. "I've always liked that about you."

"Thank you, Sire."

"You may go," Othelwaite said, with a dismissive wave of his hand. "But do remain within the palace. I have not yet decided *precisely* what I will do with you."

"Thank you, Sire," the financial minister replied again, this time with a bow. He turned to go, but then paused and turned back to the king, as if he'd suddenly remembered another matter of importance. Lord Fodge had one more throw of the dice to take, double or nothing.

"Ah... and one more thing, Your Majesty," he added gingerly, "if I may be permitted? Allow me to offer my sincere congratulations on your recent, somewhat... efficiently-consummated nuptials. I do admire your – shall we say *discretion*? – in opting for a small, private ceremony. So often royal weddings are such ghastly and lavish affairs, and in poor taste, in my humble estimation. Your... restraint in this regard is to be admired, I think."

"Yes..." said Othelwaite, slowly. He seemed to be torn between anger and amusement at Fodge's not-so-subtle insinuations. "Sadly," the king added, with the slightest hint of a smile, "it was the most elaborate celebration that the bride's father could afford. But true love... you know how it is." He opened his hands in a gesture of resignation, smiling a little more visibly now, in spite of himself.

"Indeed, Sire," Fodge replied, with only the polite trace of a grin. "Indeed, I do know it very well."

# Chapter 4:
## The Throne of Tunber

King Mulrin of Tunber sat by himself in his chambers and contemplated the future of his realm. With the arrival of the princess Dophne, all of his plans, which had seemed so well-laid and secure, were suddenly thrown into doubt. Throughout his long life, he had carefully built his kingdom through diplomacy and cunning, and he had hoped to die in a time of peace, leaving the troubles of the world for his eldest son to manage.

But war with Drey now seemed not only inevitable but imminent, and without the aid of Furgathor, it seemed almost certain to be a war that Tunber would lose. Diplomatic relations with Furgathor were strong, but King Edral was not yet Tunber's ally, and his aid in such a war was uncertain. Mulrin had hoped that the marriage between Halvik and Nalya would move the two kingdoms closer together, but that marriage had not yet taken place, and even if it did, there was every chance it could backfire. Narev, Nalya's older brother, might well see Halvik as a rival to his own power, rather than as a close relative and a friend.

And then there was the problem of Roal. Ideally, he would serve as his brother's confidant and capable right hand. But Mulrin knew better. A certain sort of man might move comfortably into such a role, but he had watched his youngest son over the years, and he knew that Roal would not be that sort of man. He had far too much ambition, and far too little restraint to stand silently in the wings. He would more likely be a constant thorn in his brother's side than a reliable source of support.

These, of course, were problems Mulrin already had, and they could possibly have been managed, had well enough been left alone. But now this princess from Drey had kicked the post from under the table, and thrown an already tenuous situation further into doubt. And Roal, to both his credit and his fault, had not hesitated in turning the disruption toward his own potential advantage.

Mulrin knew that he would have to allow the marriage; there was no plausible way for him to prevent it without creating even greater turmoil, and nothing else to be safely done with the girl, now that she was already here. She was dangerous, married or not, that much was certain, but so was his youngest son, come to that. As he thought about it, it seemed prudent to the old king that he should bind these two dangers together, so that they might be more easily managed. When in doubt, it is often best to keep your dangers conveniently organized.

But if each was a danger alone, together they might be truly perilous, and not least of all to each other. There was little reason to imagine that they would find love in the match, but Mulrin suspected that their shared ambition might prove a stronger bond even than love, in the end. If left to play itself out, the eventual end of that emerging drama was impossible to foresee. Whether Dophne and Roal would eventually destroy Tunber, or Halvik, or Drey, or each other, or all of the above and more, Mulrin could not guess. But the old king was certain of one thing – their drama would end as a tragedy, not a comedy nor even a romance.

When they were still children, having two sons had seemed wise; a worthy precaution in an uncertain world. But now that they were grown it had become a matter of unfortunate excess. The old king found himself faced with a thorny problem, and not one which could be resolved immediately, or without risk. But Mulrin of Tunber had not maintained his throne all these years by being either hasty or timid.

------------------------------------------------------

Mulrin, of course, was not the only one contemplating the impact of Princess Dophne's arrival in Hinwahl. Halvik had said little and thought much, as he usually did. Roal, on the other hand, was busily congratulating himself on what he regarded as a major triumph. As he saw it, fate had intervened in his favor, and he himself had been swift to exploit the opening. Now, he was doing his best to taunt his older brother, but Halvik refused to take the bait.

"What a pity," Roal said, with mock disappointment. "The sole heir of Drey, suddenly available, and you're already engaged. I'm sorry for your loss, Brother."

"As things stand today," said Halvik evenly, "I think there is very little chance she will ever see that inheritance."

"Some might regard that as a gamble worth taking."

"Why gamble over something," Halvik asked, "which, with a little patience, can be easily won?"

"That's a simple question for the elder brother," replied Roal, with a bitter grin. "Others of us find such opportunities must be *made*. Are you jealous that I might have the better prize?"

"No." replied Halvik. "The princess Nalya is an ideal match for me. I find her every bit as beautiful, far more gracious, and of more even temperament than this exile from Drey."

"*Power* is beautiful, brother. Nothing else."

"I might remind you that there is power in Furgathor, as well as in Drey."

"But you won't be king there," said Roal, tauntingly. "That title will go to her older brother, unless some kindly soul does you the favor of killing him before his time."

"Diplomacy is a slow and careful process, Roal. You've never understood that."

"Caution is an empty field," Roal replied, "where fortune goes to seed, unharvested."

Halvik smiled broadly, and shook his head.

"I do suspect that this exiled princess will make for you an excellent match, in terms of rank and temperament," Halvik conceded, "But I do not envy you in the slightest regard. Be certain of that."

He looked his younger brother in the eye.

"And know this," he cautioned, "such matches as the one you are pursuing rarely last into old age. You see her as a ladder to be climbed, but I think you might be closer to the mark if you left off the "L" from the start of that word. Be wary in your ruthlessness, for yours is not the only cunning mind at work in these affairs."

Roal glared back angrily, but his brother's voice was calm and even, and he did not look away. After a few taut moments, Halvik continued.

"If you wed with this princess from Drey, it is likely that the union will be short. I have little doubt there will be more than enough venom for all concerned, in your mutual nest of vipers. You still have many years before you, but there are also many ways to die. I, for one, find no cause for trust in her. Your domestic affairs are your own matter, but all the same, I would advise you to keep an eye to your porridge, Brother."

# Chapter 5:
## The Innkeeper's Daughters

It was a busy night inside the Speckled Crow.  Valand, the son of Lord Vildar, had arrived early in the evening with half a dozen of his father's soldiers.  They had quickly disappeared into the back room, and Mida was tending to them there while her younger sister and father served the inn's other guests.  A larger crowd than usual had gathered in the Crow's main room, with some unfamiliar faces seated among the various rogues and other regulars.  Gurin and his younger daughter were kept quite busy, shuttling a steady stream of food and drink out to their customers, then bringing the empty mugs and plates back into the kitchen again.

Saren was weaving her way nimbly through the maze of benches and tables, carrying a loaf of bread in one hand, and a bowl of soup in the other.  As she passed by his table, one of the inn's frequent patrons, who that night had indulged perhaps a bit too vigorously in the house cider, reached out an open hand and slapped her firmly on her rear. Saren was already tired, and not in a good humor.  She whirled about, and immediately spotted the culprit.

"Was it you that did that?" she asked, smiling broadly.

"Aye!" said the man with the scruffy brown beard.  "Shall I do it again?"

The two men sitting with him laughed loudly at this.

"No," said Saren, sweetly, as she flipped the bowl of soup into his lap.

The man shouted in surprise, and suddenly everyone in the room was watching them.  More than a few of the other patrons laughed. Drenched in soup, the man jumped up, and grabbed at the girl with both hands, but she was too quick for him. She pulled the kitchen knife from the loaf of bread in her other hand and raised it high, pointing it toward the drunken man's wavering eyes.

"I don't like killing customers," she said, still smiling through her clenched teeth, "but I do make exceptions from time to time."

A hush of anticipation fell over the room as the drunkard's friends tried to prevent him from foolishly drawing his own weapon or lunging at the girl. Red-faced, he stared at the knife with both alarm and fury, as he uselessly tried to shake the soup off his arms and clothes.

"You're square-boned, Girl!" the man shouted, with his hands balled tightly into fists. "You should be grateful of a friendly pat now and then! Who'll have you? You're not your sister; you're half-mad and half the world knows it!" He struggled angrily with the two men who were still holding him back.

Just when it appeared that the fight might escalate in earnest, Gurin emerged from the back room. Though he made it his habit to be politely servile – even to his most rough-hewn guests – the innkeeper was a large, powerful man, and an intimidating presence when he chose to be. He did not tolerate brawling, and was quite capable of restoring order in his own house. He'd heard the commotion, of course, and looking at the scene before him he could make a fair guess at what had happened.

"Saren!" he bellowed. "Get back into the kitchen with you. Go!"

"Absolutely Father," Saren replied in mock obedience. She kept the knife high for a moment longer as she took a step backward, then she turned and walked casually toward the kitchen. She'd almost reached the doorway, when she stopped. She took a satisfied look back toward her soup-drenched customer, and added "I'll tell mother that the stew isn't hot enough."

She stabbed the knife deep into the wooden doorjamb, and disappeared into the kitchen as the room roared with laughter at the drunken man's expense. A few of the most enthusiastic cheered aloud and some whistled appreciatively. Within moments, however, the commotion had ebbed, as the crowd returned to their food and drink and other topics of conversation. Gurin went to mop up the mess, apologizing for his daughter's behavior and trying to make amends to the angry customer as best he could.

Mida had watched the end of the fight, peering out from the half-open doorway to the back room. But once she was sure that Saren had safely escaped to the kitchen, she closed the door again. She envied her sister's courage, but she did not envy the beating she would likely receive at their father's hands later in the evening. Mida wished that Saren could be more like herself, or perhaps she wished the reverse. She shook her head sadly, and set aside any further wishing.

She returned her attention to her duties in the back room, where the soldiers were laughing and arguing as usual, absorbed with their cards and their wagers. But she saw that for some reason Valand was not among them. He sat alone in the far corner, silently nursing a mug of ale. She walked over to him. It was clear to Mida that he had brought the men there that night, and yet, he was not a part of their game. She thought it odd.

"No luck with the cards tonight?" she asked.

"Not tonight," Valand replied. "My heart just isn't in it."

"Something troubles you?"

"Yes," he said, "since you ask. Everything troubles me, it seems."

"You're not yourself, that's plain," Mida said, smiling gently. "I don't know that I've ever seen you in this mood."

"I don't know that I've ever been in this mood before," he replied. "I had hoped..." He paused mid-sentence, and looked at his half-empty mug of beer. He set it down, rested his elbows on the table, and turned up his hands in resignation. He looked Mida squarely in the eye.

"I had hoped," he began again, "that one day I would ask you for your hand."

"For my hand?" replied Mida. For a moment she was genuinely startled, but she quickly recovered herself. She had plenty of experience fending off amorous advances. "Whatever would you do with it, I have to wonder? You seem to have two of your own, and I promise you, I have need of both of mine."

"Please," Valand replied, his face thoughtful and earnest, "don't make a jest of it."

"Then what is it you mean?" Mida asked, cautiously. "You can't be serious."

"But I am."

"I don't believe you; and surely you'd have to ask my father first."

"I don't *like* your father," said Valand, bluntly. "I never have. And I am given to understand that he is already married."

"You *are* playing fun with me," Mida replied with some relief.

"Sadly, no," said Valand, looking down at the table. He took a breath to steady himself, then looked up at the beautiful young barmaid again.

"I had meant to ask *you*," he emphasized, "because without your answer, your father's assent would've meant nothing to me. And if you *would* have me, then I'd never have let him stand in the way. But that cannot happen now."

"Is this some cruel riddle?" Mida asked, frowning. "I don't understand what you mean to say. Are you asking me, then? Or aren't you?"

"I am not," he said, looking her again in the eye. "I cannot. I am no longer my own to give. Aglor, my older brother is dead and gone, and I am now my father's only heir. He will dispose of my life as he sees fit. All choices are taken from me. I am sorry, for I do love you so."

Mida closed her eyes and stopped breathing. Behind her, she heard the soldiers shouting over their game of cards, oblivious to the little pas de deux that had been playing out in the corner of the room between their favorite barmaid and their lord's only remaining son.

She opened her eyes again and looked squarely at the young man before her. "There has been some difficulty," she said quietly, "in the main room. If you will excuse me."

Mida turned and walked slowly across the wooden floor, exiting through the narrow door that led into the kitchen. Berla, her mother, was there, methodically chopping vegetables and adding them to the large stewpot that hung on an iron hook over the open fireplace. Kersin and Nera – two local peasant girls that her father sometimes hired on as extra help – were also hard at work. Kersin was hauling buckets of water in from the well outside, and Nera was hastily rinsing the worst of the grime off of the plates and bowls that came back from the main room, before filling them up to be sent out again.

Saren was there as well. She had just carried in a fresh bundle of dry kindling for the fireplace, and now she was carefully adding more wood atop the coals that were glowing orange and black beneath the simmering stewpot. That done, she leaned a hand against the stone mantle, bracing herself for balance as she grabbed a ladle and stirred the bubbling stew.

Mida walked over to her.

"If you'll take the back room for a bit," Mida said, "I'll help Father with the front. There's too many of them out there for him to manage alone."

Though Mida had spoken softly, just above a whisper, her mother had overheard her. Berla stopped working, and looked up from her cutting table long enough to reprimand her daughters.

"You're for the back room, Mida," she declared firmly. "You know that. You've got to manage the soldiers. We've enough trouble with this one already!" She pointed angrily at Saren with her knife.

"There's only a handful of them," Mida argued, patiently. "And they're intent on their cards. Saren can handle them every bit as well as I can tonight. Better, even. And Valand is with them; he'll see to it that there's no trouble."

"And that's all the more reason you should be back there tonight," Berla said. "Son of a lord and *unmarried*, as if you didn't know."

"Do you want more trouble in the front room?" Mida countered, pointedly. "If a fight breaks out we'll have broken furniture and who knows what all else to deal with. They're already restive, and it won't help matters if Father can't keep up with their food and their beer."

"Ah, do what you will," Berla groused, giving up the argument. She angrily returned to chopping the vegetables.

"Please," Mida whispered to her sister, with a nod toward the back room. "I can't go back in there tonight. Don't ask me why."

Saren met her older sister's eye with a look of genuine concern. Mida *always* tended the soldiers, and it was not like her at all to argue with their mother. The two young women gazed at each other in silence for some time before either of them spoke.

"All right," said Saren, gently.

"Thank you," Mida replied.

# Chapter 6:
## A Grand Wedding

On a moonless night, at the height of summer, Prince Halvik of Tunber and Princess Nalya of Furgathor were to be joined in sacred wedlock. The wedding would take place on a great wooden barge anchored in the center of the Silent River. The venue was a sort of symbolic compromise and – like the marriage itself – was settled upon through careful diplomacy.

The river marked the border between the two realms, and by holding the wedding ceremony in the midst of the stream, neither kingdom was favored, either in terms of prestige or convenience. Each royal retinue could remain encamped on its own respective bank of the river, within its own territory and at its own expense. And, by keeping the two camps separate, the likelihood of some careless supernumerary committing an unfortunate diplomatic faux pas was greatly reduced. Wine could flow freely, while gossips could gossip and jesters could jest, and no insults would be given or taken – or at least none would be heard by those most likely to take offense.

To be sure, the two sides mingled upon the great wedding barge. But there, only the elite few were allowed. Anyone with sufficient wealth and status to be invited into that innermost nexus of royal privilege was adept enough at the game of politics to keep their most incendiary remarks to a polite whisper, and to pretend not to overhear the polite whispers of others.

Even Roal, who was not known for his polish or restraint, could maintain a dignified silence for a few requisite hours. And remain silent he did. While aboard the wedding barge he kept to the railings most of the time, and spoke little if at all, leaving the spotlight to his older brother. If anyone noticed him smiling more than he typically did, they assumed that he was merely enjoying the festive occasion. Only his brother and father knew the real reason for Roal's uncharacteristically jovial mood.

As for Mulrin, he had intended for this wedding to be his last and greatest triumph of diplomacy. It marked – if not quite a full alliance with Furgathor – at least a bold gesture in that direction. In a treacherous and uncertain world, there was nothing he could do to fully ensure Halvik's future success, but in securing for him the best conceivable mate, Mulrin rightfully felt that he had managed to slip his eldest son an extra ace under the table. How the next king of Tunber played his cards from this point forward would be largely his own affair.

For his part, Roal's high spirits were largely due to his anticipation of acquiring an ace of his own – even if he had to snatch it himself, and from the bottom of the deck. As Roal saw it, fate had handed him a seat at the political gaming table, and it was his lot in life to make the most of it. Even if fate had not dealt him an ideal hand, he had no qualms about playing to win.

The princess Dophne, it should be noted, was *not* in attendance, and her tentative betrothal to Roal was still – at least officially – a matter of utmost secrecy. Mulrin thought it safest to keep the exiled heir of Drey neatly sequestered in Hinwahl, for the time being. He certainly was not going to take the risk that her presence might jeopardize the current festivities. She was a marked card, and one that Mulrin would keep well-hidden at least until Halvik's marriage was signed, settled and fully squared away. First things first.

The ceremony itself was a lavish and splendid spectacle, carried out with clockwork precision. No expense had been spared on any detail, and everyone in attendance was dressed to the nines in their most opulent finery. In the torchlight, the grand and gilded wooden barge – filled to the railings with powerful men and women in brightly-colored clothing – glowed like a richly bejewelled version of the sun, rising above the dark water.

The forward portion of the barge held the royal couple and their respective attendants, the wedding officiants and various high-ranking religious figures, and the most favored of the royal guests from both kingdoms. The aft portion was laden with wedding gifts: Fine tapestries, great sacks of coins; ornately carved wooden chests filled with gems; glittering necklaces, rings and brooches; as well as myriad other trinkets of gold and silver; all displaying the finest work of the finest artisans from throughout the known world.

The ancient prelate officiating the ceremony spoke glowingly of love, as if that emotion had played some role of significance in these arrangements. It had not. But Halvik and Nalya were each satisfied enough with the partners fate had assigned them. Halvik was wealthy and handsome, Nalya was wealthy and beautiful. Raised from birth in full awareness of the narrow confines of their pedigrees, neither had ever imagined better for themselves, though both had privately dreaded far worse. It was as happy a match as either could reasonably have hoped for.

Nearly every aspect of the entire event went perfectly. From the martial splendor of the honor guard, to the chorus of children singing along the riverbank, to the braided ropes of gold and silver that symbolically encircled the wedding altar, each separate element came off, as the saying goes, without a hitch. It was, in the end, an almost flawlessly theatrical blend of religious and political propaganda.

The only blemish on the whole affair was so slight as to escape the notice of almost everyone in attendance. In fact, it was not noticed at all until more than a week after the ceremonies had concluded, and Mulrin's scribes were calculating a final tally of the wedding gifts and the related expenditures. It was then discovered that some thirty-odd pieces of silver were missing from one of the many large sacks of coins amid the bridal dowry. Everything else was perfectly accounted for, aside from one small piece of silver jewelry, which had apparently been misplaced in transit.

The scribe who discovered these discrepancies dutifully made note of them. However, given the vast extent of the marital treasure hoard, such minor inaccuracies were fully expected. When the matter was brought to the king's chief accountant, he was not in the least concerned, and dismissed the apparent loss of those few items as a simple, though somewhat unfortunate clerical error.

It is, however, worth mentioning one small intrusion that no one in attendance at the wedding had noticed. At the very height of the ceremony, a small dark figure briefly slipped beneath the aft railings of the royal barge, lingering there for only a few moments, before silently disappearing again into the shadowy waters below.

# Chapter 7:
## Summer

Summer was the season of weddings, and throughout the three realms, young men and women of every social standing busily engaged with each other in the age-old practices of flirtation and courtship, neatly arranging themselves into matched (or mismatched) pairs, formally (or casually) binding themselves together by marriage contract (or some more temporary arrangement) and setting about the timeless recreational labor of producing further generations of young women and men, who would in time find themselves busily engaged in similar endeavors. And so the circle turned.

But if summer was the season of weddings, it was also the season of pilgrimages and other sorts of travel. Couples recently married (or soon to be) would customarily make offerings to Balikan and Bikala, respectively the god and goddess of lechery. Happy couples would beg *The Pair* (the somewhat pejorative term by which Balikan and Bikala were most commonly referred) to leave them alone, and not to tempt their partners to infidelity. Unhappy couples would (usually in secret) ply The Pair with requests of a somewhat different nature.

There were other important couples among the gods. Neldor, the god of the sea, and Githran, the goddess of the sky were chief among them. They were the Greater Gods, eternally estranged from each other, and yet bound together, side by side. Neldor was generous, but temperamental, and prone to fits of violence. Githran was wise, but mysterious. She would light the sun every morning, but draw veils of cloud across it when the mood struck her. She would shine the moon by night, but slowly hide it behind her cloak as the days passed, until it was totally hidden. Then she would gradually reveal it again.

The only other major deity was the great goddess Abzag the Destroyer. She was complete to herself. She did as she chose, and had no mate. In all the world, there was only one temple devoted to her, and that was the one maintained by the Sisters of Piety. Pilgrims did not visit there. Abzag had no need of worshippers, and craved no offerings in sacrifice. If she desired a thing – whatever it might be –

she took it, at a time of her own choosing, and without question or remorse. There was no refuge from her will, in either the earth, the sky, or the sea. She was above the concerns both of mortals and the lesser gods, and even Githran and Neldor held no sway with her.

But among the pantheon of the Three Realms, there were many lesser gods and goddesses, and journeys of pilgrimage were most often taken to shrines and temples devoted to the minor, earthly deities. These sites tended to be small and specialized, and each of them in some way reflected the character of the god or goddess they were meant to represent.

Every inn in every town had its shrine to Foll, the god of tavernkeepers, travellers, and wayfarers. There were also many shrines to Foll's elusive wife Athra – the goddess of thieves and highwaymen – but her shrines were hidden in out-of-the-way places, and were always kept very small and secret. Theirs was a stable, but somewhat dysfunctional marriage. Foll was loyal, trustworthy and kind; Athra was secretive, wild and unpredictable. They would fight constantly, separate frequently, and reconcile passionately. Above all, they were madly in love, and could never be apart for long, one without the other.

Woodsmen would wander deep into uncharted forests, seeking out the hidden shrines to Tarinor, the god of hunters and prey. Such ventures were a difficult, but necessary part of any hunter's life. It was Tarinor's nature to strive for balance, and so he did not always take the hunter's side. He courted Myris, the goddess of the forests. She resented his predations of the creatures that she cared for, and would eternally elude him, but still he sought to earn her favor. Those who hunted wastefully, or with needless cruelty would draw Tarinor's ire.

Merchants and tradesmen would seek shrines devoted to the deities concerned with their particular professions, while those with simpler aims were often drawn to the simpler pleasures afforded by deities such as Sendra, the goddess of good food and companionship, or her sometimes suitor Mosig, the brown-clad patron of simple farmers, and good beer, and keen perception, and wit.

Pilgrimages were a diversion for the rich, or at least for the modestly well-to-do. Though peasants might occasionally journey as far as a neighboring town – either to obtain some necessity that could not be had at home, or to barter some of their meager belongings away for a copper coin or two – any peasant that travelled further was generally some sort of refugee, either fleeing from war, or famine, or plague, or some other manifestation of doom. For a peasant, the world around them was filled with manifestations of doom. A peasant's life was not one to be envied.

# Chapter 8:
## Hillside

Trea had walked for many miles through the hills, and was not certain where she was. It had been two days since she'd last come upon a village or town, and though she had kept to a steady westward course, she could not be certain if she was now in Tunber or Drey. She was confident, at least, that she was no longer in Furgathor, and was somewhere in the sparsely populated hills below the Last Mountain, in the shadow of the dragon.

In the early afternoon, she struck what must once have been an old roadway. She was immediately reminded of the ruined highway that the soldiers' caravan had followed to reach the dragon, but she knew it could not be that same road. She was too far south for that. Still, she suspected this was another route that had been laid in the days of the old kingdom, now largely abandoned. And, as with that other road it cut a smooth grade through the hills, and even though partly overgrown, made for a much easier journey than she'd had while crossing through open country.

Eventually, that antique highway struck another, better-maintained road heading north and south. She followed it north, and soon found herself at the bank of a broad and slow-moving river. The road ran directly to the water's edge, and continued on the other side, though there was no bridge.

She took off her shoes and trousers and travelling cloak, and waded in, finding that the water was not as deep nor as cold as she'd expected. The riverbed was covered with large flat stones, and at its deepest point, the water only rose to a little above her waist. Even with most of her belongings held high over her head, she had little difficulty crossing to the other side. The lower part of her shirt and vest were thoroughly soaked, but otherwise most of her gear was kept dry.

She dressed herself, wrung as much water as she could out of her shirt, and after another hour of walking was nearly dry again. By this time, the sun was getting low, and the shadows were lengthening. Trea had almost decided to search for a suitable place to camp for the night when she spotted a little cottage ahead on the road. The cottage was dark, and she saw no people about, but by the time she reached it, she could see a second cottage further on, and a third higher up the side of the hill. Suspecting that she must be approaching a town of some sort, she kept walking.

A few minutes later, as she came around a gentle bend in the road she could see ahead of her a large, wood-framed building. The sun was fully down now, and the first stars were beginning to appear. Trea still had not seen any people, but there was light in some of the windows, and that seemed hopeful. As she drew nearer, she could see a large panel-board sign which read *The Speckled Crow*. The lower half of the sign showed the image of a large crow in flight, its feathers spangled both black and grey from its head to its tail.

*"An inn,"* Trea thought with enormous relief. She'd not had a full night's sleep in a bed for nearly a week.

She opened the front door and found herself in a great open room filled with many benches and tables. Scattered here and there throughout the space were various clusters of people, sitting and eating and talking quietly. A large open fireplace stood at one end, but most of the light in the room came from a great wooden chandelier, hanging between two of the heavy beams that ran below the rafters of the ceiling.

A few of the customers glanced at the door as Trea came in, but soon returned to their conversations. Not far away, she saw a large, barrel-chested man, weaving his way toward her through the room. She guessed that he must be the innkeeper. "I'll be with you in a moment, lad!" the man shouted in her direction, as he dropped a loaf of bread and a bowl of soup in front of a thin and balding man who was sitting by himself, hunched over a mug of beer.

As the innkeeper approached, he leaned forward and peered at Trea a little more closely. "Well by Athra's cowl!" he stammered hastily. "Forgive me, Miss! Never trust my eyesight across the room. I can see now I took you wrong, but I don't think I've seen you before, have I? I do apologize. I'm Gurin, and welcome to the Crow. What can I do for you tonight?"

Trea had not been at all bothered at being mistaken for a boy, and was a little disappointed that the innkeeper had realized his error. But in the end it made little difference, and she let the matter drop.

"Thank you," she said as politely as she could, "but I've been on the road for several days now and I'm afraid I'm a bit out of my reckoning. I wonder if you could tell me... well, what town is this? Where exactly am I?

"Oh, this is *Hillside*, Miss," the innkeeper replied. "Not much of a town, to be fair. We're in the farthest corner of Glaen in the farthest corner of Drey. They forget about us down here, often as not. But if you came at us from the east then you must have come up the road from Tunber, and you've been in Drey ever since you crossed the river. Rugged country if you came that way, but the road's good enough, or so I'm told. You must be headed to somewhere in Drey, then?"

"Yes..." Trea said hesitantly, "I'm on my way north."

"Going west, you mean, surely," the innkeeper said. "There is no road north from here. The road to Drey runs along the river for miles and miles yet. North from here is open country, and you wouldn't want to go *there*. Nothing in that direction but the Sisters and the dragon, Miss, if you don't mind me saying so."

"Of course," Trea said. "I meant west and *then* north. As I might have said, I am somewhat out of my reckoning."

"Yes'm," Gurin said apologetically. "Very sorry, Miss. Just trying to save you some trouble is all. Bit of confusion, nothing more. Now I've other guests and the kitchen to attend to, but grab yourself a bench and a table anywhere you like, and I'll send someone 'round to see to your supper, if that suits you."

"Yes, thank you," she answered, but the innkeeper had already bustled off toward the kitchen, and likely never heard her reply.

Left to herself again, she looked around the room and chose a secluded bench along one of the outside walls, as far as possible from the other guests. She sat down, and was just trying to make herself comfortable when she had the disturbing sensation that she was being watched.

Trea looked up to see herself confronted – there was no other word for it – by a girl in a dark brown dress. The girl was standing on the other side of the table with her feet wide apart, her fists resting on her hips, and her head cocked slightly to one side. She was plain of face, of average height, neither pretty nor ugly, neither heavy nor thin. In fact there seemed to be nothing remarkable about the girl at all, aside from her assertive posture and her shoulder-length, shock-red hair.

"Well look at you," the strange girl said with some amusement. "What are you, fourteen, fifteen? About my age; no older than me, I'd guess. Bit young for a thief, aren't you?"

"What?" Trea replied. She was too startled to say anything else.

"Well now!" the red-haired girl exclaimed, "I look at you closer, you're not a boy at all, are you? Oh, now there must be a story behind *this...*"

"I'm not a thief," Trea replied brusquely, still trying to catch up with this sudden conversation. "I'm just a traveller; I'm on my way north."

The other girl was obviously not convinced.

"You're sitting in a thief's chair. That bench belongs to Halfmoon. He'd be angry if he found you in it."

"Then I'll move."

"I wouldn't bother; I doubt he'll be in."

"I don't mind."

"I doubt he'll be in; they hung him last year. Damned shame it was. He had a sense of humor, and he always treated me well. 'Halfmoon' was what I called him. Never learned his real name; too late for that now. He'd been dead a month before I found out about it; one of the soldiers told Mida; that's my sister. They always like to brag about this or that after they've had a few; the soldiers I mean. So I can't say I shed any tears about it. He was long gone by the time I heard. Not a shock exactly; sooner or later they get everyone. That's how it is. Hate to lose a regular, though."

"Saren!" the innkeeper shouted from the open doorway to the kitchen, "don't annoy the customers!" He turned and disappeared again.

"That's my father," said the girl, with a nod toward the kitchen. "You might have guessed. Tells me not to annoy the customers. Who else am I to annoy, I have to ask you? I'm not my sister, with a herd of glassy-eyed soldiers following behind her like a bunch of lost ducklings. I have to make my own company, such as it is. You'll be wanting food, I expect?"

"If it's not too much trouble," Trea replied cautiously.

"Oh, don't worry Love, you're in good care. They're all thieves in here. Thieves or travellers; soldiers in the back room. No one'll bother you. No one wants trouble here under the dragon, not even the soldiers, most of the time at least. They won't risk upsetting my father. They've all got the eye for my sister of course. It's a rope walk sometimes, but you'll be the least of their worries. I'll fetch you something to eat. I trust you've got a few coppers? Never worry if your purse is short, you can make it up another time if you have to. I'll have Mida overcharge the soldiers if it comes to that, but don't tell my father or he'll throw a right fit. He bristles at *charity*, or that's what he'd call it; but we're all friends here, and everything comes back around. Need a name for you, though. I'll have to think on that. Rest easy and I'll bring you something hot. And something to drink, I suppose? Do you favor ale or cider? If you won't tell me I'll have to guess."

"Water?"

"You *are* a puzzle, aren't you?" said the girl, with a wry smile. "Don't worry, your secret's safe with me. Need a name though. It'll come to me; give me time."

The girl spun on her heel, and quick as a springing fox she was off toward the kitchen. Trea blinked her eyes and stared at the empty spot where the young barmaid had been standing only a moment before.

# Chapter 9:
## A Room for the Night

Candle in hand, the innkeeper led Trea up the rickety wooden staircase to the inn's upper floor.  At the top of the stairs he turned toward the back of the building, and followed the long hallway to the third door.

"It'll just be two coppers more for the room, Miss, since you've already paid your supper," he said.  "The room's not much to look at, but the bed is comfortable enough."

Trea stopped a few feet short of the doorway and frowned.  Even from the hallway, she could easily hear the clatter of dishes and furniture echoing up through the floorboards of the room, punctuated by a few angry shouts that rose above the general rumble of low conversation.  The innkeeper noticed her hesitation.

"Don't mind the noise, Miss," he added hastily.  "That's just the soldiers, in the back room below us here.  Gambling, I'd suppose.  They make quite the racket sometimes, to be sure.  Wouldn't be surprised if a fight breaks out, but we'll hope for the best.  Nothing to be done about them, I'm afraid.  Mida's tending the room – that's my older daughter, if you will – so they're a bit quieter tonight than some.  But I won't lie to you, they'll likely be at it till late.  That's how they are."

Trea wanted nothing to do with soldiers, and didn't relish the thought of trying to sleep with a troop of them carousing under her feet.

"Is there a quieter room I could have?"

"Well Miss, I don't know.  The front corner room is open.  There's better moonlight, and it's got a view to the road, but it's a good deal larger than this one, and I'd have to charge you more."

"I'd like to see it," Trea replied.

"Well, we can, if you've a mind," said the innkeeper reluctantly. "But the room right here is only two coppers, since you've already paid the dinner.  That front room'd be five coppers more.  That'd make seven in all, and that's *over* what you've already paid."

"I'd like to see it," she said a second time.

"If you like," replied the innkeeper with a shrug. "I'm sure you know your business, Miss. Whatever suits you." He pulled the door to the little room shut again, and squeezed past her in the narrow hallway to lead her in the opposite direction.

The front corner room was indeed quieter, brighter, more spacious and altogether better in almost every way than the dark little room the innkeeper had shown her first. There were two windows that looked out across the road to a small patch of trees. Two wooden beds were along the right-hand wall, and on the left was a small table where a pitcher of water and a crockery basin were set. Between the windows was a little writing table, with a wooden chair.

"Merchants favor this room, mostly," said the innkeeper, probingly. "The door's got a good bolt, and the window-shutters lock, if that's something that matters to you."

"Thank you," Trea replied. "This will be fine." She'd already gotten a silver coin ready in her hand, even before she first asked about a room for the night. Now she handed it to him.

"I'll have to run back down to get your change for this, Miss. I won't be a moment."

"Don't bother," she said. "That's good enough."

"From a full silver?" the innkeeper asked with astonishment. "You could have the room for a week for that."

"It doesn't matter," said Trea, and it was true. The money didn't matter to her at all, but now she was worried that she might have made a serious error by overpaying. The last thing she wanted was to draw any further attention to herself.

"I should say," she added pointedly, "that it doesn't matter so long as I'm not disturbed. And I *will* take the room for a week, come to think of it. I have business to attend to, and I'm not certain when I'll be coming back, but I'd like to be sure of a good bed when I do."

Trea did her best to sound forceful and confident, as if she were accustomed to giving such orders. She managed it fairly convincingly, and hoped that would be enough to quell the innkeeper's curiosity, at least for the moment.

"That's understood, Miss, and thank you," he replied, almost groveling. "As I said, I'm sure you know your own business; and a good night's rest to you. There'll be breakfast in the morning, and of course you can come and go as you please. I'll see to it that you're not troubled by anything, and I'll make sure the room's kept ready for you."

"Good night," Trea said. She hoped that would be the end of the conversation.

"Good night; good night; good night;" said the innkeeper, as he backed out of the room and closed the door. The latch clicked, and he heard the bolt slide on the other side.

Once the door was closed, Gurin stood for a few moments in the hallway, puzzling. He saw his share of peculiar customers, and he'd always made it a rule to ask no questions. But sometimes that was a hard rule to keep. She was a strange girl, there was no doubt of that. She was dressed like a man, but hardly pretending to be one. Where did she come from and where was she headed to? And what *was* she? Daughter of a merchant, perhaps, or a nobleman even. But if she were, she'd surely have arrived by a coach, or on horseback at the very least. And yet she'd never even asked about the stables.

He couldn't guess at her age, but she was a tiny enough thing. A good gust of wind might carry her away. How did such a wisp of a girl even come to a place like Hillside, on foot and *alone*, no less? But by Foll, she was free with her money, and that was answer enough to make Gurin the innkeeper swallow his burning curiosity and keep an eye to his good fortune while it lasted.

He bit the coin gently, to make sure it wasn't just a patina of silver over a disk of lead or tin, but it was solid, and genuine, and it had come from Furgathor or he didn't know his coinage. Everything about the girl seemed to be one mystery after another. He shook his head in wonder and ambled back down the hallway toward the stairs.

# Chapter 10:
## The Way to Ruin

Trea rose before sunrise, dressed, and gathered her few belongings. She unbolted the door, but didn't open it. Instead, she went to one of the room's two windows, opened the wooden shutters and looked out. The village was silent, except for the night sounds of a few crickets, and a lonely tree frog singing in the copse of trees and brush across the road.

Seeing no one, she climbed out the window. The inn's front face was neither sheer nor smooth, and she was able to clamber most of the way down before she had to let go and drop into the narrow patch of grass between the building and the road. She rolled with the landing, more out of habit than for any real need. It wasn't that much of a fall, and the tussocks of dew-wet grass were thick and heavy.

She followed the road west until she was out of sight of the inn. Then, with a quick check to make certain she hadn't been seen, she cut northward and made her way through the light brush that covered that side of the hill, gently rising away from the road and the river.

The world turned slowly grey as the sun climbed toward the edge of the horizon. By the time the sky had taken on a rosy glow of morning, Trea was well beyond Hillside, and working her way steadily north, over the lightly wooded hills. She still did not have a clear sense of precisely where she was, but she knew that as long as she kept the rising sun on her right hand side, she would be heading in more-or-less the right direction.

After about an hour of walking, she came upon a low, unmortared wall of fieldstone. It was roughly laid, but not abandoned, as it was free of brush and seemed to be in good repair. She guessed (correctly) that the wall marked some border or pasture belonging to the Sisters of Piety. She followed the wall, as it wove a meandering path more or less in the direction she had already meant to go.

About a mile further on, the wall abruptly ended at a shallow stream that ran down a swiftly winding course, finding its way westward through the hills and south toward the Grey River. She had crossed several other streams already, little different from this one, but the ending of the wall left her to suspect that this was the same brook that ran below the bridge at the front of the Sisters' compound.

Trea wondered briefly if Malessa might be somewhere nearby, either tending to a garden or minding some of the animals at pasture, but she didn't dwell on the notion for long. Trea wanted nothing more to do with the Sisters, if she could help it. Still, that strange encounter in the temple returned to her mind from time to time, unbidden, as she continued on her way.

Not far from the stream, she finally found what she had been looking for. She crested a low ridge of dirt and stone, and suddenly before her – stretching away to the east and west – was the ancient highway that the knights' caravan had travelled some months before. She turned to the east, and followed that dishevelled road up the side of the Last Mountain.

By the time Trea reached the ruined city, the sun was high and the mountain air had lost its morning chill. In the open courtyard where the soldiers had made their camp, she stopped to eat and rest for a few minutes. She'd brought a loaf of bread and some cheese with her from the Speckled Crow, but after a few bites she decided she wasn't hungry after all. Her stomach was churning.

The courtyard had changed, but Trea was certain it was the same place. All around the site were fresh heaps of broken and blackened stone, where the dragon had brought new destruction that fateful night, but otherwise there was no clear sign that the soldiers had ever been there. The wagon, and all the other trappings of the caravan were gone. Trea wondered if the scholar and the wagon-drivers might have fled the city before the dragon's attack, and escaped his wrath, but she suspected that they had not. She shuddered, whether in terror of the dragon or at the memory of her imprisonment she could not say.

She left the courtyard and ventured into the ruins, following the same winding path by which Captain Harbek's scouts had once led the three knights. She was surprised at how easily she remembered every step and every turn. The city was less bewildering by day than it had been at night, and there were obvious markers in the ruins to guide the way: A distinctive half-broken wall to one side of the street; the posts and lintel of a stone doorway on the other, where no wall remained; The shattered frame of what must once have been a public well, beside a narrow avenue that angled away to the right; and so on. Her eyes strayed always and again up the mountain, expecting at any moment to see there the dark silhouette of the dragon. But she saw nothing beyond the ruins other than the stark and silent mountainside.

It was early in the afternoon when she reached the grand plaza, and there she was even more surprised than she had been at the courtyard. She had expected to find the upturned wagon and the broken remains of her iron cage in the center of the ring; but they were gone. She did not know that the Sisters of Piety, with slow and patient industry had returned to that place many times over the summer months, gathering all the debris that remained and disassembling the heavy metal cage, until all traces of the knights' caravan were cleansed away from those sacred ruins.

Once again Trea glanced up toward the mountainside, and for the first time she saw what she'd both hoped and dreaded to see. The dragon was there, perched on that same shaft of rock where Harbek's scouts had first seen him months before.

With a gasp she crouched low and hid herself behind a broken patch of wall that still stood at the plaza's edge. A bead of sweat rolled down her cheek, and her whole body was taut with fear. Had she been seen?

*"Of course you've been seen,"* she thought, angrily reprimanding herself. *"He sees everything; you knew that before you came. Take hold of yourself, and remember why you are here."* She took a long, deep breath, while her mind wrestled against the terror. Slowly she mastered her fear, and finally sat on a bit of rubble, with her back to the wall.

Not yet daring to take a second look toward the dragon, she reached into her satchel and drew out what appeared to be a little bundle of rags. She unwrapped the light brown cloth to reveal a brooch – a small silver bird, perched among summer leaves that were carved from some pale green stone. It was a lovely thing; by far the finest article she'd taken in nearly three months of thievery in Furgathor.

She stole another glance up toward the mountain and saw that the dragon was still there. He was facing west, not looking toward the ruins at all, but Trea knew he was watching her. She pulled herself back behind the wall and shook her head. The whole idea had been mad from the start. She should not have come back. And yet, here she was. Turning back now – abandoning the one thing she had come to do – would be even more absurd than the effort to return here at all. She looked again at the brooch and sighed. It was too little; a meaningless gesture. It was not enough. She could not imagine anything that would be enough.

But perhaps it didn't matter. *"The dragon is a collector of beautiful and useless things,"* the hermit had told her. Surely this was both. She wrapped the cloth around the brooch again and closed her eyes, taking another slow breath to steady herself.

She opened her eyes again and stood up, stepped out from behind the wall, and walked slowly, deliberately forward. She kept her gaze downward, facing the paving stones, letting their concentric rings guide her to the center of the plaza, where the wagon had once been and where her cage had fallen. There, she set the little bundle carefully on the ground, turned, and walked back the way she had come. She did not look up, did not look back over her shoulder to see if the dragon was coming for her. If he chose to kill her now, she reasoned, that was his right. She owed him that much and more.

# Chapter 11:
## Soldiers on the Road

Returning down the ancient highway, Trea felt as if a great weight had been lifted from her. She had done what she'd come there to do. The dragon had seen her, she had left him a gift, and once again he had let her go. She felt redeemed somehow, both energized and exhausted; she almost felt happy. But mostly she felt simple relief. The fading glow of the sunset was in her face, and the darkling shadows of the trees and stones were stretching out far behind her.

The world seemed different to her now. She found herself more aware of her surroundings, not only of specific details, but of the connectedness of things. The curved surface of a stone by the road; a green tendril of vine wrapped around the lowest branch of a young tree, the fading hue of a falling leaf in the wind. Each piece of the landscape seemed to her not separate, but a part of a whole. The branch gave meaning to the vine, the leaf defined the wind, the stone revealed the essence of the breathing earth. She felt herself dislodged somehow from time and place, and yet immersed in both. All her senses were filled with the world, with the texture and the weave of a greater fabric of things.

And then it was over. The sensation had passed, and she was herself again, walking through twilight, down the mountain along an old and neglected road. She shuddered, not with cold or fear, but with the jolt of a dreamer suddenly waking. She stopped walking. She could feel herself breathing.

Something was wrong; there was someone or something up ahead. She had not yet seen or heard anything other than the wind and the birds and the rustle of the trees, but she felt it as clearly as if she'd walked into a spiderweb that had been strung across her path. Silently she slipped into the deepening shadows of the brush and trees south of the road and inched her way forward.

Soon, her suspicions were confirmed. A number of horses were tied in place among the trees on the north side of the old highway. Someone had made camp, not far from the little side road that led to the Sisters of Piety.  But why would anyone be camped here, so close to the dragon?  As Trea crept closer, she saw a large wagon and perhaps a dozen men gathered around the glow of a campfire.  They were talking in quiet voices.  She could see enough of their weapons and gear to guess what sort of men they were.

"*Soldiers...*" she thought with disgust.

She strained to try and hear their conversation, and to her surprise she discovered that even though she was across the road, perhaps thirty yards from their camp, she could hear what they were saying as clearly as if she'd been sitting among them.

"It's nothing but a fishing trip and we're the bait," said one voice.

"You may be right at that," said another.  "All I know is they sent a boy to do a man's job.  Why is he waiting for nightfall?  We should already be done with it.  This won't end well."

"Don't go blaming the boy," said a third, as several other voices muttered their assent.

"He's a good enough lad; I've known far worse."

"He's following orders just like we are."

"It'll all come to nothing, I expect."

"It's a bad piece of business," said the second voice again, "that's all I know, and it has been since Flapham Abbey.  It's one thing to gather supplies, but that was beyond the line, if you ask me."

"Maybe no one asked you."

"Peasants and farmers, it's all in a day's work.  But priests and temples?  It's asking for trouble, that's what it is."

"The King's justice is the king's justice."

"You know so much do you?  There'll be an accounting, I tell you."

"Follow orders and hope for the best.  That's my rule."

"I want no argument with Abzag, that's all I'm saying.  Nor with Mosig, come to that."

"I can't argue with you there," said an older man with a gravelly voice.  "Beer's been a good friend to this old soldier."  Some of the men laughed.

"Aye to that," one of them said, "Aye to that."

Trea slowly crept away from the soldiers' camp until she was safely out of earshot, then hurried south through the brush. Before long she'd found the little stream, and could see the road and the bridge that led to the Sisters' walled compound.

Trea wasn't certain what exactly she was hoping to do, but she could think of only one reason that a troop of soldiers would be here – they must be preparing for a second attack on the dragon. And if that was so, it meant that some other girl might even now be locked inside the Temple of Abzag as she had been, expecting to die tomorrow. Trea didn't know how she could stop it, but she was determined she would not let that happen.

But she could do nothing while it was still light. The sun was already down, but it would still be some minutes before the twilight had fully faded. After that, darkness would depend on the moon and the clouds.

She found an old twisted tree near the bank of the stream, not far from the road and the bridge. Though autumn was fast approaching, there were still enough leaves to keep her hidden, so she climbed up into its lowest branches to wait. From that elevated perch she could easily see the main gate of the Sisters' compound, the bridge, and much of the road to either side.

A tree can be a cozy place to rest, when you're young and nimble and light of frame. Trea settled herself comfortably onto a large branch, where she could lean against the trunk and brace her feet on another limb just below. She took a long drink from her water bottle, and reminded herself that she had eaten only very little since the early morning. She found the now somewhat-stale loaf of bread she'd started to eat for lunch, splashed a bit of water onto it to soften it, and patiently nibbled at the crust while she waited.

She had not yet finished the bread when she heard the slow clop of hooves on the little road. Soon a man came into view, walking toward the bridge and the front gate. He was carrying a torch in one hand, and leading his horse by the reins with the other.

Seeing her opportunity, Trea dropped silently from the tree. She knew that with the man's approach, all eyes would be on the gate. Leaping nimbly across some of the larger stones that jutted out of the shallow water, she crossed the stream without so much as a splash, and was soon hidden in the deep shadows at the base of the wall. The smoothly hewn stones were well laid and tightly set, but not so tight that she couldn't find a hold for her fingers and toes. In only a few seconds she had climbed to the top, and a moment later was over and inside the Sisters' compound.

To her right, she could see torchlight moving near the wooden gate. She slid carefully in the opposite direction, following the inside of the wall. Seeing no one, she dashed across an open avenue to a small stone building, and vanished into the shadows along its eastern side.

Trea did not know precisely where she was, but she knew where she was going. The Temple of Abzag was at the very heart of the compound, and she'd seen it clearly enough when the knights' caravan had brought her there the first time. She was sure that was where the soldiers would have taken their sacrificial prisoner, just as they'd done with her.

Moving carefully from building to building, she had little difficulty in reaching the temple. She'd seen none of the Sisters on the streets, and guessed that they were all either indoors or standing guard along the wall, or otherwise distracted with the soldier. She circled to the east side of the temple, the side furthest from the main avenue, where the shadows were deepest.

She had to get inside, but she couldn't exactly go in through the front door. Fortunately, the decorative carvings that covered the building's exterior offered convenient hand and foot-holds, which allowed her to scale the outer wall effortlessly. The overhanging edge of the roof presented some difficulty, but she found a jutting stone spar at the northeast corner – probably a spigot for rainwater – where she could pull herself up. The slope of the roof was quite shallow, and she was easily able to crawl across it toward one of the open skylights.

Lying flat on the roof, she looked down through the opening. The heart of the temple was every bit as unearthly and forbidding as she remembered. A single candle was burning somewhere below her, and the whole of that great shapeless interior seemed to roll and weave in the uneasy dance between its faint amber glow and a relentless shadowy gloom.

Her worst fears were confirmed. She could see a small cot in the center of the room, and lying on that cot was what appeared to be a young woman, wrapped in a white blanket. Trea's spine clenched. She felt as if she were gazing down at herself in her own darkest memories. But what could she do? She didn't know how she might save this young woman from reliving her own ordeal, but she was determined to do it, somehow.

She couldn't risk calling out to the girl. The room seemed to swallow up every sound, but still there was too great a chance that someone would hear. And in any event, the ceiling was too high for a prisoner to get out through the roof. They would have to escape by the front door; it was the only way.

Trea lowered herself down through the opening, dangling from the edge of the skylight by her fingertips before letting herself drop to the floor. It was difficult to judge the distance in the darkness, and the fall was more than she expected. She rolled with the impact, and felt lucky that she'd not injured herself. But she'd not landed silently.

The girl under the blanket stirred at the sound, and raised her head. "Is someone there?" she said.

"Quiet!" Trea whispered fiercely. "I'm here to help you."

The girl turned toward her and sat up on the edge of the cot. Even in the pale gleam of the candlelight, now that she could see her face, Trea knew her instantly.

"Hello, Trea," Malessa said, without any hint of surprise. "I was sure I would see you again, though I did not expect it now. Thank you for being alive."

# Chapter 12:
## The Summons

"Matron," said Sister Niren, formally, "I am sorry to disturb you at this hour, but we have guests. A small troop of soldiers is encamped along the ancient road. This young man has come forward to speak for them."

The matron was seated on a wooden chair, looking across the stone table of her conference chamber toward the earnest young man who was standing in the lamplight, just inside her open door. She sat there in silence for some time. The young man was tall and reasonably handsome, with brown hair and a strong, serious face. She could see from his tan and scarlet livery that he was a knight or some other person of rank, but she could not recall offhand which noble family wore those colors. A broad-bladed sword was hung from his belt, and he wore a jerkin of dark leather. His iron helmet was not on his head, but was clasped politely in his gloved hands. He looked in every way the proper soldier.

Under the matron's penetrating gaze, the young man did not flinch, nor move, nor look away, though his fingers fidgeted unconsciously with his helmet as the silence dragged on.

"Thank you, Niren," the matron said, eventually. "Leave us for a moment, if you would be so kind."

"Certainly, Matron," Niren replied. She took a step backwards out of the room and closed the door.

"This is a pleasure," the matron said, with no hint of a smile. "We have so few visitors here, and yours is a face that I do not recall. Have we met before, or am I in error?"

"We have not met before," the young man replied.

"Ah," said the matron, lightly, "and what is your name, young man?"

"I am Gevf, the third son of Lord Wilett of the province of Jurn, and a knight of the realm of Drey."

"I see," said the matron.  "I once knew your father, if memory serves, but that is a matter of little consequence, I think.  And to what do I owe the pleasure of your company?"

"I am here by royal decree," the young man said with pride.  He lifted his chin slightly, in an effort to emphasize his authority.  "The king summons you.  You are commanded to return, under our escort, to Nyl."

The matron's face did not change.  "I see," she said again, after a moment's pause.  "And if I refuse?"

The young man looked startled, in spite of himself.  "You may not refuse," he replied.  "The king commands it.  I have my orders."

"I see..." said the matron, yet again.  "And are you ordered to kill me if I will not comply?  You are welcome to do so, if you like."

This was not a response the young knight had expected.  His eyes widened momentarily, then he furrowed his brow, uncertain as to how he should reply.  The matron noted his hesitation.

"Does that puzzle you?" she asked him.  "Perhaps I can offer some clarity: I will not go with you willingly, and you cannot compel me through threats, or through force or by violence.  You are left with only two choices: You may either kill me, or you may leave this place empty-handed.  You have no other alternatives."

The matron paused only long enough to gauge her visitor's reaction, then spoke again without waiting for him to reply.

"You see, the Sisters of Piety know a great deal about death.  We do not fear it.  Each of us waits for it, like a distant lover that will return to us in time.  For my part, I am well prepared to go with Abzag this very moment, if she might wish it so.  But I will not go anywhere with *you*.  And should you choose to lay either weapon or hand upon me for any purpose, I cannot ensure your safety; and there are so many ways that a man can die."

The young man was becoming visibly unsettled, and despite his efforts to maintain an air of politic formality, his hand – involuntarily, perhaps – strayed to the hilt of his sword.

"Do not misunderstand me," the matron continued, her face still calm and expressionless. "I have no intention of killing you myself; you are my guest here, and that would be uncivil of me. But hospitality has its limits, and were you to exceed the boundaries of our polite conversation, there are others here that might take it upon themselves to reprimand you accordingly. Indeed, they would see it as an obligation."

Suddenly aware of himself, the young knight released the hilt of his sword and once again clutched uncomfortably at his helmet. Several times his lips opened, as if he were about to speak, but he stopped himself each time without a sound. He swallowed hard and said nothing.

"So you see," the matron continued, "you have been given an order which you cannot obey. You were not ordered to kill me, but to bring me to Nyl *alive*, which you are unable to do. If you return empty-handed, it seems likely that you will be punished. How unfair life can be. How cruel. It is hardly my concern, but I think the fault more truly lies not with yourself, but with those that elected to give you such an order; one which – now that I think on it – they must surely have known you could not possibly fulfill. And yet they sent you anyway. Why would that be, I wonder? Perhaps it was their intention from the outset that you should fail, or die in the attempt. Perhaps, you are not held in such high regard with your masters as you once imagined. That is merely idle speculation on my part, but it may be something that you will find value in considering."

For the first time since the audience began, the matron's face changed its expression. She raised an eyebrow, ever so slightly, as if she were now openly daring the young man to reply. She waited. He did not take the bait.

"You seem uncertain," she said evenly. "You want to please your king, but faced with such a difficult choice, you are left to wonder what would he have you do? I think I can help you there. If I know Othelwaite's mind in this – and I assure you, I know it better than you do – he is hoping you will disobey his orders. Oh yes... faced with this intractable problem, he hopes that you will rashly kill me. As he has not ordered you to do so, he will be absolved from any responsibility in the matter. It will be *you*, not he, that draws Abzag's vengeance, and I can promise you, he hopes that vengeance will be swift. For if such things came to pass, you would very quickly become an untidy loose end, which would need to be tied. Even if your valor prevailed, and you managed somehow to escape from this compound with your flesh still surrounding your bones, upon your return to Nyl you would be swiftly tried, found guilty, and executed. For murder, and for sacrilege. It is as certain as the rising moon."

The matron fell silent again, carefully studying the young knight's reaction. Once she was satisfied that he had sufficiently digested the things she had told him, she continued.

"And now," she said with a motherly smile, "I believe our little visit is at an end. You may go, as you came, and you may take this message with you to the make-believe king of Drey: That if Othelwaite wishes me brought to Nyl he should fetch me himself, and if he does so, he should bring an army, and one that he is prepared to lose. Tell him that, when next you see him, if you would be so kind."

# Chapter 13:
## The Heart of the Temple

Trea was astonished. "Malessa? What are *you*... are you the sacrifice?"

"Sacrifice?... no." Malessa replied. "I'm a novice of the temple. We take it in turns to sleep here and dream. I say 'we'... I don't know if the others dream, but I do. Tonight was simply my turn; the others are in their usual beds elsewhere, or more likely up and whispering about the soldiers, I expect. Girls do such things."

"What are the soldiers doing here? Where is the sacrifice?"

"There is no sacrifice; not that I know of."

"But what about the dragon?"

Malessa shook her head. "I see," she said with a smile. "No, the soldiers have come to annoy the matron, not the dragon. Unless I am much mistaken, they will leave here tomorrow, returning the way they came with nothing more than the very same things they brought with them. What will happen to them after that, I cannot say."

"Then there's no prisoner?"

"Were you hoping to rescue someone?" Malessa asked, her eyes sparkling. "But there is only me. I don't need to be rescued, not yet at least, but I'm glad you are here all the same."

Relief and despair washed over Trea in equal measure. She'd been so intent on saving the imagined prisoner that she'd given no thought to herself, and now she was trapped in precisely the last place she wanted to be. She looked up at the skylight so far out of reach, and knew she could not escape that way. "How stupid could I possibly be?" she muttered to herself, and wrapped her arms around her head. She might even have wept.

Malessa put a hand gently on her shoulder. "Have no fear; a moment ago you were mistaken, and now you're mistaken again. It's only right that you are here, and you're in no danger at all. We are friends, and I promise that you will leave again, in secret if you wish, and more easily even than you came. I will make certain of it; on my life, I will. Put yourself at ease. I am so happy to find you alive again. We have so much to talk about, and little time for it."

---

Hours later, Trea was still in the temple. She was utterly drained, both in her mind and her body. She'd been so intent, so focused on rescuing an imagined prisoner, that once that purpose had been taken from her she collapsed, like an archway with its keystone gone. She no longer had the strength to fight or flee or panic. She surrendered herself to the fate of the moment.

But there was something about her companion as well, something that put Trea at ease in spite of herself and all that had happened. Malessa had an unshakeable serenity about her, not merely of acceptance but of a simple, genuine delight in each passing moment. She seemed to find joy in every detail of existence, both the splendid and the terrible. She could marvel at ordinary things, and yet nothing ever seemed to surprise her. Every new discovery, whether for good or ill, became in her eyes a fresh source of wonder.

Malessa was eager to hear whatever Trea was willing to tell her, and Trea found herself telling almost everything that had happened, from the moment of her arrest in Nyl, to the dragon and the ruined city, to her escape across the border into Furgathor. For her part, Malessa had much to talk about as well.

"It is my belief that the matron was glad you escaped," Malessa said. "It was a difficult thing for her, I think, to help the soldiers. She certainly wished no ill to the dragon, I am certain of that. She is not a cruel woman, at heart. She is hard, but fair. I think she would be kind, if she dared to be. It seems to me that she carries within her a deep and private despair."

"She was not kind to *me*."

"We are servants of fate," Malessa explained, "and the constant journey of the infinite circle. We do as we feel we must. That is a comfort for some, for others a burden. It is a burden for the matron, I think. She was only fulfilling the prophecy, or so she thought at the time. But that leads me to a question. What *was* the prophecy?"

"I don't know," Trea replied.  "I was going to ask *you*."

"We understood only that it called for the sacrifice of a maiden, and that you had been chosen."

"Then it must have been false.  The dragon didn't take me."

"Either that, or perhaps even the soldiers did not know the truth of it."

"What do you mean?"

"*Predictions* are often untrue," Malessa said with a knowing smile.  "Prophecies, less so.  Nothing can be decided, if we do not know what the prophet really foretold."

"There was a boy..." Trea said, painfully turning her memory back, "at the abbey.  He gave me water.  He told me he had heard the prophecy."

"What did he say?"

Trea strained to remember that dark night.  "*This is all wrong*, he told me. *You are not a princess...* That's all I can remember."

"I think," Malessa said, "that in time, you will need to know more."

"I want nothing to do with any of it," Trea said firmly.  "I'm making a new life.  The sooner I put the past behind me the sooner I'll be free of it."

"The past is a part of you," Malessa told her, "and the very foundation of whom you've become.  You are both of you, the old and the new.  And now you carry a weapon at your side."

Trea flinched ever so slightly, startled by the sudden shift of topic.  "I've... never used it," she said uncomfortably.  "It was given to me."

"By the hermit," Malessa replied, nodding to show her understanding.  "May I see it?"

To her own surprise, Trea drew forth the white dagger and placed the hilt gingerly in the hand of the young novice of Abzag.  Only after she'd done so did a wave of panic wash through the more rational part of her mind.  She'd just handed a deadly weapon, the most precious thing she owned in all the world, to a very dangerous young woman; a bizarre and unpredictable girl who was at least partly insane.  But Malessa clasped the hilt very gently, using only the tips of her fingers, and stared at the blade with the same casual sense of awe with which she greeted every new discovery. She turned the dagger slowly in the air, to see the candlelight flicker along the glistening blade.

"This was carved from a dragon's tooth," she said quietly. "Abzag's hand is in it."

She looked back to Trea, and stared deeply into her eyes.

"You do not merely *have* a destiny," Malessa said, "you *are* one. And my own is entwined with you in a way that I do not yet understand. But all things return with time."

She handed the dagger back to her friend, and smiled at her warmly.

"But now the moon is down, and dawn will be fast approaching. You must go, or else you will not be able to leave in secret, as you desire. Come, and I will show you the way."

Trea took the dagger back and sheathed it, then silently followed the young novice across the rolling floor of the temple to the hidden exitway. They passed through and saw no one on the main street of the compound. The moon was indeed down, and it was very dark, though here and there a lantern burned in a window, or at a crossing where two paths met.

The two young women moved quickly through the streets, darting from shadow to shadow like hunting cats. Soon, they were in sight of the outer wall of the compound. The young novice gave her friend a quick hug of farewell, then put her hands on her shoulders while she explained her plan.

"You must take those stairs," Malessa whispered, pointing to a narrow flight of stone steps that led to the top of the wall, "and then over and across the pasture to the forest. But there will be a sentry. Give me a moment to clear the way."

Malessa gave Trea another brief embrace, then released her and walked out into the open. Trea pressed herself more deeply into the shadows, and watched as Malessa worked her way toward the faintly lighted corner of a nearby building. From her hiding place, Trea could see a woman in white, standing atop the wall not far from where her friend now stood.

"Sister Delse?" Malessa called out quietly, "may I speak with you a moment?"

The older woman jumped with alarm, before turning and walking a few steps toward the young novice. She looked down at the girl standing in the dim pool of light.

"Malessa?" she asked in a harsh whisper, "You should be asleep in your cot. What are you doing outside the temple at this hour?"

"I'm distracting you," Malessa replied truthfully, "so that my friend can escape unseen."

Trea did not wait to hear Sister Delse's reply. She was already over the wall and racing across the open ground toward the trees.

# Chapter 14:
## A Knight Errant

Trea spent the rest of that night in the light woods to the northeast of the Sisters' compound, huddled against a stone wall that marked the outer boundary of their pasturelands. Wrapped in her travelling cloak she slept fitfully for an hour or two, but before long an early pre-dawn glow began to fill the sky and she roused herself, trying to shake the damp and the cold out of her bones.

She ate the last of her bread and cheese for breakfast. It was not much of a meal, but it was enough to take the edge off her hunger at least. She'd talked with Malessa even longer than she'd first guessed, and had stayed inside the temple nearly the entire night. When she left the Speckled Crow the morning before, she certainly hadn't intended on sleeping in the woods, and had only brought enough food for that one day.

She had been so determined to return to the ruined city and the dragon that she'd given little thought to what she would do after that. For want of a better plan, she'd vaguely imagined that she'd return to the inn at Hillside, resting there for a day or two perhaps, then eventually making her way back to Furgathor. But all that had now been cast aside. For whatever reason, whether it was doubt or suspicion or simple curiosity, she felt that she had to make certain of what these soldiers were going to do.

She walked north until she struck the ancient highway again, and followed that cautiously back to the clearing where the soldiers had camped the night before. She found the place easily enough, and though the men were gone, they had not been gone for very long, as the ashes and coals in their firepit were still hot. Trea took a few minutes to inspect the remnants of their camp, but she found no answers there. The brush was beaten down all around, and some branches of dead wood had been gathered for their fire and left unused, but otherwise the soldiers had left nothing behind.

They had not continued on up the mountain toward the dragon, that much was clear: They couldn't have taken their wagon past the spot where Trea had been sleeping without her being aware. That meant they must have gone west, as Malessa had predicted.

Still uncertain exactly why she was doing it, Trea decided to follow them.

---

If Trea had gotten little sleep the previous night, the soldiers' leader had gotten less. The young man known as Gevf – Knight of the Realm of Drey and the third son of Lord Wilett of Jurn – had not slept at all. After leaving the Sisters' compound, he'd slowly walked his horse back to the camp, where he disappeared into his tent without a word to anyone. When the soldiers rose at first light, they'd found him sitting alone on the bare ground, staring at the embers of the campfire which had long since burned itself down to nothing more than a darkly glowing bed of coals.

When asked about the matron, he would say only that he had spoken with her, and nothing more. He ordered the men to strike the camp, and prepare to depart as quickly as possible.

Until that previous evening, Gevf of Jurn had lived a life of simple duty and obedience. He had served his father, and his father had served the king, and all was right with the world. If his father's will was unquestionable, then by extension the king's will was positively sacrosanct. Adherence to a royal command was the very essence of honor; to disobey was unthinkable – a violation of the natural order of things.

But his brief encounter with the matron had not merely unsettled him; it had shaken him to the very core. In less time than it would have taken him to brush his horse, she had toppled the pillars upon which he'd built his entire sense of self. And she'd done it effortlessly, casually, as if she'd merely lit a candle in a dark room, or brushed a crockery bowl off a wooden table, to see it shatter on a cold stone floor.

---

It did not take Trea long to catch up with the soldiers. Though there were two horses pulling the wagon, and the company's leader rode a horse of his own, most of the men were on foot, and they did not seem to be in any hurry. She marked them at a safe distance, but even keeping herself out of sight, she had no difficulty matching their pace.

The day wore on, and the soldiers held to their slow and steady plod until late in the afternoon, when they reached the crossroads where the ancient highway met the Great South Road. There the caravan halted and made camp, which Trea thought odd, as there were still some hours of daylight remaining. Within sight of the crossroad she found a suitable tree, climbed up it until she was well-hidden by the foliage, and settled in for the night.

When morning came again, the soldiers were still there, and this time seemed to be in no hurry to strike their camp. She could see men shuffling around, bundling the tents, harnessing the horses and so on, but there was no urgency in these actions. Though she could not make sense of it, and didn't dare to get close enough to eavesdrop, it seemed to Trea that they were waiting for something.

---------------------------------------------------

It had taken Gevf most of the day to sort through his bewilderment, but by the time he and his men had reached the crossroads, he had made up his mind about what he was going to do. When the morning came, he called the oldest of his soldiers to his tent. The old veteran's name was Prace, and Gevf considered him the most reliable and trustworthy of all his men.

"You will be in charge of the caravan from here," Gevf told the old soldier, handing him a letter that was carefully sealed. "You must deliver this letter to my father, and you must do it before you return to the king's palace, do you understand me?"

The veteran soldier was mystified. "Begging your pardon Sir," he asked, "but do you mean to say you're not coming back with us? Not back to Nyl, I mean."

"No, I am not," Gevf replied firmly. "I have learned a great many things in the last few days; and now it seems there is another matter for me to attend to."

"Well, surely we can help you with that, Sir," Prace said, choosing his words carefully. "They're good lads, most of them. We've done our best for you all this way."

"You've done well," Gevf replied, "all of you have, and I've said as much in that letter. But this is something for myself alone. I'm sorry that I can't speak of it more plainly, but that can't be helped."

"Well of course, your business is your business," the old soldier replied obediently. "If that's your order, I've no need to know more."

"Spoken like a true soldier," the young knight said. To his own surprise, his voice betrayed more than a hint of irony in the remark, but Prace didn't seem to notice. "Be sure to keep that letter safe," Gevf added. "There will be trouble when you arrive at my father's castle, if that seal has been broken."

"You needn't worry about that, Sir," the old soldier replied. "There's not a man among us who could read it anyway. I'll keep it safe on my person until I put it in your father's hand."

---

The sun had been up for more than an hour when the men finally broke camp and left the crossroads, and curiously enough they did not all leave together. As Trea watched, still hidden amid the branches of her tree, the common soldiers – along with their horse-drawn wagon – walked off along the northerly track which led toward Albria, and eventually on to Flapham Abbey and to Nyl. But the young man with the horse remained behind. Trea guessed from his livery that he must be a knight, but why he had not gone with his men was a mystery. He watched them go until they were out of sight, then returned to the campfire and sat for a while by himself.

Trea wondered how long he would stay there, and suspected he must be awaiting some other rendezvous. But after a time, he stood up, mounted his horse and rode away at a gentle trot. When she saw that he was finally leaving, Trea had imagined that he would either follow his men, or head towards the ferry at Piyl, or possibly even turn back toward the Sisters of Piety. But to her great surprise he had taken the road she'd least expected. He was heading, inexplicably, toward Hillside.

Trea dropped from her tree and followed as best she could. She couldn't hope to keep pace with the horse, but something told her that she would not have to. There was something oddly familiar at work in all of this, and Trea felt strangely confident that if she held to her purpose and followed the horse and rider just a little longer, the mystery would solve itself in time.

In point of fact, Trea would never see the young man again.  Later that day however, in the middle of the afternoon, she found the answer to her riddle.  She smelled woodsmoke, somewhere between the road and the river, and with a little searching she found a clearing where someone had made – and left burning – a sizable campfire.

There was little else of interest to be found in the clearing, aside from a few fresh hoofprints in the soft ground.  But at the edges of the fire, not wholly burnt, a few scraps of tan and scarlet cloth could be seen.  Finding those, it was clear to Trea that it was the young man who had built the fire, and that he had used it to burn his livery.

At once Trea's thoughts returned to the pearl-studded blue dress, tangled in the broken cage, from which she had once torn herself free.

# Chapter 15:
## A Moment's Rest

It was not a quiet night inside the Speckled Crow.  For the first time in weeks, the inn was entirely free of soldiers, and so the regular guests found themselves in high spirits.  Tonight's revelries were not constrained to the back room, but flowed freely among the general clientele.  Near the fireplace, one of the local herdsmen was singing an old song about a clever fox that outwitted a pack of hunters.  It was a long and well-known tune, and some of the other guests would join in at the end of each verse with a rousing chorus, which they shouted more than they sang.

With no soldiers to manage, Mida was free to work the main room with her sister, while their father roamed about making friendly conversation with the various customers and "minding the store" as he called it.  He would occasionally bark an order at one or the other of his daughters, but that was hardly necessary, and mostly for show.  Saren and Mida knew their jobs and worked hard at them, and still would have done so even without his oversight.  They could manage the room full well on their own; in truth they could likely have handled it far better without their father's interference.  But shouting orders from time to time made Gurin happy, and that was reason enough inside the Crow.

It was an hour or two after sundown by the time Trea finally made her way back to the inn and slipped in through the front door.  She stood there for a moment, weighing her options.  Seeing that the crowd was mostly clustered into two groups – one in the center of the room under the great chandelier, the other at the far end by the fireplace – Trea quietly made her way through the shadows along the outer wall toward the same bench and table where she'd sat three nights before.  There was a comfortable familiarity to claiming the same spot, and it was, conveniently enough, also the least-crowded part of the room.

And – as with the previous time she'd come to the Crow – she'd barely managed to settle herself into her seat before she was greeted by one of the innkeeper's daughters.  This time it was Mida who spotted her first.

"Welcome to the Crow," she said cheerfully, "yours isn't a familiar face.  I'm Mida; what can I get you?"

Trea looked up to see the most lovely young woman she'd ever laid eyes on.  Mida was tall and slender, with long, flowing hair and entrancing eyes.  Everything about her, every movement, every angle and line in her face and figure had an otherworldly gentleness to it, like a soft wind across a clear stream, or a single feather of eiderdown, drifting earthward on a calm day.  She almost seemed to glow in the shadows of the room, and yet, her beauty seemed effortless, careless, as if she herself were entirely unaware of it.  Trea sat spellbound for a moment, before she could force herself to speak.

"I've... been here before," she stammered awkwardly.  "I've taken the front corner room upstairs."

"Oh!"  Mida gasped with surprise.  "I took you for a young *man* at first blush.  I apologize for that; the light's not good on this side, but the error was entirely mine.  Though I must say your kit suits you, all the same.  Will you be wanting supper now, or just a drink to clear your throat with?"

She gave Trea a smile that might have tamed an angry sea. "Supper, please," Trea replied.  "And just some water to drink, if that's all right.  Thank you."

"I'll fetch it for you presently," Mida said.  She turned to go, but took only a few steps before turning back momentarily to take a second look at the strange young woman seated on the bench in the shadows.  Then she gave Trea another smile before gathering up the empty dishes from one of the nearby tables, and gliding away across the open room.  When she reached the doorway to the kitchens, she met Saren, who was on her way out with another round of drinks for the revelers by the fireplace.  Mida took the chance to pull her sister aside.

"Is that her?" she asked.  Her hands were still full, but she pointed with her elbow in Trea's general direction.  Saren looked across the room toward the bench where Trea was seated.

"Yes!" she replied excitedly.  "Did you meet her?"

"I like her, I think," Mida responded.  "It's hard to be sure.  She doesn't say much, and there's something very odd about her."

"No doubt," Saren said with a smile.  "She's so quiet it's hard not to notice her."

"She wanted supper, but only water to drink," Mida said.  "Shall I take it to her, or would you rather?"

"I'll do it," said Saren.  "Thanks for pointing her out to me.  I'd begun to wonder if she'd even come back here at all."

"All right.  Good luck then," Mida replied, as she disappeared into the kitchens.

A few minutes later, Trea found herself looking up once again at the familiar face of Gurin's effervescent younger daughter.

"Hello, Nightfinch!"  Saren said, cheerfully setting a bowl of hot stew and a large loaf of bread on the table in front of her.  "Welcome back to the Crow.  I'd begun to wonder if you'd gotten yourself lost in the woods, or found better lodgings elsewhere.  We're not the most stylish of accommodations, I'll grant you that, but I think it's safe to say we're the best in Hillside, and a far sight better than starving to death in the wilderness.  Mida said you wanted dinner, so I thought I'd take the chance to say hello.  You look well enough.  And I've not forgotten your drink, but I've only got the two hands to work with; I'll be back with it in half a wink.  Are you sure you won't try the cider?"

"Just water," Trea replied, "thank you."

"You'll never know what you've missed," Saren coaxed her.  "The cider's especially good tonight."  She leaned across the table and gave a nod of her head toward the fireplace.  "I think it's even inspired old Holvor's singing, to be honest.  He's doing far better than usual.  Closer to the tune, I think."  Then she shrugged her shoulders and hurried away, without waiting for an answer.

---

An hour later, Trea was once again following the burly innkeeper along the narrow upstairs hallway toward the front corner guest room.

"I've kept it locked for you, while you were away, Miss," Gurin said fawningly.  "I try to do right by my guests, and I've not forgot you wanted your privacy."

"Thank you," Trea replied, as he slipped the key into the lock and opened the door for her.

"There will be breakfast ready in the morning, if you've a mind?" Gurin said.  He'd meant it as a question, and he paused for a moment, hoping Trea would give some indication of her plans, but she did not. "And the room's still paid for three more days, of course," he added politely.

"Thank you," she said again, before adding firmly, "Good night."

Gurin took the hint.  "Good night; good night," he said bowing his head up and down almost comically.  He stepped backward out of the room and pulled the door shut.

Trea slid the bolt, and listened to Gurin's footsteps receding down the hallway.  She'd come to realize that she didn't particularly like the innkeeper, though she wasn't entirely certain as to why.  Perhaps it was because he seemed a little too curious about her, or it might have been because he was so clearly only pretending to be polite.

Trea pondered briefly if there was any real difference between being genuinely polite or merely pretending.  She suspected that there was, but she did not intend to lose any more sleep over it.  She'd had an exhausting day, after an exhausting week, at the end of an exhausting summer.  She got herself undressed, crawled into bed and pulled up the covers, and within minutes she was sound asleep.

She did not know that it wasn't Gurin the innkeeper who was keeping the most careful watch on her room.

# Chapter 16:
## The Muster of Drey

As the summer drew to a close, and the days began to shorten, Othelwaite began to muster his army. Dozens of messengers were quietly sent out to every corner of the realm, carrying secret orders for the various lords and royal ministers of each province. Soon, all the men-at-arms that could be spared from Drey's northernmost provinces slowly began to make their way toward Nyl, most of them travelling in small companies ranging in size from as few as ten men to no more than thirty.

Those companies that were in the service of wealthier lords were well-organized, and generally well-supplied for the long journey south. Other groups – leaderless or led only by poor knights from lesser houses – often functioned little differently from random mobs of brigands, plundering what food and other goods they could find from the scattered farms and villages of the countryside as they went. These *irregulars*, as they were sometimes called, differed from brigands only in the sense that they had official license to rob their own people in the king's name. But for the peasants and tradesmen they plundered, the end results were exactly the same.

For Drey's most northerly regions – such as Toule, which had little arable land – men could be as easily spared in the fall as in any other season. Most of the more southerly provinces still had fields to harvest, but there would be time enough for that in the coming weeks, as the realm's northern muster sifted its way toward the capital. It would be at least a week – perhaps two – before the bulk of the northern soldiery reached Nyl. By then, the lords of the middle provinces would have begun moving their men toward Albria, where Othelwaite's main force would gather perhaps three weeks hence. With Lord Fodge's help, Othelwaite had carefully mapped out this timetable with as much precision as was possible, given the exigencies of his sprawling realm and the practical limits of both travel and communication over such distances.

Othelwaite had long understood that he would eventually have to launch a war against one or the other of his neighbors, though he had never been fully certain as to which.  But one thing *was* certain: his military ambitions had far overstretched the limits of Drey's economic resources, and without some infusion of plunder, his kingdom was at the brink of either open revolt or outright collapse.  Had his knights' quest against the dragon been successful, he could have chosen an enemy at his leisure, and his first inclination would have been an assault on Furgathor.  His diplomatic relationship with King Edral had rarely even been cordial, and Othelwaite hoped that in the event of such a war, the Grey River might help defend his southern border while he campaigned north of the mountains, through the broken lands of Karvik.  But Abzag, it seemed, had intended otherwise, and the events of the last few months had fallen out entirely contrary to Othelwaite's earlier plans.

It was now clear that the coming war would instead be against Tunber; the princess Dophne had decided the matter for good and all when she chose to flee there.  Her present exile was more than just a personal insult to Othelwaite, it was a festering injury to his political power.  He knew well enough that the longer she remained abroad in Hinwahl, the more sympathy for her was likely to grow among the lords of certain provinces in Drey.

And then, looking further to the future, there was the looming problem of Othelwaite's eventual legacy, and the royal line of succession.  Assuming that his new queen would at some point bear him a son, there could be no doubt that the exiled princess Dophne would one day pose a direct threat to his chosen heir – a threat that would likely be fortified by King Mulrin, or whichever of Mulrin's sons eventually inherited Tunber's throne.

No, Tunber would have to be dealt with now, before the onset of winter.  And Othelwaite could only hope that when the time came, King Edral of Furgathor would sit idly on his hands, and not choose to intervene in the conflict on Tunber's behalf.

# Chapter 17:
## An Unsilent Partner

It was shortly before sunrise when Trea woke and quietly dressed. Once again, she unbolted the door to her room but did not open it, instead lowering herself out through the open window, and dropping silently into the grass below.

"Hello, Nightfinch.  Sneaking out?"

Trea leapt to her feet with a start, and whirled around to see Saren, the innkeeper's youngest daughter standing not five feet away.  She was wearing a dark travelling cloak over her brown dress, with the hood up covering her bright red hair.  She had a large satchel slung over her shoulder, and a smaller one hanging from her belt.  Beneath her cloak, the outline of a small sword or long-bladed dirk could be clearly seen.

"You!?"  Trea whispered in surprise.  She was equally alarmed at having been seen, and relieved that it wasn't some soldier or brigand standing there.  Her hand flew instinctively to the grip of her dagger, but relaxed somewhat as her assailant only smiled, and did not reach for her own weapon.

"You got away last time before I could catch you," Saren whispered back, with a broad grin on her face.  "Clever going out the window, but trust me to get wise to a trick like that the second time around."

"You've been watching me."

"Every chance I've had."

"What for?  What do you want?"

"Quiet!"  Saren cautioned, "or you'll wake half the inn with shouting."  Every trace of her lighthearted smile had suddenly disappeared.  "I'm coming with you," she said firmly.

"What?"

"I'm coming with you.  You're leaving, and I can't stay here."

"What?..."  said Trea again, still not believing her ears.  "Are you insane?  Not on your life."

"I've already told my sister, and it's not like my parents will miss me.  Mida's the golden child; I'm just the changeling girl they don't know what to do with.  They've been wishing I'd run off ever since I first learned to walk.  And it won't be any loss to the inn, I can assure you.  Within two miles in either direction there's a dozen girls our age who'd dance a jig to take my place here, just to have a good meal once a day.  Girls that'd be glad to jump at my father's orders, and smile politely at customers and blush all over from head to toe; Squeal when pinched from behind.  For them, it'd be an *improvement* over what they've got now, I know it all too well.  You'll be doing more than just me a good turn."

"Did it never occur to you," Trea said, with no small measure of exasperation, "that maybe you should *ask* me first?"

"Yes it did."

"And?"

"All right," replied Saren, politely.  "May I come with you?"

"NO!"

"There, see?"  said the barmaid, throwing her hands into the air in frustration, "That's why I didn't ask you.  I knew you'd say 'no', so there wasn't really any point in it, was there?"

She crossed her arms and leaned forward angrily, but did not even pause to let Trea get in a word of reply.

"If I stay here, Father'll marry me off to the first woodchopper who'll have me, or worse.  I don't mind men, but I've no desire to spend the rest of my life with one, not by half a mile in a strong wind.  There's nothing here for me to do except not be my sister.  And that gets old before long, I promise you."

"Go off on your own, then," Trea growled in response, still trying to keep her voice below a shout.  "Or take up with one of those regular customers you brag on."

"What, and be murdered in the woods, or worse?"  Saren scowled, derisively.  "Your average highwayman's polite enough *inside* the inn – here under the dragon's shadow with my father and who-all-else roaming about.  But I don't fool myself that they'd still be on their best behavior after half a day out on the road."

"Well, put to it," said Trea, "it looks like I might have to murder you myself."

"You might at that," conceded Saren, "but I don't think so.  I've known my share of murderers, and you don't seem the type.  But either way, if it came to a fight, I think I'd stand more than half a chance.  I'm five-six in my bare feet, and you can't be an inch over five-foot-nothing, if that.  And I've probably got a good twenty pounds on you as well, or I'm no judge.  But I don't want to fight you, Nightfinch.  Neither of us needs that; we're not drunken soldiers looking for something to prove.  I want to *learn*."

Trea slowly shook her head in amazement.  "What could you possibly learn from me?"

"Somehow," Saren whispered fiercely, "you're managing to survive in the world *on your own*.  I want that.  I've learned all I can here.  I talk to thieves every day.  A quarter of them are madmen and most of the rest are flat stupid.  I daresay I know more about the trade than half the rogues who come through Hillside.  I know the name of every shady dealer in stolen goods from Albria to Hinwahl.  You'll have to have somewhere to take your booty to, won't you then?  You must be unloading things to *someone*."

"I... have a debt," Trea said, hesitantly, "to an old collector."

"Ahh... I knew it," Saren replied, misunderstanding.  "Teach me Nightfinch.  I know you can."

"No!"

"Why not?"

"Why not?  For starters, I don't need your help."

"It's always good to have a partner."

"I travel alone."

"Well I knew that," said the barmaid, as if stating the obvious.  "You haven't got any friends, or they'd be with you, wouldn't they?  And you're not exactly social.  You like to sit by yourself in a dark corner, and that makes people like my father very curious.  He's been puzzling about you for most of the last three days.  But that's all right.  I can be social enough for the two of us, and I'll be useful as well.  I can pick a pocket; I've done it more than once. And I'm a good cook, which I'll wager you're not. And, if you're looking to pass as a boy it can't hurt to have a girl along to provide a little contrast. At the very least, I'd draw more attention, leaving you free to do as you like without so much as a never-you-mind. When you've had to compete with my sister all these years, you find ways to get noticed when you want to, or you get lost among the furniture. I have skills of my own, Nightfinch; skills that you could make good use of, with a little imagination."

"I thought you were a barmaid," muttered Trea, with considerable incredulity. "To hear you argue, you're more than half a *barrister*."

"I have had a bit of an education, you know," Saren replied. "I can read, and I can do arithmetic."

"So can I," snapped Trea, defensively.

"Can you now? Really?" said Saren. "Well I can't say I'm surprised. I knew there was more to you than you let on. Most of the cutthroats who come through the Crow can't do more than count to ten on their fingers, and even that high only if they still have them all."

"What is this all about?" demanded Trea, angrily. "What are you after? What do you want from me?"

Saren looked her in the eye, and pointed a finger for emphasis.

"I want the one thing I don't have now," she said, slowly and precisely. "I want control of my life. I don't care if it makes my life shorter; I don't care if it makes my life worse; I *want* it. All I've ever seen of the world is what passes through the front door of this inn, and then it passes out again and I can't do anything but watch it go. I'm in a cage here, Nightfinch, and I don't like it."

The word *cage* hit Trea like a sack of horseshoes. She spun around, turning her back to the other girl, and reached out her hand to touch the wall of the inn. She stared at the ground and tried to think, but she couldn't make her head do it. For the first time since their conversation began, Saren said nothing. She just stood there silently, waiting.

Eventually, Trea made up her mind.

"I was right the first time," she said, turning back to face the girl in the cloak. "You *are* insane. Why is it always the crazy ones that find me? If you're not the death of me it'll be fair punishment on both of us, I suppose. Be sure you never get what you wish for."

Still, Saren said nothing. She could tell that the discussion was over, but she wasn't at all sure how it had ended, or what decision had been made.

Trea turned away, and started walking down the road to the west. After about ten steps, she stopped, and turned back.

"Well," she said impatiently, "are you coming or not?"

# Chapter 18:
## A Humble Wedding

On the night of the full moon, six weeks after Prince Halvik's wedding to the Princess Nalya of Furgathor, his younger brother Roal was himself married to the Princess Dophne of Drey. And though the young couples involved in these weddings were of similar rank, the second was a far less celebrated affair than the first. The ceremony was, to be sure, carried out with a requisite measure of pomp and public fanfare, but by royal wedding standards, the proceedings were kept quite private and subdued.

Officially, Roal and Dophne's wedding was kept small because the couple wished it to be. This was, of course, a conveniently diplomatic untruth. In reality, neither Dophne nor Roal had any inclination to be discreet. As far as they were concerned, the more notice their wedding drew, the better.

In reality, the decision to keep the celebration small had been entirely Mulrin's, and as he was the king – not to mention the one footing the bill – his was the vote that counted. Mulrin never explicitly stated a reason for his choice; he didn't need to. Everyone involved, however, had their own guess as to his motives. Halvik assumed that the ceremonies were kept to a minimum to forestall any possible backlash from Furgathor. It would not do to have the refugee princess from Drey upstaging his own regal bride. Roal, similarly enough, assumed that it was to keep himself from upstaging his older brother. His entire life, he had become accustomed to this sort of second-hand treatment.

For her part, Princess Nalya assumed that her new father-in-law was simply economizing. A royal wedding was a considerable expense, not only for the royal treasury, but also for the realm's nobility, who would naturally be expected to provide gifts appropriate in scale to the other festivities. With her own wedding so recently concluded, a similarly lavish affair would likely strain the finances of all concerned. Princess Dophne, on the other hand, guessed that Mulrin's primary aim was to avoid antagonizing King Othelwaite by further flaunting his daughter's defection. Dophne regarded this supposed motive as a disappointingly timid concession on Mulrin's part, made in fear of her own temperamental father's wrath.

Each of these theories made perfect sense in its own way, and by the same token not one of them was correct. Only King Mulrin himself was privy to his true motivations, and he fully intended to keep it that way.

The wedding was held in the king's private temple, inside the royal palace, with many of Tunber's most important lords and ladies in attendance. Afterwards, a royal procession paraded through the streets of Hinwahl, to the enthusiastic (and mandatory) cheering of the assembled populous. A day of feasting was declared, and the revelries continued on into the night. It should be noted that for their part, Roal and Dophne did indeed make a handsome couple.

-------------------------------------------------------

That evening, after his brother's official wedding ceremony was fully concluded, Halvik took it upon himself to visit his own bride in her chambers. Though he and Nalya had been married for several weeks, the royal couple still did not know each other particularly well. Their very public pairing marked a formal and legal agreement, but that had far more to do with politics – and their fathers' diplomatic agendas – than it did with their own decisions. Halvik hoped that in time he could enlist his young bride, not only as a mate and political partner, but as an ally and confidant as well. That was a relationship which Halvik knew might take years to fully develop. Such trust and cooperation would have to be carefully established and gradually earned.

In keeping with that long-term goal, the crown prince of Tunber was, in his own measured way, patiently working to gain a clearer understanding of his young bride's frame of mind. The topic of his brother's wedding seemed as good a place as any to begin.

"It was a... *modest* ceremony," Halvik ventured cautiously, "would you agree?"

"Yes," Nalya replied diplomatically. "I think your father managed it as well as he might have. He chose for it a handsome little chapel."

"Have you had occasion to speak with the princess Dophne?" he asked, as casually as he could. "I am curious to know what you might think of her."

Nalya paused for a few moments, considering how best to respond. She nonchalantly brushed an invisible speck of dust from her shoulder, before looking her husband carefully in the eye.

"In time, I will surely be as fond of her as propriety requires," she said warily. "I do not think it likely that I will ever love her as a sister, if that is your question. Nor will I regard her as the heir of Drey – which she might once have been – for she is certainly no longer that now. I expect with the passage of time that she will remain, in my eye, neither more nor less than she truly is. In short, my husband's younger brother's wife."

Halvik smiled. "As fair an assessment as any, I suppose," he replied. "I am confident that in time we will come to know her better. For my part, I think she seems bold, and perhaps even clever. She has no doubt taken charge of her own future in a surprising way."

"Do you think," Nalya asked, "that your brother has chosen wisely, in marrying her?"

Halvik was somewhat startled. This was a more direct question than he had expected, but apparently his new bride could be blunt with her inquiries. He found this strangely encouraging; perhaps in time they might become friends after all.

"I think he has acted according to his nature," he answered. "My brother is not given to hesitation, not when he sees an opportunity that he believes might lead to his own advantage."

Nalya gave her husband an inquisitive look. "I hope you will not think it indelicate of me to say so," she said, "but I have come to suspect that your brother is more than half a fool. If I am in error, I would be happily corrected."

Halvik laughed aloud at this, more from surprise than anything else. It was both heartening and unsettling to discover that – at least in private – his new bride was quite willing to speak her mind.

"My brother can be rash, and impulsive," he said, conceding the obvious, "and I think it would be fair to say even a bit *naive*. But he is not a fool. Quite the contrary. He has ample wit, though far too often he neglects to make use of it."

"If one does not *use* it," Nalya replied with a meaningful glance, "there is little point in *having* it, is there?"

She gave her husband a coquettish smile, to make certain that her double-entendre was not misunderstood. But Halvik had fully grasped her meaning, and the young couple set aside any further conversation for quite some time.

-----------------------------------------------------

"Your brother seems the timid sort," Dophne said bluntly. "I find boldness easier to trust."

Roal and Dophne were in her chambers in the royal palace, alone together for the first time as husband and wife.

"My brother is somewhat cautious," Roal replied with a nod, "but my father is the cunning one. Halvik makes it a habit to keep all his cards well-hidden, while Father carefully reveals exactly those few cards that he wants you to see."

"I cannot read your father," Dophne admitted. "But it is clear to see that your brother does not like me."

"I would not put it in quite that way," Roal said. "I think, rather, that my brother quite *admires* you, after his own fashion. I do believe, however, that he thinks you are dangerous."

"Indeed I am," Dophne replied.

"Oh, yes..." Roal said with an unabashedly lurid smile, "and I find that intoxicating."

"Do you think me beautiful?"

"In so many ways," Roal replied. "Have you any cause to doubt me?"

"I doubt everyone," Dophne said, with a smile of her own. "Except myself. *Myself*, I know very well indeed; she is a woman beyond all doubt."

"I cannot argue with that."

"It is not an ideal state of affairs," Dophne said, pointedly. "Being a woman, I mean."

"In what way?" asked Roal, not quite sure where this conversation was now leading.

Dophne stepped toward him, held up two fingers and lightly tapped them against his chest. "We were born into a world in which men might make choices," she explained, "but women can only choose between *yes* and *no*. Often not even so much as that."

Roal cocked his head to the side and raised both eyebrows, giving his new bride a sharply quizzical look. "It is no festival, being a younger brother either," he replied. "But for what little it may be worth, I am glad that we each chose *yes*, when given the opportunity."

"Some opportunities are given..." Dophne said, as she turned away from him, and stepped toward the marriage-bed, "and some are made." She let her robe slip to the floor and turned back to face her husband.

"As are future heirs to the throne," he said, smiling broadly as he moved slowly toward her.

They kissed, and fell to the bed together.

---

In a dark and narrow corridor that ran beside Roal and Dophne's bedchamber, four men stood with their weapons drawn. They would wait there until the room was quiet, then they would enter and do the bloody work they had been paid to do.

The room's heavy wooden outer door was locked, and securely bolted from the inside. But there was a secret side-entrance – hidden in one of the paneled walls – which the young couple knew nothing about.

That hidden door was securely locked as well, but Mulrin had provided these men with a key.

-- The End of Book Two --

# Book Three:

# Prophecy and War

## (Fall)

# Chapter 1:
## The Great South Road

It was approaching mid-day, and Saren and Trea were walking west along the Great South Road.  They'd spoken little since leaving Hillside early that morning.  Trea was in a foul mood, and though she'd agreed to let Saren travel with her, she certainly did not seem at all happy about the partnership.

Fully aware of how tenuous this current arrangement was, Saren had done her best to hold her tongue.  She was hoping that if she just gave her new companion a measure of space, sooner or later things would smooth over.  She held to that decision throughout much of the morning, but as the hours dragged on the silence increasingly wore on her, and she couldn't help trying to make some conversation.

"You've still not told me where we're going," she ventured, cautiously.

"Perhaps that's because I don't know," Trea replied.

"Oh," Saren responded sagely.  "Well, if we keep on this way, we'll hit the ferry at Piyl in a few days.  We could cross the river into Tunber there, though we might as easily have done that back at Hillside.  I've never been on that side of the river.  To be honest, I've never been much of anywhere.  So really, I'm fine to go wherever you like.  I've heard of all these towns and places, but to actually go there, it's all new to me wherever we are."

Saren waited for a reply, but she didn't get one.  This was turning out to be even harder than she'd thought, but she couldn't bear the silence any longer.

"Why do you dislike me, Nightfinch?"

"Why do you call me that?"

"You've never told me your real name."

"You've never asked."

"If I had, would you have told me?"

Trea frowned. She stopped walking, leaned her hand against a tree by the side of the road, and took off one of her shoes. "Why that name, and not some other?" she asked. She peered inside the shoe, then turned it over and shook a small stone out of it.

"I don't really know," Saren replied. "I gave it some thought, and that was the name that occurred to me. And I had to call you something. I'm not my father, after all, every guest a *Sir* or a *Miss* or a *Madame*."

Trea pulled her shoe back on, and the two girls walked along in silence again for a while.

"I do know why, now that I think on it," Saren said at length. She stepped in front of Trea, and turned to look her in the eye. "It's because you are small, and you are quick, and you are dark. You sing little, and softly, but I think there's much that you see and have seen, and secrets that you know and have told to no one. You're young, no older than I am, and yet I see centuries in your eyes."

For a moment Saren almost seemed embarrassed at herself, if that was possible. Then she suddenly turned away and started walking down the road again. Trea stood in silence for a few moments longer, then jogged forward to catch up with her. Neither of them said anything more for several minutes, as they continued side by side.

"Trea," she said eventually. "That's my name, if you were wondering."

"I'm Saren," the former barmaid responded, without breaking her stride.

Nothing else was said between them for the rest of that morning, but it seemed to Saren, if she stole a sideways glance at her companion, that the hardness of the air around her had softened, if ever so slightly.

------------------------------------------------------

By early afternoon, they were approaching the crossroad where the young knight and the soldiers had camped two nights before. Aside from a few brief detours – when they stepped off the road and hid themselves among the trees to avoid being seen by other travellers – the two girls had walked all day without a break. Both of them were tired, though only Saren was willing to say so.

"Can we stop for a bit?" she asked. "My legs are hating me right now."

"You're the one who wanted to come along," Trea reminded her.

"You might be used to this," Saren replied, a little defensively, "but I'm not. I'd be on my feet all day at the Crow, but I've never walked this far before; not in a straight line at least."

Trea was not entirely sympathetic. "If you can't keep up, that's not my fault then, is it?"

"Well for someone who doesn't know where she's going, we're wasting no time getting there," Saren grumbled. "That's all I have to say."

"Oh, I doubt that," Trea retorted. "But either way, there's a spot up ahead here where we can stop for a bit. There's a clearing over there in the trees, out of sight from the road."

"Anyplace is fine with me, so long as we can sit for a few minutes, and get out of this wretched sunshine."

"Is there anything you won't complain about?" Trea asked, impatiently. "What's wrong with a little sunshine, I'd like to know."

"I'm a ginger, Nightfinch. We *burn*?"

"You're hardly a ginger," Trea scoffed. "More like an angry radish."

"Hah!" Saren smiled. "So you *do* have a sense of humor after all. That's good to know. I'll confess, you had me worried."

They found the clearing, and sat there quietly for a while, drinking from their waterskins and nibbling at some of the food they'd each brought with them from the Speckled Crow. They'd been eating off and on while they walked, so they weren't terribly hungry; but now that they'd stopped, they felt the need to have something like a mid-day meal all the same.

After a few minutes had passed, it was actually Trea who broke the silence.

"I lied to you," she said, suddenly. "I do know where we're going."

"Well, I assumed as much," Saren replied, "but it's some relief to finally hear you say so. I don't suppose you're going to tell me *where*?"

"Flapham Abbey," Trea said.  "Have you heard of it?"

"All right," Saren answered her with a nod, "that's as good a place as any, but I can't see why you'd want to go there."

"Why do you say that?"

"Well, I've heard good things about their brewhouse, but you don't even *drink* beer; that is, unless you've been holding out on me."

"I need to speak with the prophet."

"You what?"  Saren said with surprise.  "But Nightfinch, the prophet's *dead*."

Trea was horrified.  "Dead?" she asked.  "How do you know?"

"I heard it months ago," Saren said.  "Word came through the Crow; I don't even remember who told me, but all sorts of news comes through there.  It could have been anyone, really; it was common knowledge.  I'm surprised you didn't know."

Trea scowled and ran her fingers through her hair.  "I've been... otherwise engaged," she said, evasively.

"You've been in Furgathor, you mean," Saren replied.  "Or at least that's what my father was guessing; and I told you he'd given you a lot of thought.  I suppose the news about the prophet didn't get that far, or maybe you just didn't hear about it.  But if you talk to people like I do, they tell you things."

"If I talked to people like you do, they'd never get the chance."  Trea grumbled.

"It's an art," Saren replied, smiling broadly.  "There's method in madness, or hadn't you heard that either?  Why did you want to see the prophet anyway?"

"I had questions for him."

"Well he won't answer them now," Saren said.  "I'm sorry to break the news to you.  But honestly, it might be for the best.  Prophecies are dangerous things; I do know that much."

"You've no idea," Trea said, shaking her head sadly.  "None at all."

"So what happens next, then?"  Saren asked.  "Do we go back the way we came?  Not back to Hillside, I hope.  To Furgathor, maybe?"

Trea sat very still for a while, staring at the ground. In the branches above them, squirrels were chattering, angrily arguing about acorns. A few birds were bathing in the dust on the road nearby, squabbling with each other over the nicest spots. Somewhere in the distance, a woodpecker was drumming loudly on an old dead tree. Eventually, Trea made up her mind.

"No." she said firmly. "We'll go on there anyway. Maybe someone else will know."

"I don't think it works that way," Saren said, skeptically. "Prophets aren't like other people; they don't just hand over the job to their next apprentice."

"I don't need a *new* prophecy," Trea said impatiently. "It was a prophecy from before he died. But I don't know what it was. I don't know what he said."

Saren was dumbfounded. "There was a prophecy about *you*?" she asked.

"I don't know," Trea admitted. "That's what I need to find out. I don't know if it was about me or not, but somehow my whole life has gotten wrapped up in it. It's why I'm here; I'd hoped I was free from it, but I'm not, that's become terribly clear. I've got to find someone who heard it; someone who can tell me what the prophet really said."

She stared at the ground again, and Saren watched her with a puzzled, concerned expression on her face. Eventually, Trea looked up and their eyes met.

"It's important." she said.

Saren nodded. "Absolutely." she replied.

# Chapter 2:
## Murder and Deceit

Tunber's capital city of Hinwahl was abuzz with the news of the murders.  King Mulrin's son Roal and his new bride had been assassinated on their wedding night, and there could be no doubt as to who was responsible.  First, King Othelwaite's diabolical scheming had driven his innocent daughter from Drey, and now – as retribution for the kindness King Mulrin had shown to the refugee princess – he had struck out against the royal family of Tunber in sinister and cowardly fashion.

That, of course, was the official story, and though it was largely untrue, few saw any cause to doubt it.  The truth however was that Mulrin himself had ordered the murders, to rid his favored son Halvik of a future danger, and to fan the flames of outrage among his populace.  It was a masterstroke of propaganda, and a bold gamble. The future of his kingdom and his bloodline were at stake, and for the moment at least, his gambit seemed to be succeeding.  The assassins had been caught and killed by the royal guard, but not before they had already accomplished their vile and bloody deed.

Above all else, Mulrin of Tunber was a master of appearances; when his guards informed him of the news he flew into a carefully calculated rage, reciting his shock and anguish with convincing passion, and regal dignity.  Naturally, blame for the murders fell fully to Othelwaite, and as such evident treachery could not go unavenged, everywhere was heard the call to arms.  "Death to the mad king of Drey!" the heralds cried, as men young and old set down the hoe and the scythe and lifted the spear.  From across the realm, knights and men-at-arms began to flow in a swift and steady stream toward the capital.  There, they were mustered into regiments and set marching northward.  Messengers were hastily dispatched to Furgathor, to inform them of Othelwaite's purported crimes, and humbly request King Edral's assistance in this sudden and unexpected war.

But regardless of any truth or falsehood in how matters were officially portrayed, the onset of this conflict was far from unexpected.

Though fear of the dragon might have delayed hostilities for a day or a year or even a generation, Mulrin understood full well the inherent fragility of peace. He had never been fully certain as to when, or against which of the other two realms Tunber would one day take up arms, but he had never held out any hope that peace could be eternally sustained. In the end men will be as men are, and will inevitably turn to war.

Now that a foe had been decided upon, Mulrin was determined to ensure that the war would take place on his terms, and on his enemy's fields. Armies on the march will despoil whatever lands they find themselves in, and the old king thought it best that such a fate should befall Othelwaite's provinces, rather than his own.

Even before Halvik's marriage to the princess Nalya, Mulrin had been preparing his forces in secret. Now, as his main army was gathering in Hinwahl, his agents were already striking the first blows of the war along the banks of the Grey River. Small groups of men were either commandeering or sinking every boat they could find, to ensure that only Tunber would be able to cross the river in force.

On the second night after the murders took place, the great ferry-barge at Piyl – the only craft on the Grey that could transport large numbers of men and horses – was quietly held at its southern docking, and not allowed to return to the northern bank of the river. The next morning, in the darkness before dawn, some three hundred knights and soldiers crossed into Drey in secret, using the ferry-barge and dozens of other small craft. The town of Piyl was fairly large, but it was not heavily fortified; it was a hub of transport and commerce, not an outpost of military power. The assault was a complete surprise to the city's overmatched defenders, most of whom either surrendered quickly, or fled to the surrounding countryside. Within hours, Piyl had been captured, with little bloodshed and only token resistance.

Now, Mulrin was riding north through the Barren Lands, with the floodgates already open for his soldiers to flow into Drey's southernmost provinces. If his men could hold Piyl until he arrived, his main force would be able to cross the river unopposed. He could then use the city to resupply and reorganize his troops, while pressing the conflict ever further into the heart of Othelwaite's realm.

Mulrin knew that Tunber could not hope to match Drey in an even fight, but he hoped that with some early victories those odds would improve. Othelwaite was not much loved by his people nor by many of his provincial lords, and if even a few of them were to turn against him, the fortunes of war might swing decisively in Tunber's favor. And then there was the question of Furgathor. King Edral was, by all accounts, a prudent and cautious man. Mulrin feared that he might very well sit on his hands and do nothing at all, but if he could be persuaded to join this war on Tunber's side, that might well prove decisive.

But still, above everything else loomed the dragon. He was the wild card that might reshuffle the deck entirely. No plan for war could account for what might happen if the dragon chose to intervene. He had watched the world in silence for so many centuries; what might incite him to action now? What were his boundaries? What might he prevent, and what would he allow?

Mulrin had given much thought to the old worm. He saw no need to provoke him, if the war were to proceed in Tunber's favor. But if the war were to go otherwise, and Tunber's victory was to be suddenly in doubt, Mulrin wondered if there might be a way for him to turn the dragon to his own advantage after all.

The king of Tunber tucked these thoughts away in a dark corner of his cunning mind, and spoke of them to no one.

# Chapter 3:
## The Visitor

As the summer days dwindled and slowly sank into Autumn, the matron began spending more and more time alone in her quarters. At first, this went largely unnoticed: In keeping with her position of authority, she had always maintained a certain degree of personal isolation. But now she became positively distant, and soon the more senior members of the order, those with whom she had always interacted most frequently, could not help but recognize the change. Whereas it had before been her practice to "make the rounds" several times a day – greeting the various members of the order young and old, and observing them as they worked at their daily chores – now she would instead spend long hours by herself, with her tower door bolted shut. On those occasions when she did emerge, she spoke little, even to those Sisters that had before been closest to her.

But even in her withdrawal from the community, she did not wholly set aside her duties. She still gave orders that she expected to be carried out, and she still took reports on all that was happening, both inside the compound and outside in the world at large. Just as Othelwaite and Mulrin had spies to gather news, the matron had agents of her own, sending regular reports from far and wide. Envoys from the Sisters of Piety – some openly and some in secret – were common visitors to the many scattered temples and shrines devoted to other deities, as well as the cities, the towns, and even the smallest of villages throughout the three realms.

The matron had long made it her business to know the business of the world, and if the uncertain prophecy and the knights' attack on the dragon had given her food for thought, those things were no less a burden on her mind than the news that came to her from other sources. She had heard, of course, of the royal marriage between Prince Halvik and Princess Nalya. She also knew that Princess Dophne had fled to Tunber, and was to be married to Mulrin's younger son. She had learned of the ongoing muster of Othelwaite's forces, and had heard hints even of Mulrin's quiet preparations. Word of the royal murders in Hinwahl had not yet reached her, but still, she could plainly see that war was brewing between Tunber and Drey – a war in which she was certain the Sisters of Piety would become embroiled, but in what manner and to what end she could not guess. With these doubts weighing on her, she called to her chambers the one member of her order that she thought might have some insight that she herself did not.

-----------------------------------------------------

The matron sat quietly at the large wooden table in her chambers, contemplating the young novice standing just inside her closed outer door. "What can you tell me," she asked, "about war?"

Malessa smiled broadly. "War is the time when Abzag dances," she replied. "War is what happens when men gather their wisdom and agree to kill one another."

In the weeks and months following the knights' attempt on the dragon, Malessa had been summoned to the matron's quarters more than once. The two women had found a sort of kinship in each other. One was old, one was young; one had seen much of the world and the other almost nothing of it at all. And yet, they each felt themselves caught up in the turning of the great circle, and each suspected that the other could see, perhaps, things that she herself could not. Together and alone, each of them was in her own way pursuing an elusive understanding of the unknowable mind of Abzag.

"Armies are gathering north and south of us," the matron said, "and soon they will be marching. War is coming, and I am uncertain what to do. Two men, either of whom would destroy the world in order to rule it, and neither has any love for me. The uncertainty of all my choices confounds me."

"Why should your choices matter?" Malessa asked. "Abzag dances when the mood strikes her, and if she is calling the musicians to play, then play they will. Whether we will join her, or sit at the edge of the circle and clap the time, I think that in the end we will each of us be party to the dancing."

"I wonder," said the matron. "Perhaps it is as you say – that we merely choose the choices chosen for us; doing only as we are destined to do. And yet, surely those choices must matter? The wheel will turn, inevitably, but whither will it roll?  Here or there or elsewhere entirely?  Even if we cannot hold the reins, is the wagon's path already decided?  Even a rudderless boat may be turned.  Might one road be better than another?"

"You have lived a life where your choices have seemed to have some importance to the world around you," Malessa countered.  "That is rare.  Many are left only to endure the choices of others.  But I think, regardless of what choices we have made, there comes a time for each of us when all our choices seem to be taken away.  And when that time comes, it is my guess that we are left only to decide how we wish to die.  I suspect as much, but in truth I do not really know."

The matron shifted uncomfortably in her chair and stared for a moment at her own clasped hands.  She opened them again, and rested them on the table.

"I was told," she said, deliberately changing the subject, "that you had a visitor.  In secret, no less."

"I did," Malessa replied, smiling once again.  "It was quite unexpected."

"So you have a lover?"

"I don't think so, Matron."

The matron gave the girl a contemplative, skeptical look, slowly drumming the fingers of one hand atop the stone table.  She sat that way for a few moments longer before she continued her questioning.

"Sister Delse tells me that a young man visited you in the temple.  Was it one of the soldiers?"

"No, Matron," Malessa said.  "The only soldier I know of was the one that was here to visit *you*."

With anyone else the matron would have taken that remark as impertinence, but coming from Malessa she almost took it in stride.  "Indeed, he was," she replied.  "But we met only briefly.  I suspect that he was sorely disappointed with our encounter, though he left somewhat the wiser for it.  But I do not presume."  The matron couldn't help smiling in spite of herself.  Malessa smiled back, though neither woman was quite certain as to why.  The matron let the moment pass.

"But enough of that.  We are discussing *your* visitor, not mine."

The young novice nodded, dutifully. "My visitor was not a man, but I did not correct Sister Delse's error, because I was not certain that you would want her to know who it actually was."

The matron leaned forward, and furrowed her brow in puzzlement. "Is that so?" she asked. "Then who was it?"

"It was Trea," Malessa said, as if the answer were obvious. "The dragon's sacrifice."

The matron was astonished. "She returned here? Why did you not bring her to me immediately?"

"She would not have wanted to come," Malessa replied, almost sadly. "I promised her that she could leave again, and I would not break that promise."

"What did she say? Did she tell you the prophecy?"

Malessa shook her head with disappointment. "No," she said. "She'd not heard the full prophecy either, but she had spoken once to someone who had. A servant of the prophet, I would guess. He told her: *This is all wrong – you are not a princess.* That was all she could remember."

The matron seemed about to reply, but then she stopped, as if she had been interrupted in the midst of a thought. She sat that way in silence for some time, staring into empty space, her eyes gazing at nothing.

Malessa waited patiently, and did not move. At length the matron recovered herself.

"Will she come here again?" she asked.

"I think she will," the younger woman answered. "I think she must, in time."

"She is, I think, a person of considerable importance," the matron said.

"I know," replied Malessa. "So I told her the first time we met."

# Chapter 4:
## The Battle for Piyl

All the land surrounding Piyl along the northern bank of the Grey River was a fertile floodplain. In the spring, the river would reliably crest above its banks, spreading far and wide into a broad, temporary marsh that covered many square miles. The town itself – which was situated on a low, flat hill about half a mile from the river – would become a sort of temporary island, perched above the slow-moving water.

The annual spring floods inundated the ground not only with water, but also with nutrients washed down from the forests and the mountains. Consequently, the fields surrounding Piyl were among the most fertile and productive in all of Drey. Every year, wheat and barley and other grains were harvested there in abundance. The floods prevented the year-round pasturing of livestock, but the river provided ample fish and waterfowl. In the smaller villages nearby, ducks and geese were raised in great numbers, and eggs and poultry were regularly shipped out in all directions along the roads.

Peasants in that area subsisted largely on a dish called *ortage* – a sort of thick, custardy, tasteless mush, made mostly with duck eggs and wheat, sometimes with a few vegetables or diced fish added in, or whatever other ingredients could be found. But the region's wealthier residents enjoyed perhaps the most complete and varied diet of any people living anywhere in the world. As so many different places shipped their foodstuffs through Piyl, almost anything imaginable could be found there, at least in the right season and for the right price. Mutton and cheese were brought in from the pastures of Glaen, along with various fruits and vegetables that were grown in the regions below Albria. Nuts and olives, beets and other root crops, and even a few exotic spices came north across the ferry from the upper scrublands of Tunber.

Piyl's singular importance as a point of commerce was largely due to the nature of the Grey River. Upstream from Piyl, reaching almost as far as the fordings near Hillside, the river was swift and rocky, and though in some places smaller fishing boats were sometimes used, the river could not be safely navigated by any larger craft. Similarly, downstream from Piyl for many miles there were sandy shoals, rapids, and other obstacles that also precluded secure crossings. Not until the Grey drew near the Great Western Sea did it calm down enough to allow reliable transit. And though some cargo was indeed transported by great ships sailing up and down the coastal waters, that route presented dangers of its own. For most of the goods and people that flowed between Tunber and Drey, Piyl was the safest, fastest, and most convenient point of exchange.

Some 3000 people lived within the city itself, though that number varied considerably with the seasons. During the spring flooding its population would nearly double, as peasants from the surrounding countryside would crowd into the city temporarily, sleeping on floors or makeshift cots, or even in the city streets until the waters subsided. Then they would filter back out into the soggy fields to hurriedly sow that year's crop of grain. It was difficult, sloppy, and yet ultimately rewarding work. The knee-deep mud of the fields around Piyl was legendary throughout the three realms. Like Abzag herself, or so it was said, the Grey River would wipe clean its portion of the world, to let the next year's grain sprout anew.

Since most other landmarks would be carried away by the slow-moving spring floods, the fields around Piyl were clearly marked out by large standing stones that were set deeply into the ground. The stones had been there longer than living memory. Most people believed they had been fixed in their places since the days of the old kingdom, or perhaps even longer than that. The stones seemed, in their own way, more eternal even than the landscape they apportioned.

Each of the great stones was deeply carved, not with runes or words, but with animal glyphs and other symbols. This one showed an ox, that one a raven, the next a rising sun. There were nearly three hundred of these stones laid out around the hill and the town, and the local farmers knew every one of them. They were the landmarks, the roadsigns and the surveyor's compass points that demarcated the otherwise flat and featureless expanses of that fertile region.

The main road through Piyl was built along an elevated causeway, slightly above the floodplain. Though there were many channels and culverts and small bridges along its path to let the waters pass through, in most years it would flood as completely as the fields did. When the waters receded it would inevitably be covered over with bracken and silt, but every year the residents would diligently clear it again, and repair the damage.  The road was nearly as ancient as the standing stones, and as far as the local residents were concerned, it had also been there forever.  Its foundations were deep below the ground, and it was paved with massive flagstones which, like the city hill itself, even the river could not wash away.

That ancient causeway met the Great South Road about a mile north of the town hill, just beyond the usual boundaries of the spring flooding.  That crossing was at the top of a low ridge, from which travellers could look southward and see the fields, the town, and the whole of the Grey River Valley stretching out east and west along the banks of the silvery water.

---

As the sun rose on the third morning following Tunber's capture of Piyl, a small army of knights and men-at-arms arrived at the crossroad north of the city, hoping to take it back.  A force of over six hundred men – nearly two hundred of them on horseback – stood arrayed across the open fields north and east of the city, deployed into battle lines.

These men were led by Lord Vildar and his son Valand, and most of them had come from Glaen.  When news of Piyl's fall came, Vildar quickly assembled all the men-at-arms that he could find and hurried west to its aid.  At the outset of their march, his force had been too small to hope that they might recapture the town, but they had more than doubled their numbers as they traveled.  Most of these additions were also professional soldiers: various guards and sentries collected from smaller villages and towns along the Great South Road, as well as many of the lord's own troops that had been stationed in the more westerly parts of his home province.  They had even been joined by some thirty members of the Piyl town garrison who – having fled in the wake of Tunber's surprise assault – had rallied behind Vildar's banner, hoping now to reclaim their homes.

At the outskirts of the city, across and to either side of the causeway road, the invaders from Tunber had thrown together a handful of hastily-constructed fortifications.  There were now a few wooden barricades and some sharpened poles set into the ground to deter charging cavalry; but these defenses were minimal, and the effort to build them was far from complete. There was, in reality, little use in blocking the causeway road anyway, as the surrounding fields were dry and firm and still high with grain. The season for harvest had only just begun, and most of that year's bounty of the floodplain had not yet been brought in. At this time of year, horsemen and other troops could cross the open ground nearly as easily as they could walk the main road.

Another reason it was odd that the invaders had bothered to barricade the causeway was that the city itself could have been far more easily defended than the road or the open fields. Not only would the houses and other buildings have provided some measure of protection, but the elevation of the hill would give defenders a significant advantage. But Lord Brale, leader of the Tunber forces, had chosen to array his troops outside of the town instead. A likely reason for this was that he did not want the city destroyed: King Mulrin would need it as a supply hub and base of operations.

For his part, Lord Vildar did not want the city destroyed either. He wanted to reclaim it for Drey, and for those that lived there. And so it appeared that the battle would take place in the open fields, and Vildar thought this would play to his advantage. Neither side had more than a handful of archers, and the opposing forces seemed to be evenly matched in numbers. But seeing few horsemen among Tunber's troops, Vildar planned to exploit this tactical advantage. He ordered his footmen to advance down the causeway road, and divided his cavalry, sending half with his son Valand toward the enemy's left flank, while leading the rest in a wide circle toward the right. His hope was that his footmen would anchor the enemy in place, while his cavalry came in from both sides to crush them.

And at first it seemed that was indeed how the battle would go. Vildar's troops steadily advanced along the road, then broke into a charge over the last hundred yards. The defenders held their ground awaiting the onslaught, as the footmen of Glaen surged forward into the barricades.

Once the two sides were engaged, Vildar led his company of horsemen around to his enemy's western flank in an all-out charge. A hundred horsemen rode beside his banner, cutting a broad, curving track through the golden fields, trampling the slender stalks of wheat that still hung heavy with unharvested grain.

It was then that Lord Brale sprung his trap. He had kept his own horsemen concealed in the city, waiting for just this opportunity, and he seized the moment. As Vildar's company of horsemen raced toward the causeway, Brale's cavalry came thundering down the slope of the city hill toward their exposed flank. Vildar tried desperately to halt his own charge, ordering his men to turn and meet this new onslaught. But it was too late. Most of his men did not hear him, and even if they had there would have been no time to rein in their mounts and reform their lines. The Tunber cavalry struck in full formation, and tore through Vildar's company, killing dozens of Glaen's finest horsemen and leaving the rest scattered in confusion and disarray.

From his vantage point on the opposite side of the causeway road, Valand had full view of the riders descending on his father from the town hill, but there was nothing he could do. The horsemen under his command were already committed to their own charge against their enemy's eastern flank. Tunber's footmen were directly between him and his father's company, and he could not ride to his aid. Across the causeway road, perhaps a quarter of a mile away, Valand saw his father's banner fall.

Now the battle was fully joined. Valand's charge seemed to have turned the tide against the barricades, where two great shapeless swarms of men were locked in a frenzied melee. Along the eastern side of that mass, the footmen from Tunber were steadily giving ground before Valand's cavalry, while on the western side, Vildar's company was being cut to pieces by Lord Brale's surprise counterassault. In this way, the two armies were turning together, rotating en masse around the battle's central point. It was as if a tiny whirlpool had been filled with men who were now slowly sinking into a placid river of grain.

-------------------------------------------------

Though strictly in terms of numbers the two sides were at first evenly matched, after the fall of Lord Vildar's banner the final outcome was never really in doubt, and by late afternoon the battle for Piyl was over. Nearly five hundred men and half that many horses were dead in the fighting; blood and corpses, broken weapons and battered armor, all were strewn about the fields. But otherwise, little had changed from the day before.  Indifferent to the carnage, the sun set that evening as usual, the Grey River flowed on as before, and Piyl was still held by the forces from Tunber.  The men from Glaen had all been driven back, or scattered, or killed, and Lord Brale's surviving troops had withdrawn into the city to congratulate themselves on their victory, such as it was, and to lick their wounds.

From the outset of the engagement, the defenders had slowly given ground along the causeway.  But their lines held intact, and for some time the two sides were locked in an apparent stalemate.  But on the western side of the battle, where Lord Vildar had fallen, his men were in disarray.  There, Lord Brale was able to regroup a portion of his own cavalry, withdrawing them from the melee and circling around to the north, while on the eastern side Valand was unable to disengage his own horsemen, who were deeply entangled in the fighting along the causeway.  Shortly after noon Brale mounted a second charge, this time against the rear of Glaen's line.  That was the decisive blow.  Caught like a hazelnut between two stones, Valand's infantry shattered into panic, and the rout was on.

As the sun rose the next morning, the peasants returned to the fields to collect the harvest of the battle.  The dead were gathered and sorted according to rank.  The wealthiest, even among the defeated, were loaded into carts in their full regalia, and their bodies conveyed to their distant homes.  Those of lesser rank were stripped of their armor and valuables and hauled in carts to the north, into the forests beyond the fields.  There they were burned in a great pit that would later be covered in earth.

The peasants went about these funereal chores under the same cloud of grim detachment with which they carried out all their labors. The dead were the dead, and in the end it mattered little to them which side had won or lost.  From the peasants' point of view, as long as men with swords were giving orders and taking their food, it did not matter much in whose name it was being done.  They would sweat and toil and still face starvation in the spring, under the nominal rule of one king just as much as under another.

# Chapter 5:
## A Stop for Apples

"Look," said Saren, "apples!"

Away down the hill to their left, on the other side of what seemed to be a pasture for sheep or cattle, Trea could see where a well-tended orchard stood, not far from the bank of a narrow brook. Saren leapt easily over the low stone wall that ran along that side of the road, and started walking off toward the trees.

"It's definitely a pasture," she said, turning back to Trea with a wry chuckle. "Be careful where you step."

"What are you doing?" Trea asked.

"Come on," said Saren, impatiently. "We can't be in *that* much of a hurry, can we? We'll grab a few and be off. They'll be in season, I expect. That's unless they're a winter sort, like Rimewine or Snowcap; but one bite will settle that for good and all. We'll know soon enough."

"No." said Trea.

"There's no one around," Saren said, coaxing her. "Come on, this won't take a minute."

"No!" said Trea, firmly. "They aren't ours."

"They aren't ours?" said Saren, incredulously. "What's the matter with you? I thought you were a *thief*. It's hardly a secret and you've said as much yourself, or nearly."

"We don't steal food," Trea replied.

"We *what*?" asked Saren.

"All right," said Trea, "you wanted me to teach you something? First lesson: Sit." She pointed forcefully at the stone wall, then sat straddling it and folded her arms.

Mystified, Saren slumped her shoulders, and walked slowly back. She hiked up her dress a little, and sat on the wall facing Trea.

"What's a handful of apples between friends?" she asked, "The trees are covered. It's not like anyone's going to miss them."

"Food has value," Trea said. "Food is precious. You'd know that, if you'd ever been really hungry. And we only steal worthless things."

"We what?" replied the bewildered Saren.

Trea held up one finger to stop Saren from talking, then reached into her satchel and took out a single silver coin. She held it up, between the thumb and forefinger of her right hand.

"Think of the life of a coin..." Trea said. "What does it do?"

She turned her wrist so her palm was facing upwards, and suddenly the coin was gone, as if it had vanished into thin air.

"It travels..." she continued, slowly turning her right hand until her palm was facing down. And suddenly the coin was there again, between the knuckles of two fingers.

"One person trades it for a room for the night... a warm place to sleep."

As she spoke, she gently rolled her fingers, and the coin danced across the back of her hand: from the index finger to the middle, to the ring finger, the pinky, back to the ring, then the middle, and then the index finger again, where it vanished once more.

"The innkeeper trades it to a farmer for a sack of grain..." she continued, as she reached behind Saren's ear with her left hand and found the coin hiding there. Once again, she held it up, pinched between her thumb and forefinger.

"...Which he bakes into loaves of bread. The farmer takes the coin and buys new boots; the cobbler takes the coin and buys leather from the tanner; the tanner takes the coin and buys hide from the butcher; and on it goes. All these things of value move from person to person – the grain, the bread, the boots – all because of a single coin. But the coin has no value of its own. It's a placeholder, a marker for all these other things. A coin is a wanderer. And so it travels freely from person, to person, to person. Until...."

With a flick of her thumb, she tossed the coin spinning into the air. Then, with a quick stab of her right hand she caught it before it fell, and clenched it in her tightly closed fist.

"The coin travels until it reaches a rich man, and there it stops."

She opened her hand again, but it was empty. The coin wasn't there.

"It sits in his pocket and never travels again. It is locked in a chest in a room. It hides in a purse with a hundred other coins. No one buys a meal with it, no one rents a room for the night, no one purchases a new pair of shoes."

Trea looked Saren squarely in the eye and slowly closed her hand into a fist once more. Then she opened it, and impossibly, the coin was there again, shining in the center of her palm.

"I do not gather wealth," she said, "nor seek to possess it, but to set it free; to let it wander again. I have *been* a prisoner, and I have great empathy for coins."

She reached out and took the former barmaid gently by the wrist. She placed the silver piece in Saren's open hand and closed her friend's fingers tightly around it.

-----------------------------------------------------

An hour later, Trea and Saren were on their way again, both of them munching happily on freshly picked apples. With only a few minutes of searching, the two young women had found the hut of the peasant family that tended the sheep and the orchard. The woman there told them that the flocks and the trees belonged to Lord Parr of Levfryn, but she was happy to sell them a bag of apples for a single copper piece. Instead, Saren gave her the silver coin that Trea had wrapped in her hand. That one coin was more money than the peasant woman had ever had to her name in her life. The apples were Shallanor, a sweet fall variety; ripe and perfectly delicious. Everyone was delighted with the exchange.

"Where did you learn to do that?" Saren asked, between bites. "That trick with the coin."

"My grandfather," Trea replied. "He was a juggler, of sorts. A clown; an acrobat, if you like. I grew up with that, travelling with him from town to town, when I was little. He taught me lots of things."

"Can you juggle?" Saren asked, excitedly. "I've always wanted to know how."

"Yes," said Trea, "He taught me all sorts of things like that. I can juggle, tumble, do little tricks of magic, like the coin bit. Not *real* magic, of course, but that's what he'd call it. I was halfway good at most of it, but I was always hopeless at the only part that mattered: asking the crowd for money. He had a way about him; he could always make them laugh, and he'd get a few coppers out of it. But I'd try my best, and people either got angry or they'd just walk away. When he died he left me alone and hungry, with a storehouse of clever skills that I couldn't get paid for."

"So that's how you became a thief."

"Not even then," Trea said. "They made me one, really. I juggled in front of a peddler's vegetable stand for more than an hour. I don't know how many people stopped to watch, and bought this or that from him. No one gave me so much as a bent copper. I asked him for a bit of food, and he told me off. So I took a turnip and ran. I felt he owed it to me. The king's guards didn't feel that way, though."

"What happened then?" Saren asked, wide-eyed.

Trea stopped walking, took a last bite of her apple, and threw the core as far as she could toward the little stream on the far side of the pasture. She looked back at Saren, then down at the dusty surface of the road.

"Nothing happened," she said, as she turned away and started walking again. "After that, nothing happened at all."

# Chapter 6:
## Pignut

The next morning, Trea felt strangely ill at ease, as if some uncertain danger were either ahead of them on the road, or following them just out of sight. She said nothing to Saren, hoping the feeling would pass, but as the sun rose higher and the day brightened, her apprehension only grew stronger.

She had finally decided to ask if Saren was feeling a similar sense of foreboding, when she caught sight of something alarming on the path ahead. They had just crested a gentle rise, where the road climbed a low hill that was lightly forested to either side. Looking down into the hollow before them they could see a dark shape lying in the middle of the road.

"Is that a body?" Trea asked.

Saren immediately put out an arm to block her way. "Stop," she said, keeping her voice low. "It's an old thieves' trick. They'll be hiding in the woods up ahead on both sides. They've already seen us, you can be sure, but if we stay here we might be able to keep them all in front of us. We don't want to get surrounded. We'll have to find out who it is, and how many of them there are. Put your hand on your sword but keep it in the sheath for now, and let me do the talking."

Trea did as Saren had advised. Even before her hand touched the hilt of the dragon-knife, she realized how angry she was – more angry than afraid – and entirely at herself. She'd felt the warning and she'd ignored it. There was no time to undo her mistake; she only hoped she'd have the chance to repent her stupidity.

"The road can't be the most comfortable spot for a nap," Saren called out in a loud voice. "You might as well get up; we've seen you, and you're not so convincing a corpse as you'd like to think."

The shape on the road rolled itself over in the dust. Trea could see now that it was a thin man wearing dark trousers, soft leather shoes, and a heavy brown overshirt. He was nearly bald, with a few stringy tufts of pale brown hair sprouting here and there at random across his broad head. As he slowly stood up, he revealed the short narrow-bladed sword that had been hidden underneath him. Three more men slowly emerged from the woods on either side. All of them were carrying weapons, of one sort or another. They clustered together on the road, perhaps ten yards ahead of the young women, and the two groups looked each other over.

"Hello, Pignut," Saren said, cheerfully. "Who've you got with you this morning?"

"Well if it isn't the little barmaid from Hillside," replied the thief who had been lying in the road. "I didn't hardly know you with your hood up. A bit far from home aren't you girl? No daddy to watch out for you here."

Saren ignored the taunt, and turned her attention to the other three men. "I don't know *you*," she said, pointing toward the one on the far left, who had black hair and a crooked shoulder. "But Halfhook there next to you is an old friend of mine, and that's Flatrock hiding in the back, isn't it? You don't need to be so worried, Flat; we won't hurt you, as long as you behave yourself."

"Won't hurt us, will you?" said Pignut, mockingly. "Little girls shouldn't be out alone on a road like this. They could find themselves in all sorts of trouble."

"Use your brain, Pignut, what little you have," Saren said. "I see four already, so what are there then, five of you in all? No more than six, I'd wager. How many have you got still hiding in the woods?"

Saren turned her head to the side and shouted "Come on out, if you're still in there! Don't be shy. We're all friends here, aren't we Master Pig? Let's have a good look at you. Hurry it up, now! We're waiting and we haven't the whole day to waste."

Saren stamped her foot in the dust impatiently and crossed her arms. A few moments later, a ragged young man with a short spear sheepishly emerged from behind a large-boled tree, just off the side of the road.

"There," said Saren with some satisfaction. She eyed the boy carefully, sizing him up. "That's better, I suppose," she added with a nod. "But you're not much to look at are you?"

She turned her eye once again toward the four men standing in the road. "Is that all then? That had better be everyone, Pig. I'd be upset if you were holding out on me."

"That's more than enough talk from you," Pignut said, edging forward cautiously. "We'll have your purses now, and your swords, and your hides too if we like, or we'll be taking them from you in a most unpleasant way. Do you catch my meaning, girl?"

"Now, you don't really want to do that, do you Pig?" Saren continued, without a hint of concern. "We're old friends, and I'd feel bad after I cut you open and fed your heart to the crows; honestly, I would. And what? The five of you against the two of us? Hardly a fair fight, I'd say, but that's your bad luck and not ours. Still, you can't even count this one, can you?" She pointed at the crook-shouldered man with the black hair. "I'll call you Coalbucket, if that's all right? Just to keep it all clear. But he's new to your little tribe isn't he, Pig? Him and the boy there. They probably don't know how you'll turn on them, just like you always do with your extra help. Like you did with Flop last year, or Bullnose the year before that. Then there was that little fellow from Piyl you were with last month at the Crow. What happened to him, I wonder? Did you cut his throat in his sleep or did you let the patrols hang him?" She turned to look at the boy with the spear again. "Pignut's not very inventive, and his partners don't seem to live very long. It's the same every year. Stick with him, and you'll soon be part of a proud tradition."

Pignut scowled, and tugged at one of the shoulders of his overshirt as if it didn't fit him properly (it didn't). The other men exchanged uncomfortable glances. The one Saren had addressed as *Halfhook* leaned in beside Pignut to have a word with him.

"Come on, then," he said quietly. "Let'er go. I've always liked the girl. She's got brass enough, and she's probably not got more than a handful of coppers on her anyway."

"And I want no trouble with old Gurin," added Flatrock.

"Gurin'll know nothing about it!" Pignut said angrily.

"And what'll you do if he does?" Halfhook countered. "She's not worth it, if you ask me."

"Let *her* go, if you like," argued Pignut, "but what about the other one?  She's got something worth taking, I'd warrant."

"Oh, that's right," said Saren, interrupting their argument.  "You've not met Nightfinch, have you Pig?  She's a better thief than you, I can tell you that standing right here.  And though I doubt that Athra cares much one way or the other about a second-rate half-witted cut-throat like you, *Abzag herself* has an eye on this one.  So mind your knitting, if you want to see the sun come up tomorrow.  She's got a *destiny*, Pignut, and I promise you, you're not it."

"Gahhh..." growled Pignut with disgust.  He spat on the ground and glared at the two young women.  "Try to frighten us with Abzag, will you?  You're all bluff, girl."

"Well come on then, Pig," she said, suddenly whipping out her long-bladed dirk and taking a step forward.  "If you don't think two little girls might be too much for you?  I'll tell you this: I'm quicker than you are and you know it.  Which of your hands shall I cut off first?  Or would you rather I start lower down?  Either way, let's get on with it.  I'd tell you to invite your friends along, but it sounds like they have better sense than you do."

Pignut glared hard at Saren, but he didn't move.  A long moment passed before anyone spoke again.

"As I thought," said Saren.  "You're all foam and no beer."

The black-haired man slipped across the road toward the boy with the spear.  Now that they were side by side, Trea could see the resemblance.  She guessed they were brothers, perhaps, or a father and son.  Saren noticed as well.

"Go on the both of you," she said to them.  "Pig's not to be trusted; and neither are we, come to that.  One way or the other, this ends badly for you, I can promise.  Stick to hunting rabbits in the forest and you'll live longer."

-------------------------------------------------------

Ten minutes later, Saren and Trea had put half a mile between themselves and their would-be assailants.  Though they did not dare to relax their guard again for some time, they had begun to feel as if they'd managed to escape their first really dangerous encounter together.  It was Trea who spoke first.

"That was my fault," she said.  "I'd had a bad feeling all morning; I should have said something."

"If you can't trust your instincts what can you trust?"  Saren asked. "But no harm done.  It worked out well enough."

"How did you know they'd back down?"

Saren took a deep breath and looked over at her companion.  "I didn't," she admitted with a grin.  "Pig's a coward, I knew that much, but I couldn't be sure about the others.  We got lucky, I guess.  To be honest, I was mostly stalling for time.  I figured the longer I could drag it out, the better our chances were.  It was worth a try at least, and what's the worst that could have happened?"

"You mean aside from them killing us?"  asked Trea.

"Not a chance," said Saren, smiling broadly now.  "You were right there with me the whole time.  I've never felt safer."

# Chapter 7:
## Edral of Furgathor

In his royal palace at Stolrik, King Edral of Furgathor sat quietly on his throne.  Before him stood a tall and broad-shouldered man with shoulder-length pearl-grey hair and a neatly trimmed moustache and beard.  His name was Lord Dornin, and Edral knew full well why the man was there.  He had come to Stolrik to plead, on King Mulrin's behalf, for aid in Tunber's nascent war with Drey.

"The way ahead is now clear," the envoy from Tunber said, bowing low.  "Othelwaite's crimes cannot go unpunished."

King Edral – as he usually did – spoke slowly, in measured tones. "Othelwaite's crimes are many," he began, "and not only against Tunber, but also against his own blood, and not least of all against his own people.  He is a loathsome, detestable man."

"Then you see the justice of our cause," the envoy continued, hopefully.  "Even now, Tunber's armies are striking the first blows against Drey's provinces along the banks of the great Grey River.  King Mulrin's banner already flies over the city of Piyl."

"I congratulate our brother to the south, on his early victories," Edral replied.

"But this war is not yet won," Dornin continued.  "The enemy's forces are gathering at Albria, even as our own men gather at Piyl. Soon, these armies will meet and there will be a great battle, one which might decide the futures of not only Tunber and Drey, but of Furgathor as well.  And as things now stand, the outcome of that engagement is far from certain."

Lord Dornin paused, expecting the old king to make some sort of reply.  But King Edral preferred to let the envoy simmer for a while, and he said nothing for a long time.  Only after Edral felt that the silence had become sufficiently uncomfortable, did he allow the envoy to continue.

"Go on," the king said.

Dornin quietly coughed into his fist, clearing his throat, and trying not to let the old king's approach to negotiations unsettle him. "I speak for King Mulrin, and he humbly requests your aid in this war. If an army from Furgathor would join us in this campaign, then our victory would be assured."

"Victory is *never* assured," the old king replied, sagely. "But be that as it may, I have now heard Mulrin's suit, and – with some reservations – I agree. Furgathor will strike against Drey as Tunber's ally, but not at Tunber's side. If Othelwaite chooses to mass his forces against you, we shall attack his undefended north, through Karvik. In point of fact, that is an order which has already been given."

"That will be of little help to us in *this* war," Dornin replied, darkly. "The heart of Drey's power lies in the fields to the south and the mines amid the mountains of the Boundary Range. There is little of value in Karvik, to Othelwaite or to anyone else."

"It is land," Edral replied, "and land has value."

"The loss of Karvik will mean little, if Othelwaite prevails against Tunber's army, and then lays claim to all the lands south of the great Grey River. Your daughter is now wed to Tunber's heir, and one day she will be queen. Surely her future must be your concern as well."

"Tunber may one day belong to my daughter's children," the old king said, still in measured tones, "but Furgathor will soon belong to my *son* and in time to his sons. That is where my responsibility chiefly lies. The Princess Nalya's future is now a matter for her husband's concern, and not for mine."

"Othelwaite's lust for mastery will not be quenched with a single war," Dornin cautioned, forcefully. "He seeks to rule the world, and if Tunber falls, his eye will soon turn in your direction, and he will have the resources to make good on his outsized ambition!" The envoy suddenly realized that his voice had risen. He clasped his hands together, and took a long, slow breath to steady himself, before pressing on.

"Should Othelwaite's armies find victory against Tunber in the south," he continued, more quietly now but still with urgency, "then the future of Furgathor will be in doubt as well."

Edral frowned, and shifted stiffly on his throne.  His face remained calm, as he stared down at the envoy, but his eyes betrayed the simmering anger underneath.  "This is *your* war," he said, with a tone of finality.  "We have no southern border with Drey, and nothing to gain there, even in victory.  Any lands taken in such a conflict would fall naturally to Tunber, and not to us.  We cannot cross the mountains, and I will not march an army through the shadow of the dragon.  There is nothing in the south for Furgathor but *risk*, with no prospect of profit."

The two men stared at each other a moment longer, in rigid silence.

"Furgathor will march against *Karvik*."  the old king said at last, with no discernable emotion.  "You may return to your king with that message, and you may also tell him that we wish our brother and ally well."

"As you prefer, Your Majesty," Dornin replied.  His voice was still politely formal, but also bitterly cold.

"That will be all," Edral continued.  "This audience is now over."

# Chapter 8:
## Redbrook

After their encounter with Pignut, Saren and Trea kept to the woods as much as was possible.  The road, which had been only sparsely travelled before, seemed to them to have become increasingly crowded, and correspondingly more dangerous.  In addition to occasional rogues like Pignut and his gang, there were also more peasants than before, as well as merchants and other travellers.  There were also large numbers of soldiers – almost all of them moving toward Albria – and they were nearly as dangerous as the cutthroats and thieves.  Trea and Saren both agreed that the woods were a safer option, where they would be less likely to meet anyone at all.

Cutting a diagonal path overland, they steered around Albria entirely, and worked their way northwest through the rolling countryside.  It was somewhat slower travelling through the forests and across the open fields as opposed to following the roads, but since their path now cut a more direct line toward Flapham Abbey, it was also a shorter route by quite a few miles.  And because the terrain in that part of Drey was not particularly rugged, in the end, hiking cross-country didn't take them much longer than they would have taken by walking the roads.

They struck the main highway again well north of Albria, near a tiny village that was only a few miles south of the abbey.  The place was called Redbrook, as was the stream that ran nearby.  The ground there was largely sandstone and thick ruddy clay, which gave the streambed the distinctive color from which the meandering little river took its name.  The soil in that region was not particularly fertile, and the dense, heavy clay was difficult to sow and till.  Consequently, the farmers of that area were particularly poor.  The only real commodity of value that the village produced was pottery.  The clay around Redbrook was far from ideal for fine ceramics, but it could be used to make serviceable bowls and goblets and other sorts of basic crockery, which the villagers would cart by hand to Albria.  There, they could barter the stoneware off in exchange for food and clothing and sundry other necessities.

Trea remembered the little village, and knew that she and Saren were now very close to their destination. They returned to the main highway, following its serpentine path through the thick patch of forest that lay north of Redbrook. After another hour of walking, they came around a sharp bend in the road and passed through the last of the trees. There, the view suddenly opened, and they found themselves looking out at the fields and farms that surrounded the former site of Flapham Abbey. But the abbey itself was no longer there. Even at this distance, the two young women could see broken piles of red and grey rubble everywhere, and the blackened remnants of huts and other wooden structures which had been burned to the ground.

At first, Saren thought that they must have come upon another ruin from the days of the old kingdom. Over the course of their journey they had passed many such places, where half-forgotten heaps of ancient brick and stone were strewn within sight of the main road. But looking more carefully she could see that these ruins were freshly made. Puzzled, she looked over at Trea, and seeing the shock and disbelief on her face, she understood that this was not what her companion had expected to find here.

"Was this the abbey?" Saren asked. "What happened?"

Trea put her head in her hands for a long time, and said nothing. She looked up and took a deep breath, as she and Saren exchanged looks of bewilderment.

-------------------------------------------------------

Trea and Saren searched the ruins for perhaps half an hour, not in the hope of finding anything of value, but simply to see if they could find any clue to what had happened. They had travelled so far to reach this destination that they could not immediately drag themselves away, not without a closer look.

Though they found nothing but scattered debris, there could be no doubt that they were indeed in the right place. The entire site was encircled by a low mound of broken stone, where the abbey's outer wall had once stood, and the foundations of the hammer-shaped temple of Mosig could plainly be seen near the center of the ring.

"There's nothing here," said Saren, eventually. "But whatever happened to this place, it can't have been more than two weeks ago – or three weeks, at the most."

Trea picked up a piece of stone and turned it over in her hand before carefully setting it back on the ground. "Why do you say that?" she asked.

"Well for one thing, I would have known about it," Saren replied. "Word would have come through the Crow. It's not the most prominent shrine in the world, but it's important enough not to go unnoticed. And it's not every day that a temple gets razed to the ground. I can't think that I've ever heard of it happening before; not in my lifetime at least. I have to wonder who could even have done it."

"Soldiers," Trea said. "Soldiers did it."

"That's hard to believe," Saren replied. "But I don't have a better explanation."

Trea shook her head and looked around at the destruction. "I saw the ones who did it," she said. "I overheard them talking about it, but at the time I didn't understand."

Trea returned to her inspection of the ruins, but Saren found herself instead looking nervously across the empty fields that stood between them and the surrounding forest. The sky overhead was clear, and the sun was still high above the horizon, but there was a dry autumn chill in the air. A cold gust of wind from the north swept through the ruins of the abbey, swirling dust and fallen leaves across the piles of broken stone. Saren shuddered, and took a long and uneasy look back toward the main road.

"Well, whatever happened, we can't stay here," she said. "There might be more soldiers on the road, and if they found us here we'd be marked as looters or worse."

Trea nodded, sadly. "All right," she said. "There's nothing left here for us to see. We can leave, but for the life of me I don't know where to go next."

"We should go back to that village," said Saren, confidently. "They'll be able to tell us what happened, at the very least, and maybe more than that. We've still got to find out about your prophecy, and there's no reason for us to give up yet."

---

Once they understood that Trea and Saren weren't there to rob them, the peasants of Redbrook were more than happy to tell them all they knew about the destruction of Flapham Abbey. Nearly a dozen of the villagers crowded around the strange young women, each of them eager for the chance to help tell the story.

"Soldiers did it, of course," said a middle-aged woman with broken teeth. "What else would you expect? Took everything they had, burned it all and tore the place down. It was terrible. Terrible."

"They broke up the brewery and the temple and everything," one of the old men added. "Didn't even take the beer, just burned the barrels and poured it out on the ground. The waste of it! Here, folk are starving, and they just went and poured it out on the ground."

"You can't eat beer, Horgil!" the old peasant's wife chimed in, reprimanding him. "But I'm sorry to have seen it, all the same. They were fair to us at the abbey. I don't know what's to become of us now. Times were hard enough."

"But why would soldiers tear down the abbey?" Saren asked.

"Why do soldiers do anything?" the old woman replied.

"*Orders*, I heard them say," added a younger man, who stood leaning on a long wooden pole. "*The King's Justice*, that's what I heard. They kept saying it over and over again, as if it meant something."

"We've a graveyard full of the king's justice," said a young woman in a patchwork dress. Several of the others grumbled their agreement.

"What happened to everyone that lived there?" Saren asked. "Were they all killed?"

"Not killed, no," said the first woman again. "Certainly not everyone. But those that weren't arrested, they scattered to Githran's swirling winds."

"They'll find a hard enough time of it," added an older man who had only one eye. "And that's no matter where they've gone to."

"Some went to Albria, no doubt," suggested Horgil. "Enough of them came south along the road, to be sure. And there's been no shortage of refugees wandering that way of late."

"Others went north to Nyl, I'd expect," said the younger man.  "Or there's rumored to be a shrine to Tarinor the Hunter, somewhere in the woods east of here.  Some of them might have gone that way, or to other shrines further off, but I wouldn't know about that."

The peasants continued to argue for some time, but it was clear to Trea and Saren that if they were to have any hope of finding refugees from the destruction of Flapham Abbey, there was only one likely place to look.  In spite of all the trouble they had gone to in trying to avoid the town altogether, it seemed that they would now have to go to Albria after all.

# Chapter 9:
## Albria

Trea and Saren had little difficulty in getting to Albria. What proved to be more challenging, however, was getting inside the town's defensive wall. The full muster of Drey was now nearing its peak, and soldiers were everywhere. They had filled the city to overflowing, and even the fields surrounding the town were crowded with tents and wagons and horses and fighting men from every corner of the realm.

Trea and Saren couldn't help but notice the soldiers, but they did not know why they were there. Having been on the road for nearly two weeks, and having done their best to avoid encountering anyone either on the road or off, they were not yet aware of the war that had broken out between Tunber and Drey. Still, it was obvious to them that something significant was afoot.

So many soldiers were crowding the road that it was impossible to entirely avoid them. But there were a great many other travellers as well – merchants and beggars and camp followers and other sorts of vagabonds – and it was easy enough for two young women to disappear among the crowds without drawing too much unwanted attention. Trea and Saren were able to reach the northern gate of the city wall without serious incident, but they could go no further: The gate was barred.

"No admittance," one of the guards announced as they tried to pass through. He was large and short, and missing a few of his less important teeth. The iron straps around his leather helmet were clearly showing signs of rust. "Soldiers only," he added with an unpleasant growl, "and those on the king's business."

"We've come a long way," said Saren. "We don't want any trouble, we only want a room for the night."

"You won't find it here," the soldier replied. "The inns are closed to travellers."

Trea had never had any love for soldiers, and she was not in a patient frame of mind. "Since when are travellers not allowed to visit an inn?" she asked, angrily.

"Since the war," the soldier said loudly, raising his gloved fist and taking a step forward. "That's as if you didn't know. Now be off with you! Where you go from here is not my concern."

Trea started to argue, but Saren took her by the arm and pulled her away. "There are other gates," she said quietly. "We'll not get in this one; he'll be watching us to make sure we don't. Come on; we've nothing to gain by arguing here."

Trea bit her lip and stood fuming for a few moments, until she had her temper back under control. "All right," she said. "You're right. I'm tired is all, and I don't like soldiers." She looked around at the tents and wagons that surrounded the city. "This whole place looks like a mercenary's carnival; it makes my skin crawl."

"Well, if someone's started a war, that explains the soldiers at least," Saren added. "It was bound to happen sooner or later, I suppose. At the Crow, we heard rumors all summer that something like this was coming."

"We don't want to be caught out here after nightfall," Trea said. "Soldiers are bad enough in the daytime, still sober and with their captains and commanders keeping an eye on them. But by dark we'd best be either indoors or hiding in the forests."

"I know a thing or two about handling drunken soldiers," Saren reminded her, "but I'm not disagreeing with you."

Trea ran her fingers through her hair and took a long look at the city wall. "Well then," she asked, "what next? We'll not accomplish anything standing here."

"I suppose we can just follow the wall until we find another entrance." Saren suggested. "Shall we try east or west?"

Trea looked up at the sky. "It's well past noon," she said, "and you're still a ginger. There'll be more shade along the wall on the eastern side."

"That's as good a reason as any," said Saren, with a smile. "And thank you for noticing. Let me know if the hair's too bright, and I can pull my hood up."

-------------------------------------------------------

It was nearly an hour later when they reached the city's eastern gate, but they had no better luck there.  It seemed that a fight had broken out earlier in the day between troops in the service of two rival lords, and now the eastern gate was not only guarded, but the great wooden doors were closed and bolted, to ensure that none of the hostilities in the soldiers' camps would boil over into the city itself.

"We could try climbing over the wall after dark," Trea suggested.

Saren looked up at the fifteen-foot tall sheer stone face of the city wall, and the overhang at the top.  She shook her head, incredulously.  "Could you really climb that?"  she asked.

"Probably," Trea replied.  "I'd have to find the right spot first.  Someplace where we wouldn't be seen."

"I've never climbed much more than a flight of stairs," Saren said.  "Maybe a few trees, when I was little."  She looked up at the imposing wall, and tried to imagine what it would be like to even attempt getting over it.  "Not a chance," she said firmly.  "I could never manage that."

"Well we might not have another choice," Trea pointed out, "if we're going to get inside.  But we've still got a few hours of daylight left.  We might as well keep working our way around the outside, for now."

"Our luck has to change, right?"  said Saren, hopefully.

"Not necessarily," said Trea.

---

But on the south side of the wall, their luck did indeed change.  There, as at the other gates, there were soldiers and travellers aplenty.  But the guards at the south gate were still allowing a few merchants to enter the city, particularly those fleeing north from Piyl, and those transporting food or other essential goods that might be of value to the king's army.  Saren scanned the line of wagons filing into the city, and spotted someone she recognized.

"I think I can get us in," she said to Trea, excitedly.  "I know that wine merchant.  How's your coinpurse?  Can we spare a couple of silvers?"

"It's only money," said Trea, reaching into her satchel.  "You should have some to carry anyway, in case we're separated."

"I'm not letting you out of my sight," Saren replied.

"Things don't always go as planned," Trea pointed out. "And a city like this is nothing like Hillside. If we do get split up, we'll try to meet back at this gate. All right?"

"All right," said Saren. "You know better than I do about that."

Trea pulled a small handful of coins out of her purse, and – taking care not to be noticed by any of the other people standing nearby – put them in Saren's hand. Saren's eyes went wide.

"This much?" she gasped. "I said two!"

"Hold on to the rest," said Trea, "just in case."

Saren looked nervously at the coins for a moment, before carefully dropping them into her satchel. She kept one in her hand, and walked toward a sturdy-looking wagon that was carrying a number of large barrels.

"Hello, Roskiff!" she said to the mustachioed man who was steering the wagon. "I never expected to see you here."

The man in the wagon squinted and leaned forward to take a closer look. "Well!" he said in surprise. "It's Gurin's youngest daughter isn't it? What would bring you this far north? I didn't know the trouble had gone all the way to Hillside yet."

"It hadn't, when I left there," Saren replied, truthfully enough. "I'm here on an errand for my father," she added, somewhat less truthfully, "but my friend and I can't get into the city. Can you help us?"

"I don't know..." said the merchant hesitantly, "like as not, they won't let me in either. And I want no trouble."

"Oh be serious," Saren said with a smirk. "If those barrels aren't empty, they'll rush you through and cheer on your horses. If they're not letting *you* in they're not letting in anyone."

"Well, that may be," said the merchant. "But I don't know... Perhaps I could take a message for you?"

"No," Saren said firmly. "I need to get in there myself. Would it be worth a silver to take your daughter and your niece through the gate with you?"

"I don't have a daughter..." said the merchant, shaking his head meaningfully.

"Please, Roskiff?" Saren pleaded, slumping her shoulders. "We're desperate. A silver for each of us, then. One now, and one after we're inside. That's all the more I have."

The merchant frowned and pursed his lips, suspicious that he was somehow being swindled.

"I'm sure my father would be grateful," Saren added, doing her best to look both sweet and harmless.

"All right," the merchant said, reluctantly giving in. "Into the wagon, both of you. Quickly. And neither of you says a word. You'll do nothing but smile and blush until we're inside, you understand me? You keep your heads covered and your jaws still. If there's any talking to be done, with the guards or anyone else, it'll be me that does it."

Fifteen minutes later, Roskiff the wine merchant was richer by two silver coins, and Saren and Trea were on the inside of Albria's city wall.

# Chapter 10:
## The Merchants' Quarter

The streets of Albria were even more crowded than the highways and fields outside the city walls. Saren had never seen so many people in one place before, and found herself lost in the noise and bustle and confusion that surrounded her. She felt entirely overwhelmed, and had no idea of where she was going, or what she was supposed to do if she ever got there.

Trea, on the other hand, was in her element. She'd grown up travelling from city to city, with her grandfather always seeking the largest crowds. She knew how to scan her surroundings, picking out the most relevant details while blocking out the noise and the general chaos of the city's bustling streets. She grabbed ahold of Saren's arm, dragging her away from the press of humanity at the south gate and on toward the slightly quieter center of town. She tried to coach her companion on the basics of city survival as they went. "Keep one hand on your satchel," she said, "and don't get caught up staring at just one thing. Let your eyes move."

They followed the main street toward the town center, and a few minutes later they found themselves in the merchants' quarter. Once they were away from the crush at the gate, Saren was finally able to catch her breath and regain her footing. "It's like the main room of the Crow on a busy night," she said, still marvelling at it all, "but it goes on forever."

Trea couldn't help smiling to see Saren so obviously flustered. "You'll get used to it," she said.

"Well, we're here," Saren said. "So where do we go now?"

"We should find an inn," Trea replied, "before it gets much later."

Saren bit her lip, and scratched at her ear pensively. "I know there are several inns here," she said, "but I can't remember them all offhand. The best one is called *The Fox & Owl*, I think, but I don't know much about it. It's not the sort of place the regulars at the Crow would usually visit."

"We wouldn't find a room there anyway," Trea said. "If it's the best of the inns, all the rooms will be taken. Do you remember the others? I expect our chances will be better at some place further down in the pecking order."

Saren looked around at the crowded streets. "I doubt there's a room to be had anywhere," she said, "but I'm trying to remember. There's one called *The Blue Hat*, I think, and *The Fat Rabbit*. But I don't know where they are."

"We'll just have to ask someone," Trea said, "and hope for the best."

The streets of the merchants' quarter were lined with all manner of trade guilds, workshops, stores, and other places of business. One of the buildings had a panelboard sign hanging in front that showed a silver needle and a bolt of red cloth. It was a tailor's shop of course, and Trea once again grabbed Saren by the arm to drag her inside.

"We can ask directions here," she suggested, "and while we're at it, let's get you something better to wear."

"What, a new dress?" Saren asked excitedly.

"I was thinking something more like this," Trea said, indicating her own attire.

Saren looked skeptical. "I'd hardly feel like a girl in that."

"What you've got on is fine for a cook or a serving girl," Trea said, looking at Saren's long brown peasant dress. "But it's not ideal for running and climbing, or for travelling overland. Trousers and a vest are much more practical for this sort of work. You're not a barmaid anymore."

Saren nodded her agreement, but still did not seem entirely convinced. "I don't know," she said hesitantly. "I suppose it wouldn't hurt to have a look, since we're already here."

---

An hour later, the two young women were back to wandering the streets of Albria, and Saren had a new set of clothes. The tailor had first tried to steer them toward a wall of colorful dresses, but he did not argue when Trea told him they wanted men's clothing instead. Saren was amazed to see some of the tailor's more extravagant offerings, but Trea insisted that she stick to simple and practical choices. "Plain and ordinary," she kept saying, over and over, and eventually Saren gave in, choosing a sturdy and comfortable pair of brown trousers, and a darker brown leather vest that fit her reasonably well. The one colorful exception in Saren's outfit was her shirt, which was a bright cornflower blue.

"It will look almost black at night anyway," Saren argued, "and it sets off my hair."

The tailor had given them directions to the inn called The Fat Rabbit, but Trea and Saren still couldn't find the place. Albria's twisting side streets were confusing and poorly marked, and after only a few minutes of searching they realized they were thoroughly lost. The sun was sinking quickly now, and neither of them relished the thought of wandering out in the city streets after dark.

They tried asking directions from some of the other people on the street, but had no luck. Everyone they approached either refused to talk to them, or was just as lost as they were. With few better options, they tried retracing their steps back to the merchant quarter, but that was no good either. It seemed that they had taken more than one wrong turn, and were now completely out of their reckoning.

There was still enough daylight that they could make a reasonable guess about which direction was which, so they decided to go south again until they hit the city wall. From there, they hoped to find their way back to one of the gates, where they might be able to get better directions from someone, or at worst simply start all over again, this time sticking to the main thoroughfares.

They made their way south as best they could. Fewer people were on the streets in this part of the city, and the buildings were mostly small houses and shabby-looking huts made of earth and wood. They had only walked for a few minutes when they spotted a large building, which stood facing a broad avenue that ran off to their left. The panelboard sign in front read *The Brown Bear*. Above the lettering, the sign showed a large bear who was holding a mug of beer in one hand and a shank of beef in the other.

"I've never heard of it," Saren said with a shrug.

"That could be either good or bad," said Trea, "but at least it's an inn."

# Chapter 11:
## The Brown Bear

Due to its out-of-the-way location in the midst of one of Albria's poorer residential neighborhoods, The Brown Bear was neither well-known nor well-trafficked by travellers. It was a local establishment in the truest sense of the word. Because it was so far from the city's major thoroughfares, most travellers were not even aware that it existed, and few of those who learned of it ever took the trouble to seek the place out. Consequently – under ordinary circumstances at least – its guest rooms were often left unoccupied. It served primarily as a mealhouse, pub, and meeting place for the impoverished denizens that lived nearby. But despite its relative anonymity – or perhaps because of it – The Bear was a pleasant enough place for an evening's respite. The mood inside was unusually calm and quiet for an inn; the local regulars regarded it as something of a second home, and treated the place accordingly.

Tonight the inn was busier than usual, but not overly so. There were people scattered everywhere around the large open room, but Trea and Saren could see several empty tables and benches as well. A warm, inviting glow came from the far end, where a few logs were burning in a brown stone fireplace. The rest of the room was dimly lit from perhaps a dozen oil lamps, hanging from various posts and beams and also along the outer walls. The air inside had a comfortable, musty smell to it, and a pale mist of bluish smoke curled around the rafters overhead.

"It feels like home," Saren muttered approvingly.

"Well, here are some unfamiliar faces," said a gravelly female voice. Trea and Saren turned at the sound, and spotted a plump and cheerful looking woman trundling her way toward them through the crowded room. "Travellers?" the woman asked, as she drew nearer. "And young girls at that!" she added with surprise as she squinted at Trea and Saren more closely. "On my life, I hope Foll watches over you both; you've picked a poor time to come to Albria. You can call me Drumma; everybody does – it's not my given name, mind you, but what's it matter?"

"Good evening!" Saren replied. "We'd like some supper, if it's not too much trouble."

"Not a bit! Not a bit!" the woman replied, laughing to herself, as if Saren had just told a ribald joke. "Find a seat if you can, and I'll send one of the girls around in a moment. I have to warn you though, we've no rooms left open if you're in need of a bed for the night. We've never seen such a crowd in the city before. But we can find you half a bite to eat at the very least. With so many people about, it's been a good week for the kitchens but not for the larder, if you understand me. And I should tell you we've no spirits either, nor even beer. It's all been taken for the knights and the soldiers. Not a bent copper did they pay us for it, either. But you don't need to know my troubles. Find a bench wherever you like; one of the girls can find you soon enough."

The woman bustled off again, moving from table to table and chattering away without ever seeming to take a breath.

"She almost talks like you do," Trea said, as they made their way to an open bench along one of the outside walls.

"Call it innkeeper's wisdom," Saren replied with a smile. "Sometimes the best way to keep conversations short is to do all the talking yourself."

Trea sat on the bench, sighed heavily, and shook her head. "How do we find anyone from Flapham Abbey in this town, I have to wonder?"

"We ask," said Saren. "I've been giving it some thought; how to go about it, I mean. I'll talk to that innkeeper later, after the crowd's thinned down a bit."

"And we still don't have a place to stay," Trea reminded her.

"We'll pay a few coppers and sleep on the floor in here, if we have to," Saren replied. "We won't find anywhere else tonight, so we might as well get comfortable."

------------------------------------------------

Several hours later, most of the inn's patrons had either returned to their homes, or retired to their rooms. Trea and Saren were feeling well-fed, but after many days of constant walking, sitting on a bench for so long left them feeling restless. Saren kept a careful watch for a chance to speak with the innkeeper, but it seemed Drumma spent most of her time running back and forth to the kitchens and giving instructions to her serving-girls. Over the entire course of the evening, there never seemed to be a good moment to bring her aside for a more serious conversation.

This time, however, when the innkeeper did finally emerge again from the back rooms, she walked straight to Trea and Saren's table herself. It seemed she was as curious to talk with them as they were with her.

"Now forgive me if I've been rushed this evening," Drumma said as she crossed the room toward them. "I haven't had a moment's peace from then to now, so I'm sorry if I've not been more hospitable. But I have to wonder, what brings these two girls to Albria without even so much as an escort? *There must be a story behind this*, I'm telling myself, so I can't help but ask."

"If you must know, we're on a sacred pilgrimage," said Saren, before Trea could make a reply. She gave her companion a meaningful look that said *let me handle this*. Trea bit her lip and clasped her hands together.

"We've come a very long way, the lady and I," Saren continued, with a nod in Trea's direction. "And in secret, as much as we could. But to speak plainly, we really don't know much about this part of the world, and we wondered if perhaps you could help us?"

"Of course!" Drumma said, dropping her voice to an excited whisper. "I'll be happy to help as I can, but the Bear's just a poor house in a poor part of the town. What sort of help do you mean?"

"We set out some weeks ago to find a certain shrine," Saren continued, "one that we understand is not far north of here. There used to be a prophet there, though an unfortunate rumor came to us that he'd recently passed away. It's a place called Flapham Abbey, if you've ever heard of it?"

"Well certainly I've heard of it," the innkeeper said with surprise. "You won't find anyone around here that hasn't heard of the abbey! But I'm sorry to say it, you've come all this way for nothing. The prophet died some months ago, and now even the abbey isn't there any longer."

"What do you mean it isn't there?"

"I mean it's gone; been torn down; razed to the ground!  The king's men did it, not three weeks ago.  Killed the abbot, too.  Executed, I should say."

"That's terrible!"  Saren remarked, with credible surprise.  "How could such a thing happen?"

"*Lies and treason*, that's what everyone was told," said Drumma, shaking her head sadly.  "It was a bad business all around if you ask me, and I've had that straight from some that was there."

"You know someone who was there?"  Saren asked, this time with genuine surprise.

"Our Gia, for one," Drumma replied.  "She was still living there when it happened."

"And who is she?"

"She cleans for us now," explained the innkeeper, "the rooms, the kitchens and so on.  She's a good worker – quiet; a bit on shy side – but that's to her credit if you ask me.  She'd been at Flapham near all her life, before this.  But the soldiers emptied the place.  They even arrested some of the priests, as I understand it.  The folk that lived and worked there scattered to Githran's winds.  A dozen or more of them came through Albria right after that.  They were all good folk, and we tried to help as we could, but we couldn't take on everyone.  I can't say what happened to the rest of them."

"But this Gia, is she here now?"  Saren asked.  "May we speak with her?"

"I suppose, if she's willing.  I'd soon be sending her home for the night anyway.  She don't like to talk much, not about the abbey or much of anything else, really.  But I expect she could tell you more than I can."

"We would very much like to talk with her," Saren said, looking the innkeeper squarely in the eye.  "My mistress would be... *grateful*," she added without subtlety.

------------------------------------------------------

One silver piece and five minutes later, the girl Gia emerged from the inn's back rooms and nervously approached Trea and Saren's table. She had a round, passive face, and mouse-brown hair that was pulled back into a simple horsetail braid. She looked to be no older than her questioners.

"Drumma said you wanted to speak with me?"

"Yes, thank you," Trea said. "Please sit down."

"I can't sit down out here!" the girl said, her eyes wide. "I'm new here; I could get in trouble if I did."

"There won't be any trouble," Saren said, reassuringly. "We were on our way to Flapham Abbey, and the innkeeper said you knew the place."

Gia nodded dutifully. "I worked there all my life, or nearly."

"What did you do there?"

"I cleaned," the girl said, as if no other answer was possible. "Same as here. I hoped I could move up to the kitchens, when I got older."

"Did you know the prophet?" Trea asked. Saren glared at her, but gave up trying to ease the girl into the conversation slowly.

"I did..." Gia replied cautiously. "I cleaned the rooms in his tower sometimes. He was a nice old man, really."

"I have a question about a prophecy," Trea said.

The girl looked startled, and more than a little afraid. "I wouldn't know anything about that."

Saren held up a hand to try to slow Trea down. "It's all right," she said to the girl, "we're only asking. Do you know of anyone who might know more? Did anyone else from the abbey come here to Albria? Anyone that you know of? Maybe one of the priests?"

"They arrested all the priests," the girl said sadly. "I don't even know what happened to them after that. And they killed the abbot. They cut off his head! They made us all watch while they did it, too; it was a terrible thing. I have nightmares about it."

"But they didn't arrest everyone?" Saren asked. "They didn't arrest *you*."

The girl shook her head and stared at the floor. "The rest of us, I don't think they cared about one way or the other. They started tearing the buildings down, and just made us all leave; ran us out with nothing but the clothes on our backs."

"I was at Flapham Abbey once," Trea said quietly. "A boy spoke to me there who said he'd heard the prophet speak; that he'd been in the temple. Would you know who that was?"

Gia's eyes went wide, and she looked back and forth between these two strange young women fearfully. She swallowed hard, looked down at the table again, and whispered an answer. "That'd have to be the prophet's boy, Miss. No one else but him and the abbot would have heard that sort of thing."

"What was his name?" Trea asked. "Do you know where he is?"

"I should," the girl replied. "He's my husband. We got ourselves married, that first day after we came to Albria."

# Chapter 12:
## The Prophet's Boy

The three young women left the inn together, and Gia led Trea and Saren along the dark and winding side streets toward her home. It wasn't far, and after only a few minutes they found themselves standing outside a small but solid-looking wooden hut with a short stone chimney. Gia opened the door and was immediately greeted by a young man who could not have been more than a year or two older than she was.

"Welcome home," the boy said, embracing her. Then he looked up at Trea and Saren. "You've brought guests."

Gia stepped into the room, and looked back toward the doorway. "I'm sorry to surprise you, but they came to the Bear tonight asking about the abbey; they wanted to speak with you." She turned toward Trea and Saren. "May I introduce Halef, my husband."

"Do you remember me?" Trea asked the young man, darkly.

The boy did not seem either puzzled or alarmed by her question. "Yes," he said without hesitation. "You were the girl in the cage. Please, come in. This is our home, and you are welcome here."

Trea stood in the doorway for a few moments, scowling and staring at the young man in front of her, until Saren nudged her forward into the room. The interior of the hut was small and cramped, but everything was clean and tidy and neatly arranged. A fireplace stood in the center of the wall opposite the door, with a bed tucked squarely into the left-hand corner. On the other side of the hearth there was a little wooden table with two sturdy chairs, and across from that was a narrow cupboard. Here and there along the walls were a few shelves stacked with the couple's belongings. A modest iron kettle hung on a hook beside the fireplace.

"Notwot left me a few coins after he died," Halef explained, gesturing to the surrounding room. "It wasn't much, but it was enough for us to get married, and to set ourselves up here, such as we have. Gia's at the Brown Bear now, of course, but I've not been so fortunate.

I'm hoping to find work as a scribe, maybe at one of the guilds. I've made some inquiries, but nothing has come of it yet."

"He's writing a book," Gia said proudly.

"It's just some bits and pieces," the boy said. "I'm trying to write down everything I know about Mosig; what I learned from Old Notwot mostly. Traditions, rites, mysteries and so on. Sacred recipes for making beer. I don't know that anyone's put it all on paper before, and after what happened at the abbey, well, what if all that learning was lost? I couldn't bear the thought of that, so I've been taking notes on everything I can remember."

"I think it's wonderful," Gia added, beaming. "It's Halef's calling, I'm sure of it. And it's holy work. I can tell that Mosig is smiling on us, and I know how proud Old Notwot would be."

"Gia, remember, I've only just started. I feel like I've already forgotten so much."

"May I fetch you a mug of beer?" Gia asked politely, suddenly remembering her guests.

"We have a keg here that we bought for ourselves," Halef explained, "just before the soldiers started to arrive in town. There's not much left to be had anywhere in the city now, not even at the inns. We don't have much to offer, but what's ours is yours, if you have a need."

"I have no need of beer," Trea replied, tersely.

"*She* might not," Saren interjected, "but I do. This has not been an ordinary week."

Gia seemed delighted by this, and hurried toward a small keg that was hidden beside the cupboard. She slowly filled two crockery mugs with a dark, richly foaming brew.

"We're not at the abbey any longer, but we're still servants of Mosig," Halef continued. "He teaches us to share what we have, even when we have very little. There will always be others who have less, and they are more deserving."

Gia carried the mugs very gingerly back across the room, carefully setting one on the table by her husband, and handing the other to Saren with a shy little smile. Saren, who had spent most of her life serving mugs of beer to other people, felt strangely out of place being handed a mug by someone else.

"I'm sorry we only have the two chairs," Halef said, "but we haven't many visitors."

"Don't mind me," said Saren, shaking her head. "I'll stand. I've been sitting most of the evening." She leaned against the wall next to the door, and took a sip of her beer. She nodded approvingly and raised an eyebrow. "It's *very good*," she said to Gia, who was now sitting on the bed, and had wrapped herself in a dark brown blanket. Gia smiled politely, but said nothing in reply.

"Please, sit down," Halef said to Trea, gesturing to one of the wooden chairs. "You've come a long way, and I'm sure you have many questions. I will try to answer them for you, as best I can."

He walked behind the little table, sat in the chair facing the door, clasped his hands together and looked up at Trea expectantly. Trea, still frowning, looked back at Saren briefly, then pulled the other chair away from the table and sat in the center of the room, facing her host. She closed her eyes and painfully sifted through the memories of her ordeal.

"That night in the abbey," she began, slowly but deliberately, "you said to me *You are not a princess*. I need to know what you meant. I need to know what was said. I need to know exactly what the prophecy was."

The boy nodded thoughtfully, and took a sip of his beer. He set his mug carefully back on the table before continuing. "At first," he said, hesitantly, "they told us the king was coming. But it turned out it wasn't the king at all, it was only one of his ministers. I don't know which one. I would recognize him if I saw him, but I never heard his name. In the temple, he asked a question. What he asked was *How might the dragon be slain?*"

Halef took another sip of his beer, then stared at the table for a few moments before looking up at Trea again. "*How might the dragon be slain?* That was the question he asked. And Old Notwot's answer was *Feed him a princess*. That was the prophecy."

Trea was crushed. "That's it?" she asked. "That's the entire prophecy? That's all of it? That's nothing more than I already knew!" She stood up and looked at Saren in dismay. "I'm sorry," she said, "we've been wasting our time."

"Wait!" said the boy, anxiously. "That was the prophecy, yes, but you have to understand how these things work. You've got to understand the *context*. Old Notwot was answering a question. That's the question the king's minister asked, and that was the answer he got. So yes, that was the prophecy, but it didn't really matter. That's what I'm trying to tell you."

Now Trea was outraged. "What do you mean it didn't matter?" she shouted, leaning across the table and pushing her chair away so angrily that it toppled over and clattered onto the floor. "I was locked in a cage and sent to die!"

"But you *didn't*," the boy replied, quietly but fiercely. "And that's a fact not to be dismissed. Now I am *not* a prophet, not by any stretch of the imagination; but I knew Old Notwot better than anyone, and I *heard* every prophecy he spoke over the last five years of his life. So if there's any value in my opinion, let me give you something more to think about. Please."

Halef looked down at the table again, and reached for his mug of beer. He took a long drink, then set the mug down, wiped his lip, and took a deep breath before continuing.

"The important part came after that," he said, looking up at Trea again. "After everyone else had gone. *It's never the right question...* that's what the old man said to me later on, after the minister and the abbot had already gone. I was helping him back to his room, and it was then, with just the two of us there, alone in his tower. He said to me *It's never the right question, had you noticed that?* At the time, I didn't know exactly what he meant; though I could make a guess. And I've thought about it a lot since then. Killing the dragon isn't the important part. That's just it. The important part is what comes after that. What matters, what's really going to matter, is what happens after that. What happens after the dragon is dead?"

He stopped talking and took another sip of his beer to steady himself. Looking back and forth between the two young women, he clasped his hands together nervously, and leaned forward to rest his elbows on the table before continuing.

"Please," he said earnestly. "Please sit down again."

Trea reluctantly picked up her chair from the floor and sat in it. Saren remained standing, holding her mug of beer and leaning against the wall by the door. Gia was still sitting on the little bed, wrapped in a dark wool blanket and trying not to be noticed.

"*Always the wrong question*," the boy continued. "That's what he said to me first, but then he added something more, and I think this was the really important part: *The treasure*, he said, *The treasure isn't what they think. But precious, yes, more precious by far*."

The boy looked from Trea to Saren and back again. "I still don't know what the old man meant by that," he admitted, reluctantly, "but maybe you do, or maybe you *will*. I don't know. But if I knew Old Notwot – and I promise you, I knew him better than anyone – then that was the most important part, out of everything he said. And the king's minister missed it, because he asked the wrong question to begin with. That was the most important part, and that's something even the king doesn't know."

Trea stared hard at the young man across from her, then looked down at the floor of the hut and rubbed her forehead lightly with the tips of her fingers. Halef took another deep breath, then lifted his mug, drained the last of his beer and set it gently back on the table. Saren, realizing she'd been neglecting her own mug, took a long drink from it. As the silence dragged on, she decided that something more needed to be said, if only to break the tension in the room.

"Thank you," Saren said, looking first at Halef, and then at Gia.

Trea slowly looked up from the floor. "I think..." she said, with some difficulty, "I think you have told me what I needed to know. Thank you."

Halef stood up from the table, and rubbed his neck wearily. "You're welcome to stay the night," he said, "if you need a place to sleep. The two of you can have the bed even. Gia and I will take the floor; we're used to it by now. I'm guessing you need a good night's sleep more than we do, and we've got the rest of our lives to sleep here in better comfort."

---------------------------------------------------

The next morning Trea and Saren made ready to depart, soon after the sun began to rise above the city's eastern wall.  They shared a light breakfast of bread and cheese with their hosts, then Halef and Gia bid them farewell.

"I'm glad you found me," Halef said, sincerely, "and I wish you the best of luck from here.  I don't know if we'll meet again, but I've long been sorry about that night I first met you, and I'm glad I finally got the chance to tell you so."

Trea reached into her satchel, and took out a small handful of silver coins.  "I would like to leave you with something," she said, "in appreciation."

Halef held up his hands to refuse.  "Money has its uses," he said, "but desire of it was one of Risby's failings.  Old Notwot understood, and it's a lesson we've tried to remember.  You've brought me the chance to make amends, and that's the kindest gift of all.  Life doesn't often allow us to address our regrets."

"Take it," Trea insisted.  "Please.  I'll have no need of it, and at the very least, I think you can make better use of it than I would."  She handed the coins to Gia, who stood beaming at her guests with wonder and gratitude.

"I think you *are* the one from Notwot's prophecy," Gia said quietly, looking Trea directly in the eye, "or you would have been, had they asked him a better question."  She blushed and looked down at the floor, leaning against her husband.

"Thank you," Halef said, "and may Mosig help you to stumble upon your own sort of happiness."

---------------------------------------------------

Ten minutes later, Trea and Saren found themselves back at the south gate.  The guards there were only concerned with stopping people from entering the city, and paid little attention as two young women, dressed as men, slipped away into the crowd outside, turned to their left, and walked off toward the east.

The two travellers walked together quietly for a long time, each of them lost in her own thoughts, until they reached the highway that led back toward the foothills of the mountains.  Once they were away from the crowds of people that still surrounded Albria, Saren broke the silence.

"Are you going to tell me what any of that meant?" she asked.  "Are we really going to kill the dragon?"

"I don't know what it meant," Trea said, truthfully.  "But I won't kill the dragon.  I don't know if that's what it meant, but I won't do it, prophecy or no."

Something in Trea's voice made it clear to Saren that the topic of the dragon was closed for discussion.  She wisely decided to change the subject, and to try to lighten the mood.

"That was an awfully good mug of beer," she said with a grin.  "You don't know what you missed."

"You enjoyed it more than I would have," Trea replied.

"And you're true to your word, aren't you?  You *do* like to set your coinage free.  I don't suppose you even know how much you have left."

"As a matter of fact, I do," Trea replied.  "That was the last of it.  I hope you've held on to what I gave you; we might need some of it before we get to where we're going."

"You've given away *all* of it?" Saren asked with surprise.  "And yes, I've still got what you gave me, minus the cost of these clothes.  Does that make me the treasurer now?"

"If you like," Trea said with a smile.

"Which leads me to my next question: where exactly *are* we going?  And don't you even try to tell me that you don't know."

"We are going," Trea responded cryptically, "to see my other friend."

# Chapter 13:
## The Deserter

It was mid-morning, and Mida was outside the Speckled Crow, retrieving kindling from the inn's woodpile. This had not traditionally been one of her chores, as her parents preferred to have her inside the inn where they could keep a more careful watch on her. But after Saren's departure, the regular orders of business at the Crow had been somewhat upended – arguably for the better – and Mida now found the firewood to be a useful excuse to get herself outside from time to time, for a breath of fresh air and at least a small measure of imagined freedom.

Her sister had been gone for more than a week, and though Mida missed her terribly, life at the inn had become somewhat easier. Their parents had taken on two more local girls to replace her, and it seemed that the daily business of the Speckled Crow would carry on as usual in her absence. Though a few of Saren's favorite regulars expressed disappointment, the innkeeper and his wife had hardly batted an eye at their youngest daughter's departure, unless it was to give voice to their perceived good fortune at the change.

With the new girls helping Berla in the kitchen, Kersin and Nera now spent most of their time serving guests in the main room. That, in turn, left Gurin free to spend more of his time doing the things he most enjoyed: loudly giving orders, sampling his own beer, chatting with customers, and generally "keeping the peace," as he liked to put it.

And inside the Crow at least, it had been peaceful. That was partly because for the last several days no soldiers had been there at all. With the outbreak of war, nearly all of Vildar's men had joined him marching west in the effort to reclaim Piyl and the ferry-barge. There had been perhaps a few more strangers on the road, and a small number of refugees had passed through as well, but otherwise the impact of this new war had not yet been felt in Hillside.

Mida had just finished bundling together as much firewood as she could easily carry, when she heard the familiar clop of a horse coming along the road at a slow walk. She hoisted the wood onto her shoulder and set it down beside the back door of the inn. Then she stood at the open door and waited for the rider to come into view.

It was not someone she immediately recognized. The horse was pale grey, heavily built and tall at the shoulder. The rider was less impressive. He was a weatherbeaten young man, with dark brown hair. He had a sword at his hip, but no helmet or armor that Mida could see. He wore a dark travelling cloak over his rumpled clothing, and was half-covered with dust and dirt, as if he'd ridden for a week without rest. Only when he drew closer did she realize who he was.

"Valand?" she asked. "Are you badly hurt? You look... I would hardly know you."

"Hello, Mida," he said. "And I shouldn't wonder. I am something the worse for wear."

"I thought you had ridden to war with your father."

"I had," he replied.

"But what happened?" she asked in amazement, "why are you here?"

"My father is dead. He fell in battle, on the fields surrounding Piyl. There are some that might tell you that makes me the new Lord of Glaen, but I want no part of it."

"I don't understand you," Mida said cautiously.

"I'm a deserter now," Valand explained, "or just another refugee." He shook his head, and patted his horse along the neck. "I've been training in the arts of war since I was old enough to ride or to lift a sword. But I never took to it. Honor and status and pride never meant that much to me. Now I've seen war, and it all means even less. At Piyl I saw proud men of honor dying on both sides, and for the life of me when the battle was over I couldn't tell them apart, not from each other or from anyone else. All dead – that was all that mattered – nothing else had changed."

Mida stood silently in the doorway staring at the young man she had once known so well, almost as if he were suddenly a stranger. In the past, Valand had always been charming and clever and carefree, quick with a joke, and as eager to lose at cards as to win. But after his brother's death he had clearly changed, and now he hardly even seemed to be the same man, as if he had aged a lifetime in a few short days.

All her life she'd heard stories of war and valor, and of the darker side of thievery and murder as well. But those things had always seemed remote to her somehow; remnants of a half-forgotten past, or legends from some distant land. But looking at this weary young knight, war and death suddenly felt very real to her, as if she were surrounded by it. More perhaps than she ever had, she felt the sudden urge to escape; to rush back inside the inn and hide herself until he went away, but she did not. She tucked a hand into the pocket of her skirt and clenched her fingers so tightly that her nails cut her palm.

"What will you do?" she finally asked him. "Where will you go?"

"I'll wander on," he said with shrug. "It's not really a plan, I'll admit, but I never was very good at planning anyway. To be fair, I don't think much of my chances; but by all rights I should probably have died at Piyl. As it happens, I didn't. So I'm leaving the game with the house's money in hand, if you like. But in truth, I have no money at all; none of my own. Do you think you could spare me a loaf of bread? I've never had to beg before, so I'll confess, I hardly know how. But I've nothing to eat, and nothing I can afford to part with in exchange. And I'm hungry. A morsel of food never seemed to matter so much before."

Mida furrowed her brow and glared at Valand hard, uncertain what she should do. "You've come all this way to beg for a loaf of bread?" she asked, scoldingly. "You know how my father detests charity. He'd have my hide for it, if he ever found out."

"I understand," said Valand, chastened. "I am sorry to have asked."

Mida frowned. "All right," she said firmly. "Wait for me here, and I'll be back in a moment, if I can. Tonight's loaves are still rising, and won't even go into the ovens for an hour yet. But there may be something left from before; I'll see what I can bring you."

-----------------------------------------------------

Five minutes later Mida returned, hurrying out the back door of the inn as if she were being hunted by wolves. She'd changed her clothing in the short time she was gone. A satchel was hung from her shoulder, and she'd pulled a dark winter travelling cloak over her skirt and blouse. Beneath that cloak, Valand could see a long dagger in its sheath, awkwardly tucked into her leather belt.

"Luck was with me," she said, taking a deep breath. "Father's napping in the back room, and mother's upstairs with Kersin, busily turning out the bedding I expect. We should hurry, though."

Now it was Valand's turn to be mystified. "What do you mean?" he asked.

"I'm coming with you," she said, "that is, if you'll have me, and your horse can carry us both. I don't think I could keep up on foot."

Valand was aghast. "I don't even know where I'm going," he said.

Mida reached into her satchel and drew out a small leather purse. She held it up and shook it gently for Valand to see. "I have nine silver pieces to my name," she said. "That's the whole of what I've managed to keep for myself over the years without my parents knowing, hiding a few coppers at a time. It's a fortune for some, I know it all too well; but too little even to be missed for others. It's all the dowry I have. I never wanted to be rescued, but I'll not have such a chance to escape again, and if I can be of help to an old friend in the process, so much the better. Will you have me?"

It was impossible, and Valand knew it. He had nothing: no hopes, no property, and no future beyond the next sunset. He shook his head slowly from side to side to tell her "no". But even as he did so, he heard his own voice saying "yes?" as if it were a question that only she could answer.

There was one moment more where the two of them stood looking at each other, unable to move, trapped in their mutual uncertainty. Then, absurdly enough, Mida *laughed*. Only a little; not a deep belly-laugh, but a quiet, ridiculous chortle that – despite the moment – she could not contain.

Valand began to chuckle as well; for sheer puzzlement at first, and then for finding himself part of a joke he hadn't heard. "I don't know..." he asked her, "...Why are we laughing?"

"I forgot," she answered him, putting her hand over her mouth in embarrassment. "I was in such a hurry, I forgot your loaf of bread."

She looked up at him and reached out so that he could help her to climb up behind him onto the horse's back. She wrapped her arms lightly around his waist, and rested her head against his shoulder.

"I do hope," she said, still with half a smile, "that one day you'll find it in your heart to forgive me."

And that was that.

They rode off to the east, and not long after leaving Hillside they forded the shallows of the Grey River and so crossed into Tunber at the same spot where weeks before Trea had crossed back into Drey, travelling in the opposite direction.

# Chapter 14:
## Othelwaite in Albria

The muster of Drey's forces in Albria was a complicated and potentially volatile operation. Not all of Othelwaite's vassals were equally enamored of their monarch, and rivalries among various factions and individuals were often fierce. Further complicating the situation was the fundamental problem of marshalling and maintaining adequate food and other supplies for such a large number of men, without adequate housing, and so far from their respective homes.

Managing this nightmarish alchemy of potential disasters was a problem of logistics and diplomacy, much moreso than a matter of battlefield tactics or prowess at arms. And so, given Lord Fodge's aptitude for this particular sort of work, Othelwaite had sent his financial minister to Albria well in advance, to ensure that the muster of Drey's army proceeded in as orderly a fashion as possible.

Not one to waste such an opportunity, Lord Fodge had acted accordingly. He began by proclaiming martial law in the city, and closing the town gates to all but "essential" traffic. He next ordered that the Fox & Owl was to be shuttered and emptied, established the inn as his operational headquarters, and moved himself and several of Othelwaite's more important lords into its most comfortable guest rooms.

By the time Othelwaite arrived in Albria, Lord Fodge had already been there a week, and had made himself quite at home. The muster had proceeded more-or-less according to plan, and though there were certainly many minor disputes and small-scale altercations, on the whole the process had been as orderly and professional as could reasonably have been hoped for.

---

"Welcome to Albria, Your Majesty," Fodge said, with a courteous nod. "I trust your journey from Nyl was a pleasant one."

"Indeed it was," Othelwaite replied. "We passed by Flapham Abbey along the way, and I think the sight of it – or what little remains of it – did my heart good. It has put me in a better mood. It has put me in the proper frame of mind, and it has whetted my appetite for more. And yet, despite that, I doubt you have any good news to tell me. You so rarely do."

"I have news," Fodge replied, diplomatically. "I will leave it to your discretion, to determine if it is good or bad."

"I dislike the sound of it already," Othelwaite grumbled.

"The bulk of your forces have arrived here in Albria before you, though more will be coming. I am confident that stragglers will continue to arrive over the course of the next week or more. However, most of them have been here for several days now, and are, if anything, eager for a fight. In fact, in many cases they have already begun to squabble with each other. They are predictably restless, and correspondingly unruly."

"I assume you have such matters well in hand."

"For now, with the able assistance of their commanders, I do. Thank you, Sire." Fodge said. "There is another matter, however, that is entirely out of my control. I do not know if you have been informed of this, but I received word this morning that an army from Furgathor is now marching into Karvik."

"I had not heard of this, though I expected it," Othelwaite replied, testily. "How is it that this report came to you here in Albria before it came to me in Nyl?"

"The message was brought by a rider dispatched from Blackhall," Fodge explained, "Lord Torinal, I suspect, feared Your Majesty might be gone from Nyl before the message reached you there, and so he sent it here, where he knew you would be bound to come. It seems likely that he sent messages to both cities, and the one to Nyl simply arrived there after you had already departed."

"It does not matter," Othelwaite said dismissively. "We planned for this. Torinal and Hargrave know that I cannot send them further assistance. Furgathor does not have a navy sufficient to blockade the city of Toule, and without a blockade there can be no siege there. And

Blackhall chasm is easily enough defended. So long as Toule and Blackhall remain loyal to Drey, the loss of Karvik means nothing. Edral's campaign there is an annoyance, and nothing more."

"Edral is cautious to a fault," said Fodge, in agreement. "Had he joined his army with Tunber's then we would be overmatched. As the matter stands, we may still hold a numerical advantage."

Othelwaite glared at his financial minister, and waved his hands in the air to demonstrate his impatience. "Are we finally getting to the matter at hand?" he asked. "I cannot help but notice that you have made no mention of the invading army from Tunber."

"Each piece of news in its proper order," Fodge replied, calmly. "I was coming to that presently. Since the capture of Piyl, Mulrin has moved swiftly, both to the west and the east. After Lord Vildar's ill-fated attempt to retake the city, Glaen was left largely undefended. And as for the provinces west of Piyl, it would seem that the lords there have either fallen in with Mulrin, or thought it best not to resist him. Lord Rill, as you may recall, has some blood relation in Tunber, and Lord Drune's wife was born near Hinwahl."

"They will be made to pay when this war has ended," Othelwaite fumed.

"Be that as it may," Fodge continued, "for the moment, at least, Mulrin now controls the whole of the Grey River Valley, from the mountains to the sea."

"And what is his next move?" Othelwaite asked, striving to hold his anger in check. "Does he march on Albria?"

"I do not think so," Fodge replied. "He has no need. He knows that you have the advantage of numbers, but that you are also poorly supplied. He already controls the most productive farmlands in Drey. If things remain as they are, his armies will be well fed, whilst yours will soon be facing starvation, either here in Albria or wherever else you might choose to winter them. In Albria, we have stores for a month, or two months at the most. But with the captured harvests from Piyl and Glaen, Mulrin can remain where he is indefinitely."

"We can retake Piyl," Othelwaite said. "We have greater numbers and the city is poorly fortified."

"It will be better fortified now than it was a week ago," Fodge pointed out, "and could be better fortified still by the time you arrived there.  But Mulrin might not even defend it.  If you were to march against Piyl, I think it likely that he might simply withdraw across the Grey River, taking the fall harvest with him.  He could leave your army starving on the northern bank of the river, and wait until spring to resume his campaign.  Then he could march unopposed through the shattered remnants of what was once your kingdom."

"Are you telling me I have no options!?!"  Othelwaite shouted, slamming his fist against the wall.  "That we can either remain in Albria and starve *here*, or we can march to Piyl and starve *there*?!?"

"What I am saying," Lord Fodge replied, calmly, "is that we have an army which we cannot sustain.  Even now they are scarcely more than a mob of rabble, and when our stores are depleted, that mob can be depended upon to swiftly turn on us and on each other.  You must seek battle as soon as possible, if only to decrease the number of mouths we will be obligated to feed."

Othelwaite glared at his financial minister, angrily at first, but then his face slowly broke into a grim sort of smile.  "I take it then, Fodge, that you have a scheme," he said quietly.  "You always do."

"Thank you, Your Majesty," Fodge replied.  "I do indeed.  If we are to prevail in this war, we must draw Mulrin's army out of Piyl.  If nothing else changes, he will take his plunder and withdraw to his own lands.  We must persuade him to *seek* battle, rather than shun it."

"And?"  the king prodded, impatiently.

"It is my advice that your army should march to the east, toward the Last Mountain."

Othelwaite was incredulous.  "Have you forgotten the dragon, Fodge?"  he asked, with no small measure of scorn.

"I have not," Lord Fodge continued, "and I assure you, neither has Mulrin.  May I remind Your Majesty, that the Princess Dophne was well aware of the salient details of the prophecy regarding the slaying of the dragon, and that she might well have made mention of such to her new father-in-law at some point prior to her unfortunate demise?  Mulrin surely knows of our earlier attempt against the dragon which failed.  But what if a second attempt were to succeed?"

"Marching an army against the dragon would be sheer folly," Othelwaite replied.

"Precisely," said Fodge.

The king eyed his financial minister suspiciously, then clasped his hands together and quietly cracked his knuckles. "Go on," he said.

"Mulrin knows that you would not march against the dragon unless you had some prospect for success. If he has heard the prophecy, or as much of it as the Princess Dophne knew, then so much the better. And let us not forget that the Sisters of Piety are also there." Fodge paused, raising an index finger to his temple for emphasis. "If you march toward the dragon, there will be doubt in Mulrin's mind. I think he will move to intercept you before you ever reach that destination. And if he does so, then your armies may do battle on even terms."

"And what if he does not take the bait?" Othelwaite countered. "What if he chooses instead to let the dragon have me, or lays siege to Albria whilst my army and I are off hiking up the mountainside?!?"

"You need not march all the way to the dragon," Fodge replied with uncharacteristic exasperation, as if the point should have been an obvious one. "And you can easily leave enough men here in Albria to securely garrison the city. If Mulrin does not *take the bait*, as you put it, you can return here within a week, and be no worse off than you already are. Or, should he choose instead to march against Albria, you could first reclaim Glaen, and then march west along the Great South Road against Piyl. In that way, you could prevent Mulrin from escaping across the river, and do battle with him somewhere between there and here."

"And what about the dragon? What guarantee do we have that he will fold his wings and do nothing?"

"We have no guarantee," Fodge replied firmly. "This is war, and war is by its very nature an uncertain business. If the dragon stirs, he is as likely to strike against Mulrin as against you, or more likely against you both. That cannot be helped. We cannot ensure against every contingency. If you successfully draw Mulrin into the field, and if the dragon does not intervene, you will have no worse than an even chance in open warfare. If Mulrin instead chooses to sit on his hands, then you will still be left with alternatives no worse than the ones you already have."

The king rubbed his neck with frustration and displeasure, then scratched lightly at his beard. He stared levelly at his advisor for a long time.

"Very well," he said at last. "We will march east tomorrow, toward the Sisters and the Last Mountain. See that all the arrangements are made. We depart with the first light of dawn."

Fodge closed his eyes briefly, and gave a subservient nod. "As you will, My Liege," he replied.

# Chapter 15:
## The Meadow

Saren and Trea stopped in their tracks, and gave each other a long look.  Not far ahead of them, lying at the side of the road, was a man.  Trea frowned and ran her fingers through her hair in disgust.  Saren shook her head slowly, sighed heavily and bit her lip.

"Not again," mumbled Trea.

"Well it's not Pignut, at least," Saren muttered in reply.  "This one's got hair on his head.  I can see that much from here."

They had left Albria three days before, and were now approaching the Ash River.  In stark contrast to their earlier travels, they had walked most of the last two days without meeting anyone at all.  The further they got from the great walled city and Drey's mustering army, the fewer people they had encountered.  Now, for some time the road had been empty of travellers of any kind, and even the farms and villages they'd passed had seemed to be entirely deserted.  This man on the roadside ahead of them was the first person they had come upon in a long while.

"Hello!"  Saren called out.  "Stand up and dust yourself off, if you like; we've already seen you there.  And the rest of you can come out from hiding and show your faces, if you please!"

The two girls waited, but no answer came.  The man did not move, and no one emerged from the grass or the trees to either side.

"I don't like this at all," Saren said quietly.

"Wait," Trea whispered sharply.  "Listen..."

At first, Saren could hear nothing but the sounds of the forest and her own breathing.  She held her breath.  Still, she heard nothing unusual; there were birds, some crickets, and the hint of a light breeze drifting through the leaves.  Then, very faintly, just at the edge of hearing, she noticed the high-pitched wavering hum of insects... flies.  The wind shifted slightly and brushed against her face.  She let herself breathe again, and her throat instantly lurched at the smell of rotting flesh.

"I think he's really dead."

The two young women drew their weapons and moved cautiously forward, their eyes searching the lightly wooded meadows that lay on either side of the highway.  As they drew closer, they could see that the man was not only dead, but naked as well, and he was not alone. Within a few yards of the road, Saren and Trea could see a number of other men lying here and there among the trees.  Those men were also dead, and had also been stripped bare.

Perhaps the most disturbing aspect of the entire scene was how ordinary everything still seemed.  The sky was blue with a few white clouds; the sun was shining; squirrels were chattering in the trees overhead; birds were singing; and all around them were dead men, lying cold and still, and slowly decomposing in the grass.  The world rolled on as it always had, either oblivious to the horror, or utterly unconcerned.

They stopped a few feet from the man they had spotted first and surveyed the carnage that surrounded them.  Each of the bodies had been hacked or carved or stabbed, by what sort of weapons they could not guess.  The corpses were scattered about, some flat upon the ground, others twisted in hideous contortions.  The man by the road was on his back, facing up.  His mouth and eyes were open, staring at the sky as if he were either rapt with the wonder of his own mortality, or transfixed by some other nameless, unblinking astonishment.

Saren and Trea held their arms to their faces, and breathed through their shirts to lessen the stench of death.  But they did not stand there for long.  They pulled each other away from the clustered corpses, stumbling forward, dragging themselves down the road until they were well beyond the sight of that carrion meadow.

"What was that?!?" Saren exclaimed, looking back.  Her hands were on her knees, and she was trying to catch her breath, now that the air was clean again.

"I don't know," said Trea, who was taking slow, deep breaths of her own.

"Thieves?" Saren asked.  "A caravan of merchants, murdered and robbed?"

"No," Trea replied. "I would guess they were soldiers. I think we've had a first-hand look at war."

"If they were soldiers, then who were they? Did they come from Tunber or from Drey? I didn't see any signs or heraldry for either side."

"I don't think it matters much which side it was," Trea said, shaking her head. "Are you all right to keep walking? We should get as far from here as we can. Whoever they were, and whenever it happened, it wasn't long ago, and whoever did it might still be close by."

"I'm fine," Saren replied. "But when we reach the river, we should stop and have a wash, or else the smell of that place is going cling to us, in our clothes and our hair."

# Chapter 16:
## The Fog of War

Ever since his arrival in Piyl, King Mulrin had made it his primary objective to collect and secure the fall harvest of Drey's most productive farmlands. All the provinces along the northern bank of the Grey River were now in his control, and the bulk of his army was encamped in the now-empty fields surrounding Piyl. To the east and west, all along the Grey River Valley, squads of his infantry were seizing herds of livestock and stores of grain, and bringing them to the ferry-barge, to be taken south across the river.

Tunber's early successes had seemingly made it possible for Mulrin to wage this war in an entirely different way than he had initially planned. He no longer saw any need to defeat his enemy in battle; by ravaging Drey's wealthiest provinces and plundering their reserves of food, he could starve Othelwaite's armies into submission. Winter would tame them, and when the spring came Mulrin could either solidify his claim to the provinces he had already captured, or march further north, into the heart of Drey, virtually unopposed.

But now, troubling news had reached his ears, and it had thrown everything into doubt. His spies reported that Drey's army had departed from Albria. However, they were not marching south, as Mulrin had expected, but *east*. The King of Tunber could only guess as to why Othelwaite would choose to march in that direction, but his suspicions put him ill at ease.

-----------------------------------------------------

"Othelwaite marches east out of Albria," Mulrin said to his son. "Why would he do this? Why *east*?"

Halvik knew that his father was not asking his advice, but testing his perception, and his understanding of strategy and the arts of war. He clasped his hands together, and sat for a moment in thought before making his reply.

"He must intend to recapture Glaen," Halvik said, at last. He did not sound as confident in his answer as he would have liked.

"No," Mulrin replied. "If Glaen were his goal, he would march first on Piyl, to either capture or sink the ferry-barge, and so prevent our transporting any further resources across the river."

"But if his muster is incomplete," Halvik persisted, "he could be taking only a *portion* of his army. In a week or thereabouts, with the muster complete and Glaen once again under his control, he could then march on Piyl from both the north and the east."

Mulrin could see that Halvik was grasping at straws, and he shook his head with disappointment. "There would be no advantage in dividing his forces in that way," he said. "If Othelwaite wished to attack Piyl from two sides, he would simply march toward us with his full army. Then, he could easily wait, and divide his troops a mile from the city, and in that way better coordinate his attack. No, I do not think that Glaen is his immediate goal. I think, instead, that he is marching toward the Last Mountain."

"If he is," Halvik said with a grim laugh, "then we can let the dragon do our work for us. We can wait here and watch; and if there are any survivors, we can deal with them easily enough at our leisure."

Mulrin was growing impatient with his son's errant guesses. "Have you forgotten the prophecy?" he asked, testily.

"Certainly not," said Halvik, "but I see no reason to believe it, or even to trust that the Princess Dophne was speaking the truth when she revealed it to you."

"And why not?" Mulrin demanded, pointing a finger for emphasis. "The Princess Dophne believed it, I can assure you, and enough so that she fled her home and her inheritance for fear that her father believed it as well. If Othelwaite slays the dragon, he will bring this age of the world to a close; and if he claims the dragon's treasure, he might very well chart the course of the next age to come. We cannot allow him to do so."

Halvik frowned, and pulled uncomfortably at his beard. "But even if the prophecy is true," he said, skeptically, "Dophne is already dead, and The Princess Nalya is safe in the palace at Hinwahl."

Again Mulrin shook his head, and heaved a weary sigh. "There are other princesses in the world," he said.

"Then what are we to do?" Halvik asked.

"Prepare the army," Mulrin replied. "If we can reach the Last Mountain before him, so much the better, but if we cannot, we must intercept him before he arrives there. In any event, Drey is already on the march, and we can spare no more time puzzling as to why. Send word to the camps that we will depart at dawn with every available man. We shall have need of all of them."

"And what if this is a trick?" Halvik asked. "What if Othelwaite is merely bluffing, to draw us into a trap?"

"Then we have no choice but to call his bluff," Mulrin said, bluntly, "and walk into the trap, hoping that we still hold the better cards."

"If it *is* a trap," Halvik suggested, "we need not both walk into it."

"And which of us would you leave behind?" Mulrin asked. "No, I am still the King of Tunber, and I must go where my army goes. It is likely that this will be the deciding engagement of the war, and so you must be there as well. Were I to die in battle, and you were not there to take command, you would have no claim to the throne other than birth, and that would not be enough. We cannot allow such things to come into question."

Mulrin walked to the window, and looked out across the Grey River toward the opposite bank, and home. "There is much that a king can do – and should do – in secret," he said bitterly. "But there are other times that he must place himself in full view. This, I fear, is one of those times. I must go. You must go. We both must go."

# Chapter 17:
## The Sisters' Compound

It was mid-morning when Trea and Saren reached the little side road leading south. Trea paused, and held out a hand to stop her friend before they walked any farther.

"What do you know about the Sisters of Piety?" she asked.

"I would see them in the Crow, from time to time." Saren replied. "They were courteous, and quiet usually. They'd pass through Hillside in groups of two or three, going to who-knows-where. Father told me never to ask their business, and I didn't. I know that they wear white, and that they follow Abzag, and that even cut-throats and soldiers will tread lightly in their presence. But I can't say that I know much more than that. Is that where we are?"

"This is the road to their compound; have you ever been there?"

"I'd never been out of Hillside, until I met you. And I don't mind telling you that their sanctuary would not have been my first choice for a sightseeing tour."

"Nor mine," said Trea. "But I *have* been here before, if not always by my own choosing. So for once, will you let me do the talking?"

"For once," Saren replied, "I'll be glad to."

They saw no one as they approached the gate. The pastures were neatly grazed as before, but they were empty. No flocks were anywhere to be seen, nor did any of the Sisters seem to be anywhere outside, either in the gardens or the fields.

As they crossed the little bridge, they could see a few women keeping watch atop the wall. When they finally reached the gate, the great doors swung slightly open, and one of the Sisters stepped out onto the path in front of them. She had a lean, angular face with dark eyebrows and a slightly crooked nose. She was of medium height, with her greying brown hair tied back into a simple braid. She looked the two young women over carefully for a few moments before she spoke.

"The Sisters of Piety greet you," she said cautiously, with a bow of her head. "It is not common for girls such as you to come to us without escort. Are you devotees to our order?"

"We are not," Trea replied.

The woman scowled slightly at this, before turning away from Trea to look more closely at the taller of the two visitors.

"You I know," she said to Saren, "or at least I know your hair. You're the daughter of the innkeeper at Hillside, are you not? I have been to the Speckled Crow more than once, on the matron's business. But I have to wonder what would bring you here, so far from your home?"

Saren folded her arms, but uncharacteristically held her tongue.

"You've not seen much of the world, have you?" Trea quipped, "if you think we're so far from Hillside. We've come much further than that, and not by the shortest road."

The woman turned toward Trea again, with a look of disapproval. "You have chosen a poor time to come to us," she said. "The matron will see no visitors today."

"We did not choose the time," Trea replied firmly, "and we are not here to see the matron. We are here to speak with the novice Malessa."

"Malessa? What is this? Novices are not allowed visitors. Who are you, and what is your business?"

"You're Sister Mildren, aren't you?"

The woman took a step backwards and eyed Trea even more suspiciously. "How is it that you know my name?" she asked.

"The crook in your nose gives you away," Trea replied. "I am the one who gave it to you, if you don't remember, and I must say it suits you well enough."

"What is your name, and who are you?" Mildren demanded. "The peasant girl that bent my nose is long dead, and good riddance to her, I say. The dragon has seen to that."

"It would be useless for me to tell you my name today," Trea replied, looking the older woman squarely in the eye, "because you never thought to ask it of me when first we met. You were too busy half-drowning me in a washtub, and wrestling me into a pearl-studded dress. But we did not come here to stand bickering at the gate. If *you* will not fetch Malessa for us, is there someone of authority who can?"

---------------------------------------------------

Ten minutes later, Sister Niren arrived at the gate, and Malessa was with her. Sister Mildren – still with a sour expression on her face – followed behind at a safe distance.

"The Sisters of Piety greet you," Niren said. "This has been a most irregular morning for us, and I apologize if we have seemed discourteous. I am Sister Niren, and I speak for the matron, as she is absent. Malessa, I understand, you already know."

"Hello, Trea," Malessa said brightly. "Who is your friend?"

"May I invite you in?" asked Niren. "You may both come, if you like. Unless I miss my guess, we have much to talk about, and we could speak in more comfortable surroundings inside."

Trea frowned and shook her head. "I've already spent two nights inside your temple, and I've no desire to make it three."

"I appreciate that your reluctance is not without cause," Niren replied. "I know something of the circumstances under which you came to us before. We were misled on that occasion, that much is certain, but that does not mean we were not also at fault. And for that, on behalf of the matron and the Sisters of Piety, I humbly apologize."

Niren bowed her head, and did not look up again for a long while. Trea looked at her uncomfortably. Being forcibly arrayed as a sacrificial victim is not an easy thing to forgive. It was Malessa who broke the silence.

"Have you learned the prophecy yet?" she asked, her voice no louder than an eager whisper.

Saren looked at Malessa with surprise, and then at Trea to see her reaction, but Trea did not hesitate to answer the question.

"Yes," she replied. "The prophet was asked how the dragon might be slain. His reply was *Feed him a princess*. Those were his exact words."

Niren, whose head had still been bowed in apology, looked up at Trea again. "That is very curious indeed," she said, thoughtfully. "You see, the matron is not here, because she has gone to speak with the dragon. There is war in the land. Two kings are marching this way at the heads of their armies, and neither has any love for the Sisters of Piety. We have been secure here for a long time; and we have depended on the dragon as our shield against the world. Now, the matron has gone to ask for the dragon's help; only he can destroy the armies that would otherwise destroy us. In the night we prepared for her a horse-drawn wagon, and she left for the ruined city, alone, shortly before dawn."

Trea looked hard at Niren, then down at the ground, pondering what this might mean. She ran her fingers through her hair, pensively, then turned to Saren. "We should follow her," she said.

Saren took a deep breath, and reluctantly nodded in agreement. "What else?" she replied, fatalistically. "I suppose I signed up for this."

"Yes," said Malessa, looking from Saren to Trea with a smile. "You were clearly meant to do so. And this time, I think I shall come with you, if I may."

Sister Mildren was outraged, and could hold her silence no longer. "You cannot go after the matron," she sputtered. "We were forbidden to follow her!"

Malessa shook her head slowly, as she turned toward Mildren. "I am not following the matron." she replied, with a mischievious look on her face. "I am following Trea, though for today at least, she and the matron may share the same road."

"I cannot know the matron's mind," Niren said, looking first at Malessa, then at Trea and Saren. "But I suspect that in this, you are correct. Abzag's hand is at work here, and none of this has happened by accident. You may follow the matron. The Sisters of Piety will not hinder you."

-------------------------------------------------------

As a Novice of the Order, Malessa had few belongings of her own, but Niren provided her with a travelling cloak, and a satchel filled with food. Malessa was reluctant to take anything at all, and tried to refuse, but Niren insisted. "The autumn air is cold," she said with a smile, "and it is already winter, high on the mountain. Wherever you are meant to go, perhaps it is my part to see that you do not freeze to death before you arrive there."

"But what if it is my destiny to freeze to death?" Malessa asked, with a winsome smile.

"That may be so," Niren said in return. "And if it is, then a warm cloak and a little food will do no harm, other than to help you live just long enough to fully enjoy it."

With the matter settled, Niren then embraced each of the young women in turn. Trea first, then Saren, then Malessa last of all. "Farewell," she said. "And thank you. I do not think that we shall ever meet again."

The trio departed without another word. They followed the path across the little bridge, and soon were beyond the edge of the pastures and out of sight.

After they had gone, Niren turned to Sister Mildren, who was now standing beside her.

"Will you please gather all the Sisters together in the temple?" she said quietly. "I will give the order to disperse."

Mildren was aghast. "That was not the matron's command!" she said in astonishment. "We were to wait until tomorrow morning. We were told to wait until the matron returned."

"She will not return," Niren replied. "The older sisters are free to do as they wish, but our time here is ending, and we are no longer what we were. As for the rest, the novices at least should abandon this place; depart into the world and dissolve themselves into the peasantry, where they can vanish like snowfall on an unfrozen lake. Perhaps they will return here in time, but that may not be for a generation or more. I cannot say."

"I will not go," said Mildren, "even if the matron does not return."

"Nor will I," agreed Niren.  "Two kings are marching this way.  I have been to both of their capital cities at one time or another; and I have met with each of them more than once over the years, as the matron's Representative of the Order.  I will wait here patiently, and I will speak to whichever of them eventually arrives."

# Chapter 18:
## The Echoes of Time

For the matron, alone with her horse and cart, it was a lonesome trek up the mountainside, following the ancient highway to the ruined city. She had walked that path many times before, but it had never seemed so long or so slow as it seemed to her that morning.

That may have been because the way was finally clear. In the past, it had always been hidden in the overgrowth. Today, the road was unobstructed, and there were no distractions. It had all become much too simple, and the journey only seemed longer because there was nothing else to be done along the way.

And as there was nothing else to be done, she had ample time for thinking. She thought of her childhood; she thought of a soldier, and a girl in a blue dress; she thought of hunger, and war, and the turning cycles of the moon.

She thought of Githran, whose clouds would hide the world's secrets, and Mosig, the drunken jester from whom nothing could be hidden. She thought of Abzag, who would destroy the world – and would even destroy herself in time – and so be reborn. Abzag, who answered to no will but her own.

And she thought of her own past. As a young woman, she'd been rich, and beautiful as well. Now, looking back through the lens of time, she thought of how that young woman had found herself caught between the love she'd desired and the destiny she'd been born to, and how fate had conspired to take them both from her. And she thought of the monastic life she had gone on to live instead.

And through it all, there was another thought that haunted her: Perhaps it all came to nothing. Perhaps there was no fate; she had no destiny; and after so many years of brooding on her life, now she was merely going insane; nothing more than that, and nothing less. She could not know.

She passed through the shattered gates of the city, and led the horse through the rubble-strewn streets. Today, she would not take her usual short-cut to the stone circle. With the wagon in tow, she would have to follow the longer path, winding through those open streets that were free from rubble and from all the other obstacles.

When she left the Sisters' compound, the sky had still been dark, and the air had been thick and heavy with dew. But soon the morning sun had brushed the dampness aside. In climbing the mountain she had risen above the fog, and now the sun was shining brightly, but still she was cold. Standing so near the summit, the air around her was sharp and thin, and carried in it the hint of frost. She could see her own breath, and that of the horse. Here, within the ruined city, winter had already come.

She reached the plaza shortly before noon, and walked to a sheltered alcove, just beyond the periphery of the stone circle. There, she tied the horse in place, out of sight from the center of the plaza. She chose that hidden spot, not to conceal the horse and cart from the dragon, but the reverse. She wanted to ensure that the horse would not see the dragon, and panic. There were oats and water stowed in the wagon, and the matron took a few minutes to see to the horse's care, before turning to her own business.

The only other item in the wagon was the great wooden chest from her tower. She unlocked it, and removed its contents one-by-one. First she took out a white ceremonial robe, and wrapped herself in it. Then she removed the great axe Brogna, and set it aside in the bed of the wagon. Last of all, she took the captain's helmet in one hand and the tattered blue dress in the other, and carried them to the center of the stone circle. Kneeling, she set the dress and the helmet very gently on the stones. Then she stood up again, and waited for the dragon.

A moment later he came. Dropping silently from the sky, with a flap of his great wings he landed softly, only a few yards in front of her. A great rush of wind blew back the woman's hair and her white robes flowed in waves around her body.

Then the dragon stepped slowly forward across the stones, until he and the woman were face to face. In contrast to the elegance of his flight, his stride was stiff and labored, as if this simple movement somehow caused him pain. It struck her how old he was. Had he lived a thousand years, or longer even than that? What had he seen? What did he know? She could not guess.

"Hello, old friend," the woman began.  "It is good to see you again."

The dragon gazed down at her, but made no reply.

"I have come to ask for your help," she continued.  "Two armies are marching this way."

She waited, but the dragon said nothing, and did not stir.

"The Sisters of Piety are in danger," she said.  "A great war is brewing on our doorstep, and neither of these kings has any love for us, or reverence for the gods, or any thought for justice or the common good."

The dragon said nothing.

The woman took a deep breath, and pressed on: "When one man possesses the world, the rest will have nothing at all," she added, firmly.  "If these men are left to do as they will, the victor in this war will restore the old kingdom.  All of your labors, the work you began so long ago, it all will be undone."

Silence.

The woman shifted her weight uncomfortably, and clasped her hands together, looking up at the dragon, her eyes imploring.  "For all my life, you have been our protector, and the guardian of our order. Fear of you has long sustained the world in peace.  And now I beg you: Destroy these armies.  Strike down these tyrants that would lay claim to the entirety of the world.  You *can* do this.  You *must*."

Still, the dragon said nothing, but now a thought came quietly into the woman's mind:

*You are mistaken.  I am not here to do your bidding.  Your designs are not my designs; your will is not mine.  You are human, and have human goals.  I am not, and do not.*

The woman closed her eyes for a moment, and took a long, slow breath, as if searching for something deep inside herself.  She opened her eyes again and looked down at the dress and the helmet, where she had set them at the center of the encircling stones.

"Do you know these tokens?"  she asked.  "You have seen them before, do you remember them?"

She knelt down, and lifted the iron and leather helm with reverence. "This helmet was worn by a man," she continued. "He is dead now, in the service of one who should never have been king."

She set the helmet gently down upon the stones, and stood upright once again.

"And as for this dress," she said, "three women have worn it. The last was a peasant girl, and before that it belonged to the Princess Dophne; but it was not made for her. This dress was mine, a lifetime ago. It was made for me, when I was a child. It was given to me by my grandfather. He adored me, and he was a great man."

The matron threw back her white ceremonial cloak, and revealed that she wore at her belt a sword. She drew it forth from its sheath, and the black and silver blade gleamed in the mid-day sun.

"This relic of the old kingdom was his, and its name is Vore."

She raised the ancient weapon, and held it aloft for the dragon to see.

"I am the eldest grandchild of Arvallin the Great," she said aloud. "I was born the Princess Ardelia, heir to the throne of Drey. The world was my birthright, and it was taken from me."

Still, the dragon did not move.

*Your birthright? And at that age, what had you done in your life to deserve so much? You resent the injustice in what was taken from you, but not the injustice in what you were given. How ordinary of you. How very human.*

The woman lowered the sword until the tip of its blade rested upon the stones of the plaza. Then, still grasping the hilt, she leaned against it as if it were merely a cane or a walking-stick. She seemed suddenly old again.

"All of these years, I have borne my sorrows without complaint, and for what?" she asked. "For this? The final indignity?" She stared deep into the infinite blue of the dragon's eyes. "I am she, aren't I?" she asked again. "The prophet's princess. Am I now to die, only so that my younger brother can rule the world? Is that my ending? Is that all that I have been for?"

*Like the most timid of wolves, or the cruelest sparrow, you have played your part. Nothing more. Nothing is due to you, nor ever was. The universe does not care.*

"And what will come of this?" she demanded. "Has it only been vanity? Will any of it have mattered?"

*The lords of the old kingdom were glorious in their day. Who remembers them now? Do you know their names? Do you know anything about them, aside from the fact that they must once have been, and now they are no more? The same fate awaits us all.*

"The same fate," she said. "And you have known it all along."

*I know the future, but shall not live to see it; just as you know the past, but cannot escape from it, or forget.*

"Why do you infest my thoughts?" she cried out. "Why do you not speak? Is my mind no longer my own? Am I now denied what had been my only refuge from the world? Is even that to be taken from me?"

*You will never know if these thoughts were mine, or your own. It matters not at all. In madness, all things are equal. In time, all things are nothing more than they are.*

"If that is so," the woman said quietly, "then you and I are equals as well."

Still the dragon did not stir. But now the Princess Ardelia, eldest grandchild of Arvallin the Great, stood tall and proud once more, with her feet apart, and raised her grandfather's sword. She looked up and met the dragon's eye.

"Kill me if you will," she said. "Devour me if that is what must be. If you are my doom, in the same breath I am yours."

They stood there motionless, the woman and the dragon, forever balanced at the edge of time. Then they fell together. The dragon struck, and the woman's hand – clutching the black and silver weapon of the old kingdom – rose up to greet him.

The blade sank deep, the fangs tore through flesh and bone, and as swiftly as the passing of an age, both the princess and the dragon were dead.

-- The End of Book Three --

# Book Four:

# The Dragon's Treasure

## (Winter)

# Chapter 1:
## The Wake

Trea, Saren and Malessa followed the old highway up the side of the mountain. Trea was anxious, and though she wasn't entirely certain as to why, she felt the need to hurry. It was late in the morning when they'd finally left the Sisters' compound, and she knew that by now the matron would already have reached the ruined city. Malessa and Saren followed some distance behind, and little was said among the three of them as they labored up that ancient road.

They were halfway to the ruins when Trea suddenly stopped. A strange and uncomfortable feeling had washed over her like a wave. She looked back at her companions, and saw that they had come to a stop as well.

"Yes," Malessa said, in answer to Trea's unspoken question. "Something has happened."

"I felt it too," Saren added.

Trea said nothing. She waited a moment to let the other two catch up with her, then turned and continued walking. But with the silence finally broken, Saren took the chance to greet her new companion.

"My name is Saren, by the way," she said, with a friendly grin. "Nightfinch isn't good about introductions."

Malessa was puzzled. "Nightfinch?" she asked. "Do you mean Trea? Why would you call her by another name?"

"It's how I knew her first," Saren replied.

Trea thought it best to interrupt this line of discussion. "It's a very long story," she said, without looking back.

"Ah," Malessa replied, as if everything had now been clearly explained. She turned to Saren again. "I am called Malessa, but you may call me by some other name, if that would please you. Thank you for welcoming me."

Nothing more was said until they reached the courtyard near the city gates. There, Trea meant to lead them toward the plaza by the only route she knew, but Malessa stopped her.

"Wait," she said.  "Are we going to the stone circle?"

"Yes," Trea answered with a nod.  "Unless you know of somewhere the matron would more likely have gone."

"That's the wagon road," Malessa said, pointing down the route Trea had meant to follow.  "But we are on foot, and there is a shorter path; I can show you."

Trea and Saren agreed to this, and let Malessa guide them along the matron's short cut to the circle.  Even in her simple gown, Malessa climbed easily over the broken walls and other rubble that blocked their way.  But for her part, Saren was glad to no longer be wearing her long brown peasant dress.

"You were right," she said to Trea, as soon as she had the chance. "Trousers are better for this.  And I haven't skinned my knees."

As they drew near the circle, Trea put up a hand to stop the other two.  "Wait," she said.  "I think I heard a horse..."

She clambered over a low pile of rubble and turned the corner past a broken wall, and there – tucked into a sheltered alcove – she found the horse and wagon, tied as the matron had left them.  Malessa and Saren were close behind her.

"That chest in the wagon is from the matron's tower," Malessa said with a nod.  "I've seen it before, and... Oh...!" she gasped with surprise as she looked in the back of the wagon.  "Look what else she's brought!"

Malessa reached down into the wagon-bed and lifted out the ornate black and silver axe.

If Saren was startled to suddenly see such a strange and ominous weapon, Trea was positively alarmed.  "I know that axe," she said.  "I have seen it before."

"As have I," Malessa replied.  "I found it on the stones of the plaza, that morning after the knights attacked the dragon.  The matron took it from me, and told me to keep it secret... I wonder why she has brought it here now?"

"Its name is *Brogna*," Trea added, frowning as she said it.  "Beldrin of Blackhall carried it.  He said it was a relic of the old kingdom."

"I had guessed that, when I first saw it," Malessa replied. "The matron thought so as well. What should we do with it?"

Trea looked at the axe uneasily. It was remarkably beautiful, but it was also a disturbing reminder of her captivity, and that fateful night in the ruins. "Put it back in the wagon," she said. She looked around the little alcove with some frustration. "We know the matron is here, but she obviously isn't *here*..." She ran her fingers through her hair, trying to contain her impatience. "And now I'm lost again. Which way is the circle?"

"This way," Malessa replied. "We're nearly there."

She led her companions back down a short and narrow street, past another pile of rubble, and along the side of a heavy wall that was still largely intact. They turned a corner, and suddenly there before them was the great stone circle.

The woman and the dragon were there, entwined in death. In the cold of the mountain wind, her white robes – torn to tatters and stained now with scarlet and crimson – flowed around them like a shroud, so that the dragon's head and the woman's body both were nearly hidden from view. His blood and hers were pooled together on the stones.

The young women halted at the edge of the circle, transfixed by what they saw. No one spoke for a long time. In the silence all three began to weep, each with a different emotion. Trea fell to her knees, and hanging her head with grief, rested her hands against the stones. Saren's hands were clasped to her mouth in shock and disbelief.

Malessa's hands were held tight to her breast. Then she opened her arms wide, as if to embrace the totality of the scene. She closed her eyes against her tears, breathing deeply for a long moment. Then she opened her eyes again, and looked out at the tableau before her, feeling delight and anguish in equal measure. "The circle turns," she said quietly, with reverence.

Trea lifted her head again and stood. She walked slowly forward to the center of the plaza, knelt down, and pressed her hand lightly against the bloodstained stones.

--------------------------------------------------

The trio did not go any further that day, as none of them knew what to do about either the matron or the dragon. It seemed heartless to leave their bodies exposed there on the mountain, but the dragon was much too large for them to move or to bury, and the matron was so entrapped in the dragon's jaws that the three girls were not at all certain they would be able to remove her either, had they even been inclined to try. They were not. The very thought of disturbing that final embrace seemed to them grotesquely irreverent.

For want of any other plan, the trio left them as they were, hoping that with the light of morning they would be better able to decide what should be done. They each agreed that, for now at least, they would return to the alcove where the horse and wagon were hidden, and make camp there.

Even in the bright sunshine of the mid-afternoon, it was cold in the ruined city, and the night promised to be colder still. There was a chill wind blowing down from the northeast, and though the little alcove provided some shelter, it was not enough to keep out the frost. Fortunately, there were dead sticks and branches to be found almost everywhere in the city, lying underneath the broken and stunted trees that grew here and there, wherever a patch of bare earth allowed their roots to take hold. The three young women spent the rest of that afternoon gathering bundles of kindling. They built a cozy fire in one corner of the little alcove, tended to the horse's needs, and settled themselves in for the night.

# Chapter 2:
## The City of the Dead

As the earliest glimmers of pre-dawn light crept into the ruined city, Saren was the first of the three girls to rise. She woke up suddenly, cold and stiff and bleary-eyed, and immediately sat bolt upright, startled at her unfamiliar surroundings. Several seconds passed before she remembered where she was.

Until very recently, she'd slept every night of her life in the same bed, and she still wasn't used to waking up outdoors, lying on the cold ground. She wrapped her cloak more tightly around her shoulders and looked over at Trea and Malessa, who were still sound asleep. She stood up and started pacing around the alcove, mostly to shake off the cold. She whispered a greeting to the horse, and gave him a friendly rub on his neck.

It had been a strange night, and her sleep had been troubled by even stranger dreams. She had been wandering in darkness, through mists and fog, and she could hear the faintest murmur of voices. Somehow, she understood that the dead were speaking to her, telling her their stories and their secrets, but she could not understand what they were saying.

Perhaps the most puzzling aspect of her dreams was how little they had frightened her. Thinking back on them now, they should have been nightmares, and yet they did not seem so at the time. She had felt herself lost, somewhere between tranquility and yearning, and unable to find her way. And now that she was awake she still felt out of balance, as if the world itself were somehow askew. Her mouth was dry.

Their fire had burned itself down to a few coals. Saren briefly considered rebuilding it, but breaking branches for kindling was a noisy business, and would likely wake her companions. She decided instead to walk around for a little while, to warm herself up and to let them sleep. She had no clear plan of going anywhere in particular, but inevitably, she soon found herself at the edge of the plaza.

She was stunned by what she saw, or rather, by what she didn't see. The dragon's body was gone. Saren rushed a few steps forward, and realized that the matron's body was gone as well. Only her robes remained, strewn in a heap at the center of the circle. All around the robes, still the paving stones were caked with dried blood.

She felt herself compelled to move toward the center of the plaza, drawn either by curiosity or sheer amazement, until she was standing at the very edge of the bloodstained stones. As she slowly inched closer she could see a torn blue dress and an iron and leather helmet, which before had been completely hidden underneath the dragon's body.

And then she saw the shattered fragments of a sword, lying beside the matron's robes. Its blade had been dark, with ornate silver tracing, much like the axe that Malessa had found in the wagon. And though everything around them was covered in blood, the broken shards of that sword were still clean and gleaming, as if they were newly made and had just been set there a moment before.

-----------------------------------------------------

Trea was awake and sitting on the back of the wagon, when Saren returned to the alcove, but Malessa was still sound asleep beside the embers of the burned-out fire.

"There you are," Trea said. "I wondered where you'd got to."

"They're gone," said Saren. "The matron and the dragon; they aren't there anymore."

"What do you..."

"They aren't there!" Saren repeated. "Their bodies are gone; they're just gone. Come and see."

Trea walked over to Malessa and jostled her shoulder. "Wake up," she said. "There's something strange."

Malessa blinked several times, looked up at Trea and smiled. "I was having lovely dreams," she said.

"Wake up," Trea said again. "Something has happened."

-----------------------------------------------------

Though Trea was every bit as astonished at the disappearance of the bodies as Saren had been, Malessa was not.

"The Sisters of Piety came here, on that morning after the knights did battle with the dragon; that night when you escaped," Malessa explained. "We found no bodies either, only their clothing."

"But what happened to them?" Saren asked.

"I do not really know," Malessa replied. "On that morning, the Matron did not seem surprised, and told us we would find no bodies. I thought then that the dragon must have taken them somehow, but now I see that it was otherwise. The city itself has claimed them, I would guess, now that they are among the dead. This is not an ordinary place."

"But we slept here all night," Saren said, still mystified, "and the city did not take *us*."

"We are not yet dead," Malessa pointed out, somewhat needlessly.

Trea frowned, and ran her fingers through her hair, as she often did when she wrestled with an unpleasant thought. "The dead were in my dreams," she said quietly.

"And mine," Saren added.

"And mine as well," said Malessa. "It was wonderful. It was almost like sleeping in the temple, and yet it all felt more present, and so very much older."

----------------------------------------------------

They gathered the remaining items from the circle together, and not knowing what else to do with them, placed the dress and the robe and the helmet back inside the matron's wooden chest. They set the axe back into the wagon, where the matron had left it, then they took a few moments to puzzle over the pieces of the broken sword, before storing them in the chest with the other relics. The sword had clearly been the weapon that slew the dragon, but what its history might have been, and where it had come from, neither Trea nor Malessa could guess.

"Arvallin the Great had a black sword," Saren said, to the surprise of the other two. "It's an old story that soldiers would tell sometimes in the inn. That sword's name was Vore, and it was supposed to have been buried with him, long ago."

"It really wasn't long ago at all," Malessa replied, "it only seems that way, because we are so young. Some of the older Sisters could *remember* the reign of Arvallin the Great. And now that I think on it, it's not impossible that the matron might even have known him. She told me once that her father was *a man of some importance*... Those were her exact words. But I wonder... She might have been a descendant. He could even have been her father."

Saren's eyes went wide. "And that would make her..." Her voice trailed off. "...that would fit." she concluded, lamely.

"Then this is that same sword," Trea said.

"I think it must be," said Malessa. "And like us, and like the matron and the axe, it did not come here by chance. Abzag's hand has been at work in all of this."

"That's probably true," said Saren, "and there's still the matter of the prophecy."

"Or that part of the prophecy that went unsaid..." Trea pointed out. "So yes, it would seem that the three of us are somehow meant to look for the dragon's treasure."

"That would be the obvious thing to do next," Saren agreed. "But this city is a maze. Where do we even start?"

"I have heard it said that his lair was somewhere above the city," Malessa suggested.

"His perch was *there*," Trea said, pointing toward a stone outcropping further up the side of the mountain. "He would sit on that one shaft of rock for hours, watching the world below. That's where we should begin."

With their destination decided, the trio gathered the rest of their gear and prepared to set out once more through the streets of the ruined city. They left the axe in the wagon bed, wrapped it inside the horse's blanket for safety, and then harnessed the horse to the wagon again. They could not abandon the animal in the ruins, and though they did not expect to find any path suitable for the wagon further up the mountain, they felt an obligation to take it with them, as far as they could.

"If we do find the dragon's treasure," Saren pointed out, "we may have a need for a wagon after all."

Trea nodded her agreement, but said nothing.  Malessa only smiled.

# Chapter 3:
## The Spiral Stair

The three travellers had expected to have a difficult time finding a suitable path through the streets of the ruined city, but the boulevard leading north out of the plaza was surprisingly clear. It wove a gently undulating course, cutting a fairly steep but manageable grade through the city's rising terraces.

That particular road had apparently once been a major thoroughfare, and the buildings facing it had been set some distance back from the street. Consequently, though there was considerable rubble to either side, the road itself was largely intact, and unobstructed. To be sure, there were places where they had to stop to clear some debris before they could get the wagon through, and more than once they were obliged to take a short detour through the side streets that twisted away to the east or west. But these were minor inconveniences, and even with the horse and wagon they made slow but steady progress, in roughly the direction they wanted to go.

They continued to gather as many dead sticks and branches as they could find, stowing them in the wagon as they walked along. Even in the mid-day sunshine it was cold, and the thought of spending a night in that place without a fire was not a pleasant one. They did not know how long it might take them to find the dragon's lair, but they all agreed that it did no harm to be careful of their supplies. They had enough food between them to last for several days, and the water barrel in the wagon was still nearly full, so it seemed that firewood might well turn out to be their most precious commodity of all.

The hour was approaching noon when they finally reached what appeared to be the highest point of the city. Looking up the mountain to the north, they could no longer see the dragon's perch, though they knew it must be somewhere directly above them. Looking back to the south, they could see the city ruins stretched out below them like a broad, crumbling staircase, stepping unevenly down the mountainside.

To one side of the boulevard they found a sheltered nook that must once have been a courtyard between two buildings. They could go no further along the main road, so they chose that place to stow the wagon, and to have a bit of lunch. They were cold, but they did not build a fire. They did not intend to stay in that spot for long.

They had spoken little as they'd climbed through the city, aside from the immediate business of clearing debris from the path, or choosing which side-roads to try when they were forced to take a detour. But now that they were stopped, their thoughts inevitably returned to the matron and the dragon.

"There are plenty of people in the world who will be happy about the dragon's death," Saren remarked, "but I'm not one of them."

"Not everyone feared him," Malessa pointed out. "The Sisters of Piety saw him as a guardian."

Saren pondered this for a moment. "I suppose I did as well," she replied, "though I never thought about it in quite that way. I had seen him several times before, but only rarely, and always at a great distance, flying and far away."

Malessa sighed and looked out over the ruined city. "Those who hope to measure time might say that we three have become witnesses to the dawning of a new age," she said. "In truth, a new age is always dawning, with every passing moment; but that is a small matter. We tell ourselves such things, if only they will help us to endure what we cannot otherwise understand."

Trea had been sitting in silence, consumed with her own reflections on the dragon, but now she joined their conversation for the first time. "I think you're mistaken," she said quietly. "With the death of the dragon, the last age has ended, but I do not believe that a new age has yet begun. We are now somewhere outside of time; the world is *between* ages. The circle has been broken, and I wonder if our task is to mend it somehow."

"What do you mean?" Saren asked, puzzled.

"I don't know what I mean," Trea replied, with a gesture of resignation. "I simply don't know."

Their lunch concluded, the trio searched all around that highest terrace, looking for any possible route that might allow them to venture further up the mountain. They had reached the upper limits of the ancient city, and above them to the north there was now only the gravelly dirt and sheer naked stone of the bare mountain. They searched for several hours before they stumbled upon precisely what they had been hoping to find.

Behind the northern wall of what must once have been a particularly large and magnificent building, Malessa found where a narrow corridor of steps had been carved into the native rock of the mountain. The staircase must originally have been well-hidden at the rear of the structure, but now that the surrounding building was gone, it lay partially exposed to the open air. With a little work, the three girls managed to clear away enough debris to climb over the rest of the way, and found themselves standing at the bottom of a long circular stairwell that led up through the mountain, slowly curving out of view.

Before attempting the staircase, they returned to the little courtyard. They checked to make sure that the horse was fed and comfortable and safe, then they unhooked the wagon's night-lantern and took it with them. They could not see very far up that curving stairwell, and did not know if they would have any light at all, once they were further inside.

As it turned out, they did not need the lantern after all. The stairwell was dimly lit by narrow windows that had been chiseled out of its southern side. Some of those windows had collapsed, or were blocked by fallen rock or other debris, but even without the lantern, in most places there was still enough light to clearly see.

The staircase spiraled relentlessly upward through the grey stone of the mountain, and though there was occasionally a broken stair or a small pile of rubble where some part of the outer wall had crumbled away, most of the stairs were solid, and wholely intact. But still, it was not an easy climb. They did not count the steps, but there were hundreds, and they seemed neverending. Each time the trio passed an open window, they would peer out, and see that the city was further below them, but still they could see no sign that they were any nearer to the top.

Then suddenly the stairs ended, and they found themselves standing in a narrow corridor, facing west. The far end of that corridor was open to the setting sun, and after being so long in the dim and shadowy stairwell, the glare ahead of them seemed impossibly bright.

Stepping out of that corridor, they emerged from the base of a sheer rock wall that towered more than a hundred feet above them. They were standing on a flat expanse of bare, unworked stone, which was perhaps ten yards wide and twice as long. In front of them, the ground tapered upward, ending in a flat and narrow finger of rock which jutted out into the open air. They had found the dragon's perch.

"You can see the whole world from here!" Malessa exclaimed with delight, as she rushed forward to the edge of the outcropping of stone. Rapt with excitement, she flung her arms wide and looked out at the broad vistas below. But the view seemed somehow out of focus, and she felt suddenly dizzy. The landscape began to move at random, as if the hills and forests were only clouds of dust, wafting aimlessly in all directions. Her head swam with the wonder of it as she stumbled and fell.

Saren caught her from behind. She wrestled her back from the precipice, pushed her down onto the bare stone, and lay on top of her to hold her still.

"Don't stand!" Saren shouted at the white-robed girl pinned underneath her. "We're a mile above the stones! Crawl on all fours unless you know how to fly!"

"But it was marvellous," Malessa said. She looked at Saren with pure delight, as if she were blithely oblivious to the fact that she had very nearly fallen to her death.

Saren glared at her with frustration. "It's going to be a challenge keeping you alive, isn't it?" she asked.

"You needn't bother," Malessa replied with complete sincerity. She was still smiling, which only irritated Saren that much more.

"Well if you could at least make a token effort at it," Saren grumbled, "maybe I wouldn't feel obligated."

"If Abzag wishes to take me now," Malessa chuckled happily, "it would be wrong of you to intervene."

"If Abzag wanted to take you now," Trea pointed out, "it would make no difference if Saren tried to intervene or not."

Malessa turned her head to the side, and looked at Trea with a peculiar expression on her face. Then she smiled again. "You are quite right," she said, with some surprise in her voice. "I find myself happily corrected; thank you both."

# Chapter 4:
## The Dragon's Perch

Aside from the narrow tunnel that led back to the spiral stair, there was no shelter to be had anywhere on that high shelf of rock. Behind them, to the east, the mountainside rose almost vertically for a hundred feet or more, and to the other three sides, cliffs fell far away to the rocky mountainside below. Standing on that lofty platform, the three young women felt isolated, exposed, and terribly naked to the world.

Malessa and Saren crawled back from the promontory, and did not stand again until they were well away from the brink, and on much less precarious ground.

"I think we've come to the end of the trail," Saren said, dusting herself off, and unconsciously flexing her arms and legs to make certain she hadn't injured herself in dragging Malessa to safety.

"It *is*..." Malessa agreed with a sheepish grin, "a long way down."

"There's nothing here," Trea said, "but the dragon must have had a lair of some sort nearby."

"Perhaps he had a cave somewhere in the cliffs below us," Malessa suggested.

"Or above," said Saren, pointing far up the rock wall. "Look."

Trea turned toward the face of the mountain and craned her neck back, but she could see nothing but bare stone.

"What is it?" she asked. "I can't see anything."

"I see it," Malessa said, now pointing to the same spot. "It's a cave; come away from the wall."

Trea walked to where the other two were standing, and looked up again. This time she could see it clearly. There was a jagged opening in the rock face, just over a narrow ledge that stood perhaps fifty feet above them. The cliff was nearly vertical, and from the base of the wall the cave's entrance had been hidden from her view.

"We'll never get up there," Saren said.  "Not without ropes or scaffolding."

"I might be able to climb it," Trea suggested.

Saren was more than skeptical.  "That's a smooth sheet of rock," she said.  "What would you hold on to?"

"I can see cracks here and there; it's not totally smooth," Trea replied.  "And there are bumps and tiny outcroppings everywhere, if you look closely.  Some of them might be enough for a finger or a toehold."

"I couldn't climb that in a hundred years," Saren insisted.

"Nor could I," Malessa agreed, "but I believe that Trea can."

---

Regardless of whether Trea could or could not climb the rock wall, they were all agreed that she should not make an attempt until morning.  The sun was already low, and though none of them relished the thought of traversing that long spiral staircase a second time, none of them wanted to spend the night on this naked patch of stone on the mountainside, either.

Before returning to the ruined city below, Malessa wanted to take a longer look from the promontory, to see the view from that high point.  Saren and Trea were reluctant to approach the edge, but Malessa was insistent, and eventually they gave in.  They had, after all, taken such pains to get there; they could not just leave again without first taking a proper look.

Saren and Trea crawled out on the ledge to join Malessa, and now – with greater caution – all three of them looked out at the slowly setting sun and the vast expanses of land below them.  And yet, even lying flat on the surface of the rock and holding very still, the world seemed to move and sway in their vision.

"I feel dizzy," Saren said aloud.  "I think..."

"Close your eyes," Malessa said, firmly.  "Keep them closed.  When you open them again, look at one thing.  Choose one single spot and concentrate on it."

Trea did as Malessa instructed, and to her great relief, the world stopped spinning. But now it seemed to draw closer, to become more precise, more clearly defined. She was looking toward a patch of forest, far away to the west, and yet she felt as if she could see every detail, every leaf on every tree. She could see deer grazing in a patch of sunlight, and if she strained her ears she thought she could almost hear the singing of the birds. Then she heard the bewildered voice of Saren beside her.

"What?..." Saren asked, dumbfounded. "What is this? This is not... what are we seeing?"

Trea turned her gaze somewhere else, and suddenly the world swam in her vision again. She stopped, chose a new point in the landscape and concentrated on it. Suddenly, that place snapped into view. She could see men, moving along a road. They were soldiers, and there were hundreds of them, maybe thousands. She could see their banners, the glint of their spears, and the rust on their helmets and shields.

Trea's mind flashed back to that moment on the road, when she became aware of the troop of soldiers even before she saw or heard them. Suddenly she understood.

"This was the dragon's perch," she said with quiet astonishment. "We are seeing the world as the dragon saw it."

"Yes," said Malessa, "I think we must be. I have no other explanation."

"I can see more clearly now," Saren said, slowly coming to grips with the strangeness of what her eyes were showing her. "I see soldiers everywhere; on the roads and along the river. They are coming this way."

"Sister Niren told us that armies were on the march," Malessa said. "And now we can see them ourselves... there... and *there*, below us. They are drawing closer to the mountain and to each other. In the morning they will meet along the banks of that winding river."

Trea had seen the soldiers, and knew that Malessa was right. She found that she could not bear to look at them any longer. She closed her eyes and took a deep breath to steady herself, then looked out toward the setting sun.

"The musicians have been called to play," said Malessa, quietly. "Abzag dances."

# Chapter 5:
## The Stone Cliff

The three young women spent the night in the little courtyard with the horse and the wagon, and when morning came they prepared to climb the staircase to the dragon's perch once again. They were hoping to return to the wagon by sunset, if not before, so they carried only enough food and water with them for the rest of that day. They took the wagon-lantern and their empty satchels, and Saren and Trea kept their weapons, but everything else was stowed in the wagon and left behind.

Malessa considered taking the axe Brogna, as she was the only one of the three without a weapon, but in the end she saw no need. It seemed impossible that they would encounter anyone there at the peak of the mountain, and she had no good means to carry the axe anyway.

"I'm more likely to need my hands free," she said, "than I am to need a weapon. If we do find the treasure, maybe I'll have a use for it later on, but I can't see any need for it today."

If anything, the spiral stair seemed even longer than it had the day before. The trio guessed that in the days of the old kingdom, the dragon's perch must have been used by the ancient kings to observe what transpired throughout their domain, or perhaps by their astrologers and mystics, to chart the stars. But whether the power of sight that was granted in that place was due to the long presence of the dragon, or to some lingering sorcery of the old kingdom, it was impossible to know. The only thing that seemed certain about the place was that whoever had carved the spiral stair that led to that high shelf of rock had clearly meant for it to be kept very secret, and well-hidden from public view.

When they reached the perch, they found it gloomy and cold, and a much more dreary place than it had seemed the evening before. Although the sun had risen above the horizon down in the courtyard below, here it was still hidden behind the mountain. There was light, but it was hazy and grey. It seemed as if Githran had concealed the whole of the world below them under a heavy veil of morning fog.

Trea stood for a long time, staring at the rock wall.  She would walk up to the cliff face and brush it gently with her hand.  Then she would walk away from it, choose another spot, and put her hand on the bare stone again, taking the sense of it, testing her grip on some tiny crack or small protrusion of rock.  Then she would stare up toward the ledge, back away from the wall again, and run her fingers through her hair, lost in her own thoughts.

Saren and Malessa sat silently in the middle of the stone shelf, watching her.  They knew she was trying to plan her climb, or perhaps trying to decide if it was even worth making the attempt.

"I think the best approach is along this side," Trea said eventually, pointing up the northern half of the rock face.  But I can't reach the first crack from here.  You'll have to give me a boost up."

Trea took all three of the shoulder satchels and hung them around her neck, along with her water-skin.  She folded her travelling cloak, and stowed it in her own satchel along with a little food.  She also kept a tinderbox and the wagon-lantern.  If the cave turned out to be very large, she would surely need a good source of light to fully explore it.

Saren was the tallest and the strongest of the three, so she planted her feet far apart and braced her arms against the bare stone, while Malessa helped Trea scramble up her back.

"I'm glad you're little," Saren joked.  "I don't mind, really, but I've never been mistaken for a siege tower before."

Trea was now precariously balanced, standing squarely on Saren's shoulders, but she still could not reach the first hand-hold.  In the end, Saren and Malessa each had to slip their hands under her shoes, and hoist her up at their full arms' length.  With Trea bracing herself against the cliff, they were just able to manage it.  Trea caught hold of the horizontal crack with both hands, pulled herself up a few inches, and planted her right foot on a round knob of rock, some six or seven feet above the floor of the stone shelf.  She was up.  She had begun.

The cliff was a far more difficult climb than Trea had faced scaling the Temple of Abzag, or even the outer wall of the Sisters' compound. It was a slow, tedious process, but for the next hour she made halting progress up the face of the cliff toward the jagged entrance to the cave.

Malessa and Saren helped as they could, by looking for promising cracks and ledges and letting her know if her route was taking her too far from the cave entrance to either side.  But for most of the time, there was little they could do but watch and hope and wait.

At one point, perhaps fifteen feet below the cave entrance, Trea came to a patch of wall where there was simply no purchase to be found for hand or foot, either above her or to either side.  She hung there for several minutes before she finally gave it up and reluctantly worked her way back down for a few feet, so she could shift herself further to one side and try again.  That was the most harrowing part of the climb for her, because she could look *up* much more easily than down.  Back-tracking meant that she couldn't clearly see where she was going, and had to work mostly by feel.

By the time she reached the narrow ledge that ran along the mouth of the cave, her every muscle ached, and her hands and feet were cramped and numb with the cold.  She dragged herself up those last few feet, crawled onto the ledge, and collapsed there with exhaustion, lying on the bare stone floor just inside the cave's entrance.

When they saw that Trea had finally reached the cave, Saren and Malessa hugged each other with excitement and relief, but they were almost afraid to cheer.  After nervously watching her climb for so long, they felt nearly as tired as she did, and now she'd disappeared from their view.

"Are you all right?"  Saren called up toward the cave entrance.

Still flat on the floor of the cave mouth, Trea turned herself around, so that she could look down at her friends below.  "I'm fine," she said, smiling wearily.  "But I need a nap."

"What can you see?"  Malessa asked.

"Not very much."  Trea replied with a shrug.  "It's a cave.  It's dark."

# Chapter 6:
## The Battle of the Ash River

If the final outcome of the Battle for Piyl was determined by planning and strategy – specifically Lord Brale's surprise counterattack from the city hill – the Battle of the Ash River, as it was later known, was not. By comparison, the Battle for Piyl was a small-scale conflict, fought in good conditions on a well-defined patch of clear terrain, and involving only a few hundred men for either side. At the Battle of the Ash River, the conditions were poor, the field of battle was spread over an enormous stretch of hills and woodlands, and the armies were larger by more than a full order of magnitude. It was a sprawling, chaotic affair.

At sunrise on the day of the battle, the lightly wooded hills that lined the banks of the Ash River were thick with fog. The chill of that grey morning seemed to swallow up the world, like a heavy rain that merely hovered in the air, refusing to fall until it had soaked every shirt and cap and lock of hair, and had coated every autumn leaf, whether they still held to the trees or had already fallen to the forest floor. The ground below was soft, and yielded damply underfoot, as the watery mud crept up the sides of boots and shoes, clinging wetly to every passing step.

The armies of Tunber and Drey broke camp with first light, and spread themselves across the landscape in clustered companies, each side preparing for battle with an enemy that they knew was there, but they could not yet see. Campfires burned themselves out, or were doused with water, and the cold damp air rushed into the voids they left behind, eager to replace them. Every surface of metal and leather and wood glistened alike with a heavy sheen of morning dew. Every toe and finger was stiff and cold. Every joint ached with chill. Every patch of skin was icy to the touch.

In their respective camps, the two kings issued final orders to their generals, but in truth, those orders would be of little use. The armies they ostensibly commanded had been cobbled together from hundreds of makeshift regiments, each led by a knight or a regional lord, and little more organized than a murder of crows. For most of these men, their only experience with battle had come in tournament dueling, or random tavern brawls, or at best in small-scale regional skirmishes. Few if any of them had ever experienced real warfare on a larger scale. In the wet and foggy conditions – with inexperienced armies fighting on uncertain terrain – any plan of battle more nuanced than *Kill the enemy as you find them* bordered on futility.

-------------------------------------------------------

Once Trea had disappeared into the cave, there was little for Malessa and Saren to do but wait. They nibbled at the food they had brought, but neither was hungry. The sun was now a little higher, and had moved a bit further to the south, and so at least some portion of the dragon's perch was no longer in shadow. In the world below them, the morning fog was gradually melting away, and as it did the landscape of hills and forests slowly came back into view.

By the time they could see what was happening along the banks of the Ash River, the fighting had already begun. Far below them, dark swarms of men drifted like slow-moving clouds across the open spaces between patches of forest, sometimes meeting other swarms and fighting, sometimes vanishing again beneath the canopy of the trees.

Saren was horrified by the chaos. "Men are fighting everywhere," she marvelled, "but I can't tell them apart. Which side is which? How do they even know who to kill?"

"I don't know that they do," Malessa replied. "For most of them, it is only about the killing now, and at the end of the day, those that have not been killed will have won."

For a long while, the two young women watched in silence, as the grim spectacle unfolded below them. Wherever Saren looked, her eye became fixed upon some gruesome detail: a severed arm, lying by itself in the grass; a body, face down on the bank of a woodland stream; a man weeping beside a dead friend. She closed her eyes and clenched her teeth, and reminded herself to breathe.

"Reduced to its essence," Malessa said quietly, "war is very simple to understand. It is human sacrifice on a grand scale. It is the consummate distillation of deliberate waste. It is futility sanctified. It is man's most delicious absurdity."

Saren looked over at the young woman lying beside her, and saw that her eyes were closed as well.

---

The battle was fought in an endless series of skirmishes and brief encounters – along the river, beneath the trees, and on the grassy hillsides. Two groups would meet and clash until one side found themselves overmatched. Then they would try to break away, either withdrawing as an ordered company, or scattering with confusion in all directions. Survivors who became separated from their regiments would wander through the forests until they came upon allies that they knew, or enemies that they could not escape. Few prisoners were taken for either side, as there were no provisions for their care. Those that surrendered were often executed anyway, as nothing else could safely be done with them. In the forests, attempting retreat was a wiser choice than surrendering, or standing to fight if outnumbered.

It was in one of those forest skirmishes that Mulrin of Tunber fell and did not rise. When his troop of horsemen found itself caught between two squadrons of infantry, he ordered a withdrawal; but his men could not hold together amid the trees. His horse was brought down by a soldier's spear, and once he was on foot, the old king was not able to flee or fight off his assailants. He was soon surrounded and slain.

His death might have been a crippling blow for Tunber's army, had it been widely known. But the battle was fought over so great an area – and the troops for both realms were so widely scattered – that few were even aware that he had fallen. The fact of Mulrin's death was not widely reported until later that evening, when the sun began to set and the fighting waned, and the survivors for each side gathered together to tally their losses.

---

By early afternoon, the chain of command for both sides had broken down almost entirely, and the larger companies had mostly fragmented into smaller groups. As the day dragged on, many of the combatants abandoned even the attempt to distinguish friend from foe. Any man that a soldier did not personally know was taken to be an enemy, unless somehow proven otherwise. Some men panicked and fled blindly through the woods. Many of these were caught by roving bands from one side or the other, and killed as either deserters or as enemies. Some few escaped, and hid themselves until nightfall, then crept back into their camps and tried to rejoin their companies. Those that stayed with their commanders did their best to follow orders, with no way of knowing whether the larger battle was going well or poorly for their own side.

Though Drey held the advantage of numbers from the onset of the fighting until its ending, it was not until early evening that the day's final outcome was truly decided. Prince Halvik had managed to hold together a small contingent of his own forces, but while trying to withdraw from the fighting in the forest they were discovered at the river's edge, and cornered there. Outnumbered, with no route to escape, his company fought to the last man, but they were overmatched and overwhelmed. Shortly before sunset, Prince Halvik of Tunber was slain along the western bank of the Ash river, leaving Tunber with neither a commander nor a king.

# Chapter 7:
## The Shadow Gate

Trea lay just inside the opening in the cliff wall, trying to catch her breath, and waiting for her muscles to unclench. But she could not stay there long. The wind that swirled about the entry chamber was bitter cold, and cut through her clothes. She took her travelling cloak out from her satchel and wrapped it around herself again.

The light that filtered in from the entrance showed nothing but a bare stone cavity, reaching far enough back that she could not see the end of it. It looked like an ordinary cave. As she stepped further inside, the wind lessened, though she could still hear the faint echoes of it murmuring around her. She lit the wagon-lantern, and put her hands against it to warm them. Then, holding it ahead of her at arm's length, she carefully made her way deeper into the mountain.

But the further she moved from the cave's entrance, the more the lantern light seemed to falter and grow dim, as if it had little power to penetrate the relentless gloom surrounding her. The darkness seemed tangible, as if she could reach out her hand and take hold of it and squeeze it in her fist, to watch it ooze through the gaps between her fingers. Soon, she could barely see the lantern, and she could no longer see the floor of the cave at all. The darkness stood before her like a wall, blocking her way.

She stepped through it.

Suddenly, there was light.

She was standing in a vast white cavern. Everywhere, she saw gold and jewels. They were piled in great heaps, strewn across the floor and against the distant walls of the chamber. Coins and precious stones clattered beneath her feet as she stepped further inside. She was stunned to amazement, awestruck with the splendor of the infinite riches that surrounded her.

Then she stumbled and fell. She looked back to see what had tripped her, and saw a spur of bone jutting up through the treasure below. Still lying on the bed of coins, she looked around the cavern more carefully now, and she saw that there were bones everywhere, thrust in among the gold and silver and jewels, half-buried. The floor beneath her, and even the walls and the white ceiling were made entirely of bones.

As she stood up again, soldiers stepped out from the walls all around her. Their eyes were dark, and their armor did not shine.

"All this treasure is yours for the taking," they called out to her.

"I have no need of treasure," she answered them.

"Who could be more deserving?" they asked. "You can rule a great kingdom. The whole of the world could be your domain. Even the distant islands will bow to you."

"You have spoken these words to me before," she replied, "as I slept in the ruined city, and in forgotten dreams inside the hermit's cottage."

Now the soldiers drew their swords and held them aloft. "There is wealth to be had in the death of others!" they cried. "There is power, and we are yours to command. Say the word, and we shall crush your enemies."

"I have no enemies," she replied, "unless they are you."

Suddenly, the world spun and whirled, as it had when she first looked out from the dragon's perch. She staggered but did not fall, and forced her eyes to focus.

Still, she was surrounded by treasure, but it was not the dragon's cave. It was a moonless night, and she was on a long wooden barge on a river. Far away at the other end, a wedding was being held. She looked at the riches all around her, and amid the gold and jewels and sacks of coins she saw a small and lovely brooch: a silver bird, perched among leaves of pale green stone. She reached out and took it, then slipped into the water below, before she was seen.

The water was terribly cold. When she surfaced again, she was naked and shivering, and standing on the bank of the little stream in front of the hermit's cottage. She opened the door and went inside, but no one was there.

She saw her rope belt, layed out on the table by the door, encircling a set of clothes and a dark-handled dagger. She reached out, and clasped the dagger's hilt tightly in her hand.

Again the world swam around her, and suddenly she was standing, still naked, at the center of the stone circle in the ruined city. The bodies of the knights and the soldiers were strewn around her, and their captain lay dead beneath the upturned wagon. A white blanket was in his hand. She reached out and took it, and wrapped herself in it against the cold.

And then she was standing in a marketplace, dressed only in rags, alone and hungry amid the swarming crowds. She could think of nothing but food, but had nothing to eat. She saw a merchant beside a stall filled with carrots and beets and other vegetables.

"Please..." she heard herself saying, "I drew the crowd to your stand... please, may I have a bit of food."

The merchant raised his fist and threatened to strike her. "Urchin!" he shouted. "Beggar! Wretch! Worthless child, be gone!"

Trea hesitated, and for a moment time seemed to stop and hover there, frozen in place all around her.

She grabbed a turnip and ran.

"Thief! THIEF!!!" the merchant shouted at the top of his lungs.

In the blink of an eye there were soldiers ahead of her. She ducked away from them, but others were on all sides, surrounding her. One of them caught her from behind and clapped his bare hand over her mouth to hold her still.

She bit him as hard as she could, and tasted blood. The soldier cried out and kicked her fiercely as she twisted free and tumbled onto the dusty ground. She drew the dragon knife and turned to face him.

It suddenly struck her that this had not happened. In the past, the soldiers had held her, and dragged her to the palace. They'd taken her to one of the king's ministers, where she'd been locked in a cage and sent to die. But now she held the dragon knife. She was not simply reliving a memory, she was *re-living* it, a second time, and differently from before.

She ran.

She ran, and the soldiers pursued her once again. She fled through the winding streets, but she could not get away. She climbed onto a rooftop, but still the soldiers were close behind her.

She ran across the roof to an open skylight, and looked down into the shadows below.  She saw a girl there, wrapped in a white blanket, lying alone on a little cot in the center of the darkness.  She knew she was seeing herself in the Temple of Abzag.  The room seemed to be gently swaying in the flickering light.

The soldiers were on the roof now, all around her.  She lowered herself through the skylight and hung by her fingers from the edge.

"Come back!"  they cried.  "We are yours to command.  Say the word and we shall crush your enemies!"

"I have no enemies," she said, "unless they are you."

"Come back!"  they cried again.  "This does not need to be.  Return what you have taken and the world can be yours!"

She looked down, but the room seemed to have slipped away.  She could no longer judge the distance; in the flickering light, she could not even see the temple floor.  She looked up, and saw the soldiers reaching out for her.

She let go, and fell into the darkness.

# Chapter 8:
## The Orb

"She's alive," Malessa said.

Trea found herself lying on the stone shelf of the dragon's perch, looking up at the cliff wall.  Malessa and Saren were kneeling beside her, and behind them the sun was sinking low.

"What happened?" Trea asked, trying to sit up.

"Don't move," Saren said, setting a hand lightly on her shoulder. "You fell."

Trea was confused.  She hurt all over, and nothing she remembered seemed to make sense.  "No, I let go," she replied.  She tried to look at Saren, but she couldn't focus her eyes.  She closed them, and let her head sink back onto the ground.  "I'm all right.  I hurt."

"You're not all right," Malessa said, "but you're not dead either, which is a remarkable thing."

"You're not supposed to fall off cliffs," Saren reminded her gently, "unless you know how to fly.  I already explained that to Malessa; weren't you listening?"

Trea started to laugh in spite of herself, but it turned to a cough, and she grimaced with pain.  She looked at Saren again, and this time she was able to make her eyes focus.  "I stole a turnip," she insisted. "The soldiers wanted it, but I couldn't let them have it.  I was hanging from the roof.  I had to let go."

-----------------------------------------------------

As a Novice of the Sisters of Piety, Malessa had learned quite a bit about medicine and the treatment of injuries, and Saren refused to let Trea sit up until Malessa had carefully checked her over.  Miraculously enough, she seemed to have no broken bones, though every part of her ached, and she had a large bruise on the side of her ribcage.

"That's where he kicked me," Trea explained.

"Who kicked you?" Saren asked.

"The soldier," she said, "after I bit him."

Once she'd had a chance to gather her thoughts, and was allowed to sit upright again, Trea told them all that had happened in the dragon's cave. Though her ordeal sounded even more bizarre in the telling than it had seemed to her at the time, neither Malessa nor Saren doubted her story. Malessa, of course, had long experience with visions and dreams of that sort (if dreams they were), and after spending two nights in the ruined city, Saren had already seen things nearly as strange herself.

Though Trea was exhausted, and far from steady on her feet, they all agreed that they could not stay where they were. They'd brought no firewood with them, and the dragon's perch was cold enough in broad daylight. Now that the sun was nearly down, and with the night winds sweeping over the mountain, they all were chilled to the bone.

The wagon-lantern was lying on the ground a few feet from where Trea had fallen, and astonishingly enough it was not only unbroken but still lit. Trea had taken all three of their satchels with her into the cave, so she handed Malessa's back to her. It seemed to be surprisingly bulky.

"This was empty..." Malessa said, curiously. "What did you put in it?"

"That must be my cloak," Trea said. "I took it off to climb."

"It can't be," Saren pointed out. "You're already wearing it."

Trea looked down at herself and saw that Saren was right; she was indeed already wearing her cloak. She was so tired and so dazed that she'd completely forgotten that she had it on.

Malessa opened the satchel and drew out a neatly folded length of heavy white cloth. Trea recognized it immediately.

"It's the blanket you gave me," she said. "I took it back from the dead captain."

Saren had thought at first that her own satchel was entirely empty, but now she opened it and looked inside. To her surprise, there was something there as well.

"Well look at this!" she marvelled, holding up a small piece of silver jewelry. "Do you know what this is?"

"That's the gift I left for the dragon..." Trea said. "I took it from the wedding-barge."

"No!" Saren exclaimed, holding the brooch up to show them. "Look at it! What do you see?"

Trea was puzzled by the question, and too weary to think it through. "It's a silver bird..." she answered cautiously, "and pale green leaves."

"It's a *finch*," Saren said, "standing in moonlight." She paused, waiting for some reply, but Trea only shook her head, still mystified. Finally, Saren had to explain.

"Nightfinch, it's *you*."

Now Trea could not help but wonder what might be inside her own satchel. She had thought that the heavy lump there was nothing more than the lunch she'd neglected to eat while in the dragon's cave, but after seeing the blanket and the brooch she was almost afraid to look. She reached in, and drew out a fist-sized object that was loosely covered by a brown rag. She carefully unwrapped the cloth to reveal a strange dark sphere. Its outer surface was transparent, like clear ice or fine crystal, but just below that surface the sphere was grey and dark, and shadowy mists seemed to slowly drift inside it.

"I don't remember this at all," Trea marvelled, holding it up for the others to see. "What do you think it is?"

Saren and Malessa stared at the sphere in amazement. It was a beautiful, mysterious, captivating thing, and they found that they could not pull their eyes away from it. The shadows inside flowed in gently swirling patterns, all around the fingers of Trea's hand.

"Surely this is magical somehow..." Trea muttered quietly. "A mystic orb of some kind, or some sort of seeing-sphere..."

"Those could be Githran's mists inside it..." Malessa suggested, her voice hushed with reverence, "but they move like the river, or Neldor's seas... Whatever this orb might be, Abzag has surely touched it."

"I have no idea what it is," Saren whispered aloud, "but it certainly isn't a turnip."

No one laughed.  For a long moment they stared at the sphere in silence, each of them filled with a powerful sense of wonder and awe.

"There is *life* inside that orb," Malessa said at last, almost fearfully. "I can feel it from here."

Trea gasped.  Suddenly she understood.  "It's not a crystal at all," she whispered in astonishment, "and it's not a seeing stone either."

She paused, and looked up at the other two.

"*This is the dragon's treasure*," she said.  "It's an *egg*."

---

Trea's injuries might not have been serious, but her exhaustion was nearly complete, and the return trip down the spiral staircase was a nightmare.  Her body simply wasn't up to the task, and her muscles refused to obey command.  She found it painful just to breathe, and she could only walk a few steps at a time before her legs began to cramp or to buckle underneath her.  Then she would have to stop and lean against the outer wall, or simply collapse onto the stairs to rest.

Malessa and Saren did what they could to help her struggle along. They could offer their encouragement, and steady her to keep her from falling, but neither of them was strong enough to safely carry her down those circling steps.  They draped the white blanket around her shoulders to keep her warm, and tried their best to keep her spirits up.

If the stairwell had seemed long when they were climbing up, it seemed interminable for the climb down.  Night had fallen completely, long before they reached the bottom, and as the skies had grown increasingly overcast there was not even the light of the moon coming through the windows to guide them.  Had they not had the wagon-lantern with them, they would soon have found themselves stumbling along in total darkness.

Hours later, they finally reached the little courtyard where the horse and wagon were hidden.  By then, Trea was shivering and covered in sweat, and could barely stand, even with Saren's help.  She collapsed into a heap beside one of the stone walls and did not move. Malessa did what she could to comfort her and keep her warm, while Saren set to work at building a fire.  Once she had a strong blaze burning, the three girls huddled around it. Trea had no strength left at all, and within minutes she was fast asleep. Both Malessa and Saren were weary to their bones, but concern for Trea kept them awake and watching over her for several hours more, before they too succumbed to exhaustion and slept.

# Chapter 9:
## The Matron and the King

On the morning after the battle, Othelwaite met privately with the lords that he had chosen as the generals of his army.

"This war is won," he said to them. "Mulrin and his son are dead, and I have seen their bodies. Tunber's army is in shambles, and has scattered in retreat in all directions from here to Piyl. We have lost many men as well, but that is of little consequence, as there is no other force left to oppose us."

"Congratulations on your victory," said the silver-haired man that sat to his left. The others nodded their assent.

"We will dispose our forces in this way," Othelwaite continued, looking at each man in turn. "Lord Parr, you will take your men and reclaim the province of Glaen for Drey. You will then ford the Grey River at the end of the Great South Road, and march south through Tunber. Lord Dalvish, you will take your men and return to Albria. Once there, you will gather any that came late to the muster, add them to your numbers and march to Piyl. From there you will reclaim our territories on the northern bank of the Grey, from Piyl to the sea. Lord Pynne, you will take whatever troops remain and march directly from here to Piyl. Once that city is retaken, you will cross the river and march south. You will meet Lord Parr at the far edge of the Barren Lands, and together march to Hinwahl. At every turn, demand surrender and vows of allegiance from all that you meet. If any resist you, they are to be killed without question. Is that well understood?"

"It is, Your Majesty."

"And where will you go, My Liege?" Lord Parr asked. "Will you ride north, to the aid of Blackhall and Toule?"

"In time, perhaps," Othelwaite replied. "But not today. Today, I will ride east. I have business with the Sisters of Piety."

"East, Your Majesty?" Lord Pynne, asked. "But what of the dragon?"

Neither the king nor any of his generals were yet aware that the dragon was already dead, but that made little difference. Othelwaite's mind was set. "We have fought the greatest battle of this age on the dragon's doorstep and he has done nothing," he spat out, angrily. "For too long, fear of him has tempered our ambition, but I do not fear him now. The dragon is no longer an obstacle, is that understood? Should he choose to interfere in our destiny, it is his ending that has been foretold. I will hear no more of the dragon. You have your orders, and I have business with the Sisters of Piety."

---

On the morning of the second day after the battle, Othelwaite arrived at the side road which led to the Sisters' sanctuary. By the time the king rode across the little bridge – in the midst of his honor guard of hand-chosen knights and lords – his soldiers had already positioned themselves around the walled compound on all sides.

Othelwaite's entourage stopped before the closed wooden gates, and his herald called out in a loud voice:

"Open your gates! The King of Drey approaches!"

They waited, but received no reply.

"Open your gates!" the herald called out again. "The King commands it!"

The gates remained closed. But a few moments after this second challenge, a single woman, dressed all in white, appeared on the wall above. "The Sisters of Piety greet you," she said. And though she spoke softly, her voice seemed to carry over a great distance without fading. Even those furthest from the wall could hear her every word quite clearly.

"Open your gates!" the herald demanded for a third time.

The woman slowly shook her head. "You are welcome here, but you must remain outside the wall. One of you may speak to the matron, if you wish. Which of you shall it be?"

Othelwaite urged his horse a few steps forward, and the herald withdrew behind him. "I am the King of Drey," he said, "and master of all the lands west of the mountains. I have won a great victory in battle, and I am not in a patient humor."

"Greetings," the woman replied.  She nodded her head courteously, but said nothing more.

"You are *Niren*, are you not?"  Othelwaite said, peering up toward the woman on the wall.  "You have been to Nyl, as I remember.  You and I have spoken before.  I am not here for servants.  You will open your gates.  I am come for your Matron of the Order."

"You are speaking with her now," Niren replied.  "Our former matron is gone with Abzag.  I have been selected as the new Matron of the Order.  If you have business with the Sisters of Piety, you may now discuss it with me."

Othelwaite fumed impatiently in his saddle.  "You will open your gates!"  he demanded.  "Or else we shall open them by force of arms.  You will submit yourselves to the king's justice."

"I see no justice," Niren replied calmly, "nor a king, come to that.  I see only men, toying with fate and death, as children might play with sticks and mud."

"This will be the downfall of your Order," Othelwaite said, warningly, "your persistent refusal to acknowledge the rightful king."

"The rightful king?..."  Niren asked, her face betraying only the doubtful hint of a smile.  "There is no such creature on land or sea or sky.  Some are born to wealth, by which they encumber the less fortunate, while others may rise to power, either by chance or by cruelty.  They each adopt for themselves a glittering veneer of reverence.  The hollow soul of kingship is artifice adorning power, nothing more.  You are not the rightful king.  There is no rightful king.  The very phrase is a perversion of language."

"This decision was yours!"  Othelwaite said through clenched teeth.  "Your lives could have been spared, but you choose otherwise.  Your rebellion will not be endured."

Niren seemed entirely unconcerned, as if she were at rest in a flowering meadow, and not standing at the top of a stone wall, facing a hostile army.  "The world makes us, and we the world, and *neither* decides," she replied.  "There is a conference of everything, and a confluence of fate, even as we choose and are chosen."  Then she raised her left hand, and drew a circle in the air before wiping it away.

"We are here," she said with finality. "You have no authority. Our gates remain closed. We shall not resist, and we shall not yield. The circle turns. Do as you will."

Othelwaite glowered at the woman in silence, then reined his horse roughly about, and rode at a slow walk back across the little bridge, with his honor guard following behind. He said nothing more until he reached the ancient highway, then he turned to one of the lords who rode beside him.

"Kill them all," he said. "They are to be executed, young and old, every single one. Let none of them escape. When that is done, you will burn all that will burn. And when the ashes are cold, you are to bring down the walls and crumble every stone."

"It will be done," the lord replied. He turned his horse, and rode back toward the compound.

# Chapter 10:
## Escape

On the morning after their descent from the dragon's perch, the trio rose late and did very little for a long time.  Saren woke up briefly at first light, and saw that the day would be grey and dreary at best.  She got up only long enough to add more wood to the fire, and to see to the needs of the horse, who had been sorely neglected the day before.  With those chores attended, she returned to the fireside and soon fell back to sleep.

Malessa spent the night deep in dreams, and did not wake until late morning.  She quietly added the last of their wood to the fire, ate a little of the food that remained, and waited for the others to rise.  It was nearly an hour later that Saren woke again and joined her.  They sat near the fire together and ate, but little was said between them.

Trea slept until early afternoon, when she woke suddenly with a start.  She looked around their little camp, as if to assure herself of where she was, then she took a deep breath, winced with the pain of it, and struggled stiffly to her feet.  Saren and Malessa went to help her, but she waved them off.

"I'm all right," she told them, though it wasn't entirely true.

"Well, we're all up," Saren said, unenthusiastically.  "What do we do now?"

Trea only shook her head.  "I don't know," she replied.  "Everything hurts, and I'm still too tired to think."

"Well, I can't imagine that there's much left here for us to do," Saren said.  "I don't think that any of us want to climb those stairs again, and we couldn't make it all the way up to that cave, even if we did.  I think we've already found what we came for.  If that sphere is really the dragon's treasure, then I don't see why we shouldn't just leave."

Malessa smiled faintly at this, and nodded her agreement.  "Last night, the dead filled my dreams again," she said.  "They would like for us to remain here. But if we do not, they are confident that one day we will return to them.  The dead can be very patient, and they have some understanding of such things. I agree that we should leave this place while we can. There is nothing more for us to do or see here any longer."

Saren and Malessa hitched the horse back up to the wagon, while Trea drank a little water and nibbled hesitantly at some dried fruit and a stale piece of bread. She was ravenously hungry, but she suspected that if she ate more than a few bites of anything she would throw it back up. Every part of her still ached, it hurt to move, and even breathing was painful. She forced her legs and arms to bend enough to pace around the courtyard for a few minutes, then with Saren's help she crawled into the back of the wagon and layed there, wrapped in the white blanket.

For the rest of that afternoon, they slowly retraced their route back toward the great stone circle. Beyond that, they had no plans as to where they were going to go. With the dragon's egg carefully wrapped in cloth and securely nestled in Trea's satchel, their only thought was to escape from the ruined city. All other plans, they left to wait until that much was accomplished.

That night they camped again, in the same alcove near the plaza where the matron had left the horse and wagon three days before. Malessa and Saren had managed to find enough dead sticks and branches on their return trip that they could build another campfire. They fed the horse the last of the oats, and even their own supplies of food and water were starting to run low. But now that they had found their way back to the stone circle, they could at least be confident of a route back toward the Sisters of Piety and out of the dead city. They felt almost as if they were safely in familiar territory once again.

A second night's sleep did wonders for Trea, not only for her physical recovery but also for her mood. Though the sky that next morning was every bit as dismal and grey as it had been the day before, Trea was more cheerful; and though her arms and legs still were stiff and sore, she felt as if she could walk, rather than simply riding in the wagon.

As they had the morning before, they took their time breakfasting and resting before they broke camp. Trea re-packed the dragon's egg inside her satchel, bundling it up with Malessa's white blanket. The egg was fairly heavy for its size, and it did not give the impression of being breakable, but the three girls were all agreed that every precaution should be taken to ensure its safety.

They returned briefly to the stone plaza, to pay their final respects. Trea once again knelt near the center of the great circle, bidding farewell to the dragon and still trying to come to grips with the fact that he was gone. Other thoughts were in her head as well, but she did not speak of them.

After that, they led the horse and wagon back down the winding path that would eventually lead back to the entry courtyard near the city gate. Saren was leading the horse, and Malessa was walking beside her, carrying the dark axe in her hand. Having found it twice, she'd come to regard the axe as hers, and neither Trea nor Saren had any inclination to disagree.

Trea was relieved simply to be on her own two feet again, and felt better than she had in days. And yet, she also felt a strange sense of apprehension, as if she had neglected something of importance, or had overlooked some crucial detail. She puzzled over it for some time before mentioning it to the others.

"Have we forgotten something?" she finally asked aloud. "I have a sense that something is terribly wrong, but I don't know why."

"Maybe we should tread lightly," Saren suggested. "I certainly don't trust this place."

"I don't think the city itself is any danger to us now," Malessa said, "but that does not mean that we are safe and secure."

Even as Malessa was saying this, they came around a sharp corner of the street and suddenly, less than a hundred feet further along the road, they saw a dozen or more soldiers on horseback, riding towards them at slow a walk. Both groups froze in their tracks, as the soldiers — who were easily as surprised as the three girls in front of them — reined their horses to an abrupt halt.

It was obvious that the trio had no chance in a fight with so many soldiers, nor was there any hope of them escaping mounted horsemen by fleeing back down the open street. There was no cover anywhere along the right side of the road, aside from a few stunted trees and some scattered piles of rubble, but to their left the street was bordered by a long wall of broken stone that was not much more than five feet tall at its lowest point. That was their only chance.

"Over the wall!" Trea shouted, as her instincts took hold and the pain of her injuries vanished in a rush of adrenaline. She quickly scaled the broken stone barrier and turned back toward the wagon to see if her friends were following her.

They were. Saren managed to clamber her way over the top as well, but they both had to help Malessa. The wall was a difficult climb to begin with, and in her robes she simply could not get herself untangled well enough to plant her feet in the crevices. She passed the axe up to Trea, so that her hands would be free, and then Saren helped to pull her up by her wrists. Once Malessa was safely over, they all three scrambled down the pile of rubble on the other side, as some of the soldiers hurriedly dismounted and started after them in pursuit.

"Don't chase them!" the soldiers' captain shouted to his men, calling them back. "You won't catch anyone in this maze anyway, not in your armor, climbing over these rocks and rubble. Chances are they know every stone of this old ruin, and you don't. So use your heads while you still have them."

The men who had dismounted to chase the three girls halted, reluctantly. One of them was already halfway over the broken wall.

"We were told to kill any of the Sisters of Piety that we found," the man at the top of the wall argued.

"Would you have them lead you into a trap or worse?" the captain shouted back. "The Sisters are cunning and dangerous. Don't be deceived by the old women we saw back at the temple. These young ones can kill you a hundred ways if you're not careful."

"There's a chest in the wagon!" one of the other soldiers shouted. "They might have been trying to flee with the matron's treasure."

"There, you see?" said the captain. "We've already got what they had that was of any value. Let them go. There's a snowfall coming, I can smell it in the air. Chances are they'll all die on the mountain, long before you'd ever catch them anyway. Our orders were to find news of the dragon, not to take foolish chances chasing after a few of the matron's handmaidens. So get back on your horses and let them go."

The soldiers did as they were told, and clustered around their commander, waiting for new orders.

"Molrik and Sharl," the captain said, pointing toward two of his men, "you take this wagon back to the compound. And don't look inside that chest, if you know what's good for you. That's for the king's eyes; he'll want to know what we've found. The rest of you, scout the ruins in pairs. Keep an eye to the mountain in case the dragon is there, and stay alert to everything around you. There may be more of those little girls about, so stay sharp, and stick to the roads as much as you can. We've lost more than enough men in this war already."

# Chapter 11:
## Snowfall on the Mountain

Trea led the way as the three girls fled through the rubble of the ruined city.  They avoided the open streets, working their way over walls and through the hollow interiors of crumbling buildings, taking whatever route seemed to offer the most concealment as they made their way to the south and east.  They had no way of knowing whether the soldiers were still pursuing them or not, but they were taking no chances.

The day had been gloomy and overcast from the outset, and before long a few scattered snowflakes began to appear.  By the time they reached the wreckage of the ruined city's outer wall, the wind was blowing steadily out of the northeast, and a light snow was falling all around them.

Once they were out of the city and into the surrounding forests, Trea led them eastward, following the southern edge of the city wall until it curved away from them to the north.  Malessa and Saren did not know for certain where Trea was leading them, though Malessa thought she could guess.  Saren's only thought at first was to escape from the soldiers, but now she was equally concerned about the falling snow.  The thought of being lost in a mountain forest at night in the middle of a snowstorm was not an appealing one.

Several hours had passed since they'd left the ruined city behind them, and the daylight was just beginning to fade, when Trea finally found what she'd been searching for.  The wind was growing stronger now, and the snow was falling more heavily, swirling about them and covering the forest floor.  But just above the low-pitched cries of the wind, they could hear a quiet murmur of rushing water.  Following that sound, they soon discovered the little river, tumbling crisply over the same set of cataracts that Trea had first found some months before.  The waterfalls were partly frozen, and ice covered all the stones.  Even in the pale grey light, the falls glistened as if they were cut from jewelled crystal.

The trio followed the little river downstream for the better part of an hour. It was difficult going, as the wind cut through their clothes, and the snow – though not yet particularly deep – was steadily increasing, making it difficult to see very far ahead. But the river was a sure guide, and just as the last light of day was fading, they spotted the little cottage on the opposite side of the stream. The windows were dark, and they could see no smoke rising from the stone chimney.

They had little difficulty crossing the river, though the water was bitterly cold. The stream was neither so broad nor so deep at this time of year as it had been when Trea crossed it earlier in the spring. Then, fed by snowmelt from higher up the mountain, the river carried more water than at any other time of the year. But now it was shallow enough for them to wade through without swimming, and narrow enough to dash across with only a few leaping steps. Rushing to the cottage, they did not pause on the front stoop to knock, nor did they take the time to peer through the windows to see if anyone was already there; they just hurried through the front door as quickly as they could.

The interior of the cottage was very dark. There was no fire, and it did not appear as if anyone had been there for a long time. It was every bit as cold inside the little hut as out, but at least they were sheltered now from the snow and the wind. There were some dry sticks bundled beside the fireplace, and all three of them set to work starting the fire. It was Saren who first got the tinder to catch, and soon they had a good blaze going. They took off their wet clothes, and wrapped themselves in the blankets that were on the beds. Then they huddled by the fire to get warm.

It took some time, but eventually the fire began to drive the chill out of their bones. The cold stone hearth of the fireplace grew steadily warmer, until the whole cottage began to feel cozy and safe. Now that they were more comfortable – and with better light to see by – the three girls examined every inch of the cottage's large single room.

"I have been here before," Malessa said, with a puzzled expression on her face. She was standing in the center of the room, with her hands held open before her and her fingers stretched out wide. "I can almost remember it. But it was not me..." she added, "and it was not here."

"Why is it," Saren asked, impatiently, "that you always sound as if you've had far too much to drink?"

Trea ignored Saren's remark, and looked curiously at Malessa. "What do you mean?" she asked.

"I don't know," Malessa replied. "But I'm certain of it."

Saren was occupied with more practical concerns. "There's food," she said, exploring the shelves and the cupboard. "Quite a bit of it, in fact. Sacks of flour, nuts, dried beans. I wouldn't be surprised to find a root cellar somewhere outside. Your hermit seems to have laid in more than enough provisions to last him the winter."

"They weren't for him," Trea said, looking around at the room and its various furnishings. "I don't think that this was ever really the hermit's cottage. He might have lived here; he might even have been the one that built this place, but if he did, it wasn't for himself. And I suspect he was really never more than the caretaker."

Now it was Saren's turn to be puzzled. "What do you mean?"

"Why would a hermit, living alone in the woods, have three beds?" Trea asked. "He wouldn't. They weren't for him. They were never for him. He didn't need them."

"Then who were they for?" Saren asked.

"For us, of course," said Malessa, with a nod of understanding. "There's a bed for each of us. It's not a coincidence at all."

"But then where is the hermit now?"

"Whoever, or whatever he was, he's gone now," Trea said with a shrug. "Along with the matron and my grandfather, and Notwot the prophet, and Arvallin the Great, and all the rest. He played his part, and then he stepped away. We were meant to come here, the three of us. We were always meant to come here. I've suspected it for a long time."

Saren rubbed her neck uncomfortably at this thought, but she did not argue. From the very start, she had hoped only to escape from the inn, and to find a different sort of life for herself. But the notion that she'd been brought here by any sort of personal destiny was difficult for her to wrap her thoughts around. She let the idea sit, and returned to more practical concerns.

"Well, if we're going to stay here for the winter," she said, looking around the room skeptically, "then it looks as if we've plenty of food on hand.  But unless there are great piles of it lying around that we haven't seen, we don't have nearly enough firewood, not even to last us a week."

"There are dead trees in the forest," Trea suggested.  "It will be a lot of work, but I'm sure we can gather more as we need it."

"I will chop the wood," Malessa said brightly, with a mischievious smile.  "I have the axe."

# Chapter 12:
## The King of Drey

The King of Drey had lost nearly a third of his army in the Battle of the Ash River, but in practical terms that meant only that he had fewer mouths to feed, and fewer salaries to pay. His enemy's losses were much greater, both in numbers and in political significance. What portion remained of Drey's army faced little opposition, and less than a week after the battle, Othelwaite's forces were marching freely into Tunber.

The remnants of the garrison that King Mulrin had left in the city of Piyl withdrew across the Grey River, and burned the ferry-barge behind them in a vain attempt to forestall what by that time had already become inevitable. Had there been a significant force of arms on the southern shore, they might have been able to repel the invaders from Drey as they crossed the river in piecemeal fashion. But Tunber's remaining troops were badly scattered and in near-total disarray, and there was no one at hand with the status or the will to lead them.

With their king and both of his sons suddenly dead, the lords of Tunber found themselves without an obvious successor to the throne, and there was no time for the remnants of that kingdom's noble families to come to any sort of agreement on which of them should be next in line to assume the crown. Most of Mulrin's most prominent and loyal vassals had been with him at the battle of the Ash River, and many of them had died there as well.

Of those lords that had remained behind in Tunber, many were at best ambivalent about their feudal allegiances to begin with, and were more than content to make the practical adjustment of quietly assenting to Othelwaite's rule. As they saw it, they were far more likely to retain their own holdings by promptly swearing fealty to the conquering king from Drey, rather than by pointlessly opposing him. For many of Tunber's more practical lords, a prompt reversal of allegiance was, in the simplest terms, a pragmatic business decision.

A similar calculation was made in northern Drey, on the broken steppes of Karvik. There, King Edral of Furgathor ordered an end to his troops' advance, after capturing only a few minor provinces. Karvik's notorious winter snows had arrived earlier than expected, bringing a premature end to the campaign season in that part of the great island. And, with Tunber now defeated, Edral found that he no longer had much interest in sustaining a prolonged military campaign against the undivided might of his western neighbor.

Within a month after the Battle of the Ash River, Tunber had fully surrendered itself to Othelwaite's rule, and Furgathor had withdrawn the bulk of its army back inside its original borders. To be sure, some scattered fighting continued, here and there, for some time into the winter season. But these engagements were merely skirmishes, with no real impact on the final outcome of the conflict. In actuality, the war was already over in every meaningful sense, and the king of Drey had been victorious on all fronts.

With the fighting largely concluded, Othelwaite sent his most skillful and trusted administrator to Hinwahl, first to coordinate the business of Drey's immediate occupation of Tunber's former capital, and then to make suitable arrangements for the ongoing governance of that newly conquered realm.

# Chapter 13:
## The Viceroy of Tunber

Upon his arrival in Hinwahl, Lord Fodge took up residence in what had once been Tunber's royal palace, and immediately set himself to work, establishing a suitable bureaucracy for the management of this freshly conquered realm.

The former Minister of Finance, as usual, found himself caught between the competing priorities of prudent administration and his monarch's unreasonable demands. Tunber's remaining stores of food, treasure, and other material goods were to be sent north, to replenish the king's coffers and to relieve those provinces of southern Drey which had most sorely felt the ravages of the recently concluded war. The challenge Fodge faced was how to extract enough wealth and resources to satisfy Othelwaite's expectations, while not so impoverishing Tunber as to incite a general revolt. It did not promise to be a simple undertaking, but it was the sort of task at which Lord Fodge excelled.

One of his first obligations, as the newly appointed Viceroy of Tunber, was to meet with the Princess Nalya, the only surviving member of Tunber's royal family. The meeting was a necessary formality, but one which Fodge was not at all looking forward to. Though he had been given no explicit orders on the matter, he well understood that Othelwaite would expect the princess to be brought to Nyl, where she would almost certainly be tried as an enemy of the realm, and summarily executed. For his part, Fodge regarded this eventual outcome as regrettable, and quite probably unavoidable.

Hoping to handle the matter with at least some degree of discretion, Fodge chose to meet with the princess privately. In his judgement, the less public attention that was drawn to her unfortunate circumstances, the better.

-------------------------------------------------------

Fodge had anticipated that the princess would be dressed in black, formally mourning the death of her husband. She was not. She wore an emerald green dress, lightly adorned with an elegant silver brocade. Though her choice of attire was somewhat unexpected, it was not inappropriate to the occasion. It was tasteful, yet understated, at least by royal standards. Her hair was loosely braided, striking a balance between rigid formality and casual courtesy. Her face was placid and composed.

Lord Fodge had not been in Furgathor for many years, and had never before met the princess in person. He was, at first glance, suitably impressed. She comported herself effectively.

"Greetings, Viceroy." Nalya began, with a curtsey and a submissive nod of her head. "The widow of Tunber's former heir welcomes you to Hinwahl."

"I thank you," Lord Fodge replied, with a courteous nod of his own. "And may I offer my condolences on the recent passing of your husband. Such are the misfortunes of war."

"Indeed," said the lady, without apparent grief. "And as some are met with such misfortune, I suppose it is inevitable that others will in turn profit by war and death. It would seem that you have done extraordinarily well for yourself in all of this, have you not, Your Grace?"

Lord Fodge could not help but be immediately engaged with the young woman's personal demeanor. He found himself so pleasantly startled by her forthright manner that he nearly smiled. He inclined his head very slightly in her direction, in acknowledgement.

"I can see that you are a plain-spoken and perceptive young woman," he said, approvingly. "But in this, you are wide of the mark. I do not relish this appointment. My only stake in these affairs – as it has been for many years – is the sanctity of my own neck, and my sincere personal preference that it remain firmly affixed upon my shoulders. I have done what I can to keep it there; nothing more."

"It would seem then," the lady replied with the faintest trace of a smile, "that you have succeeded admirably."

"Again, I thank you," Fodge replied. "But I cannot dwell for long on these simple pleasantries. I am afraid that I have an unfortunate duty to attend to.

"Do not allow me to detain you."

"It is a matter that concerns you directly," Fodge continued. "You are to be sent north, to the royal palace at Nyl."

"I see," Nalya replied calmly. "And what will the king of Drey do with me, once I have arrived there?"

"I cannot say," Fodge replied, choosing his words with suitable care. "But Othelwaite is not the most... *contemplative*... of monarchs. I have tried, in my own way, to convey to him some appreciation for the advantages of discretion and mercy, and of weighing decisions carefully before making them. But he remains rash and vindictive, and not given to subtlety."

"Do you think that he will permit me to live?"

Fodge raised an eyebrow, and sighed. "You seem quite clear-minded and capable," he said, approvingly. "These are admirable qualities, in my *personal* estimation, but they are also attributes which I anticipate the King will look upon with disfavor. I think it is not unlikely that he will regard you as a lingering potential danger."

"And why should I present any danger for the king of Drey?"

"In the first instance," Lord Fodge replied, "one might anticipate that you would be inclined to seek some measure of vengeance for the death of your husband. If I may be permitted to make note of the obvious."

"For what reason would I wish to cast my life away, avenging the death of a husband whom I did not choose? A man I scarcely knew?" Nalya asked, pointedly. "I think not. Were I to have died suddenly, in childbirth perhaps, or from some other cause, Halvik would quickly have replaced me with another bride. In this, I see little difference."

"I can see the logic in your argument," Fodge said, sympathetically, "but such reasoning is unlikely to persuade King Othelwaite."

"You hold some influence with the king, do you not?" Nalya suggested. "You could speak on my behalf."

Fodge shook his head lightly, with some small measure of regret. "My chief concern in these affairs, from the very outset, has been the preservation of my own neck," he repeated, bluntly. "Nothing more than that."

"And mine as well," Nalya countered. "We have that much in common."

"If I may speak to the point," Fodge continued, "though I may find myself somewhat sympathetic to your plight, I can see no clear reason to place my neck in harm's way on your account, or anyone else's. The circumstances in which I find myself are precarious enough."

"You are unmarried, Lord Fodge, are you not?"

Fodge was somewhat taken aback by this apparent shift in topic. "I have never found myself so inclined," he replied, cautiously.

"And you have no heir."

"My younger brother has a son."

"But none of your own," Nalya continued, decisively. "You see, I now find myself unmarried as well. Might I suggest that you and I might find in each other a compatible partner?"

Lord Fodge crossed his arms and looked at the young woman with genuine surprise. "It has never been my inclination to seek... *companionship*... of that sort," he replied, meaningfully.

"I am proposing a strategic and diplomatic alliance," Nalya said, with careful emphasis, "not necessarily a romantic one. I think that you would find me a satisfyingly cerebral companion, regardless of any... alternate preferences you might retain. And perhaps you could, at the same time, establish for yourself some small measure of favor with my father, which might prove to be advantageous, at some point in the future. But those are not the only advantages I can offer you."

"Indeed?" Fodge asked, raising a curious eyebrow.

"I carry a child," Nalya said, bluntly. "It will be born in the early days of summer. It could be yours."

"That seems.... somewhat... *implausible*," Fodge replied, skeptically.

"Not in the least," Nalya replied, confidently. "My departed husband was tall and thin, with brown hair. *You* are tall and thin as well, and I can see that your hair must once have been brown. And let us not forget that the child will be partly mine. Her appearance will be such that it could easily be associated with yours."

"There *is* the matter of timing..." Fodge reminded her.

Nalya dismissed this with a wave of her hand. "The timing would be of little concern," she said. "Some children arrive early and others arrive late. As of this moment, you are the only person I have told of this. Even my departed first husband did not know so much, as I was not aware of it myself until he had already ridden off to war. Such are the foibles of matrimony."

Lord Fodge found himself unexpectedly intrigued. "Why would you seek to do this?" he asked. "Once your skin has been saved, what assurance could I have that you would wish to maintain such an arrangement over time?"

"It is my purpose to see to my own line," Nalya said. "The heir to Lord Fodge, I think, will be better positioned for success in this world than the orphaned offspring of a soon to be forgotten kingdom."

"And why should I wish to raise a child that is not my own?" Fodge asked. "Other men fight duels when they find themselves so cuckolded, but you would have me walk into such a condition with open eyes."

"Who is the truer father?" Nalya asked, pointedly. "The one who plants the seed, or the one who nurtures it while it grows? There is much that you could teach a child. You have a wealth of wisdom and cunning that you could bestow. I could supply you with the common clay, and you could shape from that a legacy of which you might be proud. You have risen in the world, as a clever man standing behind the throne. You could raise a clever progeny, who could rise in the world as you have done. You have *a legacy of the mind* that you could bestow. You will one day inevitably die, as all men must. But the line of Lord Fodge need not end when you do."

Fodge stood for a moment, pensively stroking his beard. He looked at Nalya, then looked down at his right hand, and moved his fingers slowly, lost in thought. "Esteemed Lady," he said eventually, looking at her once again, and with a polite bow of his head, "you have made for yourself an excellent case. And I shall consider it."

# Chapter 14:
## Abzag

As the winter deepened, Trea, Malessa, and Saren remained safely hidden in the little cottage in the woods. They found no shortage of ways to pass the time and to entertain each other, each after her own fashion. There was always more work to be done, of course, particularly in gathering wood and tending the fire. But they attended to that work in their own time.

When the mood took them, they would sing, and each of them would eagerly learn whatever songs the others knew; and they often told each other stories, sometimes long into the night. Once they had run themselves out of familiar songs and stories to tell, they invented their own, and discovered that they enjoyed those even more.

Malessa taught Saren and Trea what she could of medicine and dreams, and the mysteries of the gods. Saren taught Malessa and Trea how to cook, and how to keep a comfortable house. Trea taught Saren and Malessa sleight of hand, and tumbling, and many other simple tricks and games. To her lasting delight, Saren finally learned to juggle.

Together, the three young women shared their labors, and waited patiently for the first signs of spring. Each of them felt happier and more at home in that little cottage than they ever had anywhere else, at any time before in their lives.

They kept the dragon's egg safely out of harm's way, resting on the folded white blanket, in an unused corner of the room. None of them knew what else they might do with it. After all, what does one do with a dragon's egg, other than to keep it safe? From time to time, Trea, with an inextinguishable sense of longing and curiosity, would lie on the floor beside it, tracing the tip of her finger lightly over its surface to watch the mists that swirled endlessly inside.

------------------------------------------------------

With the conquest of Tunber finally achieved, King Othelwaite found himself one step closer to his ultimate goal, and with fewer obstacles remaining in his path. The dragon was never seen again, and though no conclusive explanation for his disappearance was ever settled upon, it was presumed that he had somehow been killed.  Years later, a popular song would attribute the dragon's death to the efforts of a brave young knight, who slew the beast to win the love of a fair princess, only to die tragically of his wounds while lying in his lover's arms.  It was a heartrendingly beautiful ballad, with the distinctly poetic advantage of being not remotely true.

The king's soldiers thoroughly searched the ruined city, but the only sign they ever found of the dragon was a great pool of dried blood at the center of a large open plaza.  Whether or not that blood had once been the dragon's, the soldiers could not say for certain, and soon the winter rains and snows had washed even that away.

At the uppermost tier of the ruined city, a spiral stair was found that circled up through the mountain to a high ledge below a sheer cliff wall.  A cave was discovered there which might once have belonged to the dragon.  As soon as the weather permitted, Othelwaite ordered a scaffolding built to reach that cave, but the men that searched its interior found nothing other than darkness and bare stone.  The cave was empty, and though men would search the Last Mountain often and again for years afterward, the dragon's great hoard of gold and silver and jewels was never found.  Some people openly wondered if the dragon had ever really had any treasure at all.

The only object that came to Othelwaite from the ruined city was an iron-bound wooden chest, which some Novices of the Sisters of Piety had apparently been trying to steal.  His soldiers had taken it from them, and brought it to him, thinking it contained some great treasure.  Its key was still in the lock, but when the king opened it he found nothing of value within.  The chest contained only a puzzling collection of torn and broken family heirlooms – his grandfather's sword, his sister's robes, his daughter's dress, and an ordinary soldier's helmet which seemed somehow familiar to him, though he did not know why.

------------------------------------------------------

Shortly after his arrival in Hinwahl, the Viceroy Fodge and the Princess Nalya were hastily married in a simple ceremony in that city's palace chapel.

By all accounts, the bride doted on her new husband, and King Othelwaite – in gratitude for the Viceroy's long service to the crown – relented.  He did not summon the princess to Nyl, and formally pardoned her for what he termed *"the unfortunate circumstances of her prior attachments."*

In the early summer of the following year, a brown-haired girl would be born to the happy couple.  The child's parentage would never be publically questioned.  Many years later, she would be wed to Othelwaite's oldest son, and when *his* time came to ascend to the throne, she would one day become queen.

------------------------------------------------

It was the evening of the final day of winter.  The sun was setting, but the air outside the little cottage had lost its sharpest edge of frost.  The forest was still covered in snow, but it was not so deep as it had been even a few days before.

As she so often did, Trea was sitting in the corner of the cottage, staring at the egg and thinking, slowly tracing her finger across its surface.  Saren watched her for a while, before her curiosity finally got the better of her.

"What do you see," she asked, "when you touch the egg?"

"I don't really know," Trea said, without looking up.  "Shadows and mists.  Nothing more than what you see when you touch it, I would think."

"I've never touched it," Saren replied.  "I've been afraid to."

"I haven't either," Malessa added.

Trea looked up at them both with surprise.  "I've seen you touch it," she said.  "You're the one that set it here."

"I only touched the blanket," Malessa replied, "not the egg.  I've always regarded it as yours, and it didn't seem right, somehow."

Trea was stunned.  "I thought surely by now..."

She picked the egg up off the floor, blanket and all, and carried it to the table.

"It's certainly not mine," she said firmly.  "It doesn't belong to me or to anyone.  And it's nothing to be afraid of, either.  Come and see."

Trea stood by the table and waited for the other two.  Saren crossed her arms nervously and kept her distance, but Malessa stepped slowly forward, torn between eagerness and apprehension.

"What do I do?" she asked.

"You don't need to do anything," Trea said, setting her hand gently against the egg to demonstrate.  "Here, like this..."

Malessa set her hand against the egg beside Trea's, and a moment later the mists below the egg's surface grew pale, and seemed to divide.  Trea pulled her hand away in alarm.

"It's never done that before," she gasped.

She looked at Malessa, and their eyes met.  Then together they turned and looked at Saren.

"You need to do this too," Trea said, nervously.

Saren swallowed hard, nodded hesitantly, and took a step toward the table.  Everyone took a deep breath, and for the first time, all three of the young women reached out to the egg at once.

As their hands touched the sphere, the grey mists inside it suddenly swirled away and vanished, and the orb became crystal clear.  They could see a pale light growing from within, like a fire slowly gaining strength.  And then, a tiny grey shape appeared at the heart of that flame and began to move and grow, stretching its wings.

-------------------------------------------------------

The long winter had faded.  Spring had finally arrived, and the bright morning sunlight gleamed through every window.

Far away, on the high throne in the king's mighty fortress at Nyl, a coronation ceremony was being held.  Othelwaite was donning the double crown, as monarch of both Tunber and Drey.  Within a year, Tunber would no longer exist, as the two kingdoms would be formally consolidated into one.  Within ten years, Furgathor as well would be crushed, and all the lands of the great island would be swept up under a single banner.  The old kingdom would be restored, with Othelwaite the Tyrant as its founder and first king, his name to be enshrined, honored, and remembered for all time.

But inside a tiny cottage, deep in a lonely pine forest on a forgotten mountainside, three young women stood around a small wooden table and stared with wide-eyed wonder at the emerging destiny of Othelwaite's new and glorious kingdom.

The egg was hatching.

-- The End --

# Acknowledgements

No book is really finished when first completed. Regardless of how careful I may have been in the initial writing, there will inevitably be errors lurking which will – by their very nature – be largely invisible to me. Identifying those flaws requires the help of others, and in polishing the final text for *A Counterfeit Princess*, I was fortunate to have the assistance of quite a few careful and perceptive readers. Their efforts were indispensable in preparing this book for publication.

First and foremost, I must thank Amy Nagi. The art she created for the cover wonderfully captures both the sense and spirit of the book, testifying not only to her skill as an artist, but also her efforts to reflect themes running below the surface of the narrative. I could not be happier with the final result. Special thanks are also due to my friend Mark Hansen, who took on the considerable challenge of translating my working copies of the book's maps into a much more suitable and aesthetically pleasing form. Readers who have not seen my original versions may never realize what a service Mark has done them.

Next, I must offer particular thanks to my volunteer editors: Doree Bedwell; Renee Retter; Rob Sartain; Jason Hayes; Cindy Kessler; Nadine Kwok; and Craig Kilgore. Through their efforts, dozens of errors – large, small, typographical and otherwise – were identified and corrected. I would also like to thank my preview readers: Debbie Heindl; Anni Hine; Sue, Zaavan, and Talmon Clear; Amy Hesting; Nicole King; Matthew Siadak; and Caroline Bedwell. As with the editors, they generously provided feedback on the sense and flow of the narrative, helping to identify strengths, weaknesses, and problem spots in need of revision.

What errors remain are purely my own, and are – in the vast majority of cases – deliberate. As some readers may have noted, I do not always adhere to the narrow dictums of Standard American English™, particularly when I feel that some nuance of meaning or rhythm of language will be better served by alternate means. To the extent that such deviations may distract or annoy some readers, the fault is entirely mine.

Doug Bedwell – June 15, 2018

# About the Author:

Doug Bedwell graduated from Indiana State University in 1987 with a degree in Theatre Arts, and later returned there to complete his M.A. in 2002. He has taught a variety of college courses, including Communications, Theatre History, and Playwriting.

He has written over fifty plays, which have been presented at professional, academic, and community theatres nationwide. In 2015, Space Bear Press published a collection of those pieces as a two-volume set. His first novel, the comic science fiction adventure *Robot Captain*, was published in 2016. He has also released a small collection of poetry, titled *Wastewood*.

The range and variety of Doug's writing reflects the eclectic nature of his literary influences. These include science fiction and fantasy stalwarts such as J.R.R. Tolkien and Isaac Asimov, but also writers of many other genres and traditions. His writing has been especially influenced by his study of dramatic literature, including the works of playwrights both ancient and modern, such as Maeterlinck, Chekhov, Shakespeare, and countless others.

*A Counterfeit Princess* is his second novel.